IMPERIUM VOLUME 2 | BOOK 3

THE CLOUDS OF CAELUS

TRAVIS STARNES

Maps available at

https://tstarnes.com/book-series/imperium/

Signup to get free previews of upcoming books before they're released at

http://tstarnes.com/preview-notification-newsletter/

Contents

Chapter 1

Greece

Ky stood outside his command tent, to the world looking like he was staring into the dying light as night set in. In reality, he had a dozen semi-transparent documents layered across his vision, going through solutions to Hortensius's latest problem, supply routes, snapshots of the latest front lines and enemy estimates, and a dozen other matters that needed his attention, organizing everything he would need to write out tonight to be messengered to whoever needed advice, orders, or instruction.

It was interesting to be in the field again. They had moved so quickly, constantly pushing the enemy, that no one had a moment to dig new trenches. The line that had been nearly consistent, torn into the earth for a year, was mobile again. It was moves and counter moves as the enemy tried to avoid direct confrontation while they worked on a solution to the sheer volume of fire the Britannians could lay down and tried to pick off weaker units they could overwhelm with their numbers.

What that meant was they'd pushed well into Greece, heading toward Pharsalus in the heart of Thessaly, which could take one of the new players off the board, easing their push north through Greece until their line was able to join into the Sarmatia line, instead of the bulge that Greece had become.

"*Commander,*" Sophus intoned, pulling the documents from his vision, allowing him to see Modius walking through the camp toward him.

"Modius," Ky said, standing. "Sorry to pull you away."

"I am always at your command, Consul," the older man said, standing.

"I appreciate that. I just wanted to ask how that new batch of recruits from Italia are doing and if you've integrated them yet? I had a report of their arrival two days ago but as of this afternoon, they were still being held in the rear and weren't moving up as we advance. We should be making our assault on Thessaly within the next two weeks and we are going to need them in the line."

"Yes, Consul. We've been working through the preliminary assessments ..."

"I know that's the procedure we had when reforming the legions back in Britain last year, but that's too slow for in the field. We have the enemy on their heels, and time is of the essence."

"Understood, Consul. The delay has been in establishing proper squad integration. Many of these recruits have never worked with our lever-action rifles."

"Then get them working with them. I don't care if they sleep with those rifles. In two weeks, they march east."

"Yes, Consul. I'll see to it personally."

"Every recruit. Every rifle. Every formation. Two weeks, Modius."

"Understood completely, Consul."

"You're doing a good job. Just keep your eye on the goal ahead of us. Dismissed."

Modius saluted and turned away, although Ky thought he could see a little slouch in the man's shoulders from the rebuke. He'd tried to soften the blow, but this was not the first time the two had needed to talk about urgency.

"He's a good man, Ky," Lucilla's voice said in his ear.

"I know he is, but it's been a long time since he commanded anything larger than a squad. And now he's leading three legions across half of Greece. This is not the time for learning curves. Not when we finally have momentum."

"Men can only be pushed so hard, Ky. It can take a little time."

"Time is not something we have a lot of. We have the advantage now, but if the Easterners hold to form, they'll eventually copy our new rifles. We need to make the most of this advantage while we can and push as close to the Black Sea as possible before the balance shifts back in their favor."

"I know, and you will," Lucilla said.

"Ever the optimist. How are things on your end?"

"Fine. More meetings with the Scandi tomorrow morning."

"I thought those details were worked out," Ky said, a little confused.

"They are, but there are still ruffled feathers about the embargos that need smoothing over. Now that they're in the alliance, it's time to switch from pressure to placating."

"This is why I leave the politics to you."

"Yes, well, threatening people into compliance is simpler than keeping them happy afterward," she said with a small laugh.

"Much simpler."

"This far north, I'm out of touch with anything but reports from Bomilcar and the training camps in Germania. How is everything else progressing?"

"On pace," Ky replied. "Valdar's second has begun establishing that new port at the tip of Africa while he and Aelius push the Egyptians south and bottle them up. I have not heard anything since he took Alexandria, however. More importantly, Medb continues to make headway with the Eastern informant. Her last message indicated she might have an idea of how to take the fight to the Easterners' homeland much sooner than we could get there with our forces. But we'll see."

"She is a clever one. If anyone could do it, it would be her. I'm glad we finally got her on our side."

"I am, too. But I am also not putting all of my eggs in one basket, as it were. It's why I pushed Modius so hard. Pushed on enough fronts and the Eastern war machine will fall apart."

"I know, but still ..." she said, and then paused as voices in the distance began saying something the comms didn't pick up. "Sorry, duty calls. Try not to terrorize any more of your officers today."

"No promises."

"I'll speak with you this evening."

The line clicked shut as Sophus muted it for her. They left the comms on and he could access it if needed or Sophus detected a problem, but she'd never been able to grasp the ability to process multiple conversations simultaneously.

Or so she said. Ky had a suspicion that she didn't like it when he listened in on her conversations and would rather present things to him instead. She was ever the consummate politician, managing the flow of expectations and information.

It didn't bother Ky. He knew she'd tell him what was important to know, and besides, there was still much for him to do.

Nile River, North of Cairo

"Signal the flotilla," Valdar commanded. "Battle formation, two hundred yards spacing."

Two other times they had made this push down the Nile trying to take this last fort. Of the overlapping sets of forts guarding the river, they'd defeated all but this one at a crook in the river. This one had proved to be stubborn.

The flag signals went up, and one by one, the ironclad vessels adjusted their positions, spreading across the width of the river to make themselves less of a collective target for the fort.

This time, at least, they didn't come alone. They'd been able to pound the other forts into submission, but this one would also have forces on the ground. Aelius's legions were moving into position. Just over nine hundred men of the ninth legion, a little understrength, as most of the legions were at the moment.

"Range to target?" Valdar asked.

"Eight hundred yards, Admiral," his gunnery officer replied.

Close enough. The river-facing wall showed recent repairs, darker stone patching older sections. Gun ports lined the upper levels, bronze cannon barrels protruding. The main gates faced north, toward Aelius's approaching forces.

"Run out the guns. Load with impact shells."

The deck vibrated beneath his feet as the gun crews went to work. Valdar checked the flag signals from Aelius's position. The legions were nearly in place, spread across a front half a mile wide. Time to begin.

"All ships, commence firing. Target the lower battlements first."

Those would be the ones the infantry would have to deal with in a moment.

The ironclad's starboard battery erupted, eight cannons fired in sequence. Smoke rolled across the water as shells arced toward the fort. The first impacts sent stone fragments cascading from the walls. More guns joined in as the rest of the flotilla opened fire, creating a rolling thunder.

Through his spyglass, Valdar watched Egyptian soldiers scrambling along the battlements. Some dove for cover as shells burst overhead. Others ran toward their own cannon positions. A section of crenellations collapsed, tumbling into the river below.

"Reload! Maintain your rate!"

Every thirty seconds, another broadside crashed out. Not the efficiency he would have wanted, but acceptable. The fort's river wall began showing damage, pockmarks and craters spreading across its face.

Horns sounded from the shoreline as Aelius began his advance. The legions moved forward at a steady pace, maintaining their formations despite the broken ground. Behind the infantry lines, artillery batteries unlimbered their guns.

Valdar adjusted his ships' fire to avoid shooting the advancing infantry. The distance was closing rapidly, and he couldn't risk dropping shells among his own men. His gun crews shifted their aim higher, targeting the fort's upper works and artillery positions.

Egyptian musket fire erupted from the walls as the legions came within range. Valdar could see the white puffs of smoke from the defenders' weapons, followed by the delayed crack of the discharges. Several Britannian soldiers stumbled and fell, but the line pressed forward without breaking formation.

Another naval salvo crashed into the fort's defenses. More sections of wall crumbled under the bombardment, creating gaps in the wall of the fortification. Valdar counted at least three Egyptian cannons silenced, their positions marked by smoking craters in the masonry.

"Reduce elevation two degrees," he ordered. "We'll open the wall at ground level."

But as he spoke, the fort's remaining artillery responded. Heavy guns roared from the protected positions within the fortress, their shells screaming across the battlefield. The Egyptian gunners had found their range on the advancing legions.

Valdar watched in grim silence as the explosions tore into Aelius's formations. Whole squads disappeared in clouds of fire and shrapnel as a reign of explosive shells fell among the lines. The neat lines wavered and broke as men sought whatever cover they could find on the exposed ground.

No. They had to keep moving forward. That was killing ground.

Aelius must have seen it too and understood that meant the attack had stalled. The retreat horn sounded a moment later as Aelius's cohorts pulled back in fighting order, carrying their wounded with them. It was the right call. With the momentum stalled, it saved Aelius's command from complete destruction, but the assault had failed against the fort's concentrated firepower.

"Closer to shore. We need suppressing fire for the withdrawal."

The ironclads moved forward through the muddy water, their shallow drafts allowing them to approach within fifty yards of the riverbank.

"Target their gun embrasures. Keep those cannons busy while Aelius regroups."

The naval bombardment intensified as the gunboats concentrated their fire on the Egyptian artillery. Shell after shell crashed into the fort's cannon positions, sending up fountains of stone and metal. The defenders' return fire slackened as their crews took shelter from the devastating barrage.

But the Egyptian cannons were well protected. The thick stone walls absorbed tremendous punishment while most of the gun positions remained largely intact, even returning fire. Shells began to hammer into the ironclads, one taking a direct hit on her forward gun, killing three crew members and putting the weapon out of action.

Valdar studied the battlefield through his spyglass as Aelius regrouped just outside the enemy guns' range, where the ground dipped down slightly, giving some protection. The infantry assault had been repelled with significant casualties, and the naval bombardment alone couldn't silence the fort's artillery.

Valdar was looking at another failed attack.

"Back us away," Valdar said now that the infantry was safe.

No reason to endanger the ships more than he had to while trying to figure things out. He was just starting to think through options when a horn sounded.

For a moment, Valdar thought Aelius was resuming his attack, except a quick check showed them still in place.

The horn sounded again and Valdar turned his glass across the field, trying to figure out where it came from. Then he saw it.

From the east, a large force was approaching rapidly. For a moment, Valdar worried this was a sallying Egyptian force, and then shells began to fire, and he knew it was Britannian from the arch of the rounds that signaled them as howitzers.

Shells began to fall across the fort's eastern wall.

Valdar stared hard at the force, trying to figure out what was happening. In the distance, he could see a banner at the rear of the force. Red and gold, not a normal Britannian standard, and yet a Britannian force. Symbols flashed through Valdar's mind until he arrived at the answer, the Ulaid royal banner. Which part of the Ulaid royal family was here?

"Signal all ships," Valdar commanded. "Coordinate fire with the eastern attack. We have them flanked now."

"I think that's Prince Cormac's banner," one of the sailors said.

The man was from Ulaid. If he said it was so, then it was. Although the last Valdar had heard, the prince was in Carthage.

The three-pronged assault developed rapidly. Cormac's cannons pounded the fort's eastern defenses while Valdar's gunboats maintained their bombardment from the river. Aelius reorganized his battered legions for a renewed assault on the main gates, having his own cannon hammering the northern side of the fort.

"Bring us back in. Concentrated barrage, all ships, same target. Let's bring that wall down."

The flotilla closed with the shore again, to maximize effectiveness against the crumbling fortifications.

The coordinated fire from three directions began to overwhelm the Egyptian defenders. Shells pounded the fort from the east, west, and north, hammering away. The stone walls, already becoming a thing of the past with the introduction of explosive shells, cracked and crumbled under the sustained bombardment.

As he watched, sections of the fort's river wall collapsed into the water. The eastern defenses fared even worse as several breaches opened in the masonry. Dust clouds obscured much of the fortress as debris rained down on the defenders.

The naval guns hammered at the weakened fortifications, each shell enlarging the gaps in the defensive walls. The Egyptian return fire had almost ceased, their cannons either destroyed or abandoned as the bombardment continued.

Large gaps appeared in multiple sections of the fort's perimeter, creating openings large enough for the attacking infantry.

Britannian infantry from both armies poured through the breaches in the fort's walls. Aelius's legions charged through the main gaps while Cormac's forces attacked from the east. In close-quarter battles like this, without organized lines of battle, the lever-action rifles gave them a decisive advantage as they fought their way into the fortress interior.

The fire from the ships slowed and then stopped as Valdar ordered them to cease fire. With their troops in the fort now, their fire caused more harm than help. The Egyptian defenders, armed with slower-loading muskets, found themselves unable to match the sustained fire from the attacking infantry. Squad after squad of Britannians advanced into the fortress, clearing the defenders.

Now was the part he hated. Limited information came his way as the legionaries cleared the fort. They didn't have time to communicate with the flotilla out on the river, whose job was now finished.

Thankfully, he didn't have to wait terribly long.

Within an hour, the resistance collapsed. The Egyptian flag disappeared from the fort's highest tower, replaced moments later by a Britannian standard.

The battle was over. Aelius and Cormac's forces were already organizing their prisoners and casualties, securing the fortress and establishing defensive positions. The river approach to Cairo now lay open, although there had been a cost.

The ironclad which had been hit in the gun port had suffered the worst of the casualties, but the other gunboats also showed signs of battle damage, their armor scarred by Egyptian shot but still seaworthy.

"Signal the legion commanders," Valdar ordered his flag officer. "Request casualty reports and operational status."

Now they had to plan their next move up the river.

Chapter 2

Hofstadir, Svealand Region, Scandia

It was cold. She'd grown up in Britannia and had dealt with its winters and regular rain in all that time. But there was cold ... and then there was Scandi.

She was leaning against the railing, watching the port village come into view, her cloak pulled tight against her to protect her from the frigid air over the waters.

She'd been here before, as a younger woman with her father when he'd come to negotiate some trade. They'd been hostile then, afraid to align with an enemy of the Carthaginians. Her father's ship had needed to sneak into port in the dead of night.

Now she was here, in the daylight, the power of the greatest empire in the known world behind her.

And yet none of it seemed to matter to this tiny collection of villages, not even with a new existential threat clawing its way toward them.

Last night, she'd told Ky it was 'just ruffled feathers,' but in her gut, not even she believed what she'd been selling. The reports that arrived after the Scandi representatives left Devnum a week ago, just after their departure, had been troubling. Someone was stirring dissent among the villages, questioning the alliance they had worked so carefully to forge.

In her experience, mysterious opposition usually meant external influence, and with the Eastern Empire still pressing their war effort, any destabilization of their carefully constructed alliances could prove catastrophic.

She had sent word to Talogren immediately, asking the Caledonian chieftain to oversee imperial affairs in her absence. The thought of leaving Titus in someone else's care, even temporarily, created a knot in her stomach that the sea voyage had done nothing to ease.

Not that she'd had any choice other than to come.

The captain called out from behind her as the ship was about to dock. Lucilla gathered her traveling cloak closer and prepared to disembark. Whatever was happening in Scandia, she would face it directly rather than allow their hard-won alliance to crumble through neglect or miscommunication.

No one was there to greet them, none of the pomp that normally accompanied her arrival. She didn't take it personally. She was determined and focused.

She and her entourage made their way to the center of the village, to the hall that her father had been to once before, larger than it was then, some of the newer building techniques recently made popular in Britannia clearly in place.

That is not what interested her, however.

What interested her was the large number of people gathered outside of it. At least that explained the lack of reception.

Inside the hall, people filled the available space, their attention focused at the center of the hall where a long table had been set up. Behind it, she saw the faces of elders she knew.

Ragnvald and Merimund were there, along with Biorngeir and Einarb from the southern regions.

Some of the men who'd been at the negotiations a week ago.

There were more. Men she hadn't met but some she recognized by reputation and some she had no idea who they were. Based on where they were seated, they had to be elders. And if that was true, elders from most of the regions of Scandia were present.

Concerning.

She knew someone else, as well. The young man standing in front of them. The young man who'd come with Ragnvald and the rest to Devnum. Like them, he was dressed finely, although more finely than any of the elders.

Her appearance had caused a stir as they entered, and the young nobleman turned toward her, a smile spreading across his face that held no warmth whatsoever.

"And here," he declared, raising his voice and pointing directly at her. "We have proof of everything I have been telling you. The Empress of Britannia herself arrives to ensure our compliance with her demands."

The hall fell silent as every head turned toward Lucilla. She kept her expression neutral, neither advancing nor retreating.

"You see how quickly they respond when their interests are threatened. Not a month passes after we sign their treaty before imperial representatives arrive to supervise our affairs. Is this the independence they promised us? Is this the respect for Scandi sovereignty we were assured would remain intact? I tell you, this alliance they have negotiated is nothing more than a carefully disguised enslavement of our people."

An elder she didn't know stood and said, "You speak of enslavement, Beruwald, but where were your concerns when Eastern ships tried to push their way north?"

"Have Eastern armies threatened our shores? Have foreign invaders landed on our beaches? No. The only foreign power that has brought hardship to our people sits in that imperial palace in Devnum. They strangled our trade with their embargo. They watched our families go hungry while they demanded our submission. They ..."

Elder Ragnvald attempted to respond. "The embargo was a problem, but we've done the same thing to other nations, in negotiations. There were misunderstandings ..."

"Misunderstandings?" Beruwald said, cutting him off. "Tell that to the families who lost their homes. Tell that to the young people who fled south seeking work because there was none here. Tell that to the merchants whose businesses collapsed while Britannian ships enforced their blockade. This is how the Britannians work. They work through economic pressure to create webs of debt and obligation. Today, it is trade agreements and military cooperation. Tomorrow, it will be Britannian governors appointed over Scandi villages. The day after that, our young men will march in their legions while our resources flow south to feed their empire."

"The terms were fair," Elder Merimund protested weakly. "We negotiated protections for our autonomy."

"Protections written in their language, negotiated under the threat of continued embargo, and interpreted by their representatives," Beruwald shot back. "How many times in history have such agreements protected the weaker party when the stronger decided their interests had changed?"

"The benefits we have gained ... Britannian merchants pay fair prices for our goods. Their knowledge has improved our tools," one of the other elders said.

"Scraps from their table," Beruwald replied dismissively. "Token gestures to maintain the illusion of partnership while they position themselves to control our future entirely. They offer you just enough to forget the pain they caused, but never enough to truly prosper independently. I speak to you today not as an enemy of progress or prosperity, but as someone who believes we can achieve both without sacrificing our independence. There is an alternative to this false choice between starvation and submission."

He paused, turning to face the audience instead of the elders.

"Hordaland, which I represent, has chosen a different path. Communities across Scandia are discovering that they can prosper through cooperation with each other rather than dependence on foreign powers. We offer mutual support, shared resources, and collective defense without requiring anyone to surrender their sovereignty. These villages have chosen self-determination over foreign domination. Communities that have discovered they can achieve prosperity through their own efforts rather than imperial charity."

"What exactly are you offering?" someone from the crowd called.

Beruwald smiled, clearly pleased by the question. "Immediate financial assistance to any community that chooses to join our coalition. Resources to replace whatever trade benefits you might lose by rejecting the Western alliance. Even some technological knowledge Britannia would withhold or offer at a price. These are not promises for the future but resources available today. Villages that join our coalition receive immediate support for their local economies. Families receive direct assistance during difficult times. Businesses gain access to new markets and opportunities that do not require submission to foreign oversight."

A murmur passed across the crowd. Lucilla frowned. She was not surprised by the offer, but the mention of technological knowledge did bother her.

"The embargo taught us valuable lessons," Beruwald continued. "It showed us that depending on foreign powers leaves us vulnerable to their whims. But it also demonstrated our resilience and resourcefulness when forced to rely on ourselves. The choice before you is simple. Will you accept the charity offered by the same power that brought you to your knees or will you join with your fellow Scandi to create prosperity through our own strength and wisdom?"

Elder Ragnvald attempted to restore order. "These are serious decisions that require careful consideration. We propose that each village return to discuss these matters with their full communities before making any commitments."

"Of course," Beruwald agreed smoothly. "But remember that opportunities like this do not remain available indefinitely. Other regions are eager to join our coalition, and our resources must be allocated to those who demonstrate commitment to our shared vision."

The implied pressure was subtle but clear, and Lucilla could see its effect on the crowd.

The formal meeting began to dissolve as villagers broke into smaller groups to continue their discussions. Supporters of each position gathered around their respective leaders, with tensions remaining high between the competing factions.

As the main crowd dispersed, several elders who had participated in the original alliance negotiations made their way toward her.

They looked worried.

"Empress," Elder Ragnvald said quietly. "Beruwald has been distributing silver to influential families throughout the region for weeks. Not just small gifts, but substantial payments that exceed what most of these people earn in a full season."

"The young man clearly has significant resources," Elder Biorngeir added. "More than any single village or even region should be able to command. We suspect outside support, but we have been unable to determine the source."

"I have the same suspicions," Lucilla said.

"But what can be done?" Elder Merimund asked. "Beruwald's supporters grow bolder each day, and his promises become more generous. Several villages have already announced their intention to join his coalition. We need to find a way to counter him."

"I know," Lucilla said. "I'll deal with him."

Of course, she had no idea yet how she'd do that.

Devnum

Talogren studied the dispatch from the southern settlements. Mostly just the normal complaints. Requests for delays in tax payments, requests for engineers to work on this or that municipal project, requests for help with some local bandit problem.

Always requests. He'd always pushed his people to be self-reliant, to deal with their own areas and look to the central leadership for coordination and under extraordinary circumstances.

The Romans had always been softer, more needy.

Still, he wasn't just the chieftain of the Caledonii anymore. He'd agreed to join this empire, and that included dealing with his softer neighbors.

Of course, that was before the Empress had waylaid him and forced him to sit on the cursed throne and deal with their petty complaints day in and day out.

"Chief Talogren, there is a captain from the docks who says he needs to meet with the Empress. He is from one of the Scandi merchant groups, I believe, although I do not recognize him," one of the aides who had been helping him work through the day-to-day issues said.

Talogren, happy to have a reprieve from the complaints of local mayors, waved to let the man in.

A weathered man in sailor's garb was shown into the room. Talogren had half expected a merchant factor of some kind. With the soft hands and fine clothes of many of the rich men who had fattened themselves over the last seven years as the logicians to the western world.

No, this was a kind of man Talogren was more familiar with. A true man of the sea, one of the rough Northmen that he had come to know in his childhood when the Romans were threats and not friends and they had needed every friend they could get.

The man looked confused to see a large, bearded Caledonian on the throne and not a much smaller woman.

"I'm sorry, I came looking for the Consul or the Empress," he said, pausing a few steps into the audience chamber.

"I am Chief Talogren, leader of the Caledonii and in line for the throne of Britannia. The Consul leads the war effort in the east and the Empress is away. If you have something to say, tell me, or you can wait. I'm sure it will only be a month or two until she returns."

Another thing that grated on Talogren. He was one of the three rulers who made up the Empire and, at the moment, had the power of the throne behind him. And yet he still had to identify who he was each time.

The man waffled for a moment and then said, "I am from Captain Yrsa's fleet. Have you been briefed on our ... I'm sorry, but I was given to understand our mission was not for public knowledge."

He stopped to look around the room at all the courtiers and officials gathered there, ostensibly to be available to do Talogren's bidding, but it seemed more so to be seen as being at court, better setting up their own position.

But he was also right. Talogren had a vague memory of an expedition sent out by the Consul almost a year ago, although he hadn't been very clear on the goal of that expedition at the time. He did, however, remember the name of the merchant Yrsa attached to it, along with the air of secrecy.

"Aye." Talogren waved his hand toward the administrators and nobles. "Leave us."

The clerks, officials, and hangers-on gathered their things and departed through the side entrances.

When the last of them had gone, the captain said, "I do not know how much you know, but the Consul sent Captain Yrsa west with three ships to a great landmass beyond the ocean, although not nearly as distant as the eastern homelands themselves. A continent sitting between two vast seas."

"I assume the Consul's information was correct?"

"It was. We found it using the course and maps the Consul provided about a month's sail to the west. The only thing he was wrong about was the size. Massive doesn't begin to describe it. We sailed days north from where we first made shore and the shoreline never seemed to end. It went on forever."

"Were you intercepted by ships along the shoreline?"

"Only small fishing ships that mostly kept their distance, but were curious about us. It reminds me somewhat of how the captains who sailed down the coast of Africa spoke of the locals they found there. Scattered villages with limited technology. We found the place the Consul advised for a colony, set it up, and began to make our way toward where the Consul indicated we'd find large deposits of nitrate, which was the main part of our mandate."

"Did you find them?"

"Eventually. Deposits larger than anything we've seen. Enough to supply our gunpowder mills for years, maybe decades."

That was the part Talogren remembered. There had been an increasing shortage of the chemical the wizards in Factorium cooked up, and he'd been hearing alarms in his briefings about supplies running low due to the high pressures of the war.

"You were able to start the mining operations?"

"To a small degree, yes. We are limited by our numbers, even when factoring in the locals we've managed to employ. But the surveys confirm the deposits are as rich as the Consul said. Although we did run into opposition."

"The same locals that you recruited?"

"Not the same. There seems to be limited coordination between the tribes, or in some cases collection of tribes, but yes, some were very hostile. They resisted our landing, fought us during construction. They caused significant casualties among our people before we established defensive positions. Some groups number in the hundreds, others much smaller. Several skirmishes cost us dearly before we negotiated arrangements with certain friendly groups and, dare I say, protection."

"You made arrangements with them?"

"Trade agreements mostly. Some tribal leaders agreed to assist with locating the deposits and providing labor in exchange for manufactured goods and our help protecting them from their enemies. They are particularly interested in the muskets the Consul sent with us."

"Were you able to deal with the hostile tribes, or are they still a threat?"

"Very much still a threat. Things are precarious without reinforcements. The colony holds its position, but larger native coalitions could overwhelm our defenses. The only thing that has stopped them so far was a fairly widespread disease outbreak among several tribal groups, but that won't last forever."

"I assume you came back seeking help with that, then?"

"Yes, that is one of the reasons Yrsa ordered me to return. We need additional legionaries to secure the territory against continued resistance, more miners to expand production, regular supply shipments of gunpowder, rifles, military equipment, and skilled craftsmen and engineers to improve mining infrastructure and even set up some processing facilities if possible."

"So in short ... everything."

"Yes. Our initial group was mostly meant to establish a foothold. We never had enough resources for a permanent settlement. I think it was always intended that we return once we accomplished that. We began the mining because we knew that was needed, but beyond that, we also need more men for the secondary objectives the Consul gave us. Additional mining of metals, accessing the very large timber reserves, and the like."

"How long do you think the colony can hold until you return?"

"The disease problem was still raging through the native populations, so things should be settled for some time. I imagine with the food we have and the farming the captain set up as soon as we got a basic camp in place, in addition to the trade with the friendly locals, they should be good through the winter, but without more manpower there will be trouble come the spring."

Talogren nodded. There was some urgency, but there was also some time, which was good.

"I see. Recruitment efforts will begin immediately. I'll make it clear the orders are for recruitment for settlements along the African coast, since we know some Eastern spies still operate within our borders, and the Consul believed it wise to keep knowledge of this new land a secret. That will at least prepare whoever signs up for an extended stay far away from their homes without giving away this continent's existence."

"A wise move," the sailor said.

"I will get together a small fleet to return with you, so that they can bring enough men and load up on supplies for the return trip. Along with men, gunpowder, more muskets, and other trade goods, I will also send some of the new rifles and ammunition for them with you."

"I actually came with our first shipment of potassium nitrate loaded in my holds."

"Really? That is fortuitous. We will get that offloaded and on a train to Factorium today. It will take some time to get the supplies and manpower together, as well as the ships. I want you to hold here if you can, so you can lead the ships to your new port."

"I have some charts showing where we are established. It is where the Consul said, so he should be aware."

"Still, I would feel more comfortable if you were here to take them in. I will try to have them prepared within the month. With sailing times that might even get them back to the colony by early winter."

"Thank you. I'll return to my ship and see that the nitrate is offloaded today, and then wait for your word."

"Good," Talogren said.

At least this gave him something to focus on instead of the inane complaints for a time.

Chapter 3

Camp Banwīhraz, Central Germania

The room was stark, one of imprisonment and interrogation, meant to give the power to the jailer and oppress the jailed.

You wouldn't know that from seeing the Easterner sitting at the simple wooden table, working his way through a plate of roasted lamb and root vegetables. Far from the standard fare for a prisoner.

"Leave us," she said to the guards.

They exchanged glances but obeyed without question, filing out and pulling the heavy door shut behind them, the lock mechanism clicking into place with finality.

Fa Jian looked up at her, but didn't pause his eating, slowly cutting another piece of meat as Medb pulled out a chair opposite him and sat, leaning back and watching him.

"Better than field rations, I'd imagine," she said. "Though I suppose we have to be careful not to make your preferential treatment too obvious."

He didn't answer right away, slowly chewing a bite before setting his utensils down.

"I do not think they see. You choose people every day for ... talking. Very smart idea. All camp thinks it is a trick. You bring people, sit for hours, ask nothing, do no hurt, almost not look at them. They think they are more smart than you when they do not talk. People you choose get help from others after. Extra food. Small things. They think they fight against you together."

"Good. That was exactly what I intended. Your government is too centralized and controlled, so most don't know any of the long-term planning, just carry out the orders they are given as the orders come down. Those that do, we question before they are put into the camp. This is just a holding pen, so if it works to screen our conversation, then I wish them luck in their opposition. I've been thinking about what you told me last time, about this resistance network among the Han. You've given me fragments, but I need to understand how it actually functions. You mentioned cells, but that could mean anything from three malcontents meeting in a barn to something far more sophisticated."

"More big than that, but less than we used to be. Old resistance try to organize like an army. Leaders, followers, one big boss. That was the time of my grandfather. Empire destroyed them in a few months. Now we work differently. Keep small and local. No more than twelve people in one group. Most groups do not know about others. Those who know have almost no contact. It limits much what we can do, but it keeps us alive."

"But surely you need some way to coordinate, otherwise you're just isolated groups accomplishing nothing. How do you even recruit in a setup like that?"

"Some of our angrier people argue the same thing. But yes, we coordinate. It is slow and careful. Through middle people. No real names, mostly fake names. For finding new people ... the army draft gives us the best chance. When the empire takes young men from villages, they make ready groups of angry people. Bitter words about leaving sick parents, fields without men to work them. We watch for these small signs. That was my main job. As a Banner Army officer, I have perfect access. Who thinks an officer moving up through the ranks the proper way is a spy? I could move between army posts, find people who might help among both drafted men and career soldiers."

"Until this war pulled you west. Do you have any idea how many groups actually exist?"

"I knew twelve in my area. If I guess from communication and other things ... maybe three hundred in all the empire. But that is just guessing. I not think anyone knows the true answer."

"Three hundred cells of a dozen or so members each, even if that is all of the cells, which is probably unlikely, that isn't even four thousand. You realize how inadequate that sounds?"

"Each active person has family, friends who help even if they do not know they help. A farmer who looks away when strangers cross his fields. A merchant who forgets to report strange buying. Active resistance is small, but the support network goes deeper."

"Still, you're talking about overthrowing an empire that's lasted centuries with what amounts to a loose association of malcontents and sympathizers. What exactly do you hope to achieve?"

"Freedom. To see Han rulers rule Han people. To end the draft that bleeds our villages. To stop watching our children marched away to die in foreign wars."

"Those are all noble aims, but I asked about practical objectives. Have you ever actually tried to act on these grand ambitions?"

Fa Jian pushed his plate aside, his expression darkening. "Fifteen years ago, three groups in Yúnzhōng worked together to attack the garrison. They beat guards, took weapons, said Han rule was back. Empire response was ... complete. Not just rebels. Their families, their villages, anyone who might know them. Public killings for weeks. The provincial governor made everyone watch."

"So now you focus on smaller goals?"

"We protect Han communities. Gather information. Help soldiers run away when possible. Survival instead of revolution, as you say."

"Because revolution requires hope, and your emperor has crushed that for generations. I'm curious about this man. I've heard similar stories from a few prisoners, but they speak of him like a force of nature rather than a man. Help me understand this fear that seems to paralyze even hardened resistance fighters."

"You cannot fear what you cannot understand. The emperor is beyond fear. He is like winter or death, unstoppable. No one has seen him for many years, but his hand moves everywhere. People who speak against him disappear. Often not even arrested and killed. They just ... stop existing."

"Someone must see him. Even hidden rulers need servants, physicians ..."

"I am sure they do. But they are kept in the palace, never allowed to leave. Locked in the same way others are locked out. They serve for life and never leave the deepest part of the Forbidden City."

"Terror alone can't maintain an empire. He must have other methods of control."

"The emperor has ten thousand eyes. In every village, someone reports to the local official. In every army unit, political officers watch for loyalty. Even in families, children are taught that reporting parents who speak against the empire is the highest good. We live in a prison of mutual suspicion that has lasted for generations."

"Every empire believes itself eternal. Every tyrant thinks his rule unbreakable. History proves otherwise. Which brings us to why we're having this conversation. Your empire attacked mine without provocation. They burned one of our ports, invaded our territories, started a war that's cost thousands of lives. That makes us natural allies against a common enemy."

"Allies. An interesting term from someone holding me prisoner."

"Would you prefer I release you to your fellow prisoners, let them know what we've been up to? I'm certain they'd welcome a Banner Army officer who collaborates with the enemy with open arms. No? Then perhaps we can discuss this like adults who understand necessity. Your emperor, and the system of oppression he has set up, threatens both our peoples. You want them gone. We want them stopped. Our interests align perfectly."

"Do they? You help us and win. What stops your people from just replacing the emperor as our master? Your empire spans from these lands to Africa. You conquered nations, absorbed kingdoms. Why should we believe you would stop at our borders?"

"I think you are confusing an alliance of countries for mutual defense and a single country. Germania, where we sit, has its own government and rules. Italia has its own government. Gaul, Hispania, Scandi. Before the war, we traded and worked together, but we were not all ruled as one. Besides, look at the distances involved. From the front lines of the war to your homeland exceeds the entire width of our current alliance, if I understand it correctly. We never tried to go to Persia and, in spite of knowing of your existence, from your emperor helping the Carthaginians, never attempted to travel to the east. Because logistically, it is a difficult thing. And even harder to maintain control outside of war."

"Your version assumes we started this war. Emperor's announcements say Westerners caused conflict. Attacked first."

"And you believe these proclamations?"

"What I believe matters little. Truth of who started this war changes nothing for my people. They remain under TianYou rule regardless."

"But that could change with the right pressure applied in the right places." Medb watched his reaction carefully. "The Han resistance lacks resources and coordination. Britannia has both in abundance. Properly applied, those resources could transform scattered cells into an effective force."

"Supplies cannot cross so much hostile territory. Even if they could, border watches would stop any support before it traveled into the empire. The watching network I just told you about ... how do you plan to bypass it?"

"That is the problem we have to solve, isn't it? What if I could get you home?"

The question clearly caught him off guard. His composure cracked slightly, revealing genuine surprise before he reasserted control.

"That's impossible."

"Is it? Ships sail many routes. Documents can be created. A Banner Army officer separated from his unit during the Western campaigns, making his way home through irregular channels, would that be so unusual in the chaos of war?"

"Political officers would question any returning soldier extensively. Slightest mistake ..."

"Then we ensure your story withstands scrutiny. You were captured early in the conflict, held in various camps, escaped during a transfer, traveled slowly to avoid recapture. Details can be crafted to match known events. I'm very good at creating believable lies."

"Even if I reached home safely, what then? One man cannot change the empire's fate."

"One man with the right connections can do a great deal. You know which cells can be trusted. Which officers sympathize with the resistance. Where to place resources for maximum effect. You could be our bridge to the resistance network."

"Supplies that still cannot reach us. You have not answered how your support could possibly reach us."

"Let me worry about the logistics. I'm asking a simpler question, if I could arrange safe passage home, would you go? Would you resume your resistance work knowing that this time, you might not be alone?"

He was quiet for a long moment before saying, "To see home again. To walk among my people. Yes. If you could truly do this, I would return. I would contact cells I trust, organize what resistance I could."

"Then we have an understanding." Medb stood. "I'll need detailed information, every detail you can remember once we work out a plan for this. You will not be a passive participant. We have resources, but the thing we lack is information."

"You truly mean to attempt this?" There was something almost like hope in his voice now.

"I've accomplished more unlikely things," she said, standing. "Tomorrow we'll start with geography, every route you know, every checkpoint, every seasonal variation, what the empire's control out into the sea looks like. Then documentation, procedures, personnel. Every detail that might help someone navigate your homeland."

Fa Jian stood as well. "I hope you are as able as you say."

"Time will tell," she said, knocking on the door. "Guard!"

The lock disengaged and the door swung open.

"Return him to general population," Medb ordered.

As they moved to flank him, Fa Jian offered a slight bow. "Until tomorrow, then."

"Until tomorrow."

She watched them escort him down the corridor; plans were already forming, pieces sliding into position. She had the inkling of a plan, but there was much to do to make it real.

Wistla River

Bomilcar stood on the muddy western bank of the Wistla, watching as fifteen ironclad riverboats turned the corner. It was still early in the day and the light was low, hiding the plume of smoke that rose off the group of them for a moment. These were all the riverboats he was able to pull together over the last few weeks for this assault.

He just hoped it would be enough.

The plan had started when the enemy had begun to dig their trenches in this sector. Along most of the line, the enemy trenches were almost half a mile back, putting everyone's artillery in range of the river, but not so close that they were susceptible to the ironclads, which could put direct fire on them while withstanding the pounding they'd take in return.

In this sector, that had not happened.

The Eastern armies' zigzagging earthworks cut close to the river, in some cases only back a few hundred meters, a new metric of distance the Consul had started drilling into the army personnel.

The enemy was too confident, and Bomilcar hoped that confidence was going to cost them today.

The Eastern sentries probably heard the ships first, before they saw them, the loud steam engines collectively making a hell of a racket, even over the sporadic artillery fire that never seemed to stop along the long front.

Bomilcar could see men running along the trench lines through his spyglass, followed by the sound of horns announcing an oncoming battle.

The lead riverboat brought her broadside to bear. Her captain had positioned the vessel perfectly, presenting her armored side to the enemy while her six rifled cannon tracked toward the Eastern positions.

The first salvo erupted in an orange flame and white smoke poured from the gun ports. Shells screamed across the four hundred yards of open water and the shells struck the forward trench line in a series of devastating explosions. Earth fountained skyward as the fused charges detonated on impact, hurling sandbags and wooden planking through the air.

Bodies tumbled from the firing steps as concussion waves rippled through the enemy positions. One shell must have found an ammunition depot, the secondary explosion sending a pillar of black smoke climbing into the morning sky.

The second riverboat fired her broadside, then the third. Each vessel added her voice to the bombardment, shells falling in steady succession along the Eastern line. The enemy trenches disappeared behind curtains of smoke and flying debris. Splinters of wood and clods of earth rained down on the defenders as they cowered in their dugouts.

Behind Bomilcar, his own artillery batteries opened fire. Dozens of howitzers added their deeper voices to the chorus, lobbing shells in high arcs over the water. The shore guns had better angles on the enemy's rear positions, their plunging fire reaching targets the riverboats could not see.

Between the two, they completely bracketed the enemy position, laying down a devastating fire.

As impressive as it was, Bomilcar knew it wouldn't be enough to win the battle itself. Artillery could stop charges and cause terrible casualties, but it took infantry to actually move the front forward.

The Eastern response came within minutes. Their artillery, positioned behind the trenches, began returning fire. The first enemy shells fell short, throwing up geysers of water between the riverboats and the shore. The Eastern gunners were firing blind through the smoke of their own burning positions, but they adjusted their aim quickly. The next salvo bracketed the lead riverboat, one shell punching through her upper works and another clanging off her armored side.

Bomilcar gave another signal.

The moment the colored flag went up, engineers emerged from their concealed positions, teams of men carrying the pre-assembled pontoon sections toward the water's edge. Each pontoon was a wooden platform two and a half meters square, reinforced with iron bracing and fitted with rope loops for lashing to its neighbors. The engineers had spent weeks preparing these sections, knowing they would have only minutes to deploy them under fire.

The first team reached the river's edge and slid their pontoon into the muddy water. The platform rode low but stable, designed to support the weight of marching soldiers while remaining easy to maneuver. The second team followed, their pontoon sliding into place beside the first. Ropes flashed as the engineers lashed the sections together, creating a growing platform that extended into the current.

Enemy rifle fire began crackling from the Eastern trenches. The engineers made tempting targets, silhouetted against the water as they worked. Bullets whined overhead and splashed into the river around the pontoon builders. One man cried out and stumbled backward, into the water.

Bomilcar turned to the centurion commanding his covering force. The man needed no orders; squads of riflemen were already moving forward, taking positions along the bank where they could fire across the water. The new lever-action rifles gave his men a decisive advantage in this kind of firefight. Each soldier could fire seven rounds without reloading, maintaining a volume of fire that no enemy equipped with single-shot weapons could match.

The riflemen opened fire in rolling volleys, their weapons crackling like burning branches. Across the water, Eastern soldiers ducked below their parapets as bullets smacked into sandbags and splintered wooden reinforcements. The covering fire was not meant to inflict casualties so much as to suppress the enemy's ability to target the bridge builders.

On the water, the battle still raged.

The third riverboat in line took a direct hit from an Eastern cannon. The shell punched through her thin armor plating near the waterline, the explosion buckling plates and starting a fire in her forward magazine. Smoke poured from the breach as her crew fought to control the damage. Her captain kept the guns firing even as water flooded the lower compartments.

That had been a lucky shot, however.

The Eastern artillery concentrated its fire on the lead riverboat, recognizing her as the flotilla's flagship. Shell after shell slammed into her superstructure, each impact sending fragments flying across her deck. Her smokestack crumpled under a direct hit, the twisted metal falling across her stern gun. Fires broke out in three places as her crew struggled to maintain their stations.

The riverboat's return fire never slackened.

It continued to provide cover for the engineers as more pontoons slid into the water. The bridge was taking shape with remarkable speed, a testament to the planning that had gone into this operation. The current pushed against the structure, but anchor ropes held it in position as the bridge reached the quarter-way point across the river.

Another riverboat moved into the line of battle, her captain maneuvering into position to replace one of the damaged vessels that was retreating. Her guns added their weight to the bombardment, shells arcing across the water to burst among the enemy positions. Even though the sun has come up all the way now, the Eastern trenches were barely visible through the smoke and dust of the ongoing barrage.

Time ticked by. As smoothly as this operation seemed to be going, it took time to build a bridge like this, especially under fire.

Next to the new arrival, the lead riverboat had developed a pronounced list as it took on water. Her captain ordered the starboard guns abandoned as water reached the gun deck, but the port battery continued firing. The bow of the vessel was settling, her armored prow riding lower in the water with each passing minute. Steam escaped from ruptured pipes in her engine room, white vapor mixing with the black smoke of her fires.

The ship wouldn't be long for this world, but it wasn't going out without a fight.

The bridge had gotten close enough that enemy sharpshooters began targeting the bridge builders directly, not just hitting with scattered fire. Engineers began to fall, dragged off the bridge and plunging into the waters to be swept downstream, as the work continued.

Bomilcar signaled for additional covering fire. Two more companies of riflemen moved to the riverbank, their weapons adding to the suppressive fire. Among them were his own sharp shooters, trying to counter the fire of the rifles on the other side.

The bridge reached the halfway point. The pontoons stretched across a hundred meters of flowing water, a narrow ribbon of wood and rope that swayed with the current. Engineers continued to work at the growing tip, adding sections as quickly as they could manhandle them into position.

An Eastern shell found the fifth riverboat in line, the explosion tearing through her pilot house and killing her captain instantly. The vessel began to drift as her crew fought for control.

Bomilcar silently urged the men to move faster. The riverboats were strong, but they couldn't take this barrage forever. He needed men on the other shore.

The Eastern artillery was finding its mark more frequently now. Their gunners had adjusted for range and deflection, walking their shells onto target. The riverboats were taking a pounding. No armor was made to stand up to this level of punishment. But they held their positions, trading damage for time while the bridge neared completion.

They weren't the only ones paying the price.

Bodies floated downstream as Eastern marksmen found their targets among the bridge builders. The engineers worked over the corpses of their comrades, lashing pontoons together while bullets cracked overhead.

More pontoons splashed into the water. The bridge was three-quarters complete now, reaching toward the Eastern shore like an accusing finger.

The lead riverboat finally succumbed to her damage. Water flooded her engine room as her boilers went cold, and her list increased until her port rail touched the surface. As she settled onto the muddy bottom her crew abandoned ship, swimming toward the friendly bank with her superstructure still visible above the waterline.

She wasn't the only one suffering badly.

Two more riverboats showed serious damage. The third vessel in line had lost her steering and was drifting sideways in the current, her crew fighting to regain control. The eleventh boat had fires burning on two decks, her crew forming bucket brigades to fight the flames.

But it was working. The bridge was almost complete.

Bomilcar turned to his waiting assault troops. Two full cohorts stood ready, their rifles loaded and bayonets fixed. These men would be the first across, fighting their way onto the shore held by the Easterners while the bridge builders completed their work.

The bridge touching the Eastern shore signaled the raising of the flag that would start the full assault. Men moved forward at the double, four men abreast in a column that stretched back along the bridge. As they reached the halfway point, the double-time march became a charge as rifle fire increased from the trench line.

The Easterners unleashed everything they had.

Men fell in groups, their bodies tumbling from the pontoons or collapsing on the wooden planks. The column wavered as soldiers behind the fallen struggled to advance over the bodies of their comrades. Some men tried to push the corpses aside; others simply stepped over them and continued forward.

Centurions drove their men onward with shouted commands and physical force. The assault could not stop, regardless of casualties. If the attack failed now, the bridge would be wasted and the entire operation would collapse. Officers pushed their way through the packed ranks, urging soldiers forward while bullets cracked around them.

The lead elements reached the Eastern shore. They leaped from the bridge onto the muddy bank, men firing away. But the defenders were ready for them. A wall of enemy rifle fire met the first soldiers to land, cutting them down before they could advance ten paces from the water's edge.

More men poured off the bridge, adding their weight to the assault. The lever-action rifles gave them a temporary advantage, their rapid fire forcing some defenders to take cover. But the Easterners held strong positions, fighting from prepared trenches while the attackers had to advance across open ground.

Bodies accumulated on the Eastern shore as the assault forces paid the price for their bridgehead. Soldiers fell in heaps, their blood mixing with the river mud.

Soldiers pressed forward from the bridge, their boots slipping in the bloody mud as they scrambled for any cover the riverbank offered. Bodies floated past in the current, grey uniforms dark with water and blood.

A squad of Britannian soldiers managed to reach a shallow depression twenty yards from the water's edge. They dropped prone and began working their lever-action rifles.

The second pontoon bridge had been started downriver from the first. It was going together much faster as the enemy was more focused on the bridgehead. A fatal mistake.

As more and more men poured into the meat grinder in front of the enemy trench, the second and then the third pontoon bridge stretched across the water, growing by the minute.

Eastern shells burst among the advancing troops, their targeting switched from the beleaguered riverboats to the new danger. One detonated directly on the first bridge, splintering pontoons and hurling men into the river. The structure sagged but held, engineers rushing forward with spare sections even as wounded soldiers crawled past them toward safety.

It was too late. The next two pontoon bridges were up, and additional cohorts were pouring across. In three places, the lead elements of these cohorts reached the base of the Eastern earthworks.

And then the first breakthrough.

A Britannian centurion led twenty men in a rush up the earthwork slope. Half fell before reaching the top, but the survivors dropped into the trench beyond. The crack of rifles intensified as they cleared the position at close quarters, working their weapons as fast as they could cycle the actions.

The enemy fire slackened to deal with the breach just as fresh troops poured across all three crossings simultaneously. The weight of numbers began to tell as Britannian soldiers established firing positions along the riverbank and poured volleys into the Eastern trenches.

More squads reached the enemy earthworks. They fired from the hip as they crested the parapet, then jumped down among the defenders. The lever-action rifles proved devastating in the confined space of the trenches. Eastern soldiers with single-shot weapons had no chance to reload between shots. They died with ramrods in their hands or fell back toward their second line.

The first squads managed to get over the rear of the trench, and head toward the rear positions. The ironclads and their artillery had started to fall silent now, as their own men were mixed into the battle.

A Britannian squad captured an Eastern cannon position. They spun the gun on its carriage and fired point-blank down the trench line. The shell exploded among a knot of defenders, clearing twenty yards of earthwork in an instant. More Britannian soldiers poured through the gap.

The breakthrough widened as additional squads flanked along the captured trenches. They moved in bounds, one group firing while another advanced to the next traverse. Grenades preceded them around corners.

Eastern officers tried to organize local counterattacks, but the rapid fire from lever-action rifles broke up their formations before they could close. Bodies accumulated in the trenches as defenders fell back or died where they stood. The systematic clearing continued in both directions from the initial breaches.

Bomilcar ordered two more cohorts forward. The bridges groaned under the weight of continuous traffic, but the structures held. The first medical teams were also sent across to work among the wounded on the eastern bank while fresh troops crossed to exploit the expanding bridgehead.

The enemy wasn't out of it yet.

The Eastern second line erupted in activity. Reserve battalions formed up behind their earthworks as eight hundred men tried to stop the rout that was forming.

They were crossing open ground from reserve trenches, not having yet built up communication trenches to the front where they could move men securely.

They were on open ground, ripe for the picking.

Britannian soldiers in the captured positions saw them coming and began firing immediately. The Eastern charge maintained its momentum through the first hundred yards. Men fell steadily, but their comrades closed the gaps and pressed on.

The volume of Britannian fire intensified. Fresh troops from the bridges reinforced the captured trenches, adding their rifles to the defensive line. The Eastern ranks began to waver as casualties mounted. Gaps appeared that couldn't be filled quickly enough.

The Eastern reinforcements disintegrated under the sustained fire. Small groups pressed forward while others sought cover or turned back. Officers fell trying to rally their men. The organized charge became a scattered rush by desperate individuals.

The attack collapsed before it could reach the now-captured trenches.

Survivors fled toward their second line, many throwing away their weapons to run faster. Britannian rifles continued to fire into their backs until they passed beyond the effective range of the rifles.

The Eastern counterattack had failed completely, leaving their second line weakened and demoralized. This was the moment to press the advantage.

Bomilcar sent in all of his remaining cohorts for the attack, pressing hard.

Britannian soldiers climbed from the captured trenches and advanced across no-man's land. They moved in open order, stopping to fire whenever Eastern defenders showed themselves.

Squads with grenades led the assault on the Eastern second line. They reached the earthworks and hurled their fin-shaped weapons over the parapet. Britannian soldiers followed immediately, jumping down among the dazed survivors.

The second line fell faster than the first. Eastern morale had cracked after their failed counterattack. Many defenders fled rather than face the rapid-firing rifles at close quarters. Those who stayed died in their positions or surrendered when surrounded.

Britannian troops pursued the fleeing Easterners beyond the trench lines. Artillery positions fell into their hands, the gun crews caught trying to limber their pieces for withdrawal. Some guns were turned immediately, firing into the backs of the retreating enemy.

Five hours after the ironclads had turned into the river at dawn, Bomilcar's command group crossed on the central bridge. Sections of the trench line were on fire, the wooden framing lit by explosions.

The breakthrough was complete.

Chapter 4

Devnum Docks

It was a good morning.

After nearly a year of work, the superstructure of the massive, completely metal ship was done and nearly ready for the water. The screw and rudder were in place, connected to the massive quadruple boilers in the center of the beast, ready to push the ship to speeds Lucan would have thought impossible even five years ago, all without the benefit of wind and sail.

There was still a lot of work to be done, however.

Yes, the ship could most likely sail on its own, but it would be simply a mechanical marvel, only able to carry cargo from place to place.

That wasn't what he was making here.

He was making what would be the greatest military vessel to ever slip across the waves, able to shrug off whatever damage one of the Eastern vessels might do to it and crush cities from the coast.

Which is where today's work began.

Arriving at the docks from his office, Lucan looked up at the massive steel hull that seemed to dwarf the caravels under construction around it. Workers moved about it like insects, both finishing the last tasks for the basic construction of the ship and preparing for the work ahead.

The hull stretched nearly ninety meters from bow to stern, its iron plates riveted together in overlapping sections that formed an unbroken barrier against the sea.

First, to inspect their work.

Lucan trusted his men, but trust did not keep ships afloat. Inspections did. His foremen had, of course, already done their checks, but for a project of this importance, he was not willing to rely on them alone.

Lucan pulled his measuring tape from his leather satchel and began his inspection at the bow, running his hands along each rivet line. He traced the curve of the hull where it met the waterline, checking that the plates maintained their proper alignment despite the tremendous weight they now supported.

The stern section drew his particular attention. Here, the propeller shaft emerged from the hull, requiring precise tolerances to prevent water intrusion while allowing the massive bronze screw to turn freely. He crouched low, examining the stern tube assembly where it passed through the hull plates. The bronze fittings had been cast according to specifications the Consul had laid down.

Even with the incredible detail of the Consul's plans, the men putting those plans to work were not sent by the gods. They were hardworking and skilled, but still men.

Which meant errors could be made.

Satisfied with the exterior examination, Lucan climbed the rope ladder to the main deck and then went down the metal ladders through the primary hatch into the ship's interior. The compartments stretched before him in orderly progression. Unlike the open hold of the caravels, these spaces had been planned to accommodate the machinery and crew requirements of steam propulsion.

He moved through each compartment methodically, checking bulkhead alignment and verifying that structural supports had been installed according to plan. Lucan made notes in his journal, marking several locations where the work had to be corrected, small errors that, while they probably wouldn't keep the ship from working, were not up to his standards.

The magazine spaces required his most careful attention. These compartments would store stacks of explosive shells, hundreds and hundreds of them. The storage arrangements had to prevent accidental detonation and had a section that would be fitted with a hydraulic lift, powered by steam from the engines, to carry the shells to the gun deck above.

There were four, one under each gun emplacement, to pull the rounds up to the gunners without having to be walked to them, speeding up how quickly the guns could fire.

This was probably the thing the sailors and gunners would be happiest about. The new cannons that were to be installed were the largest he had ever heard of, let alone seen, and the shells would be equally large. And heavy.

He was sure the men would appreciate not having to carry the shells up a ladder by hand each time one was needed.

His inspection complete, Lucan descended into the engine compartment where the real heart of the vessel awaited.

The space was full of activity as workers made final adjustments to the four massive boilers that would generate steam for both propulsion and to power the hydraulic systems. Each boiler stood nearly three meters tall, its iron construction reinforced with steel bands to contain the tremendous pressures required for efficient operation.

"How are the pressure tests progressing?" Lucan asked the man in charge of this section.

One of Hortensius's people, he had worked on most of the early steam projects and been involved in creating similar, if smaller, setups on the riverboats. He was a wealth of knowledge in this area, and Lucan was happy to have him.

"All four units are holding at maximum working pressure," the man replied, wiping sweat from his brow. "We've tested the relief valves and pressure blow off, and it's as ready as it ever will be."

"Good, good," Lucan said.

He hadn't expected anything different, but this step was needed before they began the work on what was left. Lucan moved to examine the steam distribution manifold. This complex arrangement of pipes and valves would direct steam to the propulsion engines, the hydraulic pumps, and various auxiliary systems throughout the ship.

The main pipes that would feed the entire ship were already in place, but that was just the start. There would have to be channels off these main pipes, controlled by a series of valves and gates, to allow steam through or to cut it off if a section of the ship were compromised, to keep from losing the steam from the engines.

And it seemed likely, even with the ship's thick armor, that those kinds of leaks would happen in battle. The Easterners had, after all, shown amazing skill at copying and getting around the Consul's inventiveness.

The main propulsion engines occupied the center of the compartment, their massive cylinders and connecting rods representing every lesson they had learned with the riverboats. Lucan checked the engine mounts, ensuring that the tremendous forces generated during operation would not crack the hull plates or damage the surrounding equipment.

"I know you did it already, but can we run the test on the governors again. I just want to make sure."

Workers cranked the throttle controls while Lucan observed the governor assemblies. These mechanical devices would automatically regulate steam flow to maintain steady engine speeds regardless of sea conditions or combat maneuvering, or as power from one boiler shifted to another.

The technology had been adapted from Hortensius's workshops and had been in the riverboats, but never to this scale and power.

Steam pressure gauges lined the bulkhead, their brass faces reflecting the compartment's lantern light. Lucan verified that each gauge read accurately and that the spacing allowed maintenance crews to service the equipment without interfering with normal operations.

Satisfied with the engine installation, Lucan climbed back to the main deck where his senior shipwrights and engineering team were assembled. These men represented the finest technical expertise in the Empire, drawn from shipyards, metalworking shops, and Hortensius's facilities.

"The hull and propulsion systems are done," Lucan announced. "Now it's time for the real work to begin."

The men all laughed at that. They had been working on this ship for a year and had gotten used to his dry sense of humor. Most had worked with him longer than that. The majority of the team had also been involved in the work on the river ironclads. Those ships, after all, had been intended both as a tool of war but also as a learning opportunity for the much more complicated work they now faced.

Those vessels had mounted fixed cannons in traditional broadside arrangements. The plan for this ship, one Lucan had almost wanted to tell the Consul was impossible regardless of the plans he'd delivered, was for rotating turrets capable of directing fire in any direction regardless of the vessel's heading.

"You've all seen the plan. Four turrets will be mounted on this deck," Lucan continued, indicating the marked positions. "Two forward, two aft. Each turret will house twin cannons capable of engaging targets at ranges exceeding that of all the cannons we have ever tested."

He walked to the forward turret position where steel support rings had been embedded in the deck structure. The turret would rest on these rings while maintaining the ability to rotate almost two hundred degrees. A second turret was positioned well ahead of him, but lower down, so that one cannon could fire over the other.

An ingenious design, really.

"We used steam pressure for some of the operations in the river boats, but not to move anything this heavy. Each turret weighs approximately forty tons fully loaded. The hydraulic pumps will generate pressure using steam from the main boilers, but the distribution system must operate independently to prevent a single failure from disabling multiple turrets."

One of the engineers raised his hand. "Is this even possible? As you said, nothing we did on the river boats got close to the pressure we're talking about here."

"The system will operate at pressures exceeding anything we've attempted," Lucan replied. "Hortensius's workshops have developed the basic technology, and the Consul assures us that even down to two boilers, we should have the power needed to operate the mechanisms. Assuming we do our jobs correctly. Follow me."

Lucan led the group to examine the spaces beneath the turret positions where the hydraulic machinery would be installed. Complex arrangements of pumps, accumulators, and distribution lines would occupy these areas.

"The turrets will rotate on bearing assemblies fabricated from our finest steel," he said. "The lower bearing ring remains fixed to the deck structure while the upper ring supports the turret weight and transmits rotational forces. These bearings must support the turret weight while still allowing rotation."

The gear reduction systems drew particular attention from the assembled engineers. Hydraulic pressure would be applied to large pistons connected to reduction gears that would translate rapid piston movement into precise turret rotation. The gear ratios had been calculated to provide both rapid traversal for tracking moving targets and fine adjustment for accurate aiming.

"I know you said it should still operate even if down to two boilers, but what happens if hydraulic power fails during battle?" the same man as before asked.

"Manual backup systems will allow continued turret operation," Lucan replied. "Hand cranks and wheel mechanisms will enable gun crews to rotate and elevate their weapons using mechanical advantage. The backup systems will be slower than hydraulic operation and require a lot of men to do it, but the crew complement on this ship is large enough to handle it."

He walked the team through the structural supports that would handle the tremendous stresses generated when the cannons fired. Each turret would mount two rifled guns capable of hurling massive explosive shells. The recoil forces would attempt to destroy the turret mechanisms and damage the ship's structure. Huge steel reinforcements would distribute these forces throughout the hull framework.

The elevation mechanisms represented another engineering challenge. Each gun would be capable of elevating from horizontal firing to high angles for engaging distant targets or shore installations. Hydraulic cylinders would control elevation while mechanical stops prevented the guns from depressing enough to damage the ship's own structure.

"The operator positions will be located within each armored turret housing," Lucan explained as they examined the turret designs. "Gun crews will control both rotation and elevation from protected positions behind steel armor. The turret walls will be thick enough to stop enemy shells while providing visibility ports for target acquisition."

Communication systems would connect each turret to the ship's bridge through speaking tubes, although it was likely once a battle commenced, runners would also have to be employed. During battle, turret commanders would receive targeting information and assigned targets from the bridge.

"We'll begin with the forward turret," he outlined. "I'm sure we will run into problems, so let's limit them to a single turret, and save ourselves the work of undoing our mistakes four times instead of one. Once those systems prove reliable, we'll complete the remaining installations and conduct full-ship trials."

The gun installation would represent the final phase of turret construction. The massive, rifled cannons would be lowered into position using the cranes the Consul had designed. These cranes had been at work in Hortensius's factories, but this was the first time something like this was needed here.

Up till now, they had used simple wooden cranes that were much easier to operate. The cannons would then be secured within the turret assemblies. Ammunition hoists would be tested with actual shells to verify loading procedures under simulated combat conditions.

We don't have to worry about the cannons themselves. Hortensius is working on those and testing them at his facility, and they will be delivered more or less intact for us. But be prepared. They will be nothing like the cannons you are used to. Or so I'm told. I want to be clear on this last point. No component enters this ship unless it meets specifications. We have the opportunity to make history here, and I will not have that messed up by a rushed job. I know we hear how important this ship will be to the war, and we have been given the time to do this right, and by the gods, I will see that we do. Questions?

Of course, there were many. Mostly technical and clarification. The men had seen the same plans he had, and knew what they needed to do, but they liked to talk their tasks out ahead of time, and Lucan let them.

He preferred them to be as comfortable as possible with their assigned tasks. They went back and forth for almost an hour, making sure they each knew exactly what their tasks in the coming months would be.

They had a timetable, and everyone knew what was expected of them. Work would begin immediately on the hydraulic and steam systems while turret assembly commenced in the adjacent workshop.

As they wrapped up, Lucan thanked each man for his expertise and dedication. They were good men, and they were doing good work. He could be a hard ass, but in truth, he liked his men and trusted them to do the work.

"Just stick to your training and experience, follow your check-lists, communicate with each other, and we'll be fine. I'm certain we're going to encounter problems, but we can handle them. This isn't the first time they've asked us for the impossible, right?"

The men laughed and began to break up, heading to their respective responsibilities to brief their men in turn. Lucan looked back at the massive structure and smiled.

Impossible. That about summed this thing up.

Forward Supply Depot, Central Greece

Medb thought she'd seen a lot since she'd come to the continent. Germania held the main training and logistics base for the western armies, where everything from Britannia and the other members of the alliance gathered and prepared before going east.

She had spent some time there before moving to the prison camp, and she imagined there wasn't another place on the planet as hectic or as full as that.

Stepping off here, at the simple Greek farming village that had become the last train stop on the line and the main supply depot for the Greek armies, she realized her imagination had not gone far enough.

Rows of canvas tents stretched across the hillside, interspersed with wooden structures that housed ammunition stores and equipment repair shops. People were moving about everywhere, and the full might of the Britannian war machine was in full swing, from the steam-powered cranes unloading artillery pieces to the telegraph lines that connected this end of the war to the rest of the alliance.

Germania might have more men and equipment in total, but none of it was concentrated like this, in such a small area.

A young tribune approached as she gathered her traveling case. "Lady Medb? The Consul received notice that you were coming and is expecting you."

He was nervous, bowing and trying not to make eye contact with her. This young man had seen war, probably fought on the front line, and yet he was terrified of her.

She suppressed a smile.

She had decided to give up her aspirations of ruling again because she could see where being feared behind the throne had just as much power as being on the throne.

Her reputation had settled in nicely.

She followed the nervous man up a winding path that led to higher ground overlooking the depot. Here, a cluster of larger tents and semi-permanent buildings had been erected around what appeared to be a small storehouse of some kind. Guards and communication equipment had transformed it into a modern command center.

Ky stood before a large table covered with detailed maps, pointing to various positions as he spoke with three staff officers.

"The Fourteenth will advance along this front. I don't want them to push north, just hold the enemy from changing their mind about their retreat once they realize our true target. Block from here to the sea; that will cut off all of these forces, and allow us to box them in. We own the water, so they can't resupply or escape. It should be a simple task of pounding them before we finally take the city and the regions around it. If we're lucky, they'll surrender."

One of the officers looked about to ask something when Medb was led in, causing all of the men to stop and look at her.

"Lady Medb," the tribune leading her announced.

"Medb," Ky said in that disconnected way he had about him sometimes. Like he was looking at something not in this room. "I am glad you arrived safely, but your message was short on details. What can I do for you?"

"I have some information that I wanted to discuss in person," she said, and then looked at the other officers in the room. "And in private."

"I see," he said. "Gentlemen, we'll continue this in an hour. You have the general idea and know where your assigned sectors will be. Send runners to your men and prepare them for the push."

The officers saluted and departed, leaving them alone in the old wooden building. Ky pulled a set of chairs from against one of the walls, setting them facing each other and gesturing for her to sit.

"I am sorry for intruding."

"Medb, you are a lot of things, but sorry is never one of them," he said with a laugh. There was no heat behind the statement. "Besides, you wouldn't have traveled all this way unless it was significant."

Medb settled into the chair and said, "I have told you about the Eastern prisoner I have been working with, and I believe we have an opportunity."

"I'm all ears."

"I want to send him back to the Eastern homeland as our asset. He's agreed to cooperate and believes he can reconnect with the Han resistance once he returns home. This represents our best opportunity to gather intelligence from inside their empire rather than just reacting to their moves here."

Again, she suppressed a smile. Ky was normally so stoic and unfazed by anything, that when his eyebrows went up in surprise, she took it as a personal compliment.

"You want to send him back? That's a considerable risk considering the distances involved, especially when the people we are fighting are between us and their homeland. The logistics alone …"

"I know the challenges. But consider what we gain if it works. Right now, we know nothing about their homeland operations, their military, their internal politics. He could provide intelligence that changes how we approach this entire conflict."

Ky stood and walked to the window, looking out over the bustling depot below. "What happens if he's captured and they discover his true allegiances? Or if he changes his mind about cooperating once he's back among his own people?"

"Any intelligence operation carries those risks, but this man has conviction. He's seen what the Eastern Empire does to its own people. He's lived it. His family was destroyed by their corruption. That kind of personal motivation doesn't disappear easily."

"Personal motivation can also make someone reckless."

"Or effective, and in this case, it's not just him."

He looked back at her, waiting.

"Fa Jian described an existing resistance network operating throughout the TianYou Empire. They call themselves the Han resistance. Approximately three hundred small groups, each with about twelve members, spread across the homeland territories."

"That's a lot of people involved," Ky pointed out.

"Yes, but they operate independently. The empire crushed larger organized groups generations ago, so now they maintain minimal contact to avoid detection by imperial surveillance. Each group only knows one or two others, and even then, communication is extremely limited."

Ky returned to his chair, his expression thoughtful. "How does he know about this network?"

"He was recruited by one of the groups years before the war started. They identified him as someone with access to military information and the intelligence to be useful. His planned infiltration of the Imperial Guards, the next rank closer to the emperor and the true seat of information, was interrupted when his unit got deployed here to fight us."

"And you believe he can reconnect with these cells?"

"Yes. He knows some of the people and how to get to those who exhibit the most control. These aren't amateur revolutionaries. They've survived for generations under one of the most oppressive surveillance systems ever created."

"And you think supporting these resistance groups could destabilize the empire from within, help us win without having to fight all the way to China?"

"Yes. Imagine if we could coordinate sabotage operations against their infrastructure, their supply lines, their communications. Or if we could get advance warning of troop movements, new weapon developments, or even political changes that might affect their war strategy."

"It's an attractive prospect," Ky said. "But the logistics are still your biggest obstacle. How do you propose to maintain contact with him? Supply him with resources? Even if everything goes perfectly, we're talking about communication delays of months."

"That's actually why I'm here. I need advice on how to deal with those problems. The lack of information I have on the region is why we started this effort in the first place, but it is also making coming up with a plan to get that information difficult. We have significant gaps in our geographic knowledge about the Eastern territories and maritime regions. Fa Jian provided useful information about inland areas, but he knows little about coastal regions or island territories that might serve as intermediate bases."

Medb knew it would be easy to dismiss this out of hand. She had worked the problem over and over, and couldn't come up with a solution.

"We need better intelligence about the TianYou naval presence and shipping routes before committing to any long-term operation. I know this. But I also know that if we don't act on this opportunity soon, we might lose it entirely. Plus, the longer he stays here, the more suspicious his eventual return becomes."

"Your best option would be establishing some sort of support base somewhere in the island chains to the east of the landmass."

"Island chains?"

"Yes, there are islands between Taiwan, which is just off the coast, and Okinawa, which is much further away. There is a set of smaller scattered islands that would be far enough from the mainland to avoid notice from the Easterners but close enough to send ships in to meeting points along the coast. The distances between here and there are vast, even if we were to go the roundabout way, by sea."

"How vast?"

"Several months of sailing for just one way of the journey. Any information you receive would be old by the time it reaches us."

"I understand that limitation, but it would still be more information than we have right now. I also want to be able to regularly supply him with materials for stepping up the guerrilla war against the empire. Weapons, explosives, whatever he needs. Things that could make the resistance groups significantly more effective."

"I understand. You know, if we could base off of Taiwan itself, we would have faster access to the mainland and the room to set up."

"I thought you said that was the island close to the coast?"

"It is, which means it's likely already under TianYou control or at least surveillance. Still, it would be nice, but we can't decide exactly where to establish a base until we have more intelligence. We need to understand how heavily defended the coastal approaches are. Whether the empire maintains permanent garrisons on the smaller islands. This intelligence would be valuable for future naval operations even if the resistance support mission doesn't proceed."

"Now you see my conundrum," Medb said.

"I do. I'll draw up detailed maps showing the geographic features and coastal areas of the Chinese mainland and surrounding sea regions. Take them back to Fa Jian and see if he can identify where resistance groups have assets or contacts and if he knows where the empire might have an established presence. Once we have more information about the operational environment, we can decide on our next move. But Medb ..." Ky said, looking at her directly. "This operation, if we proceed, will require resources we can't easily spare. Ships, men, equipment, ongoing supplies. All for an uncertain return on a timeline measured in years rather than months."

"I have considered all of that and I think it's worth it."

"Fine. I'll support a thorough analysis of the possibilities. If your man's answers show the operation is feasible and the potential benefits justify the risks and costs, then yes. But I won't commit resources to an operation based on hope and good intentions."

"Fair enough. How long will it take you to prepare those maps?"

"A few hours."

"Then I'll take the train back as soon as I have the maps, and we shall see."

Chapter 5

Memphis, Egypt

Aelius studied the city ahead of him, its limestone walls and mud-brick buildings rising from the riverbank, and hoped his scouts were right. They had reported that there were no signs of defenders. No fortified positions, no soldiers in the streets, and no sign of Egyptian scouts.

He had sent two more groups of scouts to follow up and confirm that the improbable report was true.

All the reports were the same. No soldiers in sight and only a few civilians, most of whom probably were in hiding because they knew there were armies in the area.

For all appearances, the Egyptians had abandoned the town.

"Tribune Marcellus," he called to the commander of the twelfth cohort, who'd just arrived at his summons. "Deploy your cohort along the main avenue and stay vigilant. I don't trust this. Send runners to all tribune commanders. They are to follow behind, advancing by sections and securing each block before moving forward. No one rushes ahead."

The man saluted and ran off to the legion's lead element. Twenty minutes later, the ninth legion began moving into the city, a thousand men moving carefully, street by street.

Aelius positioned himself at the highest point outside of the town that he could find, to get a view of their movement until he could move into the city and get a better position.

The first centuries penetrated three blocks without contact. In spite of that, everything still felt wrong to him. He'd entered enemy cities before, and they weren't like this. Even abandoned settlements showed signs of recent habitation. Here, nothing moved at all.

Thirty minutes of steady forward momentum later, a runner came galloping back toward his command post. "Sir, the twelfth reports they have reached the central plaza and still see no sign of resistance."

"Tell the tribune to halt at the plaza's edge and wait for the flanking cohorts to reach his position before advancing further. Pass the word that we are moving our command post just inside the city."

As the man saluted and rode away, Aelius shifted his command staff inside a taller building, climbing up to the roof, which gave him a fairly good view of most of the city.

The nineteenth and twenty-second cohorts took positions to the west of the twelfth, while the twenty-third and twenty-fourth took positions to the east of them. That gave them a small amount of control of the center of the city, although they still had a lot of the northern section of the city uncleared, waiting on his remaining five cohorts to move in and clear them.

Once all the men in the center were ready, the cohorts began to move forward into the central plaza.

The ambush erupted without warning.

Muzzle flashes bloomed from dozens of concealed positions, rooftops, windows, and doorways that had all appeared empty moments before. The sharp crack of rifle fire filled the air as bullets slammed into the advancing legionaries. Men dropped instantly.

The attack wasn't just in the center of the city, but across it as every building seemed to suddenly come alive with fire.

In the plaza, the neat formation dissolved as legionaries dove for whatever cover they could find.

Aelius cursed. He'd felt that something was wrong, but he'd still sent his men forward. He knew that was his only choice. He couldn't leave an uncleared city at his rear, and there was no way to clear it without marching in, but he'd felt there was a trap here, and it pained him to have to spring it.

The Egyptians had prepared well, turning the plaza into a killing ground with overlapping fields of fire from elevated positions. His men were pinned down in the open, unable to advance or retreat without exposing themselves to the crossfire.

"Send the fifty-fourth cohort up, order them around those buildings to the east and try to bring in flanking fire on those positions," he barked to his runners.

It took time, but they began to get his reserves into position, putting enough pressure on the enemy to allow his men to untangle themselves. From there, his men began to work on clearing buildings, including those that were considered at their rear an hour ago.

Although there was still live fire happening in the area, Aelius moved his command post to a stone building overlooking the plaza where he could direct his men more effectively. Through the windows he watched squads using doorways and building corners for cover, laying down suppressing fire while their comrades maneuvered for better positions.

The only thing that saved them was their new rifles. He had no way of knowing how many Egyptians were out there, since they were well established in hiding points, but the volume of fire suggested a fair number.

In spite of that, his men were out-firing the Egyptians several times over. Where Egyptian riflemen needed precious seconds to reload after each shot, Britannian legionaries could maintain continuous fire. The sustained volleys forced defenders to keep their heads down, giving assault squads opportunities to advance.

The fifty-fourth finally got into position, moving through the maze of side streets, emerging behind the eastern buildings where Egyptian marksmen had established positions. The sudden appearance of Britannian rifles at their rear threw the defenders into confusion. Some tried to reposition to meet the new threat, others attempted to escape through interior passages.

Across the plaza, a squad from the twenty-third breached a doorway, their sergeant leading with a fin-shaped grenade. An explosion blasted through the building, followed by the rapid fire of lever-action rifles as the legionaries cleared each room. Smoke poured from broken windows while defenders stumbled into the street, only to meet concentrated fire from other squads.

His men began to clear building by building. Aelius coordinated the assault through his tribunes, maintaining pressure on multiple fronts while preventing his men from advancing into prepared kill zones. Each structure required careful assault, grenades to clear fortified rooms, followed by close combat with bayonets and rifle butts.

There was a particularly fierce engagement in a three-story structure where Egyptian marksmen had dominated one corner of the plaza. Two squads from the twenty-second approached from different angles, one going up a neighboring building and jumping from one roof to the other while another breached the ground floor. The defenders, caught between converging attacks, fought for all they were worth.

Rifle fire erupted from the building's interior as legionaries and Egyptians engaged at point-blank range. Windows exploded outward from grenade blasts, sending fragments of glass and stone into the street below. A defender appeared at a second-story window, rifle raised, only to be cut down by crossfire from squads positioned across the plaza.

The tide turned gradually as Britannian firepower overwhelmed the Egyptian positions. Each cleared structure became a stronghold, extending Britannian control deeper into the city.

Hours passed in continuous fighting. Aelius moved between his tribunes, coordinating attacks and ensuring wounded men were evacuated to secured areas. The urban battlefield demanded different tactics than open-field engagements, close coordination between small units, careful use of grenades in confined spaces, and constant awareness of multiple firing angles.

A messenger reached his position as the afternoon wore on. "Sir, Tribune Ailpein reports the northern sector is secured up to the government buildings on the south side of the plaza."

The city was far from theirs while heavy enemy sightings continued in the southern third of the city and along the western and eastern portions. His men had adapted well to urban warfare, using their superior weapons and training to overcome a well-prepared defense. The Egyptians had fought harder than expected, showing determination and tactical skill.

"Move our command post inside the government building and begin the push into the southern half of the city."

The government building provided an excellent command position with clear views across Memphis's southern approaches. Runners established communication lines to his cohorts while the wounded were being moved to secure areas in the northern sector, and ammunition wagons rolled through the captured streets to resupply the forward positions.

He was just passing his first orders when a tremendous roar erupted from the southern edge of the city.

Thousands of voices raised in unison, Egyptian battle cries rolled across Memphis. Aelius rushed to the window. Beyond the buildings, a massive force charged into the city from the south, where it must have been concealed, waiting to reinforce or counterattack. Egyptian infantry poured through the streets.

The enemy had been waiting. While his scouts had focused on the obvious defensive positions, an entire army had remained hidden outside the city.

His forward positions retreated from the threat. Cohorts, spread along the main avenue in defensive positions, opened fire immediately, but they were spread throughout the city, tied up in house-to-house fighting.

Britannian squads found themselves under pressure from multiple directions. The situation was deteriorating rapidly. His men were giving ground, falling back from positions they had fought hard to secure. The retreat wasn't panicked; his tribunes maintained good order, but the momentum had shifted to the Egyptians' favor.

Street fighting erupted at close quarters where retreat routes converged. Britannian squads found themselves trapped in narrow alleys as Egyptian infantry closed from multiple directions.

He needed something to change the situation, and quickly. His own artillery had started to drop fire on the southern side of the city, but he didn't have enough pieces to change the tide.

Aelius moved to his runner. "Get in contact with Admiral Valdar immediately. I need him to fire on the southern third of the city.

Enemy units are entering in force and we need heavy bombardment to give us a fire break and time to counter."

The runner dashed out of the building to the signal station set up on a roof far in the rear.

Aelius counted the seconds, knowing that naval gunnery required time to calculate firing solutions and train the big guns onto land targets. But his cohorts needed help, and they needed it quickly.

The first naval shells screamed overhead with a sound like tearing cloth. Massive explosions erupted in the southern districts as rifled cannon sent their projectiles deep into the city. Buildings collapsed in clouds of dust and debris while the concussion of the blasts rattled windows throughout Memphis. The bombardment continued in a steady rhythm as Valdar's gunners also worked their pieces.

Egyptian formations scattered as the naval fire disrupted their formations. The coordinated advance faltered when shells demolished buildings where reserve troops had been waiting. Aelius watched through his glasses as the enemy assault lost its momentum, officers struggling to reorganize their scattered units under the falling artillery.

But the pressure on his forward positions continued. Egyptian infantry, who had already committed to the assault, pushed forward despite the bombardment falling behind them. The naval fire helped prevent reinforcements from reaching the front, but couldn't stop the forces already engaged in the street fighting.

The twenty-second cohort fell back another two blocks. Aelius could see his men retreating through the streets, their gray uniforms distinct against the pale stone buildings. They moved in good order, squads covering each other as they abandoned positions, but the steady withdrawal threatened to become a rout if the pressure continued.

Dust clouds rose from the southern sector where naval shells continued to impact.

The bombardment created a barrier of fire and debris that isolated the attacking Egyptian forces from their support elements. But ammunition was limited, and the ironclads couldn't maintain this rate of fire indefinitely.

Thankfully, something did show up that changed the tide of the battle as horns sounded from the north, from his rear. Aelius turned to see the banners of Prince Cormac's legion entering the city.

Their reinforcements had arrived. Five thousand fresh men on the double march to the front lines.

Cormac himself appeared at the command post within minutes, his sword belted at his side and his uniform bearing the dust of hard marching.

"What's the situation?" Cormac asked without preamble.

"Egyptian relief force hit us from the south about an hour ago," Aelius replied. "A full army. They've pushed my cohorts back pretty far. Valdar's providing fire support, but I need infantry to stop their advance. The fighting has been brutal."

"Where do you need my legion?"

"Push down the east and west sides of the city, bend the flanks to the center while they're committed to the main assault. My tribunes can hold the northern line and we can put fire on them from three sides."

The prince nodded and departed immediately, his staff officers following to coordinate the deployment. Within minutes, fresh troops began filing through the northern districts.

Cormac's legion struck the Egyptian flanks like a hammer blow.

The tactical situation reversed almost immediately. Egyptian forces that had been pressing forward confidently suddenly faced fire from three directions. Their formations wavered as officers attempted to redeploy troops to meet the new threat, but the enclosed urban terrain made rapid maneuvering impossible.

As before, Britannian firepower dominated the engagement.

Cormac's legion had been blessed with a full battery of artillery, which also came into action, howitzers positioned in the northern sector where they could fire over friendly troops into the contested areas. The air-burst shells exploded above Egyptian formations, sending fragments of metal into packed ranks of infantry. The psychological effect proved as devastating as the physical casualties; troops who had been advancing confidently broke and ran when artillery fire found their positions.

The coordinated pressure from two legions, supported by naval bombardment and field artillery, shattered Egyptian cohesion.

Egyptian officers attempted to rally their men around strong points, stone buildings that could provide cover from rifle fire and artillery fragments. But the Britannian advance gave them no time to consolidate. Fresh troops pressed forward relentlessly, clearing each building with grenades and close combat, denying the enemy any chance to establish new defensive lines.

The naval bombardment shifted targets as Valdar's gunners adjusted their fire to support the advancing infantry. Shells fell on escape routes and assembly areas, preventing organized Egyptian withdrawal. The combination of land and naval firepower created a killing zone that trapped enemy forces within the southern tip of the city.

The retreat accelerated as more Egyptian troops abandoned their positions. Buildings that had been defended stubbornly fell silent as their garrisons fled rather than face encirclement.

In less than an hour of Cormac's arrival, the Egyptians had fully fallen apart and were in full-out flight.

The city was theirs.

Western Caledonia

Hortensius trudged up the rocky slope toward the construction site, his boots finding purchase on the loose stones scattered across the Caledonian hillside. He could hear the men working on the steel frame that poked up into the sky before he saw them; the sounds of hammering and shouted instructions floated down the hill toward him.

The drilling platform dominated the coastal bluff, its latticed steel beams forming a tower that would have seemed impossible to build just a decade before. Workers scrambled across the structure securing the final support members with heavy bolts and reinforcing brackets. Hortensius paused to catch his breath.

He was getting too old for this kind of exertion.

Septimus, one of his longest-serving foremen and the man put in charge of the project, approached from the supply area, wiping his hands on a cloth stained with grease and metal filings.

"We're ahead of schedule," he said without preamble. "The final beam placement should finish within the hour. Getting everything in place over the rough ground took longer than expected, but the men adapted well enough."

Hortensius nodded, already moving toward the platform's base. The foundation anchors were as impressive as the drawings said they'd be. Massive steel pins driven deep into the bedrock, each one capable of holding several tons under stress. He knelt beside the nearest anchor point, running his hands along the metal surface to check for any signs of movement or stress fractures.

"Four meters into solid granite. We hit softer rock at three meters but kept driving until we reached the hard stone beneath. Hard work with pick and shovel."

"That's good though," Hortensius said. "According to the Consul's notes, the drilling mechanism will generate substantial vibration. We need something to be able to stand up to that."

"It will. I triple checked the specifications and did the math several times, based on the Consul's calculations. It will handle everything we throw at it."

Hortensius completed his circuit of the platform and looked up at the steel tower. The engineering satisfied him, but engineering was only half the challenge. The real test would come when they started drilling.

"As soon as the last beam is in place, let's get started," he said.

Just under an hour later, Septimus gathered the engineering team together at the base of the tower. They were good men, most of whom had worked on factory installations or railway construction, but drilling operations presented unique challenges.

"We'll start with the drilling mechanism mounting," Septimus announced once they were all together. "Watch the specifications and let's make sure everything is aligned just like it is in the instructions. Remember the warnings the Consul included about how much stress this equipment will be under and the importance of having everything just right. Questions?"

There were none.

Two men began operating the block and tackle system, lifting the drilling mechanism's main housing toward the platform. The device weighed nearly two tons.

Hortensius kept out of the way.

This was Septimus's project, and he'd let the man take the lead, but he wanted to be here for its first practical test before he stepped away and let the foreman get to the real work.

"Support the base as it comes up," Septimus called out.

The drilling mechanism settled into position with a satisfying metallic clank. Septimus immediately moved to check the alignment, using tools the Consul's notes had also included. He made small adjustments with pry bars and wooden wedges, fine-tuning the placement until the measurements satisfied him.

"Looks good. Connect the pipe."

The drilling pipes lay arranged in order beside the platform, each section roughly three meters long and manufactured to exacting specifications. Hortensius had spent considerable time getting the threading system just right so that the pipes connected securely while transmitting rotational force from the surface mechanism down to the cutting bit.

Septimus and two other men lifted the first pipe section and demonstrated the connection process.

"The threading must engage completely before you apply torque. Partial connections will strip under load, and we don't have spare pipes if you damage these."

He showed the engineers how to align the threaded ends, how to turn the pipe sections to engage the threads properly, and how to use the specialized wrenches to tighten the connections without overstressing the metal.

He then stepped away and let the engineers have a turn at it. It was always easier to do hands-on learning before all the pieces were attached, limiting complications to one or two things.

Each man practiced the procedure until Septimus satisfied himself that they could perform it correctly under working conditions.

"Once we start drilling, pipe connections happen quickly," Septimus explained. "We can't stop the drilling mechanism for extended periods or the bit will bind in the hole."

While they trained on the pipes, other workers began hauling steam engine components up from the supply wagons. The steam engine had been significantly improved and had the river boats to thank. A smaller, more compact version of the large engines used in the factories, it was designed to be portable and rugged while still being able to deliver the sustained power needed for the operation.

The engine components required careful assembly. The firebox and boiler came as separate units, connected by precisely fitted pipes and valves. Septimus supervised each connection, checking that gaskets were sealed properly, since any leaks would reduce efficiency and potentially create dangerous operating conditions.

Next, came the collection system. Unlike the drilling mechanism or steam engine, the collection tanks and piping had to handle the viscous fluid. If the Consul was right, it would come out of the ground under enough pressure to flow easily, but Hortensius had his doubts. He'd seen the liquid once, bubbling out of the sands on a trip to Egypt four years ago. It had been thick and sticky and didn't seem like it would flow at all.

The tanks connected through a network of pipes and valves that would allow operators to direct the flow between different containers as they filled. Septimus again checked all of the valves' operations, making sure that they would open and close properly to control the movement of the liquid.

After hours of work, all of the major components were in position, the team prepared for the first operational test. They started up the steam engine.

Hortensius positioned himself where he could observe both the drilling mechanism and the steam engine. The first few minutes of operation would reveal any major problems with the installation or assembly procedures. Minor issues could be corrected. Major failures might require extensive repairs or component replacement.

The steam engine reached operating pressure with a steady hiss from the pressure relief valve. Septimus engaged the drive mechanism gradually, allowing the drilling apparatus to begin rotating at low speed. The platform vibrated slightly as the drill bit engaged the prepared starter hole, but the structure remained stable.

The drilling continued smoothly as the bit encountered the transition from soil to solid rock. Hortensius was pleased to see the drilling mechanism handled the increased resistance well and that the steam engine was able to keep up with the additional load.

The drill penetrated several meters of rock with a consistent performance. Hortensius examined the cuttings brought up by the drilling mud, noting the changing color and composition as they passed through different geological layers. The granite gave way to sandstone, then to limestone, each transition clearly visible in the drilling samples.

The drilling continued through increasingly varied rock formations. Septimus had a sheet of paper and was making detailed records of depth measurements, drilling speed, and sample characteristics. Hortensius smiled. For years, he'd drilled into the man the importance of consistent record-keeping.

He was glad someone finally got the message.

The information would prove invaluable for future drilling operations and for understanding geological conditions they might encounter at other sites across the Empire.

"Consul's geological notes suggest it will take some time before we reach the correct depth," he said offhandedly to Septimus. "Keep the drill speed slow. I don't want to push it too fast and break the mechanism."

The difference between success and failure depended on patience. Drill cuttings would change color and consistency the closer they got to their goal, often becoming darker and more granular. Drilling mud might take on different characteristics, and the penetration rate could change as they encountered different rock types. Sample collection had to be systematic and thorough, with every meter of material examined for signs they were almost to their target.

"Make sure to inspect the equipment regularly. Aside from just general use, the salt in the air and general weather here in Caledonia will corrode and wear the equipment," Hortensius added. "Change out any parts that seem to be under stress. Replace components before they fail, not after they break."

"I know, I know. Prevention beats repair," Septimus agreed, repeating the engineer's oft-repeated mantra.

Hortensius watched for another hour as they slowly drilled, deeper and deeper, into the rock.

Finally, he said, "It looks like you have everything under control. I'll leave this in your capable hands. Keep me up to date on what's happening."

"I'll send daily progress reports once we get the telegraph lines out here," Septimus said. "I promise."

"Good. I know you will," Hortensius said, clapping the man on the shoulder.

Chapter 6

Pharsalos, Thessaly

Ky crouched behind the stone wall of a collapsed mill on the city's western edge, looking out on the maze of narrow streets and tile-roofed buildings that formed Pharsalos. The ancient city sprawled across the valley floor before rising toward the imposing fortress that crowned the central hill. Smoke drifted from several points where his advance cohorts had already engaged Eastern defenders.

The first tribune's horn sounded three sharp blasts from the northern district. Contact established. Ky tracked the movement of gray-uniformed figures as they flowed between buildings, their lever-action rifles already crackling in rapid sequences that distinguished Britannian forces from the slower and deeper sound of fire of the Eastern weapons.

A runner appeared at his elbow, breathing hard from his sprint across open ground. "Sir, the tribune reports the first cohort has secured the outer marketplace. Resistance moderate but organized. Eastern forces withdrawing to prepared positions in the residential quarter."

"Casualties?"

"Seven wounded, none dead yet, sir."

Ky nodded, then flinched as a rifle bullet cracked past his position, splintering stone fragments from the wall. An Eastern sniper had spotted his command post. He shifted left, keeping low, as two more shots rang out from a bell tower four hundred meters to the northeast.

"Sergeant Kellor," Ky called to his senior non-commissioned officer. "Detail two men with rifles to suppress that tower. Third window from the left."

The sergeant acknowledged his command with a sharp nod. Within thirty seconds, rifle fire began hammering the bell tower's stone frame. The enemy sniper's shooting ceased.

Ky nodded, returning his attention to the urban battlefield. This had become the new style of battle, as the Easterners set up strong points in cities and villages, abandoning trench warfare. They were still withdrawing too quickly to establish solid positions, and cities were almost as good as the trenches, where every building was a pillbox.

Had the Britannians been more ruthless and accepted leveling every city to the ground with artillery, they might have had to find a new tactic, but Greece was part of Europe and a people the Western Alliance would have to deal with for decades to come.

It would not help their cause to level every city and then ask to be friends.

A tremendous crash echoed from the northern district as the first cohort brought down a barricade with explosives. Dust clouds billowed above the rooftops, and the tempo of rifle fire increased sharply.

Eastern troops were repositioning, abandoning their forward positions to establish new defensive lines closer to the fortress hill.

The second runner of the morning appeared, this one from the southern approach where his third cohort had been probing the enemy positions. The man's left sleeve showed fresh bloodstains.

"Contact with the enemy at the warehouses. They have artillery in the buildings and are firing into the open streets," the man reported.

With explosive shells and straight-firing cannons, that was going to be a problem. From his position, Ky could see that there was a break between the warehouses and the rest of the city, probably meant for protection from fires, but it also meant open ground his men must cross to storm the fortified buildings.

"Tell the tribune to hold position and mark those gun positions. Do not advance until further orders. Runner," Ky called, looking behind him. "Go to Battery C and order them to fire on the warehouses. He is to keep his fire contained to just the warehouses. Limit spreading out the fire."

Another horn call, this time from the eastern approach where the second cohort advanced along the main thoroughfare. The sound carried a different note, contact under heavy fire. Ky shifted his attention toward that sector and immediately saw the problem. Eastern soldiers had barricaded themselves in a cluster of two-story stone houses overlooking the avenue, creating interlocking fields of fire that caught his men in a deadly crossfire.

"Runner, find the tribune of the second and tell him to pull his cohort back fifty meters and await further orders. They're walking into a prepared killing ground."

The messenger departed at a sprint. Ky studied the eastern district more carefully, noting how the defenders had positioned themselves. The buildings formed natural choke points, forcing his troops to advance through narrow spaces where their numerical advantage meant nothing. Smart. The Easterners had quickly become masters of urban warfare.

Rifle fire erupted from three directions simultaneously as his scattered cohorts pressed their attacks. Ky watched through his field glasses as a squad of his men stormed a baker's shop, disappearing through the doorway only to emerge moments later dragging two wounded comrades. Gray smoke poured from the building's upper windows.

Slowly, the buildings were cleared, although not without casualties. His men were being made to pay the price for each building they took.

Back at the warehouses, the artillery was doing its job and was pounding the warehouses heavily. The first salvo struck the warehouse district with devastating effect. Fused shells burst against the wooden structures, sending splinters and debris cascading across the defensive positions.

The second volley found its mark with even greater accuracy. Shells punched through the warehouse roofs before detonating inside, the black powder charges turning the interiors into a shrapnel-filled hell. An Eastern cannon position disappeared in a cloud of smoke and debris as a shell struck their ammunition stores. The explosion rippled through the building, collapsing an entire section of the structure.

Return fire from the Easterners' positions grew sporadic as the bombardment intensified. Their riflemen, pressed flat behind whatever cover remained, found themselves unable to maintain coordinated volleys. The Britannian gunners adjusted their range with each salvo, walking their fire methodically through the warehouses.

Within twenty minutes, the warehouse district stood largely abandoned, smoke rising from a dozen separate fires. The Easterners had pulled back to their inner fortifications, leaving behind cannon too damaged to move and ammunition they could no longer safely transport.

He was about to issue additional orders when his attention was drawn by the booms of artillery. Ky's head snapped toward the fortress as smoke billowed from the ancient walls. A shell screamed overhead and exploded in the street behind his observation post, showering debris across the mill ruins.

Another shell burst among the buildings where his northern cohort fought, collapsing part of a workshop roof. Ky could see his men scrambling for cover as Eastern cannons began a systematic bombardment of the lower city. The elevation gave the fortress artillery a commanding view of every street and square where Britannian forces advanced.

"Sir!" The centurion pointed toward the eastern district where a building suddenly erupted in flames. "They're setting fire to the structures rather than let us take them intact."

Ky cursed under his breath. They might be hesitant to raise a city to the ground, but the Easterners didn't seem to mind. Worse, it slowed his men down as they tried to get around the fires, making them targets for the artillery on the hill. His troops were pinned down in a burning city under accurate artillery fire from an elevated position they couldn't reach.

"All artillery batteries are to shift fire to the fortress. Bring it down," Ky ordered.

As the runner departed, another shell burst near the northern cohort's position. Ky could see that his men were pinned down, unable to advance, while the Eastern cannons commanded the streets. The fortress had to be neutralized before his infantry could complete their mission.

A few minutes later, the first Britannian cannon answered, sending its shell arcing toward the fortress. Ky watched the projectile's flight until it struck the outer battlements in a shower of stone fragments. Eastern cannons replied immediately, but their shots fell short of the Britannian artillery position.

"Good range," Ky said. "Order all guns, commence firing. Target the gun embrasures and outer walls."

The remaining howitzers opened fire in sequence, their shells bursting against ancient stonework with thunderous detonations. Dust and debris cascaded down the hillside as each impact carved chunks from the fortress walls. The Eastern riflemen tried to maintain their targeting of forces in the lower city, but the artillery duel forced them to abandon exposed positions.

It would, however, take time to reduce it to rubble. The fortress was old but its walls were thick and the range was long for his gunners.

Ky returned his attention to the urban battle below. With rifle fire suppressed and the fortress guns now focused on his own cannon, his cohorts resumed their advance through the residential districts.

A squad of his men approached a barricaded house in the northern sector. The leader motioned his soldiers into position on either side of the door while two more moved to cover the windows. When everyone was ready, they rushed the entrance simultaneously. Rifle fire erupted from inside the building as Eastern defenders fought from the upper floor. Within minutes, the shooting ceased and gray-uniformed figures emerged from the structure.

Similar scenes played out across multiple districts as Britannian forces methodically cleared each building. The Eastern defenders fought stubbornly but lacked the firepower to stop the determined assaults by troops armed with rapid-fire weapons. Building after building fell to coordinated rushes supported by concentrated rifle volleys.

The fortress artillery continued dueling with Ky's howitzers, but the Britannian guns were winning. Ky could see gaps appearing in the ancient walls where repeated shell impacts had breached the stonework. Eastern cannon fire from the hilltop became increasingly sporadic as defenders abandoned damaged positions.

They had managed to hit two of his artillery in return, but the weight of firepower was still very much on the Britannian side.

More so when a tremendous explosion suddenly shook the fortress as one of the shells found an ammunition store. Flames leaped skyward from the central courtyard while secondary detonations sent burning debris tumbling down the hillside.

The downside of being hemmed in a fortress, with enough explosives packed in for your cannon, you run a high risk of the powder stores being set off.

"Now we have them," Ky muttered, signaling for another runner. "I want the fourth and fifth cohorts to assault the fortress now. The fifth is to go up the direct approach, slow and under cover, while the fourth is to attack their flank through the damaged eastern wall. Coordinate with the artillery to lift fire when they begin their advance."

The messenger departed just as Modius, who had been closer to the battle, returned.

"That puts the fifth cohort in a bad position," he pointed out, clearly hearing the orders just given. "They'll be going straight up the main road, where the Easterners are sure to be watching."

"It's why I sent them that way. It will take time for the fourth to get around and I want the men in that fortress watching the assault they expect. Once it's committed, they will hopefully think that is our attack and lose focus on their exposed flank. We will take some losses, but if successful, the fortress will fall fast, and with less close-in fighting, which is where it will be very dangerous."

Ky looked back at the fortress. Smoke poured from multiple breaches in the outer walls where howitzer shells had destroyed the defensive perimeter. Eastern soldiers could be seen abandoning the outer battlements and withdrawing toward the inner keep.

The guns continued their bombardment, concentrating on the remaining Eastern positions. Each shell burst sent more defenders scurrying for cover in the central courtyard. The fortress that had dominated the battlefield minutes earlier was rapidly becoming untenable for its garrison.

Hundreds of gray-uniformed soldiers emerge from the city streets and began their advance up the winding road toward the fortress gates.

At first, the resistance was stiff. Regardless of Ky's order, there was not a lot of cover on the path up to the fortress, which was by design. There was a large commotion in the fort. From above, through the drone, Ky watched as men who'd run to the courtyard came running back out to help repel the assault they saw coming for them.

Joining the men from the courtyard were about half the men from the side wall, near the breach.

Exactly as Ky had hoped.

It wasn't until the men of the fourth cohort were at the wall that they seemed to notice and began to fire at them. Between the cohort keeping fire discipline, the frontal assault, and the artillery fire, they just hadn't even noticed their approach.

The opposition they did put up, once they saw the assault, was far from enough. Men poured through the breach with few casualties, their rifles putting too much fire on the few men left to defend that area. The few that survived the first few minutes of assault ran, the men of the fourth cohort right on their heels.

In ten minutes, the entire outer defense was cleared, opening the way for the fifth cohort to join them as both pressed into the central keep.

Once inside, the images from the drone were no longer helpful, and he was forced to wait ... just as did all of the other leaders who sent men into combat.

He hated it.

Thankfully, he didn't have to wait long. Twenty minutes after the men disappeared into the fortress, the banner at the top of the tower was cut away, falling down the side of the fortress. The hilltop stronghold had fallen, eliminating the artillery threat that had pinned down his urban assault.

With the fortress neutralized, the remaining Eastern defenders in the lower city began falling back toward the eastern exits. Ky could see organized groups of enemy soldiers withdrawing through the streets in good order, but his cohorts were closing in from multiple directions. The city would be his within the hour.

Or so it seemed until a massive explosion suddenly erupted in the market square where the third cohort was advancing. The blast collapsed an entire building and sent a column of smoke and debris skyward. Through the drone feed, Ky could see scattered bodies in gray uniforms lying motionless in the rubble.

Before he could react, another explosion rocked the northern district. This blast was even larger, demolishing two adjoining houses and leaving a crater where a squad had been advancing moments before. More of his men lay scattered in the wreckage.

"They've mined the buildings," Ky realized with growing horror.

The Eastern forces had prepared explosive charges throughout the city, turning their withdrawal into a deadly trap for pursuing Britannian troops. Every structure could potentially become a bomb.

As if to drive home the point, a third explosion destroyed a workshop in the western sector where another squad had been clearing rooms. The blast hurled fragments across the street and buried several soldiers under collapsed masonry.

"Halt all advances," he ordered a nearby centurion. "Get the word to every cohort, no building is to be entered until it's been checked for explosives. Move the wounded back to safe positions and organize rescue parties."

Which meant the scattered enemy forces were going to get away clean. He had a chance to wipe out this entire force, and they'd snatched it away from him.

He still held the city, but not the victory he'd hoped for.

The advance ground to a halt as his troops carefully extracted casualties from collapsed structures while searching for additional charges. Every doorway, window, and staircase now represented a potential death trap that could detonate without warning.

Two more explosions followed in quick succession, both in areas his men had previously cleared. The Eastern demolition plan was sophisticated, with charges positioned to maximize casualties while denying the city to Britannian forces.

The forces not involved in finding the demolitions had to help clear debris so that forces could keep moving through. In between both of those were medics carrying wounded soldiers away from the destruction. The casualty count was rising with each detonation.

Hours passed before engineers declared the remaining buildings safe to enter. The final sweep of Pharsalos revealed that Eastern forces had completely withdrawn, leaving behind more than a dozen crude bombs made up of casks of gunpowder.

While they waited, Ky, Modius, and the command staff headed to the fortress where they had identified the command post of the forces that had been defending the city.

The room at the heart of the fortress remained intact amid the destruction of the majority of the building. Britannian soldiers had already secured the perimeter and were beginning to search the interior for intelligence materials.

"Sir, this might be of interest to you," the tribune standing in the room looking through documents said.

Most of the forces here were Greek, which meant some people other than Ky had a chance to figure out what the documents said.

The man wasn't wrong with his estimation. The letter Ky had been handed was a notice to pull all of their forces out of Thessaly and consolidate in Macedonia and across the Dardanelles in Anatolia.

They were giving up on this part of Greece entirely. Considering how quickly this front had collapsed, with almost a month of their armies straight retreating, the orders were not much of a surprise.

Ky didn't see anything about explosives, so that must have been the commander of these forces' idea, which made Ky wish he had gotten the entire force themselves. He did not want to have to deal again with a man that clever.

Still, the orders confirmed what he'd suspected. Pharsalos represented the last organized Eastern resistance in Thessaly. With its capture, the entire region lay open to Britannian advance toward the next phase of the campaign.

Camp Banwīhraz, Central Germania

The camp stretched across the muddy plain in orderly rows of canvas and timber, its perimeter marked by earthworks thrown up by alliance engineers. Claudius guided his horse past the sentries at the main gate. He'd never been here before, but it was as impressive as rumor had said it would be. Guards checked him twice before allowing him through.

Warfare had been completely transformed several times over the last ten years, but some things remained constant. Soldiers drilled, men marched, and armies built things.

Medb waited outside the command building, arms crossed over her chest. The former queen of Connacht had adapted well to her role as intelligence chief, though she still carried herself with the bearing of royalty despite her plain woolen tunic and leather breeches.

"Took you long enough," she said.

"The roads from the coast are mud. It was slow riding."

"Excuses already? How Roman of you."

Claudius frowned and dismounted, handing his reins to a waiting soldier. He knew she didn't mean anything particular by her snobbery. It was just how she was sometimes.

"I am what I am. You said you had developments with the Eastern prisoner."

He knew she liked for people to stand up for themselves and looked down on those she considered 'weak.'

As if to prove the point, she offered him the faintest of smiles and said, "I do. Come."

They walked through the camp, past drilling soldiers and into the wired-in prison camp, through a maze of wire-covered paths to a low building near the prisoner quarters, its windows barred with guards posted at regular intervals.

"I wrote you about the prisoner I'd found, Fa Jian?"

"Yes. He seems very interesting."

"He seems interested in my proposals, which is what matters. More importantly, he's provided insight into something we barely suspected existed when I started this journey. A resistance network that's been operating within the TianYou Empire for generations."

Her messages had been terse, even for her. He'd read between the lines and understood that whatever she had to say, she thought it was too important to let slip into someone's hands.

"What kind of resistance network?"

"The people who ruled the TianYou homeland lands before their empire emerged were known as the Han. According to Fa Jian, they never truly accepted their conquerors and, over time, persisted and became a resistance in spite of brutal suppression. Since then, they have been waiting for an opportunity to set things right, as they see it."

"And you believe we can work with these groups?"

"I believe we must. Our armies can defeat theirs in the field, but conquering an empire that spans a land mass that, according to the Consul, is many times larger than the area controlled by the Western Alliance. That could take decades and cost hundreds of thousands of lives. Better to let them tear themselves apart from within while we apply pressure from without."

"That sounds great, except my understanding is that the Easterners' homeland is very far from here. How do you propose getting him from here to there without someone noticing and getting suspicious?"

"That's the problem. We can't just release him at the front lines. His officers would interrogate him immediately as to where he's been and, if they know he was in our prison camp, how he escaped. At worst, they would just execute him as a deserter or spy. At best, they'd send him straight back to the trenches."

"So my question stands. How do we get him in play? It sounds like you have a plan."

"Yes. I just returned from Greece after discussing this with the Consul, trying to come up with alternatives. A way to get him into their heartland, not back to the war zone."

"I assume he came up with one," Claudius said.

It was a statement, not a question.

Claudius had only been in the Consul's presence a handful of times, but had always found the man to be ... otherworldly. There were times he would be talking to you but would seemingly be focused on something far away, yet he was still completely engaged in the conversation.

And that didn't count the multitude of miracles he produced right as the Empire needed them. Claudius assumed that if she spoke to the Consul, he'd come up with a solution.

"A suggestion, although not necessarily a plan. At least not without more information. He's identified potential locations for establishing a forward base. Islands east of the Easterners' homeland that could serve as staging areas for operations."

"East of them? We were already talking about impossible distances. Your alternative is an area even further away?"

"Yes. I know the logistics are staggering. From his estimate, we are looking at a two-month voyage by sea under ideal conditions just to get there. But the concept is sound. We can use the islands he has identified for supplying the rebels and gathering intelligence. Our real problem now is determining which ones are suitable without alerting the Easterners to our interest."

"Which is where your prisoner comes in."

"Exactly. I'm not sure exactly how this will play out, but I'm assuming I will need you involved, so I wanted you in on this as early as possible."

"You've been talking to this man for a while, so I assume you've given him more information than a standard prisoner."

"I have. There are still some precautions. We share nothing about our military limitations or current troop deployments. Nothing about our supply situation or industrial capacity. For what he needs to do, he doesn't need to know about our dispositions here. But we can be relatively open about what support we're willing to provide the resistance."

"Which is?"

"Weapons and supplies equivalent to what we were selling our allies before the war began. Rifles, ammunition, basic explosives. Nothing cutting edge. We keep their military technology at least one generation behind anything we use ourselves, preferably something that blends in with the Easterners' own technology."

"Which means someone with technical know-how will have to either be in charge of supply shipments on this end or go with the expedition."

"I have already considered that. But first, we need Fa Jian to help us understand where we can operate safely before we can start thinking of what this base will include."

"Then I guess we should stop stalling and see him," Claudius said.

Medb nodded and led him through corridors meant to confuse someone trying to escape from the interrogation area, some with barracks for the men guarding the prisoners, to a series of interrogation rooms at the end of one of the halls; two praetorian guards flanked the entrance.

The room itself was bare, a single table sitting in the center, a small man sitting at it, gorging himself on a bowl of food.

He looked up as they entered, his eyes widening a bit at the sight of two people coming to talk to him, instead of one.

"Fa Jian," Medb began, "this is Tribune Claudius, one of my associates."

Claudius noted how she introduced the prisoner, not as a captive, but by name, with a subtle implication of respect. The Eastern man stood and offered a formal bow, which Claudius returned with a measured nod.

"Tribune," Fa Jian said in accented but surprisingly understandable Latin.

"You speak Latin?"

"Some. Lady Medb has been ... instructive."

"We've developed a potential plan," Medb said. "But we need your assistance with information of your homeland's territories."

"I will help where I can."

She took a seat and gestured Claudius to do the same.

Once seated, Medb produced a rolled map from a leather tube. She spread it across the table, weighing down the corners with small stones. Fa Jian leaned forward, and Claudius saw the exact moment recognition struck. The man's careful composure cracked, revealing genuine shock.

"This is ... how do you have such ...?" Fa Jian's voice trailed off as he studied the map.

The detail was extraordinary. Every major coastal feature for a fairly wide area was rendered with precision. Mountain ranges, rivers, even smaller island chains. Claudius knew the Consul had provided this from his mysterious sources, but to Fa Jian it must have seemed impossible.

"We have our methods," Medb said calmly. "What matters is using this information effectively. We need to understand where your empire maintains its presence."

Fa Jian's hands hovered over the map, not quite touching it.

"I have never seen my homeland rendered with such accuracy. Even our military maps ..." He stopped himself.

"We need to know where we might operate without encountering your naval forces," Claudius said.

"I understand." Fa Jian studied the map more carefully. "Though I must confess, my direct knowledge is limited. I have never been to the coast, never sailed these waters. What I know comes from stories, reports that filter through the resistance network."

"Any information helps," Medb encouraged. "Even rumors and secondhand accounts give us more than we currently possess."

Fa Jian nodded slowly, then pointed to the large island chain northeast of the mainland.

"We call the people of this place the 'Wa.' They have been under Imperial control for generations."

"Complete control?" Claudius asked.

"Yes. A large number of their male population has been drafted into the conscript armies. I have fought alongside them in the western campaigns. Many of their women have been conscripted for ... other things."

Medb exchanged a glance with Claudius. "If they serve in your armies, might some be sympathetic to resistance efforts?"

"I do not think that is possible." Fa Jian chose his words carefully. "They tend to hate anyone from my homeland with a fiery passion. Executions in the conscript army are high among their people. I would not hold hopes of them doing anything to help end our own enslavement. I would assume they have their own resistance movement, but working with them would be another thing."

"Then we will ignore that for now. Any others?" Medb said.

He pointed to a large island just off the mainland. "This large island, stories reach us of great shipyards there. The resistance believes much of the Eastern fleet originates from those facilities."

"Military vessels?"

"All vessels. Merchant, military ... the distinction matters little to the empire. Everything serves the state. Many Han have been relocated there to work in these facilities."

"Relocated?"

"Taken from their villages and sent across the water. Few return."

He paused.

"This is possible," he said, moving to a point on the coast well south of that island. "This region is known as Wujiang. There is a fishing settlement that appears loyal to the empire but is actually controlled almost entirely by resistance members."

"An entire village?" Claudius couldn't hide his surprise.

"Small communities can hide such secrets when they are remote enough. The empire's eyes cannot be everywhere, though they try."

"That is interesting. If we were to deliver supplies, that would be a logical point to do it," Claudius said.

"I agree," Fa said.

"The islands we were thinking of using might be too far, if that is the point we want to use," Medb said. "There are these very large islands to the southwest. It has a few smaller islands just off its coast, almost parallel to the province you mentioned. That would be a better spot. Do you know the empire's control in this region?"

Fa Jian shook his head.

"I have no direct knowledge. But it is well known for pirate activity. About eight, maybe nine years ago there was a big push to deal with the southern pirates, with large amounts of the empire's resources sent to end the pirate menace forever. Then the campaign suddenly stopped and we heard no more about the pirates."

"Because they were beaten?" Claudius asked.

"I don't think so," Fa said. "Had they been defeated the empire would have paraded their leaders through the streets and had public executions. Instead, they just stopped talking about them."

"Around the time they began helping Carthage in the war," Medb pointed out. "Maybe they decided to reallocate resources and that the pirates were not enough of a problem."

"I would not know," Fa said.

"Still, it seems like our best option," Medb said. "We can start there. If they're unoccupied, they could serve our purposes. Close enough for operations but hopefully beyond regular patrol routes. If not, we fall back to the Consul's original destination and deal with the complications that brings."

She paused and looked to Fa Jian.

"We're planning an expedition. Ships that will sail around Africa to establish a base and deliver supplies to your resistance network. A demonstration of our commitment."

Fa Jian's eyes widened. "You would undertake such a journey?"

"The journey is nothing compared to what comes after. We need to establish regular supply runs, communication, all without alerting your empire to our presence."

"The logistics …" Fa Jian shook his head. "The Han have dreamed of outside support for generations, but this …"

"Will take time to organize properly," Medb finished. "Months of preparation. Which gives us time to plan your return."

"My return." The words carried weight.

"You're no use to us or to your resistance sitting in a Britannian cell. But your return must seem natural, above suspicion."

Fa Jian nodded slowly. "An escape that is not an escape."

"Precisely. We'd need several prisoners to make the escape believable," Claudius said. "A group escape would draw more attention than a single man disappearing."

"That makes sense," Fa said.

"Before we can plan that, we need more information. Other prisoners who might be sympathetic to resistance efforts. Men who could be recruited or who might already be members of your network."

"You want me to identify potential allies among the captives?" Fa Jian asked.

79

"Yes. Can you do that without raising suspicions?" Medb asked.

Fa Jian considered carefully. "Possibly. I will need some time, weeks, maybe a month, to get the right men and do it carefully."

"That we have. We will begin preparing things on our end for the voyage while you find us the men we need to cover your escape," Medb said.

"And then I go home?" Fa Jian asked.

"And then you go home."

Chapter 7

Northern Italia

Llassar studied the sour faces across the long table from him. He'd been so close to settling down and putting all of this behind him, but the Empire he had helped create kept needing him to come back.

First, it had been to Sardinia, to find out why that island was resisting the unification of Italia, and once Italia was unified, getting it integrated into the alliance.

Now it was helping the people of this peninsula improve their lands, to produce and distribute more goods and make the work more efficient, freeing up men and material for the war effort.

This is what brought him to this cramped room full of nervous men, all demanding more from him. Ledgers and correspondence directing those improvements he had been assisting in covered the table's surface.

The regional prefect, a thin man named Baalius Tanitor, straightened in his chair and cleared his throat.

"My lord, on behalf of our provincial government, I extend our deepest gratitude for the Empire's assistance in this endeavor. The scale of what we're attempting here is greater than anything that has ever been undertaken in Italia. The engineering challenges alone would have been impossible without Britannian expertise and resources."

Llassar kept his face neutral. That was one thing he hated about this place. They were worse than the Romans ... or at least the Romans of Britannia. They never said what they meant and often didn't mean what they said, always using words to try to dull the senses.

They were here to review specifications for a new trunk line that would run through the mountainous terrain before cutting east across river valleys toward the Adriatic coast, as well as secondary routes that would branch off, connecting smaller settlements to the main artery.

"We, of course, are happy to assist our friends and neighbors," Llassar said diplomatically. "My chief engineer, Tarbantu, will provide us with the detailed progress report."

Tarbantu stood, a stocky man with calloused hands and ink stains on his fingers. His accent marked him as from Hispania, one of the many to leave their homeland and travel to Britannia to find their place in the world.

"The primary trunk line running north through the foothills has encountered bedrock formations that weren't indicated in our initial surveys," Tarbantu began. "The granite outcroppings required extensive blasting operations, which delayed our schedule by three weeks. We used twice the anticipated amount of black powder and brought in additional crews from the quarries near Florentia. Cost overruns were substantial, but we maintained forward progress. The section through the hills is now nearly complete, with track laying proceeding at the planned rate."

Shifting through some documents, he pulled out a large map which he unfolded and spread out on the table.

"Our crews are working in the main river valley. The terrain here is more favorable, and we're making good time. The bridge construction remains on schedule, with the first span completed last week. The secondary routes, however, are going to be an issue. The amount of steel available for civilian projects has been reduced again, and we are competing with the pacified areas of Greece and some projects in Germania for what is available."

"Without these branch lines, the railway's economic potential remains limited," Baalius said.

"Then ask your government for higher allotments," another official added.

"I have sent a request already and explained our need, but I assure you, if that were possible, it would have already been done,"

Llassar said. "You need to remember, this is not like the war with Carthage. We are facing an enemy on near equal technological footing who apparently has a larger industrial base. The volume of material needed for the front is staggering. The strategic priority is completing the main trunk line. Rapid movement of legions and supplies throughout the peninsula cannot wait for agricultural connections. Branch lines, while important and planned, are secondary compared to the needs of the moment."

Baalius frowned. "But the economic benefits to the region would be substantial. These towns produce the grain that feeds our workers and soldiers."

"They can continue using existing roads. Focus your efforts on the trunk line. In the meantime, we can divert some resources to help improve those roads using local resources."

"Fine, but that is not the only issue," Baalius said. "The railway's success depends on more than just the tracks themselves. Our main western port must be upgraded to handle the volume of trade the railway will generate. We are already having issues with our current facilities loading cargo onto these large caravels of yours."

"That project has already begun," a portly man at the far end of the table said. "I oversee the port modernization project. We've completed plans to begin dredging the harbor which should be finished well before the rail line is done. We also have plans to improve and increase the piers as well, although our initial talks have faced unexpected resistance."

"What kind of resistance?" Baalius asked.

Llassar had the same question. This was new information that hadn't appeared in the morning reports.

"The local dockworkers' guild has been vocal to our surveyors once they learned what we were doing, saying that we were bringing in trained workers to do the work on specialized equipment. It has only gotten worse since the first steam dredge, something Master Lucal built using one of the riverboat models, appeared in the harbor," the man continued. "They are angry that their employment is threatened and concerned at hearing how fast our steam-powered dredge will work as opposed to the more traditional methods. I think they are worried about the economic factors."

Llassar had encountered similar guild resistance in Caledonia when introducing Britannian manufacturing methods. Traditional craftsmen feared obsolescence, but progress couldn't be held hostage to their concerns.

"How much resistance?" Llassar asked.

"Sabotage of equipment, intimidation of workers, and political pressure on local magistrates to intervene on their behalf," the port overseer explained. "They've convinced the town councils that construction will lead to massive unemployment and my foreman was actually arrested yesterday."

"This has been an ongoing issue," Baalius expanded on the problem. "The improvement projects over the last several years have created unexpected economic disruption across the region. The massive influx of Alliance funds has established a new class of contractors who operate outside our traditional power structures. These new contractors have capital to buy up local resources and labor at rates the established merchant families cannot match. The disruption extends beyond just construction work."

Another official nodded. "The Calidian family has operated the largest grain trading business in the province for three generations. Last month, a contractor backed by Alliance gold outbid them for exclusive rights to transport grain from five major farms. The Calidian family lost their primary source of income overnight."

"Similar patterns are occurring throughout the region," Baalius continued. "New money is displacing old establishments, creating deep resentment and political instability that our government struggles to manage. Traditional families feel abandoned by their own government. They see us favoring outsiders over citizens who have supported the province for generations. This resentment translates into opposition to Alliance projects and could threaten broader cooperation."

"The people themselves will benefit from these projects," the port overseer said, confused. "Don't they see they're hurting the people they claim to speak for?"

"I don't think they speak for anyone but themselves and their own coin purse," Baalius said.

Llassar considered the interconnected problems. He felt for some of the people losing their livelihoods, and he knew economic disruption like this was inevitable with the speed of change, but the war effort demanded solutions, regardless of political sensitivities.

"The need for these facilities is paramount. Men and material flowing through Italia are critical for the war effort. Local political squabbles cannot delay projects essential to the entire Alliance."

"We understand the military necessity, but the social consequences ..."

"Those who obstruct progress will be bypassed. If that port doesn't want to work with us, we will find a new one that wants the money we are bringing in and reroute the rail line. Only those who can deliver results will get the contracts. These established merchant families must work with us or be replaced."

Baalius's face darkened. "You're asking us to abandon citizens who have supported this province for generations."

"I'm telling you to prioritize victory over tradition. Established families can adapt by offering competitive wages and services. Those who cannot will make room for those who can."

"The political consequences could destabilize the entire region."

"And how much would an Eastern victory destabilize it? Talk to the guilds, offer them some concessions, but at the end of the day, workers can learn new skills or find other employment."

The officials around the table shifted uncomfortably. Llassar knew there would be a future cost to that kind of stridency, but the needs of the moment outweighed that concern.

"We have a similar issue," Tarbantu said. "The engineering crews report that local resistance has slowed material procurement. Quarry owners are demanding premium prices, with similar complaints."

"Pay what's necessary to maintain progress," Llassar said. "As with the port, either they get the supplies we need to us, or we find a new supplier."

Baalius was clearly not pleased with that answer and was opening his mouth to respond when he was interrupted by the door to the room opening, admitting a uniformed Britannian courier.

There were two types of telegraph wire being run across the continent, usually next to each other. One for civilian use and one for the military, with the military lines being operated by a new sub-branch of the praetorians.

The uniform indicated this came from more official channels and not civilian ones, so it was no surprise when the man walked directly to Llassar and extended a folded telegraph message to him.

Llassar accepted the message, unfolding and reading it quickly. It was from the Empress, and it was concerning. A nobleman in Scandia was using unexpected wealth to undermine the agreement to bring the northern peoples into the Western Alliance. Lucilla suspected foreign interference and requested Llassar's personal attention to the situation, similar to the work he'd done in Sicilia to ensure the unification of Italia happened.

Llassar refolded the message and rose from his chair. The Italian officials watched him, probably expecting some sort of explanation.

"I have been recalled by the Empress. My deputy will serve as Alliance liaison for your projects."

"When will you return?" asked Baalius.

"I do not know. Until then, my deputy will handle resource requests based on trunk line progress. Military necessity remains paramount."

"And the guild resistance?"

"Solve it. Use whatever methods necessary."

"But ..."

"Figure it out," he said, turning his back on them and leaving.

Devnum

Hortensius pushed through the crowds of workers streaming between the packed dockyards. The massive steel hull of the warship dominated the harbor, its ninety-meter length casting shadows over the smaller vessels clustered around it like iron chicks beside their mother. Steam hissed from various work sites where steam riveting operations continued.

Lucan's message had been short, talking about issues delaying the progress of the construction, but from what Hortensius could see, they were working at full tilt.

Looking up at the deck, he spotted the shipwright standing near the forward turret installation, his arms moving in emphatic gestures as he addressed a cluster of engineers. Even from this distance, Hortensius could see that the man was agitated.

The gangplank flexed under Hortensius's weight as he climbed aboard. Workers moved around him with the careful efficiency of men who understood they were building something unprecedented. The boilers were lit and running. He could feel the subtle vibrations in the hull from the massive steam engines.

"About time you got here," Lucan turned from his group of engineers, dismissing them with a curt nod. "We've got problems that go beyond anything I know how to solve."

"That's why I'm here. Show me what's happening."

Lucan moved to a control station mounted beside the turret base. A series of brass valves and pressure gauges clustered around a central lever system that should provide precise control over the turret's movement. Later, this system would be piped inside the turret, but for now, during testing, it was housed outside of it.

He grasped the main rotation control and pulled it through its full range.

The turret mechanism groaned. Steel components shifted with reluctant, jerky movements, barely traversing. The massive assembly managed perhaps thirty degrees of rotation before grinding to a complete halt, hydraulic fluid weeping from overstressed seals.

"That's with full boiler pressure," Lucan said. "Watch what happens when I try elevation."

He operated a secondary control system. The large barrels were already installed and the system managed to lift them perhaps five degrees before the hydraulic cylinders reached their limit and stopped. The entire mechanism shuddered under the strain, producing sounds that suggested imminent mechanical failure.

"The pressure meets the specifications in the Consul's notes and should be enough to provide full rotation and elevation ranges. What we're getting is maybe twenty percent of the movement we need, and it's fighting us every step of the way."

Hortensius could see what he meant. He examined the pressure gauges clustered around the control station. The readings showed adequate steam pressure from the boiler systems, but something was clearly wrong with the power transmission to these massive components.

"How much pressure are the boilers generating?"

"As I said, exactly what your calculations specified. Four separate boiler units, each one larger than anything we've built before, all feeding into the main steam distribution network. The problem isn't steam generation," Lucan said, waving him toward a hatchway that descended into the ship's interior. "Come look at the distribution system. I think the problem is in the network itself, but I want your opinion before I start tearing apart functional systems."

They descended through narrow companionways lined with steam pipes. The engine compartment sprawled across the ship's central section, dominated by four massive boilers that filled the space with heat and a constant rumble. Steam gauges and pressure release valves clustered around each boiler unit, all showing nominal operating parameters.

Hortensius followed the main steam distribution lines as they branched from the boiler compartment toward the ship's extremities. The network resembled the circulatory system of some mechanical creature, with primary arteries splitting into secondary branches that fed individual hydraulic systems throughout the vessel.

"The pressure readings here at the source look good." He tapped a gauge mounted near the main distribution manifold. "What are you seeing at the turret locations?"

Lucan produced a portable pressure gauge from his toolkit and connected it to a test point near the forward turret connection. The reading showed a noticeable drop from the main distribution pressure.

"About fifteen percent loss by the time steam reaches the forward positions. The aft turret shows similar losses."

Hortensius worked his way along the distribution network, testing pressure at various points. The readings confirmed a steady decline as distance from the boilers increased, but the losses seemed within reasonable parameters for a system of this scale.

"The pressure drop isn't excessive for the distances involved. Let me see how this compares to our riverboat systems."

They climbed back to the deck and crossed to one of the ironclad riverboats moored nearby. The smaller vessel's hydraulic systems had proven themselves in months of combat operations, providing reliable power for gun port operations and rudder control.

Lucan operated the ironclad's gun port mechanisms, demonstrating smooth, responsive movement as the large steel hatches raised and the guns ran out. The hydraulic cylinders moved with none of the clunkiness.

"These work perfectly," Lucan said. "And look at the pressure readings."

Hortensius examined the ironclad's steam distribution system. The boilers were smaller, generating lower overall pressure than the steel ship's massive units. The distribution distances were shorter, but not dramatically so. Yet the hydraulic systems operated with flawless responsiveness.

He measured the distances between the ironclad's boilers and its hydraulic systems, comparing them mentally to the steel ship's layout. The differences were significant but not enough to explain the performance gap they were experiencing.

"The steam pressure here is actually lower than what we're generating on the steel ship. And while the distances are shorter, they're not that much shorter." Hortensius frowned, running calculations in his head. "I'm not sure I agree it's a power deficit."

They returned to the steel ship, where Hortensius stared at the frozen turret mechanism. For a long several minutes, he thought about it, about what could cause the mechanism to grind to a halt like that.

He had Lucan run the tests again, and then a third time. Each time it ground to a stop at about the same point. Not exactly at the same point, but close.

And then he had it.

The answer had been in front of him the entire time, hidden in decisions made months ago under pressure from production schedules and material availability.

"I think I know what the problem is," he said, moving closer to the turret assembly, looking at the steel components with a new perspective. "With all the war material we've been producing, the production demands forced us to use thicker steel plating than originally specified, since we didn't have time to stamp it out. I tested the changes for buoyancy calculations, made sure the ship would still float properly with the additional weight."

"But?"

"But I didn't recalculate the mechanical force requirements. I was focused on displacement and stability, making sure we wouldn't sink when we launched. But I never considered how the heavier components would affect the hydraulic systems."

Hortensius pulled out his calculation notebook and began sketching rough estimates of the weight differences. Among other things, the Consul had been giving them new ways to think about numbers and math as the engineering complications had become more challenging. It had been work, but it also opened up a large door for him to a new universe of understanding.

In this case, it was that the thicker steel plating had increased the mass of each turret assembly far beyond the original specifications.

"The original turret designs called for steel plates twelve millimeters thick. Production constraints forced us to use eighteen-millimeter plating because that's what the mills could deliver on schedule."

"Eighteen millimeters doesn't sound like much of a difference."

"It's a fifty percent increase in thickness, which translates to roughly the same increase in weight for every component. These turret assemblies don't weigh forty tons like the original specifications called for. It's closer to sixty tons each."

"And the hydraulic systems were designed to move forty-ton assemblies."

"Right. We're asking the hydraulic cylinders to provide fifty percent more force than they were designed for, and we're trying to do it through a steam distribution network that's already operating at design limits."

Hortensius could have kicked himself for the mistake. He'd thought he'd been so thorough. He had conducted thorough buoyancy tests with the heavier steel, ensuring the ship would float properly and maintain stability in various sea conditions. But he had never tested the turret mechanisms with the actual steel thickness they ended up using.

"So how do we fix this?" Lucan asked.

"We need to increase the steam pressure to the turret operations. I'm thinking about installing larger pressure chambers directly connected to the boiler systems, designed to build up and maintain higher steam pressure specifically for the hydraulic systems."

He pulled out a sheet of paper and sketched a rough version of a modified boiler feed system that would allow higher pressure. The design isolated the turret hydraulics on a separate high-pressure circuit while keeping the rudder and other mechanisms on current pressure levels.

"We can then modify the boiler feed systems to generate higher pressure for turret operations without affecting the rest of the ship's hydraulic needs. The turrets require massive force for rotation and elevation, but they don't need to operate continuously like the rudder systems."

Lucan studied the sketches. He'd been working on these ships long enough that Hortensius hoped the shipbuilder grasped what he was defining.

"So we build dedicated high-pressure systems for the turrets while leaving everything else on current specifications."

"Exactly. The pressure chambers would build up steam pressure above normal operating levels, then release it in controlled bursts to provide the force needed for turret movement. Between operations, the chambers would recharge from the main boiler systems."

The modifications would require significant work, but they appeared technically feasible. Hortensius sketched additional details showing how the pressure chambers would integrate with existing systems and what safety mechanisms would prevent over-pressurization.

"The isolation valves would allow us to maintain normal pressure for ship operations while building higher pressure specifically for turret movement. When a gun crew needs to rotate or elevate their turret, they would open the high-pressure valves and get the force they need. Before we do this, though, I want to review the calculations with the Consul. The modifications should work, but nothing in his notes suggests what the max limit of the boilers is, or if they can handle those increased pressures. I would rather be sure that this won't set us back further."

"So we wait?"

"Yes, but we don't have to sit idle. We can begin preparing the pressure chamber installations and hydraulic modifications while we wait for the Consul's review of the enhanced boiler operations. The fabrication work will take time regardless, and having the components ready will allow rapid implementation once we get approval."

"How long do you think it will take to make?"

"Two weeks for the chambers themselves, assuming the steel mills can provide the materials on schedule. The installation and system integration will require another week, maybe ten days, depending on how extensively we need to modify the existing steam distribution network."

"Well, then I guess we should get started," Lucan said.

Chapter 8

Camp Banwīhraz, Central Germania

Medb sat in the guard tower, watching the holding cell, observing the final two prisoners. The confines of this cell were much less comfortable than the standard camp, with some bedrolls on the dirt, little cover from the elements, and three dozen men crammed into a small area.

Used to hold prisoners waiting to be transferred to another part of the camp or waiting to be assigned to one, they'd told these men their section of the camp needed maintenance and they were being confined temporarily while that happened.

A lie, although the maintenance was still being done, to keep up the ruse.

In reality, Medb wanted to watch the last candidates Fa Jian had identified among the captured Eastern soldiers in a more pressure-filled environment, and not just the status quo that they'd grown used to.

The one called Zhang Min paced the small confines like a caged wolf. When another prisoner accidentally knocked over one of the water rations just after they'd been delivered, Min had erupted into a shouting match that required three other captives to restrain him from throwing punches. The man's anger burned hot and immediate.

Chen Wei presented the opposite temperament. He sat calmly, cross-legged against the far wall, methodically observing the other prisoners while appearing to meditate. When two men began arguing over sleeping positions yesterday, Wei had quietly intervened with a few chosen words that defused the situation without either combatant losing face. The man possessed the patience and good sense of social awareness.

What intrigued Medb most was how the two men complemented each other. They knew each other and Min often checked in with Wei, deferring to Wei's judgment, while Wei seemed to appreciate Min's directness when dealing with more stubborn prisoners. Her end plan didn't call for them to work together, but this could feed into the escape if played right.

"Bring Zhang Min and Chen Wei to interrogation room three," Medb said to one of the guards as she made her way down from the tower.

They quickly separated the two men from the group and escorted them toward the central camp building. Medb followed at a distance, her mind already going over the conversation ahead. These prisoners represented her best opportunity to establish reliable assets within the Eastern front lines and get Jian out of the camp without arousing suspicion, but convincing them would require careful manipulation of their loyalties and fears.

The interrogation room contained only a wooden table and three chairs. Medb entered after the prisoners were seated and positioned, studying their faces as they realized this might not be one of the odd interrogations where they were left to sit alone, unbothered and unquestioned, that many had gone through lately.

"Hello," she said in their native tongue, her pronunciation rough but understandable. "I'd like to speak with you."

Min sat straighter in surprise as she spoke. Soon enough, speaking to them in their native tongue would not be uncommon as interrogators were taught the Easterners' language, but that was taking time and they had yet to get any to the level of fluency needed to question hostile men.

So she made sure to keep the knowledge that she could speak their language a secret, to be used only for just this sort of moment.

"You speak our language," Wei said carefully, not exhibiting any of the surprise of his friend.

"Poorly, but enough for what we need to discuss." Medb settled into her chair. "Including that I know you both are part of the Han group resistance fighting against your rulers."

The words had the intended impact. Even the more controlled Wei couldn't keep his surprise off his face.

"We are simple soldiers," Wei said. "We know nothing of these people."

"Caution is wise. But consider this. I am clearly someone with power in the Western military. You can see that the guards follow my orders. I have learned your language and know about the existence of the Han. I know about its failures when it tried to go against the empire many years ago. I know about its more careful path now, how it split into hundreds of small groups across the empire for safety. I know its Han roots and its goals." She leaned forward. "Consider how I know all of this when deciding if I am somehow trying to trick you."

The two prisoners exchanged a look.

"What do you want?" Wei asked finally.

"I want your help to not only end this war but to end the current empire and help a more reasonable government regain control in your homeland," Medb said. "I want peace."

Min snorted. "You want to replace our current rulers with yourselves. That is what all conquerors claim."

"Others I have talked to felt the same when I first approached them. Your suspicion is understandable and shows wisdom. But let me ask you to consider something. Compare how Britannian forces handle prisoners versus how the TianYou Empire deals with captured enemies."

"We do not take prisoners at all."

"Exactly." Medb let the word hang in the air between them. "When was the last time you heard of TianYou forces feeding enemy captives, providing medical care for wounds, or allowing prisoners to maintain their dignity? When has your empire ever shown mercy to those who opposed it?"

Neither man had an answer for this.

"Let me also ask if your current resistance efforts against Eastern rule are succeeding? Have generations of Han resistance achieved results against an empire with vast resources using brutal suppression? Are your people closer to freedom now than they were when your grandfathers fought the same battles?"

"What exactly do you want us to do if we agree to cooperate?" Wei finally asked.

"I'm developing plans to provide material support to the resistance operating within the Eastern homeland, but I need reliable contacts and intelligence to make such efforts effective. For you specifically, I need your help at this end first. I want you to return to the Eastern lines where you can gather information about military operations to help us get those supplies deeper into your homeland and potentially influence or limit what your commanders can accomplish," she said, purposefully implying the supplies would be going overland and not by some other, indirect method. "I can establish secure communication methods that would allow you to pass intelligence back to Western forces. You would need to maintain your cover as loyal Eastern soldiers while secretly working to undermine the military effectiveness."

"How would we return to Eastern lines without making our commanders suspicious?" Min asked.

"A staged mass prisoner escape that would provide cover for your return and help grow your reputations at the same time," Medb said without hesitation. "The key is making it appear completely authentic to everyone involved."

"How? It has to be obvious that an escape from a place like this would require some kind of inside help?" Min pressed.

Medb had anticipated this question and spent considerable time developing the answer. "Western guards will create a deliberate weak point in the camp's perimeter fencing during our 'maintenance' and arrange an obvious changing of guard rotations. This will provide you with the opportunity to discover the weakness and rally other prisoners for a coordinated breakout attempt. You'll be able to claim full credit for organizing the operation when you return to the Eastern forces."

Wei frowned, his brow furrowing with concern. "And the other prisoners?"

"I am willing to let them escape to secure your safe position back inside your lines. They will genuinely believe they're attempting a breakout. The mass escape must appear completely authentic to maintain your cover, which means convincing fellow captives to participate while secretly ensuring the attempt succeeds according to our predetermined plan. You will be notified during your next interrogation when the guard changes will happen and where to look for the compromised fencing. From there, it is up to you to ensure the plan works, although know that the guard reaction will be slow and confused, but the guards themselves will not directly know of the escape attempt, to ensure it is authentic."

"What guarantees do we have that you'll honor your promises?" Wei asked. "That you won't simply use us and discard us when convenient?"

Medb met his eyes directly, holding the contact for several heartbeats. "None, beyond my word and the evidence of how we've treated you compared to how your empire treats prisoners, and the fact that I know what I know, you have no guarantees. But consider this: if we wanted to eliminate the Eastern threat through pure conquest, we would need decades and hundreds of thousands of lives. If we can destabilize the empire from within, we save both Eastern and Western lives while achieving the same goal."

"And if we're discovered?" Min asked bluntly.

"Then you'll die as martyrs to your cause, which was always the likely outcome of resisting the empire regardless of your methods." Medb's tone remained matter-of-fact, neither sugar-coating the reality nor dwelling on the brutality. "The difference is that your deaths might actually accomplish something meaningful rather than simply adding to the count of failed rebels."

Silence stretched between them as both men wrestled with the decision. Finally, Wei looked at her.

"If we agree to this, there's no going back," Wei said. "Once we cross that line, we become something different than what we are."

"You already made that decision when you learned of the Han resistance and did nothing to stop it and even joined it," Medb replied. "The only difference is that this time you can actually do something."

The two prisoners sat in contemplative silence, the weight of decision pressing down on them. Finally, Wei spoke.

"We'll do it."

Macedonian Coast, Greece

The landing craft pitched as another waterspout erupted fifty meters off the port bow, close enough to send a sheet of cold spray across the men huddled on deck. The sea, once placid, was a chaos of intersecting wakes and explosions. Modius kept his eyes fixed on the shore. Above the continuous roar of the surf, the sounds of the deeper, percussive impacts of the naval guns were a physical force, a series of shocks that traveled through the boat's hull and up through the soles of his boots. The Britannian fleet, a line of caravels and schooners standing a kilometer offshore, was engaged in a systematic demolition of the Easterners' coastal defenses.

He could distinguish the different shell types. Some struck the crude earth-and-timber bunkers directly, the impact fuses detonating with a sharp crack and a burst of black smoke, blowing fortifications apart causing showers of splinters and dirt. Others were airbursts, the timed fuses exploding twenty meters above the trenches, spraying a wide cone of deadly fragments down onto the exposed infantry. It was this second type of shell that was most devastating, clearing entire sections of trench line with each detonation. Return fire from the shore was weak and uncoordinated. A few puffs of white smoke would be followed seconds later by a geyser of water far from any Britannian ship. The Easterner gunnery was abysmal, although moving ships could be a difficult target.

The first wave's landing craft were already on the beach, dark shapes against the brown strip of rocky ground at the edge of the sea. Through his field glasses, Modius watched legionaries disembark and form up. Squads advanced in a staggered line, one providing covering fire while the other moved forward. They were closing on the first line of trenches. The faint, rapid popping of their lever-action rifles was just audible over the naval gunfire. They were not waiting for the enemy to recover from the bombardment; they were pressing the assault immediately, maintaining the pressure.

He couldn't wait any longer, climbing down a rope ladder to long boats that had just returned from dropping off the first wave to load up the second. By the time they reached the shore, the first wave had already moved well inland.

Modius was one of the first off the long boat, his cohort splashing through the knee-deep, debris-filled water behind him. The beach was a landscape of destruction. Craters were all along the shore, some large enough to swallow a supply wagon, some just shallow enough to twist an ankle. The wreckage of an Easterner gun emplacement lay half-buried, its cannon barrel bent back on itself like a piece of wilted foliage. He stepped over the still forms of several Eastern soldiers, and sadly, some of his own troops, their padded cotton uniforms soaked and dark. Medics were already at work on the Britannian wounded, their white armbands a stark contrast to the grey of the uniforms and the darker grey of the sky.

He led his men forward, quickly catching up to the first wave, which was more actively engaged. They had already secured the coastal road and were pushing on.

The speed of the initial landing had been exceptional, exceeding even the most optimistic projections. The Easterner defenses, which on paper had looked formidable, had been undermanned and collapsed under the weight of the naval guns and the swift infantry assault that followed.

Over the next thirty minutes, more waves came ashore as the remainder of the lead cohort landed, and then the second, and then a third. It would take the better part of the day to get the full legion on dry land, but a cohort was enough to push inland.

Back on the beach, Modius could see the beginnings of the logistical train coming ashore: mules loaded with ammunition crates were being led up the beach, engineers directing the placement of pontoon sections for a temporary jetty. Order was being imposed on the chaos of the landing zone.

As he was getting his own men organized from the push, and deciding where that push should be, a messenger showed up, delivering orders from the Consul.

The orders were short and simple. Push forward to the mountain pass that separated this low beach area from the inland plains. He'd already known that was an objective, but it was originally planned for the second or third day of the landings, as more men were brought ashore, since the assumption had been it would take them at least a full day to establish a foothold on the coast.

The Consul was taking advantage of their rapid progress and moving the time tables up.

"New orders," he said when nine of his ten centurions came in for a quick council meeting before getting the men moving. "We've had our orders pushed up. The Easterners are on their heels and making a run for the mountain pass. We are to stay on them and hold the pass for the remainder of the legion in support of our push inland. It's an hour's march, and you need to push your men hard. The enemy will have sent word of our landings by now, and it won't take them long to rally reinforcements. They know this land and will know that pass is their best place to hold us, so it's a race. And I don't want to lose it. I want your men on the double march in the next ten minutes. Supplies are just coming up, so get what you can before we march out, because we will be operating on our own for a while until the rest of the legion gets organized and comes up to support us. Our orders are to hold the pass until they do. Any questions?"

There were none.

"Move out."

The cohort detached from the larger force, its column of nine hundred men a grey serpent winding its way up a narrow, rock-strewn track that led away from the sea.

The terrain changed quickly. The soft earth of the coastal plain gave way to hard, unforgiving stone. The track twisted through a series of dry ravines and over low ridges making it slower going than Modius would have wanted. Once or twice, the retreating Easterners had briefly rallied from their rout and attempted to re-engage his forces, but their men were too rattled and never held for longer than a few minutes before running again.

An hour later, one of the forward scouts jogged back down the trail, his rifle held across his chest. "Enemy patrol ahead, Captain. A dozen men. They're dug in on a rocky outcrop that overlooks the trail."

"How far?" Modius asked.

"Four hundred meters ahead, where the trail bends sharp left."

"First Century, halt," Modius ordered. He turned to the centurion of his lead unit. "Take two of your squads and fix them with suppressing fire. I want a steady rate of fire, keep their heads down. Take another two squads and move them up that dry wash to the right of the trail. You'll come out on their flank, about fifty meters from their position. Once your flanking element is in place, you will initiate the assault. The rest of the cohort will hold here and provide support if needed. Execute."

The centurion relayed the orders, and his men moved with quiet efficiency. The lead squads fanned out, taking cover behind rocks and dropping to their knees. A moment later, their rifles began to speak, the sound sharp in the stillness of the hills. The fire was not a frantic barrage, but a steady, aimed series of shots that kicked up dust and chipped stone all around the Easterner position. The other two squads, moving in a low crouch, disappeared into the brush-choked ravine. Modius watched through his glasses. He could see the puffs of smoke from the enemy's muzzle-loaders as they returned fire, but their shots were wild, panicked by the volume of incoming lead.

The flanking squads emerged from the wash, rising as one. Their volley, delivered at close range into the exposed side of the Easterner position, was decisive. Half the enemy patrol went down in an instant. The survivors, shocked and overwhelmed, broke. Two were shot down as they tried to run. The rest vanished over the ridge. The entire engagement had lasted less than five minutes. His men advanced and secured the outcrop, finding the bodies of seven Easterner soldiers.

The pass was just beyond the ridge. It was a deep, narrow cleft in the hills, perhaps a hundred meters across at its widest point, flanked by sheer rock walls. It was a superb defensive position. Modius immediately began to lay out his defenses. He walked the entire length of the pass, from one end to the other before assembling his commanders again.

"This is where we will make our stand," he announced to his gathered his centurions. "First and Second Centuries will occupy the high ground on the left flank. Third and Fourth will take the right. I want every position to have an interlocking field of fire with its neighbor. No dead ground. No covered approaches for the enemy. Fifth and Sixth Century will remain in reserve at the rear entrance to the pass, to guard our back and act as a counter-attack force if needed. The remaining four centuries will take the center position in the low ground."

He waited for the commanders to look toward their assigned sections. "Clear away all loose scrub and any rocks large enough to offer cover to an advancing soldier. Use them to reinforce your own positions. I want low, two-man fighting pits like you learned in training. Optios are to establish clear lines of sight between themselves and their centurions. Communication is paramount. If you can't see, you can't fight together."

His men set to work, the clatter of the small spades each man was assigned creating a cacophony as it was amplified by nine hundred men working as one.

He could also hear the grumbling, but ignored it. Soldiers complained more than they fought; it was the way of things. They were tired, but they were good men and would do their duty.

Modius oversaw the placement of every squad, correcting angles, ordering positions moved a few meters left or right to gain a better field of fire. He paid special attention to the elevated squad positions, ensuring they had clear arcs of fire that covered the entire approach to the pass.

As he watched his men labor, he felt a prickle of unease. The natural cover was sparse. The rock was solid but offered little protection from plunging artillery fire.

"I want every man below ground level," he reiterated to his commanders as he watched the men work. "I don't care if they have to chip their way through solid granite. They will dig."

The order was met with weary groans, but still they did their duty. Modius knew he was pushing them hard, but he also knew what was coming. They'd never managed parity with the great hordes of men the Easterners had managed to put together, and here they would be even more outnumbered.

The enemy had also learned some hard lessons. They wouldn't try to overwhelm them with infantry alone. They would try to pulverize them with artillery first. There were no trenches here, so the shallow foxholes they were carving into the rock were their only hope of surviving the inevitable barrage. He walked the line, observing the slow progress, urging the men on. Every centimeter of depth they gained was another man who might live through the coming fight.

It was during this frantic preparation that the first civilians appeared. Even in enemy territory, civilians swept forward when armies marched, keeping out of the way of a foreign army, often made of men who would stop their march to give in to their baser desires.

There was a thin stream of them, trudging up the valley floor from the direction of the coast, a flight of fear, not destination. They were a motley collection of farmers and villagers, their worldly goods piled on rickety carts pulled by donkeys.

Modius sent a squad to intercept a family that was out ahead of their lines and bring them to him. He needed information. An old man, his wife, and two younger men who were clearly their sons were escorted to him. They looked at his grey uniform and the rifles of his men with unconcealed terror.

Modius softened his voice, polishing off his very rusty Greek. "Don't be afraid. We aren't here for you. Where are you coming from?"

"From our village," the old man stammered, gesturing vaguely behind him. "The army of the foreigners came. They took all the food. They are marching this way."

"Can you tell me how many men?"

"Thousands," one of the sons said. "The road was full of them for hours. More men than there are stones in this valley."

"Did they have cannons? Like those?" Modius asked, pointing to his own tube as an example. "Did you see them? Were they large? On wheeled carriages?"

"Yes," the old man nodded vigorously. "Big guns, pulled by teams of oxen. Many of them."

Modius processed the information. A force of several thousand with supporting artillery, and they were close.

Not good.

"Go. Head for the coast. You will be safe behind our lines," he said to the family before waving over a runner. "Find the Consul. Tell him the enemy is advancing on this pass in overwhelming force, at least four thousand infantry, supported by at least one battery of artillery. I am dug in and will hold the position. I request immediate reinforcement. Go now, and do not stop for anything."

The runner did not need to be told twice. He turned and sprinted down the trail. Modius stared out at the empty valley. For now, it was quiet. But it was the loaded silence before a storm.

Less than an hour later, they came. A dark mass appeared at the far end of the valley, resolving itself into columns of marching infantry, spreading out to form a broad front as they advanced. Behind them, lumbering teams of oxen hauled heavy cannons up the opposing slopes. The Eastern commander was making no effort at stealth. He had the numbers, and he intended to use them.

Modius raised his field glasses. Infantry regiments formed up in successive waves, ready to feed men into the assault. He counted twelve guns; their crews were already swarming over them, preparing to fire. His own force of nine hundred men and two field pieces seemed pitifully small.

"Take cover!" The shout was passed down the line from man to man. "Artillery!"

The men of the cohort vanished, disappearing into the foxholes they had so painstakingly dug. The world held its breath for a heartbeat. Then the opposite ridge erupted in a line of smoke and fire. The first salvo of shells screamed across the valley. They fell short, exploding in plumes of dirt a hundred meters in front of the Britannian line. Ranging shots.

The next salvo would be on target. And it was.

The pass became a cauldron of fire and thunder. The twelve Eastern guns fired in relentless sequence, their shells pounding the confined space. The ground shook with the constant impacts. Explosions tore at the rock faces, sending razor-sharp splinters scything through the air. The noise was a physical entity, a crushing weight that hammered at the skull. The air was choked with dust and the bitter smell of explosives. Modius flattened himself in his pit, the world reduced to the patch of brown earth in front of his face as shells walked their way up and down around his position.

He occasionally peeked up to see the positions of his men. During one of those, he saw a direct hit on a position to his left, men who'd been there a moment before completely erased from existence.

This was a battle of attrition, of enduring punishment. The foxholes were everything. Men hugged the earth as the storm raged above them, the shallow pits of dirt and rock the only thing keeping them alive. His own two howitzers, hidden in a deep ravine behind the main line firing indirectly, began to fire back. Their shells were a drop in the ocean against the enemy's battery, but it was what he had. One of them was silenced twenty minutes into the fight, an unlucky hit turning the gun and its crew into a tangle of twisted metal and torn flesh.

The bombardment lasted for what felt like an eternity. Through the swirling smoke, Modius saw the first wave of Eastern infantry advancing. They marched forward in dense ranks, shoulder to shoulder, moving through the explosions of their own artillery. It was a brutal, inhuman tactic, sacrificing some of their own men to keep the defenders' heads down until the last possible second.

Modius waited, his heart pounding in a cold, steady beat. He let them come on; let them close the distance across the open ground. Four hundred meters. Three hundred fifty.

"Up," he yelled, getting his men out of the bottoms of their foxholes and ready to fire. As the enemy hit two hundred fifty meters, he yelled. "Fire!"

The order, relayed by optios and centurions, unleashed the cohort's reply. From one end of the pass to the other, the lever-action rifles opened up. It was not a single volley, but a continuous, rolling torrent of fire. The disciplined ranks of Easterners wavered, then broke as hundreds of rifles tore into them. Men fell in swathes. The front rank ceased to exist, replaced by a line of writhing bodies. The disciplined advance turned into a confused mob as the men behind tripped over those who had fallen. The first wave dissolved two hundred meters from his line, the survivors fleeing back the way they came.

They tried again. A second wave advanced over the bodies of the first, only to be met by the same relentless, rapid fire. The Britannian rifles, capable of seven shots in the time it took an Easterner to reload his muzzle-loader once, created a wall of lead that the enemy could not penetrate.

For hours, the battle raged. The Eastern commander was stubborn, sending wave after wave of infantry to their deaths. The artillery bombardment never fully ceased, although it did move further back in his line, the shells continuing to fall among the rocks. Ammunition became a critical concern.

Decanuses ran from pit to pit, redistributing cartridges taken from the dead and wounded. The barrels of the rifles grew scorching hot. The men's shoulders were bruised from the constant recoil. But they held. Modius moved along the line when he could, crawling from position to position, offering a steadying word, directing fire, ensuring the line remained unbroken.

His remaining piece of artillery had been desperately trying to counter the battery fire, but so far they had only removed one of the enemy tubes because it had to move after each time it was fired to keep from being targeted in return.

The enemy took no such precautions.

He was in his foxhole, watching as they finally took out a second enemy piece, when he heard a new sound, from the rear. The deep, powerful cough of Britannian howitzers, and a lot of them. He looked back down the valley, and for the first time in hours, felt a surge of hope.

The Consul had arrived. Three fresh cohorts were advancing up the trail at double-time, not in a single column but already deploying for battle.

They did not pause. Nearly two thousand men immediately began to ascend the hills on either side of the valley, a sweeping maneuver that widened their line and increased the number of guns that could hit the enemy.

The Consul's own artillery battery, ten guns, was already unlimbering, their crews moving with haste. The remaining cohort advanced directly into the pass, adding their firepower to Modius's beleaguered line.

Within minutes, the new guns opened up. Their fire was not a general bombardment but targeted counter-battery fire. Shells slammed into the Easterner gun line with devastating accuracy. One cannon was flipped into the air. An ammunition caisson detonated in a spectacular gout of fire and smoke. The Eastern artillery, now under attack from an unexpected quarter, faltered. Their rate of fire slowed, then stopped almost completely.

The tide had turned. The Eastern commander, his artillery silenced and his attacks collapsing, tried to pull his infantry back into a defensive posture, but it was too late.

That was what Modius had been waiting for.

"Forward!" Modius bellowed, clambering from the foxhole. "Advance! On them!"

A raw, ragged cheer went up from the survivors of his cohort. They surged from their foxholes, men who had endured hours of hell, and charged forward. They were no longer defending. They were attacking. They swept down the slope, firing their rifles from the hip, joining the fresh troops pouring into the pass. The combined force, nearly three thousand strong, hit the disorganized Eastern line like a tidal wave.

The enemy resistance crumbled. What had been an army moments before was now a terrified mob. They threw down their rifles and fled, their disciplined formations dissolving completely. The final fight in the mouth of the pass was a short, brutal affair, over in minutes.

Bugles calling a halt to the advance sounded from behind him.

The Britannian advance slowed, then stopped. The battle was won. Modius stood panting, leaning on his rifle, the sounds of the dying replacing the sounds of combat. He looked back at the pass he had held. It was a charnel house, a testament to the ferocity of the fighting. He had lost hundreds of men, good men. But they had not died for nothing. He looked down the valley at the fleeing remnants of the Eastern army.

The pass was secure. The coastal landing was safe and they were behind the Easterners' army, ready to catch them between two lines and annihilate them.

A good day's work.

Chapter 9

Factorium

"Ready, Master Sorantius," one of Hortensius's workmen said, stepping away from the huge iron vessel surrounded by copper tubing, gauges, and steam pipes.

"Good. Good. Tell your master thank you when you see him next," the chemist said in way of dismissal before turning to the group of technicians gathered around a few steps away. "Gather around. I know you all have the instructions, but I want to go through it all before you start production."

Not that this should surprise them. This was how he did it every time a new piece of equipment showed up in one of his factories.

"Coal tar contains many compounds," Sorantius said. "Some useful, others dangerous. Specifically, for the new gunpowder project, we need to process this to create a chemical the Consul calls aniline, which will, in turn, be made into diphenylamine for the new gunpowder project, as well as a chemical called benzine, which will have other uses. To do so, we will heat a solution of coal tar and hydrochloric acid in this contraption."

"I don't like working with that stuff," one of the techs said.

"It is ... difficult, I agree, but these acids are also key to unlocking many of the chemicals the Consul has identified for us. Unlike in some of the other projects, the Consul's notes on this one instruct us to add the acid slowly, one drop at a time, until we reach the set amount. Too much acid, and violent reactions will destroy the equipment.

"That will be a very slow process," one of the other men said.

"Yes, it will, but this work rewards patience and punishes haste. You all know how much work it takes to produce the coal tar and acid in the first place. The last thing we want is to ruin the entire batch and waste the materials. We are going to do a small batch, together, to make sure you all understand and then will be able to get your individual crews up to speed as quickly as possible. Two things are very important in this process: maintaining the heat and the pressure. You," he said, pointing to one of the men. "Monitor this gauge. If the pressure gets close to this line, then turn that valve to release some of the pressure. Stop before it drops below that line, which would be too little pressure for the process to work."

The man nodded, looking at the indicated gauge as if it was the most important thing in the world. He chose his men for their seriousness and propriety. None of the foremen running crews were the type to slack or be too cavalier.

Pointing to another one of the men, he said, "You are to watch this temperature gauge. If the temperature reaches this point, you will release this valve to reduce the amount of steam going to the autoclave, but not so much that it drops below this point. It is important that both of you keep your assigned tasks inside these very specific ranges. Once it has run for the set amount of time, you are then to increase the temperature to this range marked here, which I will explain in a minute."

Both men nodded.

"You two will handle the materials," he said to two of the other men. Measuring out the coal tar, transferring it, collecting the compounds as they finish, and bringing in additional acid as needed. You will be in charge of adding the acid as he adds the coal tar. Watch carefully."

Sorantius added coal tar to the container and put on thick coated gloves that would give some protection before lifting up and tilting a small clay jar, one that would not pit or be damaged by the acid. A tiny amount of acid poured out, nearly a single drop, which hung for several seconds before falling into a port in the now closed autoclave.

"Count each drop. The Consul's formula requires number of drops for the weight of coal tar. The acid acts as a catalyst, helping separate the compounds that make up the coal tar. The acid interacts with impurities in the coal tar, allowing the benzine and aniline to vaporize, rise, and travel through the copper tubing where they cool and condense back into liquids. Benzine vaporizes first, at the lower temperatures. Once the processing has gone on long enough, you will have converted the bulk of it and can raise the temperatures to the range in which aniline vaporizes. Before you raise the temperature, you will turn this valve here, which will switch the collection path, allowing the aniline to flow into a separate chamber. Right? Your turn. Remember, one drop at a time. You two, man your gauges. Once the acid is introduced completely, I want you to begin adding steam to raise the temperature."

The man took the small amphora and mimicked the tilt of the container that Sorantius had demonstrated, but a little too steeply. Acid began to flow in a thin stream instead of individual drops. Sorantius immediately grabbed his wrist, steadying the container and preventing the acid from spilling.

"Stop. You're pouring, not dropping." Sorantius took control of the container, demonstrating the correct technique again. "See how I hold it? The angle determines the flow rate. Too steep and the acid pours out uncontrolled."

The man nodded sheepishly.

"Feel how the container balances in your hands. The weight distribution tells you when you have the right position."

The man practiced the motion several times without actually dispensing acid, looking to Sorantius each time, who shook his head when it was done incorrectly.

Finally, the motion looked correct to Sorantius and he said, "Better. Now add one drop to the dish."

The man tilted the container carefully, forming a single drop that fell as instructed. He looked up with obvious satisfaction.

"Good. But remember, you'll be doing this while steam heats the autoclave and pressure builds inside. Concentration becomes more difficult when other procedures happen simultaneously. If it fails, the autoclave could rupture, destroying equipment and injuring anyone nearby. Adding too much will cause the pressure to spike. If that happens, immediately close all steam valves and allow the system to cool. Hopefully, it will only ruin the one batch and not become anything more volatile."

They spent the next hour practicing all the steps for loading the coal tar with wooden tools, to keep from affecting the tar, and adding the acid, giving each man a turn at each position, to ensure they all knew every step and could teach their crews.

"Loading complete. Now we seal the autoclave and begin heating." Sorantius lifted the heavy iron lid, checking that the sealing surfaces were clean. "Any debris between the lid and chamber will cause pressure leaks."

The lid weighed nearly fifty pounds, and required two men to position it correctly. Sorantius and one of the men lowered it carefully, ensuring proper alignment with the chamber rim.

"Tighten these bolts in sequence," Sorantius said, indicating the eight bolts around the lid's perimeter. "Start with opposite bolts to maintain even pressure on the seal. Check for leaks before applying heat."

Sorantius opened the steam valve slightly, allowing low-pressure steam to enter the autoclave. He listened carefully for any hissing sounds that would indicate loose seals.

The system remained silent. Sorantius moved and checked the pressure gauge as steam entered the chamber. "Pressure is rising gradually. No obvious leaks. Now we begin the actual distillation cycle. The initial heating phase lasts thirty minutes. Temperature should reach sixty degrees during this period. We will start with the valve turned to the benzine container."

Moving again, Sorantius opened the main steam valve, allowing full pressure to heat the autoclave. The iron chamber began warming immediately, and the coal tar inside started liquefying.

This was the hardest point. With nothing to do but watch the gauges, the men's attention could falter. For thirty minutes they waited and watched, adding and removing steam to keep it in the defined range. After thirty minutes, they let the temperatures rise, turning the valve to the container that would collect the aniline.

Finally, another thirty minutes of heating had passed. Shutting everything off, they went to the collection containers for the two chemicals and found liquid condensing inside.

The trial run was successful.

The autoclave had cooled sufficiently to be opened safely. Sorantius and one of the men removed the lid, revealing the remaining coal tar residue inside the chamber.

"This residue contains compounds we don't need for current production. Clean the chamber thoroughly between batches to prevent contamination, which might be the hardest part of the whole process." The men laughed, but Sorantius did not. "Training complete."

Macedonian Coast, Greece

Captain Indibilis stood on the quarterdeck of the caravel Cawr, his weathered hands gripping the rail as he watched the heavily laden merchant ships disgorge their cargoes onto longships, sending them toward the Macedonian coastline. Ox-drawn wagons lined the beach in orderly rows, their wooden beds filled with artillery shells, rifle ammunition, and provisions for the Consul's advancing army.

They had been unloading for three days, moving supplies onshore in steady waves. This was the third merchant fleet to come and unload their goods. An army marched on its stomach, and there were almost five thousand Western soldiers marching toward northern Greece, and hopefully a port city where unloading supplies could be done faster from less exposed positions until rail lines could be stretched forward to this new section of the front.

Honestly, his position here felt almost ceremonial. The Britannian Empire had controlled the Middle Sea completely since the Carthaginian War. There was, however, still the odd Egyptian pirate, which meant orders demanded a warship escort for major supply operations. The Cawr, with her complement of twenty-four rifled cannons and experienced crew of sixty, represented the smallest acceptable protection for such a valuable convoy.

Indibilis turned his attention to his gun crews, who were using the quiet hours to maintain their weapons. The port battery had been run in for cleaning, each cannon receiving careful attention from its crew. Powder charges sat ready in their protective containers, and shells lay secured in the magazine below.

Another six or seven hours and he could clear off, return to Italia and the next supply fleet. The fastest of the merchant vessels, already cleared of cargo, were weighing anchor and setting course for the open sea where they would wait for the full fleet to gather for the return trip.

He was just contemplating a short break, leaving the operation to his first mate for an hour so he would be fresh for the task of getting his charges together and all sailing in the same direction.

That plan was crushed by a call from the mainmast lookout above.

"Sail ho! Northeast bearing, multiple vessels!"

Indibilis snatched his spyglass and trained it in the indicated direction. The northeastern horizon revealed what he'd never expected to see in these waters. Twenty dark hulls emerged from the haze, their distinctive square-rigged sails and low profiles unmistakably Eastern in design.

But how could they be here?

They must have come through the Bosphorus from the Black Sea, but that was a nearly landlocked body. How had they gotten there? It wasn't possible they'd slipped across the length of the Middle Sea, into the Black Sea, only to turn around and come out swinging.

Was there some kind of hidden base? Had they managed to build that many ships in the Black Sea itself?

"Signal the fleet," Indibilis commanded. "General scatter, weigh anchor and make for open water immediately."

His signal officer raised the appropriate flags while crew members throughout the Cawr responded to the emergency. A command like that was never given in drill and was saved for when the situation was most dire. The men on the merchant ships needed no elaboration. Ships still anchored began cutting their cables rather than wasting time hauling up their anchors.

Indibilis studied the approaching Eastern fleet through his spyglass. The enemy ships maintained a tight formation, clearly intent on intercepting the scattered merchants before they could reach safety. The lead vessels had already begun spreading into attack formation, positioning themselves to maximize their firepower when they closed range.

"Hard to port, bring us about," Indibilis ordered. "Run out the starboard battery and prepare for action."

The Cawr swung toward the enemy fleet. Gun crews hauled their cannons into firing position while powder monkeys brought up charges from the magazine. The ship's carpenter and his assistants prepared damage control equipment, although in modern naval combat, it seemed unlikely they would get the chance to use it.

The explosive shells used by both fleets left little to be repaired.

The ships that had already unloaded and started to pull away would make their escape easily, but the ones closest to shore would need time to escape. Several remained dangerously close to shore, their holds still partially loaded, and their crews working frantically to gain headway.

Eastern cannons erupted in coordinated volleys. Explosive shells arced across the water toward the nearest merchant vessels, their trajectories visible as dark streaks against the sky. The first impacts sent geysers of water skyward, but the subsequent shots found their targets.

A cargo vessel took a direct hit amidships. The explosive shell penetrated her wooden hull and detonated inside the hold, blasting a massive hole through both sides of the ship. Secondary explosions followed as stored ammunition ignited, breaking the vessel completely in half. She sank within minutes, her crew having no time to launch boats.

Indibilis was confused. With one warship and a score of merchant vessels, he would have thought their first target would have been the only ship that could fire back.

And yet more shells found targets among the fleeing merchants. One projectile exploded against a ship's stern, obliterating the rudder and steering gear while setting the wooden deck ablaze. Another shell burst destroyed the mainmast of a sailing vessel, bringing down rigging and canvas in a tangle of rope and timber. The wounded ship wallowed helplessly, unable to maneuver or maintain its speed.

There was nothing he could do to save them. With so many enemies bearing down on them, it was unlikely his ship would survive, let alone be able to rescue the wounded ships.

Indibilis focused on the merchant vessel struggling closest to shore. The ship moved sluggishly, unable to gain sufficient speed to outrun the approaching Eastern warships.

"Bring us between that merchant and the enemy fleet," Indibilis commanded. "We'll cover her withdrawal."

The Cawr altered course, positioning herself directly in the path of the Eastern attack. Her starboard battery trained on the nearest enemy vessels, gun captains adjusting elevation as their targets approached. The range closed rapidly, both fleets converging at speeds exceeding twenty knots.

Eastern gunners continued their systematic destruction of the merchant fleet. Explosive shells tore through wooden hulls and superstructures, creating fires and casualties among the defenseless cargo vessels. The enemy fleet had clearly planned this operation, timing their approach to catch the merchants at their most vulnerable moment.

"Fire as they bear," Indibilis ordered.

The Cawr unleashed her starboard battery in a coordinated broadside. Twelve rifled cannons hurled their explosive shells toward the Eastern fleet, the projectiles screaming across the water at velocities that compressed the air around them. The ship shuddered under the recoil, her timbers groaning as tons of metal and gunpowder were expelled in fury.

The first salvo scored multiple hits. An explosive shell penetrated the bow of an Eastern warship, detonating inside the forward hold and blasting debris high into the air. Another projectile struck amidships, the explosion tearing a gaping wound in the enemy vessel's hull below the waterline. A third shell burst against the stern of another ship, destroying steering equipment and killing the crew manning the tiller.

And just like that, the reprieve his ship had gotten ended as Eastern commanders responded by concentrating their fire on the

Cawr. And not just one. Multiple ships altered course to engage the Britannian warship, reforming into a coordinated line of attack.

"Port your helm, maintain distance," Indibilis commanded. "Gun crews, reload and maintain your fire."

The Cawr entered a fighting retreat, her superior sailing qualities allowing her to maintain range while trading shots with multiple opponents. Her crew worked frantically, each man performing his assigned task without hesitation. Powder charges slammed home, followed by the deadly explosive shells, gun captains ordering the next load almost as soon as the previous was fired.

The running battle developed, the Eastern ships pursuing aggressively, their commanders understanding that they must destroy the Britannian escort to complete their mission against the merchant fleet. The Cawr serpentined through the water, trying to offer as difficult a target as possible to the wall of fire coming toward them.

Explosive shells from both sides created towering waterspouts when they missed their targets. When they found their mark, the results proved devastating. It was much easier for the Cawr, who had a wall of targets to choose from. They scored direct hits on three Eastern warships in rapid succession. One enemy vessel lost her entire bow section when a shell detonated inside the forward magazine, the explosion lifting the front third of the ship completely out of the water before it crashed back down in splintered wreckage.

Another Eastern ship suffered catastrophic damage when a Britannian shell struck her mainmast at deck level. The explosion not only destroyed the mast but fire spread rapidly through the rigging while the collapsed mast crushed several cannons and their crews. The vessel fell out of formation, her captain struggling to maintain control as flames consumed his ship.

The third damaged Eastern warship took a shell burst directly amidships. The explosion penetrated the hull and detonated inside the gun deck, killing most of the port battery crew and destroying four cannons. Secondary fires started immediately, forcing the crew to abandon their weapons in order to fight the flames threatening the main magazine.

Despite these successes, Indibilis knew it was futile. The Eastern fleet still outnumbered him four to one, and their coordinated attacks were beginning to tell. His ship had suffered damage to her rigging and hull, while several of his gun crews had taken casualties from near misses and flying debris.

The best he was going to do was slow them down and allow as many of his charges as possible to escape.

The merchant vessel he'd protected had gained some distance but remained vulnerable. Her anchor had finally broken free, allowing improved speed, but she still lagged behind the other escaping ships. Eastern commanders had not abandoned their primary mission, with several vessels continuing to pursue the fleeing merchants while others engaged the Cawr.

Multiple shells struck the water immediately around the Cawr, their explosions sending fragments of metal and wood across her deck. One shell fragment grazed the port rail, the explosion killing two sailors and wounding several others.

"Surgeon to the port side," Indibilis called, maintaining his position on the quarterdeck while chaos erupted around him.

A coordinated enemy salvo bracketed the Cawr with devastating effect. Three explosive shells struck simultaneously, one penetrating the hull near the waterline, another destroying part of the port battery, and the third exploding against the stern rail. The combined impact staggered the ship, her forward momentum faltering as water poured through the hull breach.

The gun deck was a scene of destruction. The shell that penetrated the port battery detonated among the cannon crews, killing almost a dozen men instantly and wounding a dozen more. Four cannons were completely destroyed, but the remaining guns continued firing, their crews working around the bodies of their fallen comrades.

"Damage control party to the lower deck," Indibilis ordered. "Shore up that breach before we take on more water."

His ship's carpenter and his assistants rushed below with lumber and tools, attempting to plug the hole that threatened to sink them. Another Eastern vessel suffered massive damage when a Britannian shell penetrated her magazine, the resulting explosion breaking her back and sending her to the bottom within minutes.

The Eastern fleet continued its pursuit, closing the distance fast as his ship began to lag from the damage it had sustained. It wouldn't be long now. Enemy gunners had found the range, their shells striking with increasing frequency and devastating effect.

A particularly massive Eastern warship, her three masts towering above the others, closed its range, her broadside erupted in a concentrated blast of flame and smoke, sending a dozen explosive shells toward the struggling Cawr. The impacts came in rapid succession, each explosion adding to the destruction.

The first shell penetrated the Cawr just above the waterline, detonating inside the lower gun deck and killing most of the starboard battery crew. The second projectile struck the mainmast, the explosion not only destroying the mast but also bringing down the main yard and the associated rigging. The third shell burst against the stern, obliterating the steering gear and killing the helmsmen.

The ship began to list badly, but the beating continued.

More shells found their targets in quick succession as the ship's galley disappeared in a fireball when an explosive projectile detonated among the cooking fires and stored provisions.

"All hands, abandon ship," Indibilis commanded, though he made no move to leave his position.

His crew ignored him, continuing the fight even as their ship settled lower in the water. The few surviving cannons continued to fire, their crews determined to inflict maximum damage before the end.

The remaining ships of the Eastern fleet, sensing that victory was within reach, were swarming in for the kill.

The largest Eastern warship fired another concentrated broadside, her shells converging on the Cawr from point-blank range. Indibilis remained on his quarterdeck, watching as his ship died around him.

Multiple explosive projectiles penetrated the hull simultaneously, their detonations creating a series of secondary explosions as they reached stored gunpowder and ammunition.

In the final instant before the magazine detonated, Indibilis allowed himself one thought of satisfaction. Through his spyglass, he could see the merchant vessel he had protected disappearing over the horizon. He'd done his job.

The explosion that followed dwarfed all previous detonations. The entire magazine contents ignited simultaneously, creating a blast that obliterated the Cawr in a towering column of fire and smoke. The explosion lifted debris hundreds of feet into the air, with the concussion felt by the retreating supply column moving away from the beach.

Chapter 10

Syrakousa, Sicilia

Sicilia. Medb didn't care for Sicilia. The last time she'd been here, it had been an annoyance, tracking down an idiot of a merchant who was smuggling goods in and out of Carthage.

At least this time she didn't have to deal with the locals. Along the dozens of merchant ships filling the harbor, three large Britannian warships rode at anchor, standing out against the smaller merchant vessels. The distinctive profile of the flagship Bellona dominated the center of the group.

Medb stepped onto the dock as sailors secured the mooring lines. Her timing had been good, as work crews carried provisions onto the anchored ships while others loaded ammunition and fresh water barrels. She approached the naval guards stationed at the gangplank, who glanced at each other as she approached.

"Is the Admiral aboard?"

"Yes, my lady."

She stepped past them, just missing hitting one with the documents case in her hand, and started up the gangplank without pausing. Neither man tried to stop her.

Instead, once she was halfway up the plank, one yelled up, "One for the admiral."

She didn't begrudge them their warning. In fact, she smirked at it. She'd always found the admiral to be a bit ... workmanlike. One of those men who saw every problem as a nail and himself the hammer. But, his men respected him. Worshiped him, even. Enough to challenge her wrath by giving their boss a warning.

And that was something.

Sailors moved about the boat, loading supplies and cleaning. The busy work of the ship. None looked up at her as she marched across the deck toward the captain's cabin, but they looked up as she passed close by, unable to stop themselves.

She smiled again. She did love it when her reputation preceded her.

Valdar was just coming out of his cabin, a junior officer posted outside his door, as she arrived. The look on his face when he opened the door was expectant but changed to barely concealed irritation when he recognized her.

Without a word, he gestured toward his cabin entrance.

The admiral's quarters reflected his practical nature. Charts covered a large table while navigational instruments occupied built-in shelves along the bulkhead. Light streamed in from the rear windows, giving an impressive view of the harbor.

Valdar closed the door and turned to face her, his blue eyes showing controlled frustration.

"I was recalled from active operations against Egyptian positions for this meeting. The least I expected was the Empress herself, or maybe the Consul, if they wanted a report on how our operations are going."

Medb settled into the chair across from his desk without invitation, setting her case on the floor next to her. "Her Majesty has more pressing concerns than traveling to Sicily to brief naval officers on intelligence operations."

"Intelligence operations? Is that what this is about? I don't have time for your games, *Your Majesty*," he said, the last part clearly as an insult, a reference to her lost kingdom. "I have a front to lead."

Medb ignored the taunt.

"And on this front, how much naval support is there really? How many ships remain in your river flotilla?"

She, of course, had seen the reports and knew the answer, but it was the question that proved her point.

"Five ironclads and their support craft."

"So there are two full legions with experienced legates in command, but you have to be there, leading them? Perhaps I am behind on my understanding of military hierarchy, but if anyone should be directing major military operations in Egypt, Admiral, it would be the legion commanders with thousands of men under their command rather than a naval officer with a handful of river craft."

Valdar didn't answer, because what could he say? She was right.

"The real fighting is being done by infantry with rifles, not sailors with cannon."

Valdar waved her off and asked, "What is the urgent business that cannot wait for the completion of our Egyptian campaign?"

Medb reached into her document case and withdrew a large, folded map. "You have orders from the Empress to assist with a mission that requires naval transport and support."

She spread the map over his chart table, weighing down the corners with available instruments. The detailed cartography showed waters extending far beyond the Mediterranean, past the oceans identified on the map by the Consul as the Indian Ocean and parts of an apparently much larger ocean known as the Pacific. Medb placed her finger on a small island off the coast of a series of larger ones clear across the world from any known Britannian territory.

"We need to establish a forward base at this location." Her finger tapped the remote position. "One that could support long-term intelligence operations against the TianYou Empire."

Valdar leaned over the map, studying the indicated position. "I assume the Consul drew this up for you. This is amazing."

"It is. This particular island offers natural concealment while remaining close enough to the Eastern mainland for agent infiltration missions. More importantly, as far as our sources can tell us, it is outside of the Easterners' territory."

"Do you see how far this is from lands we control? The journey would require two to three months of continuous sailing through waters no one on this side of the world has set eyes on. I've made the voyage around Africa to reach these Eastern waters, and even with favorable winds, the distances are enormous."

"You said it yourself; you have sailed successfully around Africa. This is not so much further."

"This is very different sailing. Along the coast, there are opportunities for resupply and shelter during storms. This offers no such advantages. How do you propose maintaining supply lines across such vast distances?"

"It is a challenge to be sure. As I understand it, this area is largely left alone by the Easterners. It is possible to come around and sail up this way," she said, tracing her finger along the islands filling the region southwest from the mainland. "It will be an effort, but the Consul believes it's doable."

"I see," Valdar said. "And can I know the point of all of this, aside from vague statements of long-term operations?"

"The base would serve as a launching point for recruiting local allies among existing resistance networks within the Eastern Empire, supplying them, and ultimately tearing down the TianYou government from within, as well as providing us with intelligence we have been unable to get so far."

"Resistance networks?"

"We have contacts that have confirmed the existence of organized resistance against the TianYou government. We have a man who will be deposited on the mainland and work as our liaison with the resistance networks. Once he is established, we will begin smuggling supplies to these rebels and bring back any intelligence we get from them."

"And how do you plan on running something like this? My men are sailors, not spies."

"And I only need them to be sailors. I am sending Claudius to command a small security detachment along with skilled workers to construct the necessary infrastructure. He will lead the operation, determine what is needed, and coordinate it with the assistance of your officers."

"It still seems hopeless. One Eastern fleet encounter would eliminate our entire expedition with no possibility of assistance."

"Everything is a risk, I don't deny that. Hopefully, the base location provides sufficient distance from Eastern patrol areas to avoid detection, if proper precautions are maintained. The chance of finally getting an intelligence base against the Easterners makes it worth it."

"How, exactly, do you expect to get the supplies this Claudius of yours will requisition from Britannia to here?"

"There will need to be supply convoys, of course. Most likely sent out monthly, once we know the base is firmly established.

"Do you have any idea how complex this is? You can't just wave it away as a risk."

"Can't I? I am aware this is a risk, but this is also an order from the Empress, not a request for your opinion on its feasibility."

The admiral's expression hardened. He was a military man. He knew a direct command when he heard one.

Valdar looked up from his notes. "The plans will be ready for review in one week."

"Good," she said, standing and rolling the maps back up. "Good."

Sena, Egypt

"Hold them up," Aelius said, holding up a hand.

Bugles sounded as the long winding body of legionaries, artillery, horses, and baggage-carrying carts ground to a halt. They stopped just short of three kilometers from the outer ruins of Sena, where the once sprawling city had contracted, leaving behind crumbling walls and sand-choked buildings to mark its former prosperity.

The Nile's eastern branch had shifted course over the last century, leaving the city stranded among the dunes, and took away its significance as a port.

Now it stood as a marker of the eastern edge of Egyptian territory, before the Sinai separated it from what had once been Persia.

Through his field glasses, Aelius studied the enemy positions. The Easterners had chosen their ground well. Their main defensive line ran along a series of low ridges flanking the city's western approach, where ancient irrigation canals provided natural trenches. Earthworks crowned each rise, dark rectangles of freshly turned sand that spoke of recent construction. Artillery pieces jutted from gun pits like black fingers, their bronze barrels catching the afternoon sun.

Aelius counted at least twelve artillery pieces in the visible emplacements, with the possibility of additional guns hidden behind earthworks or among the ruins. The infantry strength appeared substantial, with movement visible throughout the trench system suggesting a force comparable to his own legion.

Maybe a little larger.

Worse, the terrain favored the defense. Open ground stretched between the Britannian dunes that would mark the beginning of the attack of the enemy lines, offering little cover for an advancing force.

Not that he had a choice. It was his task to open up the eastern approaches while Cormac held Upper Egypt, suppressing lingering Ptolemy resistance and Easterner presence and pushing down into Lower Egypt.

"Deploy the men," he ordered grimly.

Behind him, the column of soldiers began spreading into a battle line, even rows under good discipline. Behind them, the batteries of howitzers were deployed, the horses uncoupled and taken toward the back, away from the earth-shaking weapons that could startle even the best-trained horses.

Further back, the baggage train pulled to a halt, putting another set of dunes between them and batteries. As soon as the train was set, they began unloading additional ammunition and other materials needed for a war. Physicians set up a forward aid station, preparing for the inevitable casualties.

Men began pulling the two large observation balloons that would hold the spotters for the artillery, allowing them to see the full scope of the battlefield.

He was proud of his men. The action was smooth, with thousands of men all shifting and moving around each other, equipment going in every direction, like an anthill that had been kicked over.

Enemy activity increased as the Britannians completed their deployment. Additional figures appeared along the Eastern defensive line, suggesting that reserves were moving forward to reinforce the front positions.

This would not be a surprise attack.

"Have Paulus deploy the nineteenth along the northern parallel canal bed, but they are to stay on this side of the dune. I don't want any sign of them above the dune; they are to move slowly to keep the dust down. Tell him I want no signs of his approach. He is to then hold there until signaled. Send Ahenobarbus and his cavalry to the southern dunes there and there," he said, pointing. "He's also to hold until signaled."

The messengers took off, headed toward one of the cohorts on the far-left end of the line. Five minutes later, a section of the line began to break off, moving north.

From his position, he watched the eastern lines another minute as the remainder of his forces got into position. Looking up at the sun, he watched it creep across the cloudless sky as the minutes ticked by. Part of him had hoped the enemy would launch an attack preemptively, but they weren't quite that reckless.

No, they'd have to be goaded out of their position.

"Commence firing."

The sound of the first howitzer shot was deafening after the long silence as the two armies waited for the fight to begin. Its shell arced high in the air before dropping toward the largest Eastern redoubt. The explosion sent sand and debris fountaining into the air.

The remaining howitzers joined it, firing in sequence. Each explosion created a growing cloud of dust and smoke that obscured the enemy's view while revealing the effectiveness of Britannian gunnery. Eastern soldiers scrambled for cover as shells burst around their positions.

The enemy response came swiftly, their own artillery opening fire. Aelius missed the days of facing solid shot as the enemy shells exploded causing similar geysers. Men died as shrapnel cut into his lines.

The battle wouldn't be won with artillery, but he would lose valuable men, veterans, before things moved to the next stage.

Word came down from the balloons floating high above them communicating the positioning of the enemy guns.

Aelius directed half his artillery to focus counter-battery fire on the enemy gun positions. The howitzers shifted their aim, sending shells toward the Eastern artillery emplacements.

A feat that the Easterners, who did not have observation balloons, could not duplicate.

Explosions blossomed among the enemy batteries, silencing guns and scattering their crews.

The artillery duel continued for twenty minutes, shells flying in both directions as gunners fought their own war. The Easterners were taking the worst of it, ripped apart by the more accurate Britannian guns.

As the Eastern batteries fell silent and Aelius's guns began to retarget their line, the enemy infantry began to move. They had little choice at this point. It was fight or let the carnage continue without a response.

The Eastern army began its advance, thousands of soldiers emerged from their trenches and redoubts, charging across the open ground. There may not have been trenches here, but the tactics were still the same. Attempts to smash through by brute force.

A terrible way to wage war.

The distance between the armies closed steadily as the Eastern assault gained momentum. Five hundred meters became four hundred, then three hundred as the attacking columns pressed forward through the artillery fire. Some shells found their targets among the advancing formations, creating gaps that were quickly filled by soldiers from the supporting ranks.

It was hard not to be impressed by the bravery of the enemy, as they absorbed the carnage and kept charging.

At two hundred and fifty meters, Aelius could see individual faces among the enemy ranks.

They had reached the killing ground.

"Open fire!"

The command rippled down the Britannian line. A thousand lever-action rifles fired simultaneously, their combined report rolling across the desert like thunder. The front rank of the Eastern assault simply disappeared, soldiers falling in writhing heaps as bullets tore through their formations.

The second volley followed within seconds, then a third and fourth as the Britannian soldiers worked their rifle actions. The continuous fire created a wall of death that no infantry formation could penetrate, bullets striking down entire companies as they tried desperately to close the remaining distance. The Eastern advance staggered, then halted as survivors sought whatever cover they could find on the open ground.

The men not cut down, hiding behind the bodies of their dead comrades, attempted to return fire from their prone positions, but single-shot rifles required soldiers to expose themselves for reloading, making them easy targets for the Britannian marksmen.

Their attack was stalled and opened up the moment Aelius had been waiting for.

"Sound the signal," Aelius said.

The runner next to him, seemingly too young to be in any army, did not wait for another command. He turned and sprinted toward the northern end of the main line. A moment later, a clear, sharp sequence of notes sounded.

A kilometer to the north, beyond a series of crumbling, sand-choked walls that marked the ancient boundary of Sena, the men of the Nineteenth Cohort began to stir.

They had been lying in the sunken bed of a defunct irrigation canal for the better part of an hour, the sun beating down on them, the sounds of the main battle in the distance. Five hundred men began to move, then a thousand.

Their approach was shielded by the ruins of the old city. They moved not in a single line. The sounds of their movement were swallowed by the din of the main battle. The Easterners, pinned down two hundred meters from Aelius's main line, had no inkling of the danger approaching their right flank.

The cohort exploded from their trench, charging forward toward the enemy line, firing as they ran. The first volley from the Nineteenth Cohort struck the Eastern line hard. Cries of surprise and pain mingled with the ongoing sounds of battle. Heads turned, seeking the source of this new attack. The effect was immediate and catastrophic. The Easterner line, already stalled and bleeding, began to disintegrate.

Paulus's cohort did not halt. They fired as they advanced, each squad providing covering fire for the others, a rolling barrage that pushed the enemy back on themselves. They swarmed over the low ridges the Easterners had used as their starting point.

The fighting devolved into a series of frantic, brutal encounters within the shallow trenches and among the dunes. The smaller, easier-to-manage lever-action rifles were devastating in this close-quarters work. An Easterner soldier, fumbling to reload his single-shot weapon, would be met by a Britannian legionary who could fire seven rounds in as many seconds.

And then Aelius sent another messenger, which resulted in another trumpet call, a different sequence of notes.

From behind a massive, crescent-shaped dune, Ahenobarbus led the Ninth's cavalry. Four hundred horsemen crested the rise, a sudden and terrible apparition against the blue sky. For a moment, they seemed to hang there, then the bugle sounded the charge, and they descended upon the southern flank of the Easterner army. The ground shook under the impact of sixteen hundred hooves.

At fifty meters, the front rank of riders raised their short-barreled rifles and fired a single, coordinated volley into the packed ranks of the enemy infantry. The effect was horrifying.

The concentrated fire punched a ragged hole in what remained of the Easterner formation, staggering the entire left wing of their army. Before the enemy could recover, the cavalrymen slung their carbines, drew their sabers, and crashed into the disordered lines.

Horsemen carved their way through the infantry, their long, curved blades rising and falling. They wheeled and turned, rolling up the enemy line, driving panicked soldiers before them. The psychological shock was as devastating as the physical destruction. An army already reeling from a frontal assault and a flank attack now found itself assailed by heavy cavalry. It was too much. The charge broke the last remnants of cohesion.

The breaking of the Eastern army was not a single event, but a contagion of fear. It started on the flanks, where the pressure was greatest, and spread inward. Men saw their comrades cut down from the side, trampled by horses, and they threw down their weapons. Officers shouting orders were ignored, then shot down or swept away in the tide of retreating men. The stalled assault became a rout. Soldiers turned and ran; a desperate, mindless flight back toward the walls of Sena.

"Advance," Aelius said, his voice calm amidst the noise. "General advance. All cohorts."

The command swept down the main Britannian line. The men of the Ninth Legion, who had been firing from their prepared positions, ceased their volleys. With a single, unified shout, they surged forward, leaving their cover and advancing across the killing ground they had created, stepping over the fallen bodies of the enemy.

The pursuit was a brutal, running affair. The faster Britannian legionaries cut down stragglers, but there was no time for a systematic mopping-up operation, allowing several to escape, running into the desert.

The priority was the city itself. Aelius spurred his horse forward; his command staff following closely behind.

The cohorts of the Ninth Legion swarmed into the Eastern forward defenses. The trenches and gun pits that had seemed so formidable an hour ago were now littered with the dead and the detritus of a defeated army. Legionaries vaulted over earthworks, clearing out the remaining pockets of resistance with swift, efficient violence. The Eastern artillery pieces, some damaged by counter-battery fire, others simply abandoned, were quickly secured.

The enemy made no attempt to form a rearguard. It was every man for himself. From his new vantage point within the captured enemy line, Aelius could see the chaos at the city walls. The pursuit was so close that the defenders within Sena could not risk opening fire for fear of hitting their own men.

The legionaries of the Ninth smashed through the fleeing mob right at the main gate, preventing it from being closed. A brutal, swirling melee erupted as the Britannians forced their way into the city on the heels of the vanquished.

The last of the Easterners not caught in the crush at the gates were scattering, breaking out of the city and fleeing east, a disorganized rabble disappearing into the vast emptiness of the Sinai. The battle was over. The field belonged to the Ninth Legion.

Chapter 11

Camp Banwīhraz, Central Germania

Chen Wei counted the paces between guard posts for the fifth time that afternoon. Forty-seven steps from the northeast tower to where the construction crews had left their work unfinished. The new gate frame stood half-built, steel posts driven into the ground, but the heavy wire panels not yet secured. Instead, it was simple barbed wire. Thick, but not insurmountable. The woman had said this window would stay open for three days, long enough for him to 'notice' it, but not so long that it seemed too unbelievable.

Zhang Min shifted beside him, the larger man's bulk creating a shadow across the dirt. The others Chen had selected were spread throughout the compound yard: two former Yi Jun deserters near the latrine block, a pair of Banner Army officers by the water barrels, three more scattered among the general population. Each had been chosen for specific reasons. The deserters knew how to move through hostile territory. The officers still commanded respect among the prisoners. The others possessed skills they would need to keep those who would run out with them together and moving in the long days ahead.

Construction debris lay piled against the fence where the workers had left it yesterday. Beneath the scattered lumber and coiled wire, Chen had secreted boards during morning exercise. Four meters long, reinforced with iron strips originally intended for the gate frame. The workers hadn't noticed their disappearance from the supply stack. Or perhaps they had and were ordered not to notice it.

It was the Britannian's plan, after all.

"Two minutes," Zhang said.

Chen didn't respond. His attention remained fixed on the guard rotation playing out before them. The afternoon shift was ending. Eight guards would converge at the main gate to hand over their posts. Their replacements would emerge from the administration building, but they always took their time. Water first. Jokes about the previous shift. Complaints about equipment. Chen had timed it repeatedly. Four minutes minimum before the new guards reached their positions along the eastern perimeter.

Just as the woman had arranged.

The scarred guard reached his turning point and began walking back toward the main gate. Right on schedule. The convergence was beginning.

Chen flexed his fingers. The calluses from years of handling grain ledgers had been replaced by harder ones from manual labor in the camp. His father would have found that amusing. All those years maintaining the merchant façade while coordinating resistance cells, and his son had finally developed working hands in a Britannian prison.

"Hong is nervous," Zhang noted.

One of the Yi Jun deserters near the latrine block was indeed looking like he might bolt. Hong had deserted from his unit after watching his squad burn a village suspected of hiding resistance members. The man's conscience made him useful but also unpredictable.

Besides, it didn't matter. The guards weren't going to notice because they were told not to notice.

The fix was in.

"He'll hold," Chen said.

"You're certain?"

"No. But we proceed regardless."

The guards from the eastern fence line were walking toward the gate now. Three more from the western perimeter joining them. The northern tower guard would remain at his post, but his attention would be on the gathering at the gate, not the construction area.

Chen watched the administration building door. Any moment now.

The door opened. The replacement guards emerged, rifles slung casually over their shoulders. One was still buttoning his jacket. Another carried a cup. They moved without urgency toward the gate where their counterparts waited.

"Now," Chen said.

He pushed off the fence and walked steadily across the yard. Not running yet. Running would draw immediate attention. Zhang fell into step beside him. From his peripheral vision, Chen saw the others beginning to move. Hong had stopped fidgeting. The two officers were walking parallel to them, maintaining distance but clearly part of the same movement.

Thirty meters to the construction area. The guards at the gate were deep in their shift change ritual. Papers being signed. Keys transferred. The replacement guards hadn't even started toward their posts.

Twenty meters. Other prisoners in the yard were beginning to notice the coordinated movement. A few stepped back, sensing something about to happen. One opened his mouth as if to shout a warning or question.

Ten meters. Chen broke into a run.

The sudden movement triggered chaos. Zhang surged forward beside him. The other chosen prisoners sprinted from their positions. Someone in the yard shouted. Then another. Bodies began to move, some running away but many more running toward them, guessing what was about to happen.

Chen Wei reached the debris pile and dropped to his knees, hands finding the concealed boards immediately. Zhang grabbed the other end of the first plank. They yanked it free and carried it to the fence section where the wire panel met the unfinished gate post. The gap was wide enough to insert the board's iron-reinforced edge.

They rammed the board into the gap. Two more prisoners arrived with the second board, jamming it in above the first. The Banner Army officers had the third. Within seconds, all four boards were in position.

"Pull!"

Eight men threw their weight against the makeshift levers. The fence groaned. Wire mesh designed to contain prisoners could not resist lateral pressure. The panel began to bend outward, creating a gap between its edge and the post.

A rifle cracked from the north tower. The bullet struck dirt twenty meters behind them. Another shot followed, equally wide. The tower guard was firing, but his aim was terrible. Worse than any Britannian fire Chen Wei had experienced in combat.

Again, probably at the woman's orders.

"Harder!" Zhang roared.

The fence panel bent further. The gap widened to half a meter. Chen could hear shouting from the main gate. The guards there were starting to move, but the surprise slowed them. Blunted their reactions. More rifles began firing. Bullets struck the ground in seemingly random patterns, always missing the main group of escapees.

The gap reached a full meter.

"Through! Move!"

The first prisoners scrambled through the opening. The quartermaster with the bad leg stumbled, and Zhang grabbed his arm, practically throwing him through the gap. Chen held one of the boards in place as more men pushed through. Ten. Fifteen. Twenty.

A bullet struck close enough to spray dirt across Chen's legs. Random chance or the inevitable result of firing into a crowd, even when trying to miss. He heard someone cry out behind him, one of the stragglers who had joined the escape without being chosen. The man was holding his shoulder, blood seeping between his fingers, but still moving.

Chen Wei released the board and dove through the gap.

More than fifty men were now running, free of the wire. A few more might get through, but the Britannians were now moving with speed.

"To the forest line! Run for the trees!"

The tree line lay a hundred meters ahead across open ground. The escapees were spreading out instinctively, making themselves harder targets. Behind them, shouts of alarm were going up across the camp.

Fifty meters to the trees. Chen Wei's breathing was steady and controlled, years of physical conditioning paying off. Some of the others were already flagging, their time in captivity having weakened them. The quartermaster was limping badly, supported between two other prisoners.

Twenty meters. The rifle fire had stopped.

Ten meters. The forest edge rose before them, thick undergrowth promising concealment.

They plunged into the trees. Branches tore at clothing and skin. The undergrowth was denser than it appeared from the camp, forcing them to slow their pace. Chen Wei took the lead, pushing through a gap between two thick pines. The woman had provided detailed maps that he'd been forced to memorize so he could get them all safely back to the Eastern lines, through lightly held parts of the Westerners' own lines.

"Stay close," he called back. "Don't spread out."

They pushed deeper into the forest. The sound of the alarm faded, muffled by the trees.

After twenty minutes of hard movement, they reached a small clearing. Several men collapsed immediately, gasping for breath. The quartermaster's face had gone pale, his leg barely supporting him despite the help of others.

"We can't stop," Zhang said.

"I know." Chen looked back the way they had come. No sounds of pursuit, yet. He knew the pursuit wouldn't be coming, or at least wouldn't come until later and would be half-hearted, but he didn't want the others to know that. "Five minutes. Then we move."

"Chen Wei."

He turned to find Hong approaching, the nervous deserter now steady and focused. The actual escape had burned away his anxiety, replacing it with the familiar rhythm of survival.

"The others want to split up," Hong said. "Cover more ground, make us harder to track."

"No. We stay together until we're clear of their patrol range."

"But ..."

"Together, or you go alone. Choose."

Hong nodded and moved back to the others. Chen used the brief rest to orient himself properly. The sun was lowering toward the western horizon. They needed to cover a significant distance before dark.

"Time," Zhang announced.

Chen called the exhausted men to their feet. The quartermaster groaned but didn't complain when Zhang ducked under his arm to support him. They resumed their eastward push, maintaining a steady but sustainable pace.

The forest grew denser as they moved away from the camp. Ancient pines towered overhead, their canopy so thick that the undergrowth thinned from lack of sunlight. It made movement easier but also left them more exposed if anyone was watching from a distance.

An hour passed. Then two. The quartermaster's limp worsened, and even Zhang Min's strength was beginning to flag from supporting him. They stopped to rest at a stream, the men dropping to their knees to drink directly from the cold water.

"How much farther?" one of the Banner Army officers asked.

"To friendly lines? A week's hard march."

The officer's face fell. "Impossible. Not with wounded. Not without supplies."

"We'll manage."

"How? We have no food, no weapons, no ..."

"You can go back to the camp if you like," Chen said, not wanting to hear any more.

The man, technically his superior, did not reply.

They pushed on as the sun began to set. The forest floor grew treacherous in the failing light. Roots and rocks became invisible hazards. They were forced to slow further, feeling their way forward.

Hong, moving too quickly in his exhaustion, caught his foot on a hidden root and went down hard. His ankle twisted at an unnatural angle, and he screamed before biting down on his own hand to muffle the sound.

Chen reached him first. The ankle was already swelling, clearly sprained if not broken.

"Zhang Min, you'll carry him."

The big man was already moving, despite the exhaustion he was feeling. He had been supporting the quartermaster for hours, and now Chen was asking him to take on another burden.

"I can manage," Zhang said simply.

Two of the other prisoners helped Hong onto Zhang's back. The deserter's face was tight with pain, but he kept silent. They resumed moving, their pace now reduced to barely more than a walk.

Another hour passed before Chen found what he was looking for, a ravine cutting through the forest floor, its sides steep enough to provide concealment and its bottom relatively flat. He led them down carefully, using roots and rocks as handholds.

"We'll rest here," he ordered.

The men collapsed where they stood. Even Zhang Min sank to the ground, his massive frame trembling from exertion. Chen did a quick count. Fifty-three had made it through the fence. Several bore minor injuries from bullets or the forest itself.

The two Banner Army officers approached him. In the dim light filtering through the canopy, Chen could barely make out their faces.

"That was expertly done," the senior officer said.

"We were lucky," Chen said.

"No," the second officer said. "It wasn't luck, it was planning. You did amazing work. You're a hero of the empire, Chen Wei."

Others were nodding agreement. Part of Chen felt … dirty at accepting their praise. Not from the Banner Army officers, they were pawns of the empire and would order innocent men to their deaths with no mercy, but the others. He was taking them from a camp where they were often fed more than they were in the Imperial army to be thrown back into the line, where many would die.

But it was for a better cause. It would help Jian get back to their homeland and get the resistance outside help. Their first real chance to topple the empire.

If it required a sacrifice of some of these men to free their children and their children's children, then that's what he would do.

He raised his hand sharply, cutting off further praise.

138

"We're not free," he said. "We're inside enemy territory with no supplies, no weapons, and injured men who can barely walk. The Britannians will send patrols at first light. Their local allies will be watching for us. Every village between here and our lines will be alerted to our escape."

The men's expressions sobered.

"This was the easy part," Chen continued. "Everything that comes next will be harder. We move when I say. We stop when I say. Anyone who can't maintain the pace gets carried or left behind, their choice. Get what rest you can. We move again in one hour."

The praise died completely. The men settled into exhausted silence. Chen positioned himself where he could watch both approaches to the ravine. Zhang joined him without being asked.

They sat in silence, watching darkness claim the forest completely. In the distance, so faint it might have been imagination, Chen thought he heard dogs barking. Too far away to be immediate danger, but a reminder that their escape had only begun.

Syrakousa, Sicilia

Valdar stood on the quarterdeck of the Bellona, watching the longboat cut through the harbor waters. The last of his captains had finally arrived from their scattered patrols. Captain Dag pulled himself up the boarding ladder, followed by Captain Mandonius. Both men looked travel-worn, their uniforms salt-stained from hard sailing.

"Admiral," Dag said.

"Thank you for coming. The others are waiting in my cabin."

The cabin felt cramped with nine captains crowded around the chart table. Valdar spread the latest reports across the polished wood surface. Red marks indicated enemy positions, blue for friendly forces, black crosses for lost vessels.

"The rumors you've heard are true. The scouts confirmed this morning that fifteen Eastern warships cleared the Dardanelles two weeks ago, wiped out a support fleet, and have sunk several ships in the Aegean since."

"Heading for our forces in Egypt?" Captain Fabius asked.

"I don't think so, or if they are, then they will be fairly ineffective. The legions are too far inland now, past Memphis and nothing in the scouting reports suggests they have ships made to go on the river, and it seems like they are armed for fighting and not delivering troops. The river boats can handle any coastal threat. I think their most likely target is to try to break up our merchant traffic. Every supply ship we lose means fewer rifles, less powder, and less food reaching our armies."

"So we're aiming to stop them before they can get into more of our shipping lanes, yes?" Fabius asked.

Before Valdar could respond, Captain Hákon said, "Fifteen ships to our nine are not very favorable odds. If it was still our new shells versus round shot, maybe, but not now that they are firing fused shells from their ships as well."

"Yes, I agree the numbers aren't ideal," Valdar said. "But we have limited choices. The bulk of the available warships are headed to the Dardanelles to shut off any possibility of reinforcement and start probing north to find where these ships came from. Besides, you lot are the finest sailors in the world. Every one of you has more combat experience than any three of their captains combined."

"Experience won't stop a shell through the hull," Dag said.

"Speed and maneuverability will. They adapted to our cannon well enough and have installed some of our sails, but their main sail plan, those long-ribbed sails of theirs, have much less maneuverability than our own. Our ships are faster, more responsive. We use that advantage." Valdar pulled out a second chart showing the waters between Crete and the African coast. "But I agree a head-on confrontation is not to our advantage, so I do not propose we just charge in guns blazing, unless conditions favor us. Instead, we are going to pick at them, cut out stragglers, and force them to keep their ships bunched together for protection. Make them react to us instead of hunting merchants. Every time they try to go hunting, we force them to chase us instead."

"Will we get any reinforcements?" asked Captain Brigid.

"Eventually, yes. I've sent word to Londinium, but we are very spread out and our building of caravels has slowed down with so much dock space going to building the river boats. It will take time. For now, we buy time and we make them pay for every league they sail west. Any questions?"

None of the men had any, but that wasn't surprising. This was not complicated. Although it had been some time since they were outnumbered and matched in firepower on the sea, they would do their duty.

Valdar rolled up the charts and ordered, "Return to your ships. We sail within the hour."

The captains filed out. Valdar followed them up to the quarter deck, watching as boats ferried them back across the harbor.

His bo's'n approached.

"Orders, Admiral?"

"Signal all ships. Prepare to sail."

The signal flags ran up the halyards, blue over white, then red. The reply wasn't instantaneous. Most of the ships had to wait for their masters before they could acknowledge and follow the given orders. As time passed, across the harbor, acknowledgment flags appeared on each vessel until all were accounted for, their ships setting sail and pulling up anchor.

"Helmsman, take us out."

The Bellona gathered way slowly, her hull cutting through the calm harbor waters. One by one, the other ships moved into line. They sailed out of the harbor, the coast of Sicilia falling away to starboard.

It was good to be commanding a proper warship again, Valdar thought.

Factorium

Sorantius stood at the terminus of the production line, looking at the large collection bin full of dark grains. He lifted a handful, feeling their weight, their density. They were not too smooth and not too rough. The Consul's specifications had been precise, as always, down to measurements that seemed arbitrary at first, although he'd allowed himself to experiment enough with the Consul's instructions to learn they weren't arbitrary at all.

Letting the grains slide from his hand, Sorantius walked to the middle of the line where one of the drying stations sat, and a technician monitored the work. Steam rose from the reclamation pipes, carrying away moisture and residual solvents that would otherwise compromise the propellant's stability. The recovery system captured these vapors, condensing them back into reusable components. Considering the time and effort it was to make many of these compounds, very little was wasted.

Another of the Consul's ideas.

The temperature gauges showed steady readings. Too hot and the compounds would break down prematurely. Too cool and moisture would remain trapped within the grain structure, creating unpredictable burn rates.

The technician looked at him nervously, but as far as Sorantius could see, the man was doing fine work. Just the nerves of workers when their boss looks over their shoulder.

Moving to the washing vats, Sorantius checked the temperature gauges on each container. As with the drying, it was all about removing and reclaiming excess solvents and chemicals that would otherwise alter the way the grains worked. The first half was all about mixing chemicals and solvents together, and the last half of the process seemed to be about pulling those same chemicals back out again.

The cutting machine was the stage he'd spend the most time on. The collection of rollers and blades processed the dried sheets into the uniform grains. He watched as a technician fed another sheet into the mechanism, watching as it was pressed to exact thickness before the cross-cutting blades diced it into cylindrical grains.

After they'd first done this stage, he'd run experiments to try and understand just why the Consul had required this specific size. He hadn't doubted the Consul, who had been right about all of this, he'd just wanted to understand it better.

As always, though, the Consul's way was best.

He'd found larger grains burned more slowly, not faster, which was counterintuitive to what he'd thought would happen. He'd assumed more of the gunpowder would burn faster, but in fact the opposite was true. The smaller grains followed the same pattern, just the opposite, burning faster and hotter with a much more erratic pressure curve.

He touched the surface of a partially dried sheet waiting to be cut, feeling its rubbery texture. The chemical transformation from liquid mixture to semi-solid, which would eventually be dried into hard pellets, also fascinated him.

After all that, the grains were then washed and dried a final time, to once again clean away surface impurities and remove excess chemicals. Large containers held perfectly uniform grains.

This had been an extensive project, taking almost a year to complete, but they had finally begun producing the first test batches of the new powder that the Consul called 'smokeless powder.'

An odd name since tests showed it definitely still produced smoke.

Admittedly, a lot less than the older powder which the Consul called black powder. This new propellant would open up more doors when it came to designing new firearms. Able to generate a significantly higher amount of pressure, when used in a rifle they should push bullets faster and farther, extending the range and accuracy of a rifleman, if he understood correctly.

Of course, Hortensius would have to build a better rifle to take advantage of that. He had tested a shell's worth of the gunpowder in current barrels, just for his own curiosity, and rounds quickly began causing warping and bending to the barrel not designed for these forces.

Artillery shells were another matter, though. This new powder could be put in as the internal charge of the shells almost right away, making the cannon much more devastating and effective.

"This looks good," he said to the men watching him closely as he inspected the line. "I want us to begin continuous operation right away and start delivering the finished powder to the armorers. I also want three more lines set up. Let me know if we have any issues."

The supervisor nodded. He'd certainly been expecting this order, as this had been the goal all along. For now, they would have to operate both lines, the black powder and the smokeless, but once Hortensius finished a new version of the rifle, they could convert the black powder lines to making the new powder and increase production again.

Thankfully, ships with the new potassium nitrate had begun coming in from the Far East, although where exactly was still a closely guarded secret. The new supply was just in time, as these new production lines would greatly strain their previous ability to create the nitrate needed for both parts of the process.

He just hoped these shipments kept coming because they would only need more.

Chapter 12

Hofstadir, Svealand Region, Scandia

Lucilla set down the latest dispatch from Germania and turned toward the window. The temporary quarters the Scandi had provided were functional but sparse, with rough-hewn timber walls, simple furniture, and a single brazier for warmth. She gazed at the village, well more of a city these days, of Hofstadir spread out below. Longhouses and Britannian-style homes mixed together, arranged in careful rows around the central building where their religious ceremonies took place.

A knock at the door drew her out of her thoughts as Cynwrig stuck his face in.

"Llassar is here to see you, Your Majesty," he said.

"Thank you, Cynwrig. Llassar, come in," she said, waiting a beat as the Caledonian entered. "You made good time from Italia."

"Your message suggested urgency."

"It is urgent. We have a problem that requires immediate attention, and I need someone on the ground less recognizable than me." She gestured to a chair near the brazier. "A young nobleman named Beruwald has emerged as a significant threat to our position here."

Llassar remained standing. "Beruwald. I've not heard the name, but I thought we had an agreement signed. Didn't they agree to join the alliance?"

"They did, but some elders are now having second thoughts. And until the final negotiations, I had not heard of Beruwald either. He appeared four months ago with considerable wealth and has been using it to undermine our alliance."

"How considerable?"

"Enough to offer substantial payments to entire villages. Silver, tools, weapons. He's promising immediate benefits to any community that breaks ties with Britannia."

"Where did he acquire such resources?"

"That's the question. He claims it comes from successful trading ventures, but no one can identify which ventures or where he traded. The wealth simply appeared."

"Eastern backing?"

"That is what I think, but he's been careful not to reveal his sources."

Llassar finally sat, his expression thoughtful. "What's his stated goal?"

"He's arguing for Scandi independence, although if he has Eastern backing, it feels like more than that. He argues that our alliance is merely disguised subjugation, that we used economic pressure to force their compliance and will eventually absorb them into the Empire."

"The embargo."

"Yes. He's exploiting lingering resentment from that decision. Many here haven't forgotten how we restricted trade until they agreed to negotiate."

The sound of multiple footsteps on the stairs interrupted them. Cynwrig opened the door again, this time to admit a concerned-looking Elder Ragnvald. Two younger men flanked him, both bearing the arm rings that marked them as village representatives.

"Empress, forgive the intrusion." Ragnvald's voice carried an edge of anxiety. "The situation has worsened significantly since we last spoke."

Lucilla gestured for them to enter. "We were just discussing him. What's happened?"

"He's no longer simply offering bribes. His tactics have become more aggressive and direct. Three villages switched allegiance yesterday and two more are considering his offer."

"What changed?"

"He's offering exclusive trade agreements. Not just payments, but ongoing access to goods we cannot produce ourselves."

"What goods?" Llassar asked suspiciously.

"Rifles, powder, and even some artillery pieces, although the description I have heard of the ones he showed was close to the ones you used in the last war."

"Impossible." Llassar said plainly. "None of your villages have the industrial capacity for such production."

Ragnvald nodded grimly. "That's what we told the other elders, but Beruwald has the weapons. I've seen them myself."

"How many?"

"At least fifty rifles at the demonstration. Three artillery pieces. He claims to have access to hundreds more."

Lucilla exchanged a glance with Llassar. "He's also supplying agricultural tools and fertilizers at prices that undercut our merchants by half."

"The tools could be produced locally," Llassar said. "Some of the Gallic factories have learned to replicate simple implements. But rifles and artillery are unlikely."

"Which leaves two possibilities," Lucilla said. "Either someone in our own territories is supplying him, or the weapons come from the East."

"Considering his sudden influx of money and what he's arguing, it seems that the Easterners are much more likely to be the source."

Ragnvald shifted uncomfortably. "There's more. Beruwald has been hosting elaborate feasts for uncommitted village leaders. The hospitality is generous, but the message is clear."

"Which is?"

"Join him or face isolation. He's building his own trade network and promises to exclude any village that maintains ties with Britannia. For communities that depend on trade for survival, it's a powerful threat."

One of the younger men with Ragnvald spoke up. "My village relies on grain imports during winter. If Beruwald controls the trade routes ..."

"You'd have no choice but to comply," Lucilla finished.

"He's using our own tactics," Llassar observed. "Economic isolation to force political alignment."

"An effective strategy, as we've demonstrated."

Ragnvald pulled a rolled parchment from his cloak. "This arrived this morning. A formal invitation to attend one of the upcoming gatherings."

Lucilla took the parchment, scanning its contents. The language was polite but carried an undertone of threat.

"He's growing bold. Ragnvald, how many villages have formally broken with us?"

"Seven so far. Another dozen are wavering."

"And our allies?"

"Holding for now, but the pressure increases daily. Some of the younger warriors see Beruwald's wealth as proof of his strength. They question why we should follow distant Britannia when one of our own offers greater rewards."

"One of your own who appeared from nowhere with mysterious wealth."

"The young don't ask such questions when silver flows freely."

Lucilla studied the map, noting the pattern of defections. The villages switching sides formed a rough line along the eastern coast. "He's building a power base with access to the Sea of Serpents."

"Probably because he is receiving shipments from Sardinia. They have a port in the far eastern portion of the sea, and we do not have control of that area yet," Llassar said.

"Most likely. Ragnvald, what do the other established elders think of him?"

The old man's expression soured. "Most distrust him. His manner is arrogant, his rise too sudden. Haimdahl called him an upstart boy playing at powers he doesn't understand. But even those who dislike him personally are beginning to fear his influence."

"Fear can be as effective as loyalty."

"More effective sometimes." Ragnvald glanced at his companions. "We should return. There's a council meeting this afternoon where three more villages will announce their decisions."

"Do what you can to delay any formal declarations. We need time to respond appropriately."

After the Scandi delegation departed, Lucilla and Llassar sat in silence for several moments.

"A direct counteroffer would be expensive," Llassar said eventually.

"And potentially counterproductive. The Scandi pride themselves on their independence. If we appear to be buying their loyalty ..."

"We'd confirm Beruwald's narrative that we see them as subjects rather than allies."

"Precisely." Lucilla moved to the window again. "We need subtlety here."

"The established elders already distrust him. We could work through them. Building on existing suspicions rather than creating new ones. The Scandi respect strength, but they respect cunning more. If we can expose Beruwald as an Eastern puppet without appearing to attack him directly, his support might crumble."

"That's the hope." Lucilla returned to her chair. "I need you to coordinate with our allies here. Speak to the elders who hate Beruwald. Don't try to charm them. You wouldn't succeed anyway."

"I can be polite long enough," he said.

"Be yourself," she said. "Give them the lines you gave me. Tell them buying loyalty feeds a habit. Tell them men who sell themselves twice don't sleep well. Then listen. Tell me the names of the ones who can stand up in a hall and discount Beruwald without my hand on their backs."

He inclined his head.

"I'll talk to Ragnvald again in the morning. He left eager to work. I'll give him the lines and he'll make them his. After that, we'll host a small meeting here with only a handful of elders, the senior ones. Men whose word carries past the coast. No spectacle. No feasts. Bread, meat, and talk. Then a larger moot called by Ragnvald, not me. This needs to be Scandi lead."

After Llassar departed, Lucilla remained at the table, studying the patterns on it, but mostly lost in her own thoughts. Beruwald's strategy was sound, but it depended on maintaining multiple complex elements simultaneously: wealth, weapons, trade networks, political momentum.

It was clever, but it was also dangerous.

He was speaking out of both sides of his mouth, and the Scandi hated that. The reason he was being heard was because he was arguing against foreign intervention, but if the Scandi themselves could prove he was a hypocrite, they would quickly turn against him.

Or so she hoped.

Devnum

"Engage the auxiliary pumps," Lucan said as he stood beside a pair of pressure chambers.

A chief fitter snapped an acknowledgment. Two stokers spun the flywheel throws on the small steam engines, easing open the valve stems. The pump pistons began their hard stroke, water driven into the chambers against the heavy accumulator springs. The needles climbed.

"Slow pulls," Hortensius said. "Keep it under two, until the lines are open."

He had posted himself at the manifold face, one large hand on the sequencing levers, eyes on the row of telltales.

"Open feed to steering," Lucan said. "Half turn. Then turret circuits, forward first."

"Half, not full," Hortensius said. "We wake it gently. Cotta, give me the steering feed. No, not that one. The marked one. There."

Cotta flushed and turned the correct handle. A faint rumble passed underfoot as the water moved into the long run aft. Lucan read the main. One point three, one point four, one point five. The line gauges followed.

"Target is two point eight on the accumulators," Lucan said. "Steering branch at one point two before the bleed."

"Good," Hortensius said. "Locking valves on the rams are shut. We don't want a jump. Get ready for a staged bleed."

Lucan flicked two fingers toward the tiller flat messenger waiting at the companionway ladder.

"Go," he said.

The boy went at a run. Lucan pictured the tiller flat out of habit, the pair of long double-acting rams flanking the brass quadrant, links and pins new enough to show machine marks, wear plates chalked.

"Boilers steady," he said. "No changes until I say."

"Aye," the engine room runner said from the hatch.

Hortensius cracked the small, dogged bleed valve with his thumb and forefinger. A whisper of water broke into the waste pipe. The steering branch gauge dipped, steadied.

"Good," he said. "Enough to charge the end spaces. Close … now."

Lucan watched the small drops of oil on the sight glass move. Clean, amber, free of grit. He nodded once.

"Locking valves shut on the tiller?" he asked.

"They confirm shut," the messenger called from the hatch.

"Bring the steering up to one point four," Lucan said.

The auxiliary pumps kept time. The needles ticked up. Two point eight on the accumulators. One point four on steering. One point two on the forward turret manifold, which was sealed for now.

"Hold boiler output steady," Lucan said. "Let the system settle."

The hull creaked in the berth. Riveters above hammered somewhere out of sight, the sound distant through the steel.

He could feel Hortensius beside him, radiating his usual impatience, but the old man kept his hands off the levers, which he knew was a trial for the ever-energetic manufacturer.

Lucan checked his list on the board hanging from a length of waxed cord. He ticked off three items with a stub of charcoal. He did not like charcoal; it smudged and left his fingers black.

"Locking valves to the steering rams open on my signal," he called toward the messenger. "Tell them to brace for a slow creep."

A hand signal came back from the boy in the hatch.

"Open," Lucan said.

The messenger relayed it. Somewhere aft, the two-wheel valves slowly opened. The steering branch sank a hair. The main accumulators held at two point eight and a shade. The pump engines did not labor.

"Good," Hortensius said. "We can move her."

"Engage the steering engine," Lucan said. "Slow. Give me full port, midships, full starboard. Then repeat at one-quarter speed, then half. Confirm at each stop."

"Ready aft," the messenger said.

"On my count," Lucan said. "Three ... two ... one. Full port."

He pictured the small engine spinning up, the governors lifting. The telemotor lever in the tiller flat pulling the valve chest slide. Water moving into one end of each ram, out of the other, through the return to the accumulator, past the check valves. The rudder quadrant turning.

"Travel's smooth," a shout came up.

Lucan ran a fingertip along the line of pressure gauges. Steering branch dipped to one point three, then climbed back as the pumps kept working. The main lost a tenth, no more.

"Hold at full," Lucan said. He paused, then ordered, "Midships."

"Midships," the reply came. "Holding."

"Full starboard."

The valves clicked in their cages. The floor trembled with the rudder's mass coming across.

"Full," the aft voice came, short with effort.

"Repeat," Lucan said. "One-quarter speed."

They ran the sequence twice more, each time faster. Hortensius had posted men at the flanges and gland nuts along the long run aft, and each called a number or shook his head at the messenger as he passed. No spray. No ooze. No stink of hot oil on steam.

"Draw-down is within margin," Hortensius said. "She eats a hair less underway than the sums, because they filed the pins clean, finally. Hold her midships. Let's see if she creeps."

"Midships and hold," Lucan said.

The tiller crew set the brake and held the handwheel steady. Lucan watched the needle on the small "position" gauge that took its signal from a simple cord drum wound to the rudder stock. It did not flicker. He counted to sixty in his head. It did not drift.

"Stable," he said. "All right. Forward turret. Bring me traverse power to the forward manifold."

Hortensius eased the turret feed open, the heavy lever groaning. The forward manifold needle lifted. Two fitters posted at the ring race called the oilers to their stations.

"Power to the rack," Lucan said. "Slow traverse. Port fifteen, starboard fifteen, then around the circle."

The crew in the forward turret carcase called back. There was no roof yet ... a circle of steel open to the sky, like a throat. The twin gearboxes hummed when the traverse pinions nestled into the great rack of teeth bolted to the turret base. The rim moved.

"Is the brake band free?" Hortensius asked toward the turret.

"Free," the turret captain called.

The turret crawled to port fifteen degrees, stopped on command, then eased back through center, to starboard fifteen. The heavy bearing responded without chatter.

"Full rotation," Lucan said. "Slow, then faster."

The rim turned. Oil shone in the grooves, clean and bright. Lucan stood with his hands behind his back to keep from touching the steel. The new bearing shells had been machined, scraped, blued, and then scraped again until there were no high spots biting. His lungs loosened as the turret came all the way around and the helpers called out each quadrant as it ticked past chalk marks on the deck.

"Brake ... on," Hortensius said.

The brake lever came down. The turret stopped dead on a chalk line. No overshoot. Good.

"Brake ... release. Step up the pace," Lucan said.

The pumps sang harder. The forward turret manifold dropped a tenth, maybe two, then held. Hortensius watched the main and the high-pressure chamber needles, both held steady.

"Elevation gear," Lucan said into the speaking pipe. "Trunnions up five degrees, down five. Repeat. No guns installed, mind your cradle stops."

"Aye," came from the forward turret.

Two elevating screws turned. The trunnion cheeks tipped up. The empty cradle moved through its short range. Rollers ran in their races without squealing.

"Sealing rings," Hortensius said. "Check."

The turret captain's arm appeared at the open trunk, two fingers raised in a sign they agreed upon. The rings were seated and dry. No weep. He waved the oilers to continue feeding through the little glass cups.

"Run the same under drag," Lucan said. "Apply the drag brake a quarter. Traverse through ninety, reverse, then through one-eighty. Watch the draw."

The drag brake pads pressed lightly on the rim. The turret power unit labored with a whisper, not a shout. The forward manifold sagged a little under the imposed load, the high-pressure chambers lost three tenths, the auxiliaries picked up the slack. All of it within the parameters.

"Good," Hortensius said. His mouth twitched under the beard. "Aft turret next."

They crossed the deck plates to the aft position. The aft turret went through the same sequence. The men had learned from the last failure and had sleeved the long steam line feeding the pumps, so it did not shed heat into the void.

They ran through the steps twice, and once more to prove it was not luck. The hand gear took it, teeth seated. No banging, no chipped spurs.

"Within capacity," Hortensius said. "We can sign those lines off. Both turrets are ready for gun installation."

Lucan's answer was to start yelling up at the riggers moving along the gantry. It took a few minutes, but soon the cannon were in position and ready to be lowered.

A whistle blew. The gantry crawled in on its rails, chain falls taut, the heavy barrel slung to reinforce and chase, tag lines steadying the drift. The open, forward turret waited ... a steel ring and the elevating slide already seated in its cradle, recoil and run-out cylinders bolted beneath.

"Bring her over," Lucan said.

The rigger boss gave a small hand sign. The barrel passed the coaming and hung above the slide. On Lucan's nod, they lowered the breech lug seated to its stop, the reinforce touched the V-blocks and the long ring key went home under a hammer's coaxing, keeper plate and taper pins locking it.

"Let the slide take it," Hortensius said.

154

They had built this for a new kind of gun. Sorantius's smokeless powder changed everything with its pressures higher, burn longer, fouling less. That made the old muzzle-loading scheme a dead end for anything this size. The interrupted-screw breech design the Consul had introduced was ... amazing. It was the first of its kind in Britannia, and really the world.

"Block," Lucan said.

The breech block arrived on a short sling. The carrier took it and two men turned the spigots through a quarter arc.

"Test pump," Hortensius said.

They rigged the small lever pump to the recoil and return connections, all powered by the gases generated as the gun fired. It was genius, once Lucan understood it.

A quarter stroke first, the slide moved back to the painted mark, then forward, steady. It went to half, then full back to the buffers and home again. No weep at the gland nuts. No chatter at the end of travel.

"Again," Lucan said.

They cycled it until the cylinders felt warm under a palm, not a punishing exercise. Then the second forward gun went through the same paces, faster because hands remembered the order without talk. Pins found holes. Caps met their faces. The breech locked and unlocked by muscle memory.

"Turn on the valves," Lucan said into the trunk.

Steam and water flowed and the turret moved under weight now. The forward manifold dipped and then steadied as the auxiliaries found the rhythm. Elevation up and down, five degrees either way. They checked the brake on and off, and there was no jump on release. The bearing stayed cool under a fingertip.

"Loading angle," he said. "Run the shell hoist for alignment."

The empty tray presented right where it should, a dummy shell was rolled into the cradle. Rammer connected and tested once, slowly, to the seating line without a bump. A single dummy bag walked through the motion with the carrier open then shut and locked. The drill was repeated until the turret captain sounded bored, which Lucan preferred over clever.

"Aft turret," Hortensius said.

Same sequence, succinct instead of drawn out.

Riggers cleared the gantries from the rings. The men lashed chain falls out of harm's way. Lucan looked over the forward turret again, seeing the thing as a whole rather than as its parts. The recoil slides, the big rack, the worm, the sealed ring, all of it meant to digest the kick from the new charges that Sorantius had provided to them. Without that powder, this was only a clever mount. With it, the guns had reach and power that the old muzzle-loaders could not match.

Hortensius came up, wiping his hands on his apron.

"It's a thing of beauty," he said.

"It really is. I just hope this range keeper the Consul and you designed does its job. The gun captains are already complaining that it is an unnatural way to fire a cannon," Lucan said.

"Says men who nine years ago had never heard of gunpowder or cannon," Hortensius said. "They'll get used to it, just like they got used to everything else. What is left?"

"Swivel cannon along the weather deck," Lucan said. "Then just integration, live fire, and a short shakedown."

"Good. We might have to do the shakedown cruise on the way to the Middle Sea. The chieftain is pushing for us to get this thing into action as soon as possible," Hortensius said, using the now common name for Talogren, who was currently in charge of the home isles.

"Then we'll hurry," Lucan said.

Chapter 13

Western Sarmatia

The office had been a grain store once. Chen Wei had kept the racks and bins in place but filled them with ledgers, tally sticks, and bundles of reed markers instead of millet and wheat.

The smell of the place still held, though, a dusty and slightly moldy fragrance of old grain. Across from him, a junior clerk's stool faced his table, a plain board laid over trestles.

He'd never had his own office before. Until now, what work he'd done had been at the front, first manual labor and then organizing supplies once his superiors realized he had a talent for numbers. But this was something new.

A reward for having orchestrated and pulled off a large prison break, returning dozens of men to the front, including one particularly well-connected officer, who rewarded him for his service. It was more than they had planned on. The Britannian woman had wanted him to use his abilities to get some kind of administrative role so he could identify other malcontents and build a network for the Han here, but neither of them had expected him to be able to move this quickly.

He'd been assigned as one of the administrators to track and deal with the vast swath of humanity sweeping west from the empire's homeland, which gave him access to the records he needed to do his real task.

One of those records was sitting on the stool in front of him now, the man, a boy really, looking nervous as any conscript would when called in front of an administrator.

The boy wore an insignia that marked him as being with one of the labor battalions. Battalions wasn't even the right word. These were hordes of conscripts that did the tremendous amount of manual labor needed to keep the massive armies of the empire running.

"They read the sentence in the market, Administrator," he said. "He was labeled an agitator, accused of insulting the authority of the emperor after Father spoke in the hall when the governor's levy demanded grain after a flood year, pointing out that the levy would starve many in the village. After they read the sentence, they took him to the square and broke his legs. They hung a placard with something written on it that said our land was forfeit because a rebellious mind could not steward a field."

"That is what I had read, but I wanted to hear it from your own mouth. You've been telling that story to others recently, men in your battalion."

"I wasn't complaining, Administrator. You had asked about my father's arrest, so I was simply informing you of it. I, of course, condemn him for his actions against the glorious empire."

"You misunderstand me; I am not here to punish you for what happened to your father and condemn his actions. In fact, I wanted to give you more information about him."

"You did?"

"Yes. This has to stay strictly between us, but I will tell you not everyone who works in the empire believes treatment like what your father received was fair."

"Ohh," he said, but the boy looked around, like someone might be watching him. Like this might be a trap.

"What made it of interest to me was because of the location of your former home, noted in your file, and in a file that came across my desk recently. Did you know the cousin of the governor of your province has a son who just arrived as an aide to one of the under-generals? I noticed that son's home is listed as the same place where your father last lived. It would seem they came into good fortune after your father's death and were given your old home for their good works."

The boy tried to hide it, but he couldn't, at least not right away. For a moment, the confusion and anger were plain on his face before he managed to submerge them.

"You've been here for what? Seven months now?"

"Yes, although before that I was at the rail repair camp."

He nodded. Liu Sheng had been part of the supply trains when Westerner boats ripped apart the river line. He'd been moved to one of the artillery groups after that, digging pits to protect the guns and moving supplies.

"How is the food on your current assignment?"

"Excellent, Administrator."

"Is it? I want to help you and your fellow soldiers. We are told you get millet, salted turnip, and some meat, but I've also been hearing some rumblings that perhaps not everyone is getting what they should be. Have you been getting the standard rations?"

The boy looked around again for a second before seeming to come to a decision. The banner and conscript armies had always been rife with graft; everyone knew it. Sometimes there would be a crackdown and examples would be made, but only ever against lesser officers who had no real connections. The real culprits, the people from the upper tiers of society, never paid for their crimes.

"No. Not always."

"Do you know what has been happening to it?"

"Quartermaster Haung takes it, says it's to ensure everything gets to us. Those who don't pay find their rations completely missing. Clerical errors."

Wei didn't know Haung, but he knew the type. If he was only a quartermaster, then there was a chance he was not well-connected; if he had been, he'd be in a higher level of the officer class. Wei made a note to check on him and, if he wasn't connected, put a word in the ear of one of the more connected officers.

They did not take kindly to a commoner getting a piece of the graft, especially if he wasn't kicking some of it upstairs. He'd have to be careful, but it was possible he could do something about this one man.

"I can't promise anything, because you know how things can be, but I will see if I can fix the problem. If not, I will try to move you to a unit without a man like Haung over it."

"Thank you, Administrator. You bring glory to the empire."

"The empire is what lets men like Haung operate. Men like the governor who had your father beaten and took your home. I am just a simple man trying my best to help others."

He had to be careful. Liu Sheng fit the standard of the disaffected that made up most of the Han resistance, but that wasn't a certainty. Many would turn in those who spoke against the empire out of fear or hope of some kind of reward.

"I still appreciate it, Administrator."

"Good. Do me a favor. Please let me know if anything else happens like this. If you and the others aren't getting the food or supplies you need. Men like you are what make the empire strong, and I want to do my best to ensure you are well treated."

"I will, Administrator."

The boy stood. He bowed low, much too low for someone in Chen's position, before turning and scurrying out of the room.

Sheng wasn't the first he'd identified and wouldn't be the last, but he seemed like a good candidate. Kept his head down but clearly had grievances against the empire, watched what he said, was careful. He could do the work if Chen could turn him.

The door closed. The murmur from the clerk's bench drifted in and died. Quiet again, except for a cart bumping past somewhere in the yard.

Chen went back to his actual job, checking for security risks and making sure each battalion had the men they needed, when the door opened again and Zhang Min slid in and shut it behind him.

"How'd it go?"

"It will be hard to get into. It's well guarded. The perimeter is a ditch, a packed dirt berm, and a palisade with watchtowers at each corner and one over the main gate. One squad per tower and three pairs walking the interior at staggered intervals. The gate has a double-doored timber frame and a drop bar that takes two men to lift. They change the gate guard at second watch and at noon. The ditch is dry and there's a culvert on the north side that drains the yard after it rains but it's narrow. A skinny boy could go through, but not me."

Chen nodded. He knew the supply depot was a difficult target, but if Zhang was going to start sabotaging the war efforts, it was also the easiest for him to get to.

Any of the other targets would be well out of his sector, which would make it hard to explain if he was caught.

"I suppose you can't get in, then."

"No, it's a fortress. Triple the warehouse capacity we expected, and they've been excavating storage bunkers on the north side for the last month. Whatever they're preparing for, it's big." He pulled a folded paper from inside his jacket, spreading it on Wei's desk. "I sketched the layout as best I could. Guard posts at each corner, overlapping fields of fire from the watchtowers. Main gate here, secondary entrance for supply wagons here. Two shifts of guards, six hours each, but they stagger the changeover so there's never a gap in coverage."

The man had an eye for detail; Wei had to give him that.

Min continued, tracing the buildings with one thick finger. "Standard storage in buildings one through five. Powder in the first two, shot and shells in three and four, provisions and general supplies in five. But building six, that's where things get interesting. That rat Shun keeps it locked down tight. His personal guards control access, and not even the duty officers can enter without his direct approval. I asked around over drinks and it seems to have started three weeks ago, right after that shipment you saw in the records."

The first thing Wei had done once getting this position was to start digging through the wealth of records at his disposal. The empire was built on secrecy and security, but an organization this big had to have records for everything. The empire was just too large to maintain without them.

It was the weakness of the kind of autocracy the empire had become. They could only control what they could track, but in tracking it, they told others what they were doing.

A series of shipments well outside of the normal supply chain had jumped out at him right away. It was unclear what was being brought in. Munitions, weapons, food. There was no way to know.

But what he did know was that they wanted no one to know, which was enough.

"I managed to observe one of the deliveries two nights ago," Min went on. "Heavy freight haulers with eight-horse teams. The crates were long but narrow, all wrapped in oiled canvas and handled like they were made of porcelain. Thirty or forty of them, though it was hard to get an exact count in the darkness."

Too large for rifles. Too heavy for smaller munitions. Artillery shells maybe?

"Yesterday morning, six wagons left under heavy escort. Twenty regular guards plus a full squad of Imperial Bannermen. I can't remember ever seeing bannermen on supply convoy duty, so whatever they're transporting, someone very high up wants it protected. The convoy headed west toward the front lines. Same type of crates that were delivered, so they're starting deployment."

Wei stood and walked to the window, watching supply wagons roll past. The empire was hemorrhaging territory with each passing month, falling back from the relentless Western advance. Their repeating rifles gave them a devastating advantage in any direct engagement. The empire needed something to level the field, and whatever sat in that warehouse, it was a good bet someone believed they had found it.

"We need to know what's in there," Wei said, still facing the window.

Min was quiet for a moment. "It's possible, but it will be difficult. They keep a pretty regular schedule, though. Shun is nothing if not lazy, once he got it up set, he's not going to want to change things. During the shift change at the second hour past midnight, there's a window. Maybe three minutes when there is a gap in coverage while the new guards settle into position. It's dangerous, though."

"I know, but we need to know what's in there."

"Tomorrow night, I'll try then," Zhang said. "It'll be a new moon, so it should be very dark."

"Don't do anything rash, just see what it is and get out. If you think you won't make it, abandon it entirely. We don't want you caught."

"I won't let them take me alive."

"You dead is also a problem. I'd rather the information."

"I'll do what I can," Zhang said.

Brzesc, Western Sardinia

Brzesc lay in a long smear of brick and gray slate, roofs stair-stepping down to the river. A slight rise north of town had been grazed bare by goats long ago and was now where Bomilcar and his staff set up their command position, a few hundred meters from the edge of the village. They had opted to come in from the north so they wouldn't need to set up crossings at the river, putting themselves under fire the whole time.

On an open field, that was worth the risk, but the enemy had cover from inside the buildings that made up the sizable village, forcing Bomilcar to opt for a safer route.

"Target buildings along the riverfront but give room for our advancing troops. Timed airbursts first, then impact, walking the shots into the village."

It was a brutal thing to do to the people who lived here, but it became inevitable once the Easterners set up inside the city.

Below, Urien's 47th cohort moved in squads, filing through vegetable plots and walled gardens toward the outer streets. Through his field glasses, he could already see the enemy falling back, away from the edge of town. They were doing so slowly, however. Each building had become a redoubt and was only abandoned as it was threatened with being cut off or it took an unlucky hit from the artillery.

From the other side of town, he could see dust plumes as reinforcements were moved up. This was a bold move for the Easterners. Since the breakthrough two months ago, the enemy had been falling back steadily, only stopping to use points such as this as brief rearguard action.

This was the first time he'd seen them bring up additional troops as if they wanted a real fight.

Even stranger considering that this wasn't a particularly important town, at least compared to some of the others they had abandoned. To be fair, the time it had taken to get his full legion across this tributary of the Wistla had been plenty of time for the enemy to make plans to counter him.

Sepucius's first shells cut arcs over the riverfront. Airbursts winked above a row of plaster buildings, white chips fountained off roofs as fragments punched into the interiors. Return flashes winked from those same warehouses even before the brick dust settled.

Urien's foremost squads reached a cobbled street that ran parallel to the river. Glass blew out above them in a brittle spray; one man pitched forward and lay still. The rest ducked behind walls, then pushed for doorways, kicked them in and went in two by two, rifles leading.

Across the street, someone had piled benches and a counter against the entrance to a shop, then jabbed timbers between sill and floor to wedge it shut. The 47th hit that barricade with axes. A soldier, no more than a boy, in the doorway swung his axe like a hammer before going down when a bullet took him under the collarbone, and two more men shoved into the gap he'd made. A rifle spoke from a second-story window across the way and dropped another of Urien's men on the doorstep.

House by house fighting was brutal work.

On the river, the riverboats added their fire on the town, almost causing a crossfire as shells came in from both the north and west.

The enemy had been ready for his boats, however.

As the boats turned at intervals and sent broadsides into the long sheds where gunfire flashed, cannon fire from guns set inside buildings, offering some protection, returned fire.

A gout of splinters flew from one ironclad's flank and men near the starboard gun staggered. An Eastern round, something with weight behind it, had found an opening and tore through the hull. The riverboat slowed, then backed water to get out of the line of fire. Another boat took a hit low on her freeboard; water spurted from a ragged hole. She, too, bent away.

"They've anticipated the boats," Gordianus said beside him.

Bomilcar only nodded.

The 47th pushed up another block. Urien himself appeared in Bomilcar's glasses for an instant, bare head, short beard, sword out because there was no room to swing a rifle indoors. He was pointing and the line jumped when he moved, then steadied again.

A column of smoke rose up from the riverfront, and a building across the way folded into the street so cleanly it looked deliberate, joists tilted like fallen ladders. Men climbed across it, trying to get out of the wreckage.

"Micron requests permission to take his cavalry in on the left," a staffer said.

"Approved. Tell him to avoid the interior streets. If he sees wagons lying on their sides, he won't be able to pass," Bomilcar said.

Micron took his lead elements into the low ground south of town, horses trotting, dust kicking up behind them in a pale tail. They disappeared and came back into view ten minutes later along a lateral road, vanished again, and then word came back that every approach was choked. Someone on the far side of Brzesc had dragged drays into the narrow openings, tipped them and spiked them.

A sharp trill came from the observation post closer to the river, and then the flagman repeated it. One of the balloon teams had sent down a message bag.

"Enemy artillery relocated," the staffer said. "Guns placed in stone buildings near the main square. They are firing down the approach streets."

Bomilcar traced the path through his glasses toward Brzesc's center where a diamond of buildings surrounded a fountain and a statue of a king no one here had ever met. The roads fed it like spokes. Put guns in three of those fronts and you could hit anything that tried to reach the open area.

"Tell Sepucius to target them. He won't get them out by weight, the roofs are too heavy. Tell him to do his best," he said.

The battle commenced, soldiers slowly fighting their way into the city. The center of the city was being pounded by the riverboats and artillery batteries alike.

Time ticked down.

The 63rd, after taking their time, began to march up from the south of town, having crossed further downstream, putting the city in a pincer.

It would not be long now. The Easterners could resist, but they were bracketed. They could either hold and be destroyed or run.

"Message from the balloon scouts. There's some additional activity by their artillery. Some new ammunition being delivered. They only noticed because the current ammunition the guns were firing was pulled and replaced by it."

"Did they have bad ammunition?" He asked Gordianus, next to him.

The tribune just shrugged.

"Tell them to continue observing and report any changes."

Whatever they were doing, it would only delay the inevitable. The 47th had pushed close enough they should be receiving direct hits from the artillery in the center of town, which would be the toughest part of the attack for them.

Except no shells came.

The enemy artillery was silent. Bomilcar was considering whether this was why they were changing out their ammunition. Perhaps they had had a bad batch and couldn't fire them.

Finally, as the men began to push toward the center of town, meeting very light resistance, the enemy artillery started up again, but it wasn't followed by explosions along the streets headed into the center of town. No breaking of the formations trying to push through the fire.

These shells were shot up and exploded among the rooftops mostly, and not even in airbursts like some of the Britannian guns had been firing. The charges in them must have been very small because the explosions were minuscule. Instead of shrapnel issuing from them, a greenish-yellowish cloud puffed out of them and started to descend on the city.

Another exploded, and then another, all with the same results. Instead of a rain of shrapnel, each issued forth a cloud of odd-colored smoke.

As it reached the ground, it billowed out, flowing down the streets in waves, like dye poured in water. Thin at first, then thicker, hugging the ground and curling along the gutter line. Men in the 47th reared back from it, hands over their mouths, then a few stepped forward again as if to wave it off. One of them stopped as if he'd hit an invisible wall. He then clawed at his throat. Another staggered beside him, dropped his rifle, and knocked his shoulder hard against a wall before he fell to his knees and then to his side. A third walked three steps, arms loose, then thumped into the cobbles and began to kick.

"Tell Urien to pull his front back fifty meters. Leave markers for the path," Bomilcar said.

The signaler had the flags moving as he spoke. In the street below, there was no time for that. As Bomilcar watched through his field glasses, more shells were exploding and the cloud of smoke poured from multiple directions, running down windows, spreading fingers through foot alleyways into the main path.

The medical team assigned to the 47th ran forward, as they were trained to do, litters bouncing on their shoulders. The first two medics reached a four-man clump and went down so fast it looked like a tripwire had cut them. The men behind them faltered, then also went in, and stopped as well. They piled up where they'd attempted to stop.

Urien had been halfway up that block when the first clouds hit. Bomilcar saw him through his glass again. He was pushing men back, shouting. He reached down and grabbed one man by the collar, hauled him up, shoved him away from the green cloud, but the man took only three steps and fell again, mouth wide.

Urien took a step, coughed once, wavered, and then he was on his knees, then on his hands, chest laboring. Two of his file leaders pulled him by the arms, dragging him like a sack, faces streaked with tears that weren't from grief. They moved three meters and dropped him because they had both started to shake.

"Signal Aulus. Move the 14th to the second line ... hold until we know where this clears," Bomilcar said. "No more units are to enter the town. Everyone pull back to the edge of the city."

It was all he could think to do.

He had seen men die in all the ways he'd learned to name. This was new. He saw the first injured men who had been touched by the cloud make it out of its midst, their faces were a mess, skin bubbling up like it had been seared, eyes puffed into slits and streaming, mouths ringed with white spittle.

The effect propagated up the street the way water does when the bucket tips. The front of the 47th came apart. Some ran into the foothills of the district, away from the river. Some ran toward the river itself, into yards, dropping rifles in reflex to lighten themselves. Men shoved other men out of the way, some of them more to keep their balance than through malice, and whoever fell in the path of the cloud did not get up again.

Riverboats, already turning to make another pass, checked their motion.

A single rider came up from the right with foam on his horse's bit and dust pasted to his neck. "Message from the 63rd. Sir... they were hit too. Same smoke. Lost half before they could pull back. Civilians had already run."

"Mark their line of retreat. Tell them to hold up on the plaza before the bridge. Keep men who have not been exposed to the gas on the perimeter," Bomilcar said.

He still wanted to take the town, but he had no idea how to do that.

"Order to Aulus. Advance to the second plaza and hold. Collect stragglers but then pull out as soon as he's gotten all he can. Do not close on the gas; leave a street between you and any fog. If you see it, withdraw through the alley with the well on the corner."

The signal flags went up again. At that moment, the survivors of the 47th began to move back like floodwater, hitting the 14th as the 14th tried to move forward.

Pathways opened up in Aulus's line, the terrified remnants of the 47th pouring through the gaps, turning them like cattle through rails.

A medic ran up, looking terrified.

"What is happening to them? What is that stuff?"

"I don't know what it is, Legate, but it is like acid on them, eating at their eyes and lungs. They are coughing up blood and foam from their chests. It's like they're suffocating."

That much he'd figured out for himself. As the stragglers made their way up to his position, they had a wet rattle, choking to get in breath. They looked like things from stories, creatures that had faced the wrath of the gods. Several who had made it back had dropped where they stood, dead before they could take another step, others lingered with shuddering torsos and the slow drag of their nails against the stone until their fingers left bloody smears.

The enemy had not advanced on them yet, probably afraid to walk into their evil smoke. It gave him a chance, and he would take it.

"We're pulling out," Bomilcar decided. "Full withdrawal across the river. They're waiting for the gas to clear before they move on us, and we're going to use that."

"Sir, the wounded ..."

"Try to get as many across as possible. Load them on the artillery carriages if you have to. Have the river boats come in close and take those who can't go the long way, but I want everyone moving in the next ten minutes."

Everyone standing there knew men too badly affected by the green smoke wouldn't survive the journey. Leaving them meant abandoning them to the Eastern forces but taking them meant slowing the withdrawal and risking more casualties.

Wagons rolled forward to collect the wounded who could endure transport, medical teams making brutal decisions about who might survive and who was already dead but still breathing.

The seventh legion began its withdrawal, cohorts pulling back in sequence while artillery maintained harassing fire to discourage pursuit, just in case. Eastern forces remained behind their chemical barriers.

Micron's cavalry formed a screen, not that it was necessary. The Easterners seemed almost stunned with how well their new weapon had worked, frozen in place. He knew that wouldn't last. Now that they knew it worked, they would adapt to use it in a more effective strategy.

Two hours later, Bomilcar stood on the west bank of the river watching the last elements of his legion cross the bridges. Smoke still poured from burning buildings, but only normal smoke from burning buildings, a black smudge in the sky. The green cloud had started to dissipate and thin out, although he couldn't help but wonder what effect it would have long-term. Soot clung to buildings after smoke from a burning building, so would there be a similar residue from this gas?

Not that it mattered from where he stood. He had been repulsed for the first time since this new advance had begun. He started the morning with a veteran legion ready to take the city and ended it with barely half his force combat-capable.

"Final count?" he asked Gordianus.

"The 47th cohort has seventy-three men reporting for duty out of five hundred. The 63rd can muster only two hundred. Every cohort that entered the city took losses, mostly from conventional fighting before the gas. The 14th and 33rd are intact but shaken from seeing what that gas does."

"Urien?"

"His men got him back to the aid station, but he died before we crossed the river. Most of his centurions also died. Same with half of the 63rd's officers. The commanders mostly stayed to try to get their men out and paid the price."

Bomilcar watched Brzesc across the waste. They had developed a weapon that killed as effectively as rifles or artillery but without putting any of their men in the line of fire.

Devious.

The seventh legion formed defensive positions two miles from the river, digging in while they waited for orders or reinforcements. Men worked in silence, many still coughing from gas exposure, others with bandaged eyes or chemical burns on exposed skin.

As darkness fell, Bomilcar finished his report to the Empress and Consul, detailing the gas attack and its effects.

He just hoped they had a clever idea to counter it.

Chapter 14

Taana, Norrland Region, Scandi

The feasting hall stretched before them, its timber walls glowing with torchlight and the roar of conversation spilling into the night. Lucilla paused at the threshold, taking in the scene. Dozens of village elders crowded the long tables, their weathered faces flushed from drink and heated discussion. The smell of roasted meat and fermented mead filled the space.

The moment she and her party stepped through the doorway, silence swept across the hall. Conversations died mid-sentence, and drinking horns stopped halfway to lips as every eye turned toward the unexpected arrivals.

She ignored it and walked in as if she belonged there.

Beruwald stood behind the high table like a host at a wedding in a striped tunic with silver bands at his cuffs. He had the sort of smile young men practiced, all welcome and no warmth.

"Empress," he said as she neared his table. "This is a surprise."

"Your invitation was for any to come and hear," Lucilla said.

He didn't flinch, not where anyone could see. "That is true, it was, and I welcome you. Be seated and be fed. There have been too many empty mouths in Norrland of late, but my hospitality will not turn away a guest."

A few elders at the high table lifted their cups at that. Others watched her without expression. Ragnvald sat near the far end, hairy as a bear and giving her the smallest of nods. He had been expecting her. She'd asked for him to be there specifically, so she had at least one ally in the crowd.

There were others she knew. Stig sat three seats from the center, his hands folded, the lines at the corners of his eyes cut deep by years. Between them sat a man she recognized by description when learning of this place, the elder of this city, Thorkel.

Apparently, a fair and even-handed man.

Beruwald gestured with courtly grace to a set of empty seats near the middle of the long table, far from Ragnvald. Llassar's grunt next to her said he saw the game too, but she sat anyway. She knew the rules of this game very well.

After a few minutes, the platters started to come around. Breads, smoked salmon, and a stew that had meat and something rooty in it. A boy filled her cup with something sweet and strong that wasn't wine. Conversation dropped to a low murmur as the men ate, although it rose again in patches. The ebb and flow of dinner conversation.

Beruwald worked the room without leaving the head table. He lifted a hand, drew men to him, leaned to listen. Lucilla cut thin slices of fish, eating slowly and steadily ... enough to be seen to be enjoying the host's food, but not so much to actually get full.

Beruwald ended up with Thorkel beside him, both men turned halfway toward each other. That alone said they'd spoken before. Lucilla set down her cup.

"Thorkel," she said. "What brought you to host this dinner tonight? From what I've been told, you have stayed neutral in nearly every debate for as long as you have led this village, rarely taking one side or another."

"Ships," he said after a moment. "And who they answer to."

Beruwald eased a smile back onto his face. "We all have our own worries, Empress. Concerns of what is right and what is wrong for our people."

"Do we?" Lucilla said.

"We do. For instance, my concern for my people is how Britannia asks our hands to sign, then binds them. Once, when we traded with who we wished, until the Britannians decided to coerce others to stop trading with us until we bent to their will. Men missed meals here so you could teach us obedience."

"You were trading with our enemy; selling them the supplies that helped them kill my people. You cannot claim to be the victim

172

when you were directly harming my people and then get mad when we defend ourselves. We did not harm you in that defense, only ensured that those of us who were being harmed by the Easterners would not help you to help them harm us more. It was self-preservation."

Thorkel's jaw worked once. "You say you didn't harm us, and yet many people went hungry here in my village because of your decision."

"Which is why we begged and pleaded with your people to end trading with the Easterners. You had centuries-old arrangements with villages in Britannia, Germania, and Gaul, and yet were choosing new friends from the east over your old friends for a little extra coin. I don't ask you to love us. I ask you to count the cost of the other road."

"You speak of friends," Beruwald said. "And yet the others we traded with made no such demand. For them, business is business. And yet our friends would dictate who we could trade with, who we could speak to, and how we live our lives. Are these friends?"

A few men grunted at that. They had the look of people who liked a hard line that fit their grievance. Lucilla kept her voice level.

"Are you that naive? Have you not seen the invasion happening right now? The hordes marching into Greece and Germania? Of course, they don't dictate what you do because they plan on conquering you as soon as they are done with those on the continent. The Easterners don't have to dictate to you because they plan on being your overlords."

"Fear," Beruwald said. "It always comes to fear from you."

"Truth," she said. "I point to what is happening now. The lives that are being lost now. The territory already conquered. Have you forgotten life under the Carthaginians so fast that you would allow a new version of them to rise? The Easterners were allied with the Carthaginians and tried to help them maintain their hegemony. But if we're going to look at what has happened, where loyalties lie, then we should examine yours, Beruwald. You have been free with your coin of late, deals, preferred trade, and even direct gifts of money. All from a man that, as far as I can find out, is little more than the son of a village elder of one of the smaller villages in Scandia. And yet somehow, in only a few years, he has a hall full of meat, barrels of sweet drink, and promises measured by the ton. Where did your fortune spring from, Beruwald? Did you find a seam of silver where your father never thought to look?"

"We trade," he said. "You may have heard of it."

Thorkel's head tilted. The faintest quirk at the corner of his mouth. It wasn't humor.

"We trade as well, but we do so openly," Lucilla said. "Everyone knows who our partners are, what we offer, and has access to our ports. We don't make veiled references to 'friends' when talking about the source of our goods. Our trade arrives in the daylight, coming into ports at midday; your trade arrives by night, and the men are paid to hide their faces on the way out. Honest men do not hide what they are doing in the dark."

"Who we trade with is our matter. My coin is honest enough, as is my generosity," Beruwald said.

"And when the Easterners are done with us, you think he will go on paying you so much coin?" she asked the room at large.

Silence settled in the near rows. Out at the lower tables, men leaned in, craned their necks to catch the words. All eyes were on Beruwald.

Thorkel spoke first. "What do you bring to the table, Empress?"

"What has already been negotiated," she said. "Favored trade with Britannia and the rest of the Western Alliance. Access to Britannian technology and contracts to build some of it here. We will teach you some of what we know, let you build it yourselves, and we will even buy what you make from you, instead of only selling to you and making you beholden to us for more. We will teach you better farming methods to allow one field to feed more mouths, better medical methods so that more sick men survive the winter. We offer you our friendship."

A murmur ran down the benches. She could see the old men weighing those words. That was the weak point in Beruwald's offer. Anyone who looked closely at it could see it for what it was.

"And if we say no?" Thorkel asked.

"Then we can't be friends. We won't be enemies, but we also won't help you help our enemies."

Beruwald laughed, quick and hard. "There it is. There is the real offer. Bow to Britannia or starve."

"No one in Britannia wants your people to starve. We fight for you, too, even if you can't see it. You want to charge us with pride … fine. That pride kept the Carthaginians from ruling the world, and did we conquer it in their wake? No. We stayed on our island and helped rebuild those nations ravaged by war. And we will do the same after the Easterners are gone. Mark my words, they will come for you eventually and you will not be able to hold them alone. That is not an insult. It is arithmetic."

"Arithmetic," Beruwald said, and let the word hang. "You put a price on our children's lives and tell us that price is fair. You show yourselves in the open and then have the arrogance to think we don't see."

"Everything we do is in the open. Perhaps you should do the same. Tell us where your bags of money come from and why they are willing to be so magnanimous." She stopped addressing him and turned to the crowd as a whole. "Do you think your people are not wise enough to see that a power would only pay you if they wanted something, and that payment is not out of the goodness of their hearts? And yet, have they been at your table and feasted with you? Have they come to you in the open and made the offer plainly, or did they buy off one of your number so that he would argue for them?"

Thorkel looked at the worked metal bands on the drinking horn in front of him, then at Beruwald.

"Enough," he said. "This is a feast to celebrate before winter, a merry event. Not a council hall for old men to argue."

Lucilla took no umbrage at the phrase. She knew what he meant.

He clapped once and spoke to a youth standing by the central pillar. The boy went to a chest and lifted out a great horn with boar carvings at the rim and a strip of hammered metal fitted along its length. A woman stepped forward with a clay pitcher and filled it to the brim. It smelled of honey and something sharper.

Thorkel took the horn in both hands and raised it high, saying, "To the winter ahead. May the gods smile down on us and bring us good fortune."

He drank, head tipped back, throat working. He lowered it and handed it to a man on his right, a square-headed fellow with a scar down his cheek. The man drank, then passed it. The horn moved to the left, toward her. Each man lifted it, wetting his lips for all to see.

Lucilla watched and thought of a legal maxim her father liked: custom covers law when law is not present.

Stig took the horn when it came to him. He met her eyes for the first time that night. He drank. He wiped his mouth on his sleeve, then held the horn out toward her.

She took the horn. It was heavier than she expected. She lifted it just enough to wet her lips, enough to satisfy the ritual, not enough to pledge without reserve. The drink was sweet and almost floral.

"*Empress,*" Sophus' voice came loud in her ears. "*Stop drinking. Spit it out. Do not swallow.*"

Lucilla froze for a beat before spitting a mouthful onto the plank floor. The liquid sprayed her boot and darkened the wood. Her throat burned like she'd licked a nettle.

"Am I in danger?" she said, too loudly.

The horn knocked her knuckles as her hands loosened and she threw it away from her, the horn clattering against a wall and spilling its liquid across the floorboards.

"*Your nanites are eliminating the trace levels of poison, but any more would have overwhelmed them. You might suffer some effects, but they will be clear by morning.*"

A shocked intake of breath spread across the entire lodge hall. Some of the men had just started to rise, cries of an affront to the Scandi people and of insults to ancestors had just started to be voiced when the first of the elders who had drunk from the horn, stood up, hands going to his throat.

The hall went silent again.

The man made a sound that was partway between a grunt and a rattle. His knees gave out and he fell forward, onto the table, his shoulders and back beginning to spasm.

Stig and a man next to him, who'd also drunk, clutched at their throats. Foam flecked their lips. Stig folded over his stool as if he meant to pick something up, then didn't move while the other sagged onto his side and his boots drummed the floor twice, his eyes bulged in a way that made him look surprised at his own death.

The hall imploded. Men yelled, standing and rushing around to see what was happening.

Llassar stood so suddenly his own stool flew away from him as his hand went to his sword and he stood behind her as chaos reigned. Cynwrig and her other guards were on them in an instant, forming a small wall around her.

Beruwald was on his feet, arm stabbing out to where she stood with the horn empty a few paces behind her.

"She spat," he shouted, jumping up on a table. "You saw it! She spat it out. She knew it was poisoned! She pretended to drink to fool us, but I see it. She came to kill those of us who would not side with her."

"That's a lie," she said, but her throat was burning from the poisoned drink, making it hard to speak.

But she knew this was a losing fight. He didn't need to prove anything, not now. He only needed noise. He needed a scene.

"She killed them!" Beruwald shouted. "She did not drink … you saw her spit!"

Lucilla forced sound through the tight burning in her throat. "You put poison in the horn and you know it."

"The Britannians have declared war upon us. Murderer! Assassin!" he said, pointing at her again before jumping down from the table and turning for the door. "I'll not remain in this hall of death and betrayal. Any true Scandi who values honor, who seeks justice for this atrocity, come with me!"

Nearly half the assembled elders followed him, their faces twisted with rage and fear. Others pressed against the walls, trying to distance themselves from both the bodies and Lucilla. The doors slammed behind the departing crowd.

Lucilla stood frozen amid the chaos, her throat still burning from the amount of poison she'd ingested. The Britannian guards had formed a protective circle around her; rifles raised but not aimed, uncertain what threat to defend against.

On the floor lay four bodies, their faces twisted in final agony. Stig and Elder Ragnar, who had both supported the alliance. Now they lay among the dead, foam still dripping from their mouths.

Elder Grimnar and Elder Thorkel had been Beruwald's men, but that hardly mattered now.

The remaining elders stared at her with a mixture of fear and suspicion. Some whispered prayers. Others simply stood in shock. The sacred horn lay on its side on the floor, the remaining mead pooling out of it.

She had been a fool and Beruwald had orchestrated this perfectly.

North of Thessalonica, Greece

The casualty station stretched along the cart track in a broken line of canvas and stacked crates. Men lay on blankets or bare dirt with their tunics cut away from red, puckered burns that oozed and wept. Others coughed until their lips went blue. Field medics moved among them with bowls of water, strips of cloth, and a kind of grim economy. Oddly, there was very little shouting or crying. They had no breath for it.

Ky walked the length of it. He kept his hands clasped behind his back to stop himself from fidgeting. One of the younger orderlies jerked a bandage tight over a blistered forearm and the patient arched, choking on a dry hack that sounded like tearing canvas.

A man nearby clawed at his own throat and mumbled for his mother in Oscan. Next to him, two corpses lay to the side with coats over their faces, feet bare and pale. A medic tied a strip of cloth over a soldier's eyes and knotted it in back, then tried to make him drink. The blinded man gagged and turned his head away.

"Don't swallow," the medic said. "Rinse and spit. Again."

He passed a tent flap that didn't quite meet the ground. The smell of the entire medical area was a mix of vinegar, salt, and something rotten.

"How did I miss this?" Ky subvocalized.

"It was not expected that chemical weapons would be something within the capabilities of the people of this timeline."

"That doesn't answer the question of how they could have done it."

"Understood, but there is insufficient data to form a viable answer. Predictive modeling relies on established knowledge and the variable in the Tian You structure you have termed unaccounted for remains operative. Their artillery, gunpowder, and other technologies, other than those copied from our own introductions, were accelerated beyond plausible endogenous development. It is reasonable to extrapolate that whatever the anomaly is that altered that technological progress is equally as responsible for the progress here."

Ky silently cursed himself. He knew that there was something in the east. It was clear that the invasion of the steppes people into Europe that had destabilized the Roman Republic and caused them to lose the Punic wars was due to something further east and he knew that the Easterners had access to gunpowder and cannon much earlier than it should have happened.

It was not a hard leap to determine that some kind of influence had happened in the east causing history to change. Yes, he'd changed things more since his arrival, uplifting the people on the British Isles, and ultimately all of Europe, into the industrial and even partially post-industrial era centuries ahead of time, and the Easterners had copied many of those changes, but that didn't mean that whatever influence had been there prior to his arrival had gone away.

They had clearly been able to develop military technology well ahead of schedule, so why wouldn't they be able to develop chemical weapons as an answer to the technology he initiated?

The chemicals he'd introduced to allow more advanced technology could have easily been adapted for chemical warfare, even though Ky had chosen not to do that, as there was too much potential not only for the spreading of technology but causing losses among his own men and civilian populations.

The Easterners clearly had no such qualms.

Beyond the emergency aid station, columns moved west on the road away from the former battle lines in staggered formations.

Packs slung low, rifles carried muzzle-down. It was their first retreat since they'd halted the Easterners the year before, and the blow stung. The men marched with heads bent low. The silence from them was eerie, with just the thump of thousands of feet, but without the chatter, joking, and regular din that normally accompanied soldiers on the march.

Carts rattled past next to them, their supplies discarded and replaced by injured men. The rear wheels of one wagon were fouled with waxy residue and someone had thrown a contaminated blanket over the side and it had smeared like soap scum over oak.

"We have to pull back across the whole line until we can counter it," Ky subvocalized.

"Projections indicate that the enemy will continue moving up artillery, forcing more retreats."

"Of course they will. If it works, why change it? We'll be forced to retreat and stop, retreat and stop until we develop a counter to it. Masks at the least."

"That will take time to produce," Sophus said.

"I know," Ky replied, turning as Modius rode up hard, reining in and swinging off the animal.

"Consul," Modius said. "Rearguard reports no pursuit by their infantry but the observation balloons show the enemy moving batteries forward along the entire front, along with multiple wagons full of ammunition."

Exactly as he'd thought, although it hadn't been particularly hard to predict.

"Naturally, we should ... Yes?"

Before he could finish speaking, one of the senior medics, an older man whose hands were stained with blood and other fluids walked up, stopping a few steps away but looking flustered.

"I'm sorry to interrupt, Consul, but we need guidance. Our treatments are useless. Whatever that smoke is, it's destroying tissue faster than we can treat it. I've lost thirty men in the last hour who were only exposed at the edges of the attack. The ones who took direct exposure are drowning in their own blood. Almost none can walk and half the wounded are blind or otherwise impaired."

"There isn't much we can do now but keep doing what you have been. Wash any new arrivals to make sure the chemicals are removed from their body, treat the visible wounds, and try to make them comfortable. I will see that more wagons are brought up to pull them further from the front. Burn the clothing of any man who was touched by the gas."

The medic nodded before turning and shouldering his way back into the river of bodies. He grabbed an orderly's elbow and put him where he wanted him, then bent over a man who had curled around his own pain and was trying to get smaller.

Modius tracked the medic until he was swallowed by the tents, then looked back at Ky.

"They're preparing for a sustained barrage," Modius said. "They'll chase us with shell and gas."

"Probably," Ky said. "The only thing we have going for us is that it doesn't seem their infantry has much protection from the gas either, which means they can't follow through on their land grabs quickly. They have to wait for the gas to clear to take the land we give up."

"Unless we give up and pull back before they attack again, in which case they can chase us from here to the coast. What's worse is that word is running through the ranks of the cohorts that weren't directly involved. Moral is down across the line, although I think it's more from the retreat than the losses. The men aren't used to this."

"I know, but I'm not going to put our whole army in danger if we can't follow through with legitimate gains. They have to move up into position though, and our cannons still have range on theirs. As they come up, we will fire on them, and as soon as they start to set up to fire, we will pull back again. They'll be able to keep pushing us, but it will slow them down and we might get lucky and hit some of their gas shells and cause some trouble for them. Keep some cavalry and a cohort with them. Everyone else pulls back to Pella."

Modius saluted. "I'll see it done."

As Modius got back on his horse and rode away, Ky looked back to the retreating men again and shook his head.

He should have seen this coming.

Chapter 15

Northeastern Greece

Zhang Min crouched at the forest edge, studying the supply depot through the darkness. It was almost midnight and, as planned, it was a new moon, making it one of the darkest nights of the year.

Thankfully, the guard rotations found it equally as dark and were helpfully carrying torches, making them stand out in the dark and ruining their ability to see at the same time.

Fools. But useful fools.

He'd studied the area in the daylight enough times now to have a feel for the layout. The depot sprawled across a cleared hillside, rows of warehouses and equipment sheds protected by a wooden palisade. Difficult, but not impossible.

Two guard towers flanked the main gate, their occupants visible as silhouettes against the lantern light. Zhang had spent the previous three nights re-mapping their routines and memorizing the patrol schedules. One of the benefits of the strict top-down control the empire favored was that no one wanted to deviate from their assignments. No one thought for themselves.

Ultimately, that meant that even security favored rigid adherence to schedules, set shift changes, and consistent patrol patterns. It made them very predictable.

He moved out of the trees toward the depot, through the tall grass, keeping low. In most cases, he was not the best person for this kind of assignment. His muscular frame, built for violence, was hardly stealthy, but he'd done this a few times now, and had learned to work around his limitations.

Reaching the perimeter fence, where his previous reconnaissance had identified a section somewhat hidden in a slight dip in the terrain, he looked over the workmanship.

It was sloppy. Retreat after retreat had forced the army to move quickly and the wooden posts here showed signs of hasty construction with gaps between the boards.

Zhang pulled a metal bar from his belt and worked it between the posts, taking a firm grip and pulling, trying to leverage them apart enough for him to fit through. For a moment, nothing happened, and then the wood started to groan softly, a slight sucking sound coming from the damp ground still wet from that afternoon's rain.

He strained, putting his weight into it; the posts started to separate from one another, creating an opening large enough for his broad shoulders. Pulling back the metal bar, he squeezed through the gap, ignoring the splinters that caught his uniform.

Although he could barely make out the buildings, he knew the depot's interior layout. Storage buildings arranged in precise rows, connected by gravel paths that would crunch underfoot if approached carelessly. Zhang stayed on the grass margins, moving close to the buildings to keep from standing out against stray starlight. Guard voices carried from the main gate as the midnight shift assumed their duties, conversation distant but audible.

He knew his target.

For two weeks, there had been an almost continual stream of wagons coming into the depot, all going into the warehouse standing third from the eastern fence. This was where those strange crates he'd told Chen about were going.

Zhang reached the warehouse perimeter and pressed himself against the wooden wall, listening for movement within. Footsteps echoed inside at regular intervals.

More guards.

He listened, waiting until they moved away, as he knew they would. Predictable as ever. From what he'd seen, they completed their circuits every eight minutes, providing brief opportunities when both sentries occupied the far end of the storage space.

A side entrance faced away from the main depot pathways, secured with a simple lock that posed minimal challenge to someone with Zhang's background. He had learned lock manipulation during punishment assignments, skills acquired from other men with poor records.

He, however, didn't even need that this night. For what he had planned, anyone seeing the lock removed would be the least of his worries. Taking the metal bar, he put it between the lock and the door frame, wedged it, and pulled with all his might. His arms strained until there was a pop as the wood gave way and the lock fell off the now broken hinge.

Zhang eased the door open and slipped inside, immediately struck by the warehouse's scale. Wooden crates, stacked from floor to ceiling, created narrow corridors throughout the space, each container marked with imperial seals.

He moved deeper into the maze of cargo, following the wall to avoid the patrols. Voices carried from the warehouse center where some of the guards were discussing duty assignments and complaining about the things soldiers like to complain about. Zhang used their conversation to track their positions while examining the crates more closely. Each container bore identical markings, imperial seals included.

He knew what he was looking for, however. He'd managed to get a look at one of the crates going into the warehouse days ago and had noticed that they had an additional handling warning on them, cautioning the bearers to be extremely careful with the contents.

It didn't take him long to find one.

The lid was easily popped open by wedging his knife under the corner, enough to reveal packed straw protecting metal objects beneath it. Zhang lifted the cover carefully, exposing artillery shells. As with the crate, these rounds carried unusual markings around their fuse assemblies. Some also had a yellowish residue staining the metal, maybe where volatile compounds had leaked during transport.

He had never been accused of being a smart man, but he was smart enough not to touch whatever that substance was.

Guard footsteps approached his position. Zhang quickly put the lid back in place and dropped behind a stack of crates as lantern light swept across the row where he had been standing. He stayed as still as he could, barely breathing as the sentry passed within arm's reach.

He remained motionless until the guard completed his circuit and moved toward the warehouse's opposite end. He couldn't stay here. The longer he did, the greater the chance that he'd be discovered. He'd gotten what Chen wanted.

To be safe, he examined several more containers, finding identical ammunition, some with the same yellowish staining around fuse mechanisms.

He should be done here. Chen's instructions were clear. Find out what was in here and how much, and bring that information back to him.

Zhang wasn't one for observation, though. He preferred direct action over all this sneaking around. Even if he tried to cover his tracks, someone might figure out that he'd been there and tighten security, making it impossible to get back in.

Better to deal with it now, while he could, and face the consequences later.

He'd blown up enough stuff over the years that this shouldn't be difficult. He didn't know what was in these special shells, but he'd seen barrels of gunpowder and several crates of cannon charges two rows over.

It didn't matter what was in these artillery shells, their fuses were made to explode setting off whatever was inside, and there was enough gunpowder in this warehouse to help it along. If it didn't, the straw used for padding in all of the crates was very flammable, and the heat might do what the explosion didn't.

One way or another, it would take care of the thousands of rounds sitting in the warehouse and make it a bad day for those bastards sitting behind the lines, sending boys to their deaths.

He moved several rows over, finding the barrel of loose gunpowder. He thought about using the powder to set off the barrel, but he worried he wouldn't be able to run fast enough to get away from it. No, he needed a better way.

Going to one of the other crates, he pulled out an armful of loose straw and stacked it around the barrel. Mounds of it.

Once that was in place, he took a little of the powder out of the barrel and put it on the edge of the straw, as an ignition source. Then he pulled flint and steel from his belt.

The flint sparked against steel, sending tiny fires into the packing material, setting the dry straw alight immediately, and flames spread through the loose tinder faster than he anticipated.

It wouldn't be long before the barrel caught, and then that's all it would take. He dashed away from the fire, down the aisle, sprinting for all he was worth. He couldn't worry about the guards now. He needed to get out of there.

He banged through the side door and kept running, sprinting for all he was worth. Shouts followed behind him. Guards had heard the racket and were running toward it.

He ignored them. Sliding down the hill to the hole he'd made in the palisade, he pushed himself through. A crack of gunpowder sounded, followed by a whizzing to his right as the first guard took a shot at him. Then another.

He ignored them, too.

He'd taken a few steps toward the forest and away from the palisade when the barrel caught fire. The explosion sent debris flying high into the sky, wooden fragments and metal shards were scattered across the depot grounds as shells began detonating in rapid succession. Each blast triggered additional explosions as heat and shockwaves reached neighboring crates, creating a chain reaction that consumed the warehouse's entire contents.

Explosions begot explosions as other warehouses caught fire. The depot was almost entirely full of cartridges, artillery, and gunpowder, and all of it was going up in flames.

No one was coming after him now. They had other things to worry about.

Zhang paused when he got to the forest edge. The entire hillside looked like it had sunk into the underworld. The explosions continued, one after another, flames shooting skyward.

Not just flames, though. There was something odd about the smoke. Instead of the gray or black clouds typical of burning wood and gunpowder, a thick greenish-yellow gas rose from the destroyed building. The strange gas began to rain down onto the burning hillside.

Zhang didn't know what it was, but he knew it wasn't good. He turned and ran into the forest as fast as his legs could carry him, putting maximum distance between himself and whatever he'd let loose.

Chen was not going to be pleased, Zhang thought, smiling to himself.

Hofstadir, Svealand Region, Scandia

"Bad?" Lucilla asked as Llassar fell into step with her.

"And getting worse. I stopped by the market as I was making my rounds and three merchants refused to sell to me. One spat at me. The people here are becoming very hostile."

The pair, and her guards, were making their way up the hill to the central assembly hall. This, the largest city in Scandi, also had the largest hall, which is why they had used it several times when addressing assemblies of village elders.

This was the first time, however, she had made the trek to an assembly not requested by her, and it made her nervous.

"This assembly Beruwald has called is certainly intended to make it worse," Lucilla said.

Llassar could only nod as he pushed the great hall's doors open, sending a wave of voices crashing over them.

The attendance exceeded anything she'd witnessed during the previous assemblies she'd attended here. Every bench was filled, with men standing along the walls and crowding into every corner and available floor space. She recognized some of the faces, men who'd remained neutral during the negotiations to push the Scandi into the alliance, but most of the men she did not recognize. Men who didn't make this journey often. What was worse, their expressions ranged from suspicious to openly hostile.

"More than I expected," Llassar observed.

187

"Which isn't a good sign."

She spotted Elder Ragnvald near the front with a handful of others who had supported the alliance, but they were islands in a sea of unfamiliar or unfriendly faces. The previous gatherings had perhaps forty or fifty attendees. There had to be over two hundred here.

As Lucilla entered, conversations died, heads turned in her direction. Someone muttered something in a language that she didn't understand, but the tone needed no translation.

Beruwald stood near the center of the room, dressed in rich furs and decorations that would have cost a small fortune. His youth made him stand out among the grizzled elders, but he carried himself with the confidence of someone who knew he held the room. When his eyes found Lucilla, the corner of his mouth lifted slightly.

"The Empress graces us with her presence. Come, take your place. We have much to discuss."

Lucilla didn't respond to his taunt, taking a position near Ragnvald, though she noticed how even some of the alliance supporters shifted away from them.

Beruwald raised his hands for silence and the crowd settled quickly, eager to hear what he would say.

"Brothers of Scandia," he began, "we gather today in the shadow of tragedy. Four of our wisest elders lie dead, poisoned at what should have been a feast of fellowship. Their families grieve. Their people cry out for justice."

Murmurs of agreement rippled through the crowd. Beruwald let the rumbling build before continuing.

"I was there, as were many of the men in this room and we all saw what happened. The ceremonial horn passed among us, as tradition demands. Yet when it reached the Britannian Empress, she made a scene, spitting onto the floor the moment she drank. So quickly, in fact, I question whether any of the tainted liquid passed her lips."

"That's not ..." Lucilla started.

"You will have your chance to speak," Beruwald cut her off. "But before we hear denials and lies, let us hear from witnesses who saw something that night that changes everything."

He gestured toward the side of the hall. Two men stepped forward, both middle-aged with the weathered look of farmers or fishermen. Lucilla had never seen either of them before and did not remember them from the night in question.

"Tell the assembly what you witnessed," Beruwald prompted.

The first man, shorter with a gray-streaked beard, cleared his throat. "We were outside the feast hall in Taana, helping with preparations. We saw the Caledonian there near the preparation area where the ceremonial pitcher and horn were being filled with mead."

The second man nodded. "I saw him too, alone and looking around to make sure no one was watching, then he went to where the pitcher sat. We thought nothing of it at the time, figured he was checking arrangements for his Empress. But now …"

"Now we know better," the first man finished. "He had time alone with the mead. Time to add whatever poison killed our people."

The hall erupted. Shouts of anger, fists pounding on benches, several men rising to their feet. Lucilla stood and said.

"That is a lie. Llassar was with me the entire evening. He was never out of my sight, and he certainly never went near the mead before the feast."

"You would say that," someone shouted from the back.

"I say it because it's true. I was not the only one there. Other men were at this festival and should be able to attest that he was with me the whole evening, if they still have honor. These men are perjurers, brought here to deliver false testimony."

A few voices called out to support her, but fewer than she would have hoped.

Beruwald spread his hands in a gesture of reasonableness. "These are honorable men from Bjornvik, a fishing village to the north, who had come to enjoy the festivities. They were brave, coming forward when they heard of the deaths, knowing their duty to speak the truth."

"Strange that I don't recognize them," Lucilla said. "I've met with representatives from every major village over the past months. Yet these two were never present at any negotiation, any gathering, any feast until now. Does anyone here know these men?"

"Bjornvik is remote," Beruwald replied. "They keep to themselves, which is why their testimony carries such weight. They have no stake in our politics, no reason to lie."

"No reason except whatever you've paid them."

The two men bristled at the accusation, putting on a show of wounded honor that Lucilla didn't believe for a moment.

"How dare you?" the bearded one said. "We came here to tell the truth, not to be insulted by foreign murderers."

That got the crowd going again.

"We've heard the testimony. We've heard the Britannian response, denial and accusation, attacking honest men rather than addressing the evidence. The truth is clear. The Britannians orchestrated this poisoning to eliminate opposition to their plans for dominance."

"Nonsense. Two of the dead men supported Scandia joining the alliance," Lucilla protested. "Why would we kill our own allies?"

"To eliminate my supporters who also drank," Beruwald shot back. "Everyone knows Britannian ruthlessness. You would sacrifice pawns to remove greater threats. It's how your Empire operates, through fear, through murder, through the elimination of anyone who stands in your way."

"That's absurd ..."

"Is it? You forced Italia and Germania into submission. You rule the city of Carthage with an iron fist. You send soldiers into Hispania to grind down opposition. Now you come here with honeyed words about alliance, but when resistance emerges, when proud Scandi refuse to bow, you resort to assassination."

The crowd's anger was building toward something dangerous. Lucilla could feel it, the way violence hung unspoken but imminent in the air.

"I drank from that horn, too. If we had poisoned it, why would I drink?"

Beruwald's laugh was sharp and mocking. "You made quite a display of spitting it out, didn't you? Drawing everyone's attention to the act. Almost as if you knew what was in it. Tell me, Empress, what antidote did you take beforehand? What Britannian chemistry protected you while our elders died?"

"There was no antidote because there was no Britannian plot."

"Then who poisoned the mead?"

"I don't know, but give me time to find out."

"Time to cover your tracks, you mean. Time to intimidate witnesses, to pressure villages, to use your wealth and power to bury the truth."

Beruwald turned to address the full assembly. "The evidence is clear. Britannian agents had access to the mead. The Britannian Empress mysteriously avoided the poison that killed our elders. Now she demands time to manipulate the investigation. I say we've heard enough. I call for the immediate and permanent expulsion of all Britannians from Scandi soil and refusal to participate in their cursed alliance."

The roar of approval was deafening. Men stamped their feet, pounded fists on benches, shouted their agreement.

"One week," she said, raising her voice to be heard. "Give me one week to investigate and uncover the truth. That's all."

"You've had days already," Beruwald countered. "How much more time do you need to fabricate evidence?"

"I need time to find the real killers. Unless you already know who they are?"

The implication hung between them. Beruwald's eyes narrowed.

"I call for a vote," he said. "All in favor of immediate expulsion ..."

"Wait." Elder Ragnvald stood slowly, his age showing in the effort. "The law is clear. Any member of a gathering can invoke the right of consideration for serious matters. I invoke that right."

"As do I," Merimund added, rising as well.

"And I," said another elder, though he looked reluctant.

Beruwald's jaw tightened. "The matter is settled."

"The law is the law," Ragnvald said. "Seven days of consideration, that has been our way for generations."

Beruwald looked ready to argue further, but several other elders were nodding. Even those opposed to Britannia wouldn't violate ancient law and tradition so brazenly.

"Seven days then," Beruwald said. "But not a moment more. And during that time, I suggest the Britannians remain in their quarters. For their own safety, of course. The people are angry, and I cannot guarantee what might happen if they move freely among us."

The threat was clear. Lucilla inclined her head slightly, acknowledging she understood.

"The assembly is concluded," Beruwald announced.

The crowd began to disperse, but slowly, with many hostile looks directed at Lucilla and Llassar. They waited until most had left before moving toward a side chamber where Ragnvald had gestured for them to follow.

Inside the small room, Ragnvald was joined by Merimund and three other elders. Their faces were grim.

"That was closer than you know," Ragnvald said.

"Beruwald's witnesses ..." Lucilla began.

"Are probably exactly what you think they are," Merimund interrupted. "But proving it won't matter if the people believe them."

"What's the situation in the villages?" Llassar asked.

Ragnvald shook his head slowly. "Beruwald's agents are everywhere, spreading the story of Britannian assassination. They're saying you murdered our elders because they opposed you, that this is how Britannia deals with resistance."

"How many believe it?"

"Too many. The deaths were shocking, and Beruwald offers them someone to blame. It's easier to hate foreigners than to believe one of our own capable of such evil. Empress, I've supported the alliance because I believed it would benefit my people. I still believe that. But if you cannot prove your innocence, if you cannot expose Beruwald's deception within seven days, your position here will become untenable."

"Then I'll expose him."

Chapter 16

Factorium

Sorantius crossed the new high-arching steel bridge, the first of its kind in Britannia, that spanned the river separating the main part of Factorium's complex of buildings and factories from the isolated construction site on the northern bank.

It was far from his other factories, but the Consul's warnings about the dangers of the black sludge coming out of the ground at the platform Hortensius had installed in the north had been explicit and often repeated. Specifically, this facility was to remain completely separated from all other industrial operations.

The foundation work impressed him immediately. Thick concrete footings extended deep into the soil, reinforced with iron bars in the new style of concrete work the Consul had called reinforced concrete. The workers had laid the brickwork for the main furnace already, allowing the mortar to set and dry before today's final installation.

As with so much of the new ways of doing things, instead of creating everything on-site and installing as they went, all of the parts that would make up this plant were created ahead of time and brought here, allowing the actual installation part to go quickly.

Sort of an assembly line for buildings.

Sorantius knelt beside the furnace base and ran his fingers along the joints, finding them tight and uniform. These bricks would need to withstand temperatures far beyond those required for their coal-burning operations, and they seemed good.

"The ironwork arrived yesterday from the main foundry," one of the foremen said, coming up to join him. "They followed the drawings exactly. The firebox is double-walled as you specified."

Sorantius nodded and walked to where the boiler sat on its heavy concrete base. The iron construction was solid, with thick walls and properly installed fittings. Steam lines had already been connected, running toward the base of what would become the fractioning column. He checked the pressure relief valves and temperature gauges, confirming each component matched his requirements.

The real challenge lay ahead. Twenty meters away, the fractioning column waited on its side, a massive, riveted iron cylinder that would serve as the heart of this entire operation. Teams of men and draft animals were gathered around the enormous piece, preparing to raise it into a vertical position.

"Ready to lift," shouted the crane operator from his position beside the wooden framework they had constructed specifically for this operation.

The system used a combination of pulleys, ropes, and the raw muscle power of sixteen oxen to provide the lifting force needed.

Sorantius positioned himself where he could observe the entire operation. The teams had rehearsed this maneuver twice with a wooden mock-up, but the actual column presented different challenges. Its iron construction made it far heavier and more dangerous if something went wrong.

The oxen strained against their harnesses as the ropes grew taut. Slowly, almost imperceptibly at first, the massive cylinder began to rise from its horizontal position. Workers guided the base with long poles while others managed the guide ropes attached to the upper sections. The column rotated upward, its weight causing the wooden framework of the crane to creak ominously.

"Steady there," the foreman called to the teams managing the guide ropes. "Keep it centered on the foundation bolts."

Sorantius watched the alignment carefully. The base of the column had to seat perfectly on the concrete foundation. It was too heavy to rotate in place, so any misalignment would require lowering the entire assembly and starting again.

As the column approached vertical, the teams adjusted their positions, the base descended slowly toward the foundation while workers made final adjustments to ensure proper alignment.

"Hold position," the foreman ordered.

He and two other workers crawled beneath the column base to check the bolt alignment. It was dangerous work. If a rope came loose or something slackened, there would be nothing to do but mourn the men who gave their lives for the construction of this place. Not a position Sorantius would want to find himself in.

Thankfully, nothing went wrong.

Everyone gave a collective sigh as the column was lowered into place and bolted down. The bolts were tightened gradually to prevent warping the base plate. Once it was secured, work began on connecting it to the wide, flanged pipe that would carry super-heated vapor from the furnace heat exchanger to the fractioning column.

The workers spread the specially prepared rope, packing around the flange faces, before positioning the heavy iron pipe, connecting it with sixteen large bolts.

The most complex aspect of the refinery construction lay in the internal configuration of the fractioning column. Sorantius climbed the wooden scaffolding that surrounded the tower to observe the installation of the perforated distillation trays. Each tray had been fabricated from iron sheet with hundreds of small holes drilled in them at set spacings.

Each tray had to be installed at exactly the right height to exploit the separation caused by the temperature gradient. As the oil vapors rose through the column, they would cool gradually. Different parts of the oil, although the Consul had kept calling them petroleum fractions for some reason, would condense at specific temperatures, collecting on the appropriate trays before draining through outlet pipes.

The workers inside the column used measuring rods and chalk marks to position each tray. Sorantius descended frequently to check their progress, as this had been the part the Consul had been very clear about needing exact spacing.

One by one, they installed all eight trays at the marked intervals.

Which meant it was then time to install the external piping system. Each tray required an outlet pipe that passed through the column wall to carry condensed petroleum products to the collection system. The positions for the holes had been measured again and again before they were drilled in the pipe. Still, as each one was connected, Sorantius worried they might have made an error. That would mean starting the entire process over again from the beginning.

The outlet pipes themselves were smaller than the main steam line but still required careful fitting and sealing. Each pipe connected to an internal tray through a specially designed coupling that allowed drainage while preventing vapor leakage. The external portions of these pipes would carry different petroleum products depending on their position up the column height, with the topmost carrying something called naphtha, which would be the next thing he would be working with, and the lowest carrying heavy fuel oil.

Some would be processed into other things. Some, like the lubricating oil and the heavy fuel oil, would be used right away. Others, like gasoline and naphtha, would need additional processing and were steps along the way to whatever the next advancement would be.

Not that the Consul ever consulted him on those things.

The outlet pipes led to the condenser system, where hot vapors would be cooled back into liquid form. This had been a complicated system to build, using long iron coils submerged in water troughs where the water was circulated until the warmed water was dumped into the river and new, cool water was brought back in, which is why the facility had to be located next to the river.

Luckily, the river here was major enough that they didn't have to be overly concerned with the flow rate, which had to be sufficient to keep the condensers cooled sufficiently.

From the condensers, the new liquid would be sent into storage tanks, each made to hold its specific product which the Consul had identified as gasoline, kerosene, naphtha, lubricating oil, and heavy fuel oil. The condensers were double-hulled and made to prevent vapors from leaking out.

Oil itself was highly flammable, as the Greeks had proven, but in this separated oil, apparently even the vapor that came off of it would be flammable, with an open flame setting it off without ever having to touch the liquid itself.

The storage tanks were positioned according to the volatility of their intended contents. The gasoline tank, which contained the lightest and most volatile product, was located farthest from any heat sources. The heavy fuel oil tank, containing the densest product, was positioned closest to the main processing equipment, although still somewhat separated from it.

Final touches needed to be done, such as the installation of temperature gauges, and valves to control or even shut off the flow of oil or its byproducts along the process, in case of problems, but the piping and equipment had been engineered for those to be added easily.

The Consul really did think of everything when he gave them instructions, which meant they rarely ran into problems with getting things like this set up … unless someone along the way made a mistake.

Thankfully, Hortensius kept his people well in hand.

As afternoon approached, Sorantius gathered the lead foreman and the horde of technicians who would operate the refinery for a final review. The group walked slowly through the entire facility, tracing the path that crude oil would follow from the initial heating through the separation process to final product collection.

They'd all read the same documents as he had, but he wanted to walk them through the entire process, each group explaining to him what they understood their jobs to be, to make sure everyone knew what to do.

The Consul had warned again and again how dangerous this process would be, and Sorantius did not want to be responsible for delaying whatever projects this process would be tied to.

Thankfully, the foremen had done a good job drilling their men, and each knew his part by heart.

Some who saw this new installation would be surprised at how quickly it went up. They wouldn't realize the work that had happened for months to prepare for this, with each piece of equipment developed and manufactured to the Consul's specifications so that all they'd had to do was install it.

Even with that, Sorantius took a moment to consider the place. So far, the chemical process they had worked on had been small installations, a vat here, a condenser there, but never anything of this scale.

It was truly breathtaking.

"Good work, all of you. It looks like we're ready. You may begin processing the first batch tomorrow morning. We are going to start with a small quantity of crude oil. Once we have the problems worked out, we will advance to full production. Remember your jobs, pay attention to your work, and let's do the Empire proud."

Taana, Norrland Region, Scandi

Llassar was not thrilled to be in this small village again. The stares he got made it clear everyone, to the lowliest of villagers, knew who he was and was not happy to see him.

He was glad he had several of Ragnvald's housecarls with him, ostensibly to aid him, but also to guard him if one of these people got some misconceived idea of vengeance into their head.

The group pushed through the narrow alley between the storage buildings, following one of Ragnvald's men who had remained here after the disastrous festival and had a better lay of the land.

"She'll be in the third building," Einar said. "She comes here to hide when she doesn't have any duties. The other servants won't speak to her. They think she's cursed, or worse."

"What do you think?"

"I think she's scared witless. But Ragnvald says you need to hear what she has to say, so that's what we'll do."

They approached a squat timber building with a sod roof, one of several that served as storage for the main hall. Einar knocked on the door, then pushed it open without waiting for a response.

"Tovi. Come out. We need to talk."

The interior smelled of musty grain and old wool. In the far corner, huddled behind sacks of barley, a young woman looked almost like a doe that had been startled in the forest. She couldn't have been more than twenty, with the pale skin and light hair common to these northern people. Her hands shook as she clutched a rough woolen blanket around her shoulders.

"I didn't do anything wrong," she said, coming out of her hiding place and stopping in front of them.

"Nobody said you did, girl. But we need to know exactly what you saw that night. This Britannian here works for their Empress and is trying to find out what happened."

At least she wasn't accusing him of doing anything. Of course, she was also the recipient of accusations, so she would know as well as anyone that it wasn't quite fair.

"What happened that night?" Llassar asked.

Tovi pulled the blanket tighter around herself and began to speak, her words coming in fits and starts at first, then picking up speed as she got going.

This had been weighing on her, and she was clearly happy to finally be able to tell someone.

"The preparations that day were just like always. I've served at dozens of feasts since I started working in the hall three years ago. This was much bigger than any of those, but the process was still the same."

"Tell me about the mead," Llassar said.

"I went to the stores myself that morning and brought up the sealed cask. We received it from the brewer the day before, picked special for the event, and that night the holy man had said words over it, asking the gods' blessing on it and those who drank it. After that, we kept it separate to make sure it's the one served at the feast and not drunk by men just looking to get warm, so it was locked up and I checked it myself to make sure it was sealed the next morning. Some boys helped me carry it to the main hall and set it up in the back, but I was with them the whole time. A few hours before the feast started, one of the stewards came by and we broke the seal and he tasted it, just to make sure it was good and hadn't turned or anything. We had that happen a few years ago and so they always check now. After that, I stayed next to it until after the speeches were made and it was time to fill the horn, again to make sure it didn't get drunk up by those in attendance before it was time to pass it around."

"Did you ever leave it, even for a minute?" Einar asked.

"I did, but only for a minute, I swear. It was strange, about ten minutes before the ceremony was to begin, after a lot of people had arrived, a man came up to me and said Elder Stig, who was already up at the head table, needed to see me."

"Is that unusual?"

"No, sometimes they want to make sure I'm ready for the ceremony, that I have the horn and everything. Normally, they send for a steward, but some of the elders like to ask me themselves."

"So you knew this man, the one Elder Stig sent?"

"No, but I assumed he was one of the elder's men. I don't know him except that I'd heard his name from people talking around me, but he was at the head table, which meant he was important, so any of his men should be listened to."

"What did he look like, this messenger?"

"Tall, taller than you, with brown hair, long and braided on one side. He wore good clothes, not fancy but well-made, which made sense for someone who worked for one of the elders. Woolen tunic, leather belt with silver fittings. His hand was why I remember him though. It was scarred. Not just scarred, almost deformed, like it had been hacked by an axe at some point in his life. I couldn't keep my eyes off it, honestly."

"So you left the cask?" Llassar asked.

"I did, but I didn't go far and I kept looking back to make sure no one else went near it. It wasn't like I could ignore an elder."

"So you went to talk to Stig?"

"I did, although that's when things got a little strange. When I said his messenger had found me and I'd come at his request, he looked confused. He said he hadn't sent anyone to fetch me and that he didn't need to speak with me about anything. I thought maybe the messenger had been confused, that he had been meant to get someone else to talk to the elder, so I just went back to my place. That kind of thing happens, especially with people from other villages who don't know any of the servants, which is why they normally go to the steward and the steward gets us. But sometimes elders like to do things themselves."

"How long were you gone?" Llassar asked.

"A few minutes. The time it takes to cross the room, wait to be acknowledged, and ask him what he needs."

"What about the man, what happened to him?"

"I assume he went off after giving me the message. He wasn't there when I got back to the cask."

"Why didn't you mention this man to anyone?" Einar asked.

"Because I thought it was just a misunderstanding, and the casket was still sealed. The only time it was opened was when the steward tasted it, and after that we poured a little more wax on the stopper to make sure it stayed closed. I mean, it wasn't much, so it would be easy to break open, but I looked when I got back and it was still sealed. The ladle and drinking horn were still on top of it just where I left them. Everything was the same. I'm telling you no one could have poisoned it. If it was poisoned by the brewer, the steward would be dead, and no one opened that cask after he tasted it until it was time to fill the horn."

Einar was about to ask something else, but Llassar put his hand on the man's arm and said, "Thank you, Tovi. You've been helpful."

Llassar waved, leading the small group with him away from her and back to the main thoroughfare, stopping just short of it so they could speak.

"We need to find others who saw this man. Someone with that distinctive scar shouldn't be hard to track."

"Are you sure?" Einar asked. "You heard her, the wax seal was still in place and if the man broke it, it wouldn't have hardened by the time she returned."

"I don't think he put the poison in the mead, I think he put it in the horn," Llassar said.

The look on Einar's face said he hadn't even considered that. "Ohh."

"We need to see who else saw this man and determine where he might have gone. It is too much of a coincidence that there was a miscommunication like that followed by a poisoning. At the very least, our scarred friend has some questions to answer."

"We should ask the servants who work in the kitchens. They would have been running food in and out of the hall all night, and are most likely to have seen something," Einar said.

That was easier said than done. Most of the kitchen staff was wary of Llassar, and those who weren't hadn't seen anything. It took almost an hour of asking around until they found two kitchen helpers who said they noticed the scarred man.

"Oh yes, we saw him," the older woman said. "Nearly knocked us down in the corridor, he was in such a hurry."

"When was this?"

"Right before the feast began. We were carrying supplies from the kitchen to the preparation area when he came rushing past us going the other direction."

"Toward the entrance?"

"Yes, straight for the main doors. He looked like he was trying to get out of the building as fast as possible without actually running. Didn't even stop to see if we were alright."

"Did you see where he went after he left the building?"

"No, we were too busy with our work. But he definitely left. If I saw him again, I would have noticed him. That hand."

Llassar thanked them and headed to the watch station where the guards who patrolled the town and manned the walls would be found. It took some more questioning to find the men who'd been on duty that night, but enough knew that Einar worked for Elder Ragnvald, and had respect for the elder, so they eventually got the answer to that question.

Eventually, the pair of guards who were on the main door of the feast hall were roused and brought to them.

"Thank you for coming. We have questions about the feast," Einar said.

He did not have to elaborate on what feast.

The guard looked at Llassar skeptically, almost hostilely, but asked, "What do you want to know?"

"You controlled the people coming into the feast well, right? Because of all the elders present?"

"Those were our instructions. Every elder announces his retinue when he arrives, and we count heads to make sure the numbers match. No one is allowed in without being invited by one of the elders. Once inside, they can move around the building as needed. But nobody leaves and comes back in without going through the main entrance again, and we keep track of everyone who does that."

Llassar described the man with the scarred hand. "Do you remember seeing someone matching that description?"

The guard frowned, thinking. "Can't say I do, but that doesn't mean much. Each elder had many men with them, but since they were with the elder, as long as the count was right, that was all I needed. If he had come through by himself later or left on his own, that I would have remembered."

"So if someone matching that description was inside the building, he had to be part of one of the attending parties."

"That's right. No other way he could have gotten past us."

"Are there other ways out?"

"There are, but they were either barred from the inside or guarded."

"But, if someone left through a barred exit, and then someone else in the hall had re-barred the door, you wouldn't have known."

"Probably not. Everyone in the hall came with an elder, so they were all to be trusted."

Outside the hall, Llassar walked slowly back toward the guest quarters where he was staying under Ragnvald's protection. Einar kept pace beside him, waiting for the Caledonian to speak his thoughts.

"The assassin didn't work alone," Llassar finally said. "He was part of someone's retinue, someone important enough to bring a large party to the feast."

"You think he was with Beruwald."

"Who else? What was put in that horn might have killed several elders, but it was meant to poison the relationship between your people and the Western Alliance."

Einar nodded grimly. "I'll gather our people and send out search parties. Every port, every road, every settlement within a day's travel. If his hand is as distinctive as everyone is saying, someone will have noticed him."

"Make it clear we want him alive. Dead men tell no tales, and we need this one to confess who sent him," Llassar said.

Chapter 17

Cairo, Egypt

"Tell him to hurry, I don't like how spread out we are," Cormac ordered, looking over the latest report from the legion still staggering into Carthage.

He'd been here for over a week, arriving by boat with a few advanced elements, after receiving word of new enemy armies making the march across the Sinai Peninsula.

Cormac had hoped, with the Consul's armies almost into Anatolia, that the enemy would have other things to worry about rather than pushing men across the desert, but that had been before the enemy's new weapons had stopped progress on all fronts.

Only the fact that they had pushed the Easterners and the small Egyptian forces up against the Axum to the south, who'd grown in size to almost the area of Nubia and never really reformed after the fall of Carthage, were looking to take more territory from their weakened northern neighbor.

For now, Cormac was happy to let them keep the pressure on, although no formal treaty existed between Britannia and the African kingdom.

He had other things to worry about now, and if it freed a legion for the defense of the northern half of Egypt, all the better.

As if to highlight the things he had to worry about, a runner stumbled into the command center still caked in dust from a hard ride.

"My Lord, their vanguard is less than five kilometers from the eastern walls. They should be here within the next hour."

That was what Cormac was worried about. It had taken too long for his men to get here, and even now, at least one cohort would not reach the city until after the battle ended.

Cormac looked down at the map of Cairo spread out in front of him. The fortress, a bastion of thick walls and robust towers, was the nucleus of the city, its stone feet planted firmly on the east bank of the Nile.

He'd received the warnings of their new gas-filled shells, and if he had his way, he would have marched out to meet them, closing fast enough to neutralize the weapon, which so far they had avoided using right near their own troops.

Unfortunately, he didn't have enough men in the city to make that work. He could probably bloody the enemy, but he couldn't stop them, and it would cost him a third of his still-scattered legion to do it.

No, he'd have to let them come to him while he pushed to get as many of his men into place as he could.

Which meant they were going to finally taste this poison that the enemy had ravaged the other legions to the north with. At least they'd have walls to hide behind.

And besides, the Consul hadn't been completely passive. He'd sent instructions for some rudimentary protections, although he'd also included warnings that these would only be marginally effective and that they should expect a more complete solution in the next few months.

Not that the war was going to stop to allow them to wait for that solution.

"Get the men to their prepared positions. We dig in and hold. And make sure the buckets we had prepared are set up along the whole line. They will have to reapply the solution."

The officers looked grim, knowing what was coming, but what else could they say or do? They knew the legion's condition as well as he did.

Leaving them to their duties, he took the winding stone stairs of the Citadel's highest watchtower. From the open-air platform at the summit, all of Cairo stretched before him. It was a sprawling, dense maze of mudbrick and stone, with smallish streets and densely packed alleys that at least made the city hell to dig out.

Cormac hoped the enemy wouldn't gas the city itself, since they would need the civilian population to work, but from what he'd seen of the Easterners, he knew it was a forlorn hope.

They tended to burn everything down and then yell at the ashes for being lazy.

He did not have to wait long. Past the green, irrigated fields that formed a buffer with the desert, a dark line appeared on the horizon. It was not a line, but a flood, a river of men pouring across the land. Cormac raised his field glasses and gazed out at the thousands of individual soldiers marching toward them. Watched them setting up in their lines. At least his own artillery had range and opened up as soon as they were in place.

Surprisingly, the enemy didn't dig in, just took the pounding as they hurried their artillery forward. Maybe they'd grown so accustomed to their gas causing the Western forces to scatter that they didn't feel like they needed to dig in any longer.

Britannian shells burst through the ordered lines, scything down men by the score, but he knew that wouldn't break them. It had become clear, even before now, that artillery could not win the battle alone. And they wouldn't go unanswered for long. He could see their artillery crews unlimbering their pieces, well within range of his own.

A few minutes later, the enemy guns opened up, with their shells arriving on target a few minutes later. As he'd worried, they weren't going to spare the city, with the first salvo screaming over the walls and slamming into the dense residential blocks just inside. Mudbrick houses disintegrated into clouds of brown dust.

For a second, Cormac wasn't sure what they were doing. Maybe they realized he still had units coming up and they were cutting off reinforcements, but that wouldn't help them much with the men he already had dug in. Then the shells started to creep back toward the wall his men were set up on, and it made more sense to him.

They were trying to get close to his men without firing on the other side of the wall. Maybe they were hoping to keep the gas contained, so their own men could move up safely, although as plans go, that was also weak.

If they wanted to take the city, they were going to have to push inside its walls.

"Tell the batteries to shift fire. Target their guns. I want them silenced," he told one of the signalmen with him. "And have the men put on their gas protection."

The artillery duel intensified. Britannian howitzer shells arced high, seeking out the enemy gun positions. Cormac saw several direct hits, blossoming into orange fireballs followed by thick green smoke as ammunition cooked off, the infantry close to it scattering to get away.

But there were too many of them for this to be solved by an artillery duel.

The Consul had sent instructions to make a chalky liquid of a substance he called sodium bicarbonate. There had been a lot of directions on places where they might find the substance, and that had turned out to be easy here in Cairo.

As soon as he started looking for it, he found that the Egyptian priests used it along with other materials in the process of pre-serving bodies for mummification, which meant there was already an industry in place here in the city and other cities to prepare it.

They'd mixed the powdery material with water and then put buckets of it all along the line. Getting the signal, the men started to dip cloths into it and tie them around their mouths and noses. They also put another cloth over their heads, tying it so that only their eyes were exposed. He'd even issued gloves to try to keep the stuff off his men's skin. It wouldn't be comfortable, and it wasn't perfect protection, but it would help some.

Shells began to explode close to his line with dull *pops*. From each impact point, a thick, greenish-yellow cloud blossomed. It was heavier than air, an unnatural fog that didn't rise and dis-sipate. It clung to the ground, sinking into the compact alleys and pouring through the shattered doorways of the houses. The labyrinthine city core, which he had counted on as his best de-fense, was becoming a poison trap. The gas pooled in the narrow channels between the buildings, a creeping, toxic tide.

The first reports that came back from the front were chaotic. The gas was as deadly as the warnings had claimed. Men caught with their makeshift masks improperly secured or knocked loose died horribly, choking and clawing at their throats. But the preemptive order was working to save lives.

Casualties were high, the highest his legions had faced in some time, but still a fraction of what they could have been if reports from the north had not been believed.

More importantly, the cohorts were holding their ground. Firing from the second and third stories of the buildings, his legionaries poured a steady stream of fire down on the attackers who had begun advancing toward the gas-saturated city.

As they got closer, he could see that the Easterners had similar protection in place, strips of cloth pulled over their mouths and noses. As with their own protection, it didn't work a hundred percent of the time and men started dropping out of their own line as they reached the city walls and started to deploy ladders while others fired up at the defenders.

The Easterners had numbers on their side, however, and it was clear they were going to break through.

"Signal the forces on the wall to pull back to secondary positions inside the city. Then signal the flotilla for fire support just over the wall. Buy our guys time to pull back."

A signalman on the tower roof began flashing the message. It took longer for the men to begin to disengage than it did for the river boats to open fire, which is why he gave the infantry orders first.

Even with that, the front-line units had only just started to pull back when the sound of naval cannons joined the rest of the firing artillery. Their heavy shells arched high over the city's western wall, crashing down just beyond the walls where Eastern forces had massed.

Cormac saw one shell land directly in the middle of a squad forming up near the main road from the western gate. The formation simply ceased to exist, replaced by a smoking crater. The naval bombardment sowed enough chaos to slow their advance, giving his men that extra time to pull back to their secondary positions.

The losses weren't just in the fighting. The retreat from the wall caused some of the men to lose their masks, dropping from the gas. The good news was that the gas was also affecting the Easterners, several of whom lost their masks coming over the wall.

Not all of them, however.

And once the first dozen were over, the doors to the city were opened, allowing the enemy to flow into the streets and the thick clouds of gas.

Quickly, the fight became a brutal, close-quarters struggle, with the retreating legionaries getting caught in the narrow, meandering alleys. The Britannians' lever-action rifles were devastating in these confines, where a single squad, positioned in the upper windows of a house, could hold an entire street, their rapid fire cutting down attackers before they could even get close.

But there were too many of the enemy, and many of those in the rear ranks got caught in the fighting. The small, enclosed courtyards that were a feature of the city's architecture became tiny fortresses, bitterly contested strong points that changed hands multiple times.

Reports coming back to the Citadel were grim. Forward positions had been overrun in the initial gas attack, but the main line was holding thanks to the masks.

The enemy had started to drop more gas shells further into the city, sending the green cloud pouring over both his secondary line and his artillery placements.

Cormac spent nearly an hour watching the fight, sending messages to plug this hole or that as need be. A clear pattern emerged from the chaos. While the attacks on the eastern and northern sectors were fierce, they were designed to hold his forces in place. The true weight of the Eastern assault was coming up the wide thoroughfare that ran from the southern gate, past a large, open market square, and straight to the southern face of the Citadel itself.

Probably in an effort to turn his flank.

He could let them get around him, or he could return the favor, push through and turn their side before the enemy could push through his reserve elements in the south.

That would mean the gas that would kill the civilian population in this side of the city.

"Signal a general advance! Push them back!"

The Britannian infantry surged forward. They poured a heavy, continuous volley into the enemy, sending forth a huge volume of rifle fire, and began to push the enemy back.

Then came the second push Cormac had in store for them.

He knew that counter-artillery fire was never going to stop their cannons firing away with those damned gas shells. So he'd set up a plan B.

The cavalry.

He'd kept them out of the fight because it wasn't really practical to put masks on horses, but they weren't out of the fight altogether. He'd sent them south at the first notice of the enemy's approach, keeping them out of harm's way until the time was right and the bulk of the infantry had marched into the city.

And now they had.

Signal flags went up, and he waited, watching the infantry slug it out in the streets below, hoping the cavalry centurion hadn't gone so far that he couldn't see the signal.

He didn't have to wait long to find out. A cloud of dust picked up southeast of the city out in the desert, a long plume signaling the thundering of horses. The enemy artillerymen, and the few infantry left behind to safeguard them, were too focused on the fight to notice their impending doom until it was too late.

The cavalry swept down on those men, tearing through them like locusts. It wouldn't do anything about the gas in the city, but it would keep them from adding any more, and it put a force in the path the enemy would have to retreat through.

It didn't take long for the rear sections of the enemy forces to realize they were being flanked and to start to panic. At first, it was a trickle, the rear-guard giving way, seeing they weren't going to get through the Britannian line and realizing their artillery and reserves were gone.

The trickle became a flood, until the attack didn't just falter; it shattered.

Eastern soldiers threw down their weapons and ran, terrified, heading for the southern and western gates. The Britannian infantry pursued them, driving them into the waiting cavalry.

"Consolidate our positions and start moving everyone we can out of that gas cloud," Cormac ordered.

Sea of Serpents

The black water of the Serpent's Sea churned, slapping against the hull of the Svalbryn. Captain Sune stood near the stern, watching the faint phosphorescence in their wake. A stiff wind out of the west filled their sails, pushing them east at a good clip.

Good. They'd make Sardinia by day after tomorrow and his work would be done. Beruwald paid well, but he was putting himself up against the biggest power in the west, and Sune wasn't sure he wanted to put himself in the middle of that.

He didn't like running without lights, that was for smugglers and fools, but the Britannian ships were everywhere lately. He was especially nervous with what he carried this trip.

Out beyond the bow, the horizon had no line, just layers of dark, the trick of night that could turn a swell into a wall and a cloud into a sail. He listened. A good captain never trusted only his eyes on nights like this. He listened to the wind against the rigging, the slap of water against the hull, the movement of sailors across the deck.

Familiar sounds.

And then there was an unfamiliar sound. Not even a sound. A change in air pressure near the sail's belly. He turned to call out to the crow's nest, but a crack of a shot beat him to it, followed by a flash of light across the waves, much closer than he would have hoped.

A white splash leapt ahead of his bow and fell back in heavy sheets. He flinched, and then he swore because men near the forward rail had flinched too.

"Hands to stations," he said.

Three more shots answered from different quarters, splashes bracketed them fore and aft, port and starboard.

Sails materialized where there had been none, like cutouts pasted onto the dark. Four of them, low and quick, all rigged for speed and pointed toward him like dogs closing on a boar. Their hulls rode light in the water. He saw the shape of forward guns mounted over their bows.

It wasn't hard to work out what those shapes were.

Britannian schooners.

There was no chance he could outrun them, not loaded down with timber. Probably not even without it.

He also couldn't outshoot them. He only had four smoothbore cannon, the old stuff the Britannians allowed to be sold to civilian ships, while they had ten rifled cannons firing explosive shells. He would be ripped apart if he tried to stand against them.

No, he really only had one choice.

"Strike the peak," he said. "Heave to."

The men knew it was the only choice, too, moving quickly to bring down the canvas and lines before the warning shots became something more serious. The great sails came down with a rush of canvas, and the Svalbryn slowed, wallowing in the choppy sea. The Britannian ships took up station around him, their decks lined with the silhouettes of soldiers, rifles held at the ready.

He felt something like bile rise when he looked back at the four shadows.

"Arrogant bastards," he said, but not loudly, before lifting a speaking trumpet to his mouth. "This is a private vessel under neutral flag. Identify yourselves and your intent."

"You will stand to and prepare to be boarded, or we will sink your vessel," a man on one of the Britannian ships said, not even bothering to identify themselves, as if everyone should know who they were already.

Arrogant.

A moment later, a small launch pulled away from the Britannian ship with twelve men on it, oars pushing it toward his ship. Another one followed after it, launching from another of the Britannian ships.

Not that they needed a bunch of soldiers to keep order. Not with the guns of four warships pointed at him.

As they came alongside, grappling hooks flew, biting into the wooden rail of the Svalbryn and soldiers swarmed aboard his ship.

Sune moved to intercept what looked like the man in charge of the group.

"By what right do you board my vessel? I am Sune, captain of the Svalbryn, a neutral Scandi trading ship. This is an act of war! I demand you state your authority!"

The man did not so much as look at him. He flicked two fingers toward his men and they peeled away in pairs, one to the fore deck, one to the stern, two to the ladderways below, two more toward the galley door. Each swinging a rifle's butt. But the shape of the deck had changed in a breath, and it wasn't his anymore.

"You will answer me," he said. "This is piracy. You will answer to Scandi law. I'll see your boots nailed to ..."

The second boat came alongside and its men came aboard the ship. On it was a man not in one of the Britannian uniforms but carrying an air of absolute authority about him.

"What is the meaning of this?" He demanded of the newcomer.

The man didn't blink, didn't answer, didn't even turn. He looked over the ship, appraising it, as if he were looking to buy it, rather than seize it.

Three men came up to him and spread to either side of him. One was clearly Scandi from the clothing and hair color. A heavier-set man with a thick beard, much younger than their leader.

"This cargo is legitimate," the captain said. "Timber and furs. We are traders, not pirates or smugglers."

Llassar stopped. He turned his face, finally, and cold, pale eyes settled on the captain. It was not a look of anger, but of something far more unnerving. It was the look of a man assessing a piece of equipment that had ceased to function correctly. A look of disdain.

The Scandi took a step toward him and said, "Enough. This ship is seized by the Britannian Navy in cooperation with the Council of Elders. I am Einar and speak for Elder Ragnvald and this is Llassar, who speaks for their Empress. We are here to apprehend a fugitive, a man wanted for the murder of four of our elders. Harboring him is an act of treason against your own people, and an act of war on the Britannians."

Llassar gestured to the Britannian soldiers. "Search the cabins. The crew's quarters."

The legionaries moved at once, disappearing down the companionways. Sune watched them go, a sliver of his confidence returning. They would find nothing. His crew knew nothing. The man was in the hold. He turned back to Einar, forcing a scoff.

"A fugitive? What nonsense is this? There is no fugitive aboard my ship. You want my ship, my cargo, so you invent this tale of murder and treason."

Llassar paid him no mind. He walked to the large, square hatch that led to the main cargo hold. He looked from the heavy wooden cover to Sune, his expression unchanged. The silent command was unmistakable.

"No," Sune said, his voice shaking slightly. "That hold is sealed. It contains nothing but timber and furs. You have no right to tamper with my cargo without proof."

Llassar gave a small, almost imperceptible signal. Two of his soldiers stepped forward. They were massive men, carrying heavy iron pry bars. Without a word, they jammed the ends of the bars into the seam of the hatch. The sound of splintering wood cracked through the night air as they put their weight into it. With a final groan of protesting timber, the hatch was forced open. They slid the heavy door aside, revealing the dark, cavernous space below. The scent of pine resin and cured hides wafted up from the darkness.

One of the legionaries offered Llassar a lantern. The Caledonian took it and, without a moment's hesitation, swung himself onto the ladder and descended into the hold alone.

Sune crept to the edge of the opening, peering down. His heart was a frantic drum against his ribs. He watched the single point of light move through the tightly packed cargo. Llassar did not search randomly. He moved with a disturbing purpose, heading directly for the forward end of the hold, toward the very section where ...

The light stopped. Sune watched as Llassar set the lantern down on a bale of furs. The Caledonian began pulling aside heavy, milled planks of lumber, tossing them away as if they weighed nothing. It was a false wall, constructed to look like part of a neat stack. Behind it, a small, concealed space was revealed.

Llassar finds a terrified, disheveled man with a distinctively scarred hand.

There were no words. Llassar grabbed the front of the man's tunic and hauled him from his hiding place. He shoved the fugitive ahead of him toward the ladder. A moment later, the man was pushed onto the main deck, stumbling and falling in front of the assembled crew. He lay there, a mask of pure terror on his face, surrounded by the grim-faced Britannian soldiers.

It was over.

Llassar handed the prisoner over to Einar. "Take him to the launch."

Einar nodded, leading the man toward the rail.

With the fugitive secured, Llassar turned his full, unnerving attention back to Sune. For the first time, he spoke, his voice low and devoid of any emotion.

"For conspiring with an enemy of the Western Alliance, and for transporting the murderer of your own people, this vessel and all its contents are seized as a prize of war."

More men came aboard, sailors from the ships this time instead of legionaries. Llassar, Einar, and the rest of the original boarding party departed with their prisoner, their launch pulling away into the darkness.

Sune stood frozen, a prisoner on his own deck, surrounded by foreign sailors. He watched as the Britannian schooners moved to escort their new prize. He could only watch as his ship, his ship, was towed away into the night.

He was ruined.

Chapter 18

Western Sarmatia

There was a lot of noise out in the courtyard. He'd heard horses and carriages for the past hour, which wasn't that unusual for a supply point, but it seemed much more active than normal.

Chen Wei ignored it, his focus on the columns of figures marching across the ledger before him, each accounting for the supplies needed to maintain this many men in combat. It was tedious work, so he also ignored the door as it opened and closed.

People always wanted something. More supplies, special favors, or a hundred other things.

They could wait.

A shadow fell across his desk. Wei did not look up immediately, finishing a character before finally pausing and looking up. His visitor was a young soldier, barely old enough to have a beard, his uniform ill-fitting, the tunic bunching at his shoulders.

An orderly or something of that kind, by the look of him.

"Administrator Chen?" the man asked, ducking his head with proper deference. "You're to report to Colonel Qian at the commander's hut immediately, sir."

Wei set down his brush carefully, keeping his expression neutral while his mind raced. He knew who Colonel Qian was.

Everyone in the west knew who Colonel Qian was.

He commanded security operations across nearly the entire western front, and his reputation was terrifying. Officers who drew Qian's attention typically ended their careers staked with wooden posts through their torsos.

"Did the colonel say why?"

"No, sir. Just that you're to come at once."

The order was straightforward, direct, and one he couldn't ignore. Running was off the table. It was tempting. If Qian was here, then it was likely he'd sniffed out what Wei was doing. If the man lived up to even half his reputation, running would only make him mad.

And his death worse.

Wei closed the ledger and straightened his uniform tunic, brushing dust from the sleeves. "Where will I find him?"

"The command pavilion near the artillery park, Administrator."

Chen Wei nodded and followed the orderly out into the afternoon light. The camp stretched out in all directions, a sprawling collection of canvas shelters, supply wagons, and cooking fires that housed nearly thirty thousand men. Soldiers moved between the tents in small groups.

The command pavilion dominated the camp's center, its yellow silk banners snapping in the breeze, two guards flanking the entrance.

"Administrator Chen Wei, reporting as ordered," he said, stopping in front of them.

The man nodded and pushed the tent flap open for him to enter.

Wei swallowed a bubble of fear and pushed through the heavy canvas flaps. Maps covered every available surface, their edges weighted down with stones and marked with colored pins showing troop positions.

In the middle of the room, behind a large central desk, sat the man who had to be Colonel Qian in fine robes and signs of his station. Two junior officers stood at rigid attention beside him, both looking as nervous as Wei felt.

Qian paused what he was saying as Wei walked in and said, "Administrator Chen, please, sit."

Wei moved to the indicated chair in front of the colonel while Qian gestured dismissively toward his subordinates. "That will be all, gentlemen. Continue your preparations for tomorrow's inspection tour."

The junior officers saluted sharply and left, leaving Wei alone with the colonel. For a long moment, Qian just stared at him, considering him. The silence stretched forever.

"I trust you're aware of the recent sabotage that has crippled our offensive capabilities?" he said finally.

"Some. I've heard reports of explosions at the supply depot, but nothing specific."

"Explosion is one way to describe it. Three ammunition warehouses completely destroyed, along with our entire stockpile of the new shells that were meant to break the Western lines. Half the rest of the depot burned to the ground in the wake of the explosion. The losses were not small."

Wei nodded solemnly. This is what he was afraid of, and why he'd almost second-guessed sending Zhang at all, knowing the man's proclivities, but he was still putting together his network. He didn't have enough men he trusted to send to look into the new artillery shells. He'd just hoped Zhang wouldn't have been stupid enough to go rogue.

He'd gambled, and he lost.

And now it was going to cost him.

"The timing could hardly have been worse," Qian continued. "We were positioned to resume our advance within days. The Westerners had been retreating steadily, their morale shattered by our attacks. Now we have to halt operations for weeks until replacement supplies arrive from the homeland."

"Enough time to reinforce their positions," Wei said, still not sure where the colonel was going, and when the other shoe would drop.

"Precisely. What makes this particularly concerning is that the sabotage came from within our own ranks. The depot was heavily guarded and there were no Western forces anywhere near the facility. This was an act of betrayal by someone in our own ranks."

Wei sat up straighter, trying to show as much outrage as he could muster, "One of our own? That's ... I can't believe that. Who would betray the empire like that?"

"That is a good question, and the very one that brings you in front of me today," Qian said, before going silent again. "You know, several officers who escaped from that Western prison camp with you have made glowing reports of what happened, how you organized the escape, studied guard rotations, and coordinated the breakout."

"I did what anyone would do in such circumstances."

"No, Administrator, what you did required exceptional organizational skills and attention to detail. The officers also noted how, even after the escape, you maintained discipline among the escapees during the journey back to our lines, even the wounded ones."

Wei inclined his head slightly.

"And your work since returning to duty has been equally impressive. Not only have you done your job, but three of your superiors, men who have not shown much flair in their jobs before now, have suddenly begun identifying unauthorized requisitions, equipment being diverted for personal use, and quartermasters selling rations on the black market. They have been lauded with commendations and honors, some even with a raise in status."

"Some men have an eye for corruption and graft and a love of the empire."

"Some men, yes," Qian said. "But not those men. You, however, I think might. You certainly are the only thing those fools have in common. And you staying silent while they took the credit says you know how things work and stay inside the established boundaries."

"As long as I serve, I'm happy."

"That I can see. But it seems that service is being wasted. Stopping graft is all well and good, but the empire has more serious problems than stolen food and boots."

Wei felt a flicker of genuine surprise. "Sir?"

"I am sending you to Varisova, to a new position. You'll serve as head of rear area security, with authority to deal with the kind of trouble that we've been facing."

It took every ounce of control for Wei to keep his face set. Being in charge of the security in that sector would give him more access than he ever imagined. Supply routes, personnel records, troop movements, communication lines, it would be like standing at the center of the Eastern army's nervous system.

"Sir, I … this is completely unexpected. I'm not certain I'm qualified for such responsibility."

"You've demonstrated your abilities already, time and again. As you have your loyalty. For the rest … you can prove yourself. What happened at that depot cannot be allowed to happen again."

Wei nodded slowly, as if considering the weight of the assignment. He was considering, alright, but the weight of it was a lot more than just the duties he was being given.

"The scope of such an investigation would necessarily be quite broad. These kinds of internal threats can emerge anywhere in the command structure."

"See, you are already proving you're the right man for this. You're right, the threats could be anywhere, which is why you'll have the power to conduct interviews with any personnel in the rear echelon, review records and correspondence, and recommend disciplinary actions as you see fit."

"Even against officers of higher rank than myself?"

"To some degree, yes. I expect some level of … tact. You will have to maintain proper decorum at all times. If situations require more forceful methods of interrogation, you'll contact me directly for additional resources and I will have those taken care of. I've already spoken with the provincial magistrate in Varisova. He understands that you carry my full confidence and that you report directly to me or my direct subordinates, not to local unit commanders."

Wei felt his pulse quicken. Independent authority, direct access to the highest levels of command, and the freedom to move throughout the rear areas without local interference. He never dreamed he'd be this successful.

"I'm honored by your confidence, sir. When would you need me to assume these duties?"

"Immediately. Your replacement here is already being briefed. Do the empire proud, Majo

Hofstadir, Svealand Region, Scandia

Once again, the assembly hall was packed to the rafters, quite literally in several places, with both high-ranking members of Scandi society and the masses who just happened to be nearby.

Lucilla counted over three hundred faces crammed into the room, with more pressed against the open doorways and clustered on the raised platform outside. The usual orderly arrangement of benches had dissolved into chaos as villagers squeezed between seated elders and representatives from distant settlements to claim standing room wherever they could find it.

Beruwald occupied the center position with the confidence of a man who believed he held all the cards. Seven village chieftains flanked him in a show of force. The young nobleman's supporters had arranged themselves as close as they could to him.

Lucilla remained seated among the dwindling alliance supporters, noting how isolated Ragnvald appeared compared to the previous gatherings. The old elder's usual commanding presence seemed almost diminished.

"Friends! Kinsmen!" Beruwald's voice carried across the packed hall as he sought their attention. "We gather today not for debate, but for action. We gave the interlopers seven days, and even allowed seven more as a solace to the status of the elders asking for it, but the time for waiting is no more. We cannot afford delays when facing murderers and assassins."

Several voices called out in agreement from the crowd.

"I call for an immediate vote demanding that all Britannian representatives must leave Scandi territory before sunset today. Their continued presence threatens every village, every family, every child in our lands."

A chieftain from one of the wavering villages, one that Lucilla had been hoping to sway to their side, stood up. "Beruwald speaks the truth. My people fear attending gatherings while Britannians remain among us."

"There is no proof that ..." Ragnvald started to say.

"What proof would the people accused provide," another voice shouted from the back. "Would you trust a wolf to investigate missing sheep?"

The momentum was building and Lucilla wasn't sure they would be able to overcome it. She'd gotten a temporary stay, and Llassar was making progress, but if he didn't return soon, then it would be too late, regardless of what he found. Fear was a powerful weapon, and Beruwald wielded it well.

"Exactly. So enough stalling, it's time to vote on ..."

Whatever he was going to say died in his throat at a sudden commotion by the main doors. For a moment, it was hard to tell what was happening, just a shifting of bodies as someone pushed their way into the chamber. And then the crowd started to part on its own accord as it realized who was trying to come in.

Llassar entered first, followed by Ragnvald's man Einar and six Britannian legionaries. Between them stumbled four bound prisoners, their hands secured behind their backs with rope.

The assembly hall erupted into chaos. Bodies pressed backward, benches overturned, voices rising in confusion and alarm. Several elders jumped to their feet demanding explanations while others shouted for the intruders to be removed.

Lucilla recognized the lead prisoner immediately. The scarred left hand stood out like a brand, exactly matching the description the servants had provided.

"Remove these people immediately," Beruwald commanded. "They have no business being here."

"The evidence will be heard," Ragnvald declared, standing up. "No vote will proceed until we understand what is happening here."

More men, and not just Ragnvald's men, stood and echoed his words, demanding to hear what was behind the interruption.

"This is Britannian trickery," Beruwald protested. "They manufacture evidence to distract you and to maintain their grip on our people."

The hall fractured into shouting matches between Beruwald's supporters and those demanding to hear what Llassar had discovered. Lucilla waited for the noise to subside, then rose slowly to her full height.

"We have already released some of the information we got from the kitchen staff in Taana and from some of the other servants, about a stranger who appeared during the ceremony and was seen near the poisoned mead. A man with a deformed hand. Now look for yourselves who has been brought before you," she said, pointing at the prisoner in front.

"I spoke with three witnesses who saw this man near the drinking horn moments before the elders were poisoned," Einar said. "He claimed to carry messages from Elder Stig, but no one in Stig's retinue had ever seen this man before."

The scarred man kept his chin high and said, "I was crew aboard Captain Sune's vessel. Nothing more. These are lies."

"An interesting member of the crew. We discovered him hidden in a concealed compartment aboard Sune's ship, a compartment used for smuggling. Moreover, the vessel was bound for Sarmatia, carrying cargo to Eastern territories."

The revelation sent new ripples of excitement through the crowd. Several elders rose from their seats, calling out questions of their own.

"String him up," someone shouted from the back. "He murdered our elders!"

Llassar turned his attention to Captain Sune, whose resignation deepened under the weight of hundreds of hostile stares. "Perhaps the captain here would like to explain his destination, and the other voyages he has taken recently."

Sune's shoulders sagged. "I carry what pays. Goods move both ways across the water. That is the nature of trade. I brought goods to customers," Sune replied weakly. "Business is business."

"And who arranged this passenger's transportation?" Llassar demanded. "Whose business were you doing this time?"

The captain's eyes darted toward Beruwald, then away. The momentary glance spoke volumes.

"Answer," Ragnvald commanded. "Who paid for his passage?"

Sune's resistance crumbled entirely. "Beruwald arranged it. Paid double my usual rates. He said the man needed to reach Eastern territories without delay."

The admission hit the assembly like a physical blow. Voices rose in outrage while Beruwald's supporters began edging away from their leader. Several elders pointed accusing fingers while others demanded explanations.

Beruwald's face had gone pale, but he wasn't ready to back down yet. "More lies to save his own neck. Any man can claim another arranged his crimes."

But he had lost too much of the crowd. Many were willing to overlook his mysterious wealth, the opposition to the senior elders, the sudden arrival of trade from new partners, to placate their fears and xenophobia.

But this was a step too far.

They were angry and betrayed, and looking for a target for that anger. Luckily, they had one conveniently at hand. The shouts demanding the scarred man's execution got louder as those close to him tried to physically push and reach through the Britannian soldiers guarding the prisoners to get to him.

The bloodlust was becoming palpable.

"Wait," he said, now visibly scared. "Wait, I ... I can explain. Beruwald hired me. I needed the money and was desperate. He provided the poison. Told me exactly how to do it. Promised safe passage east and enough payment to live comfortably for years."

The confession unleashed a storm of fury. Elders shouted for immediate execution while villagers pressed forward demanding justice. The assembly hall had become a lynch mob, and only the presence of armed guards prevented immediate violence.

"Lies extracted through Britannian manipulation," Beruwald yelled, although his confidence had faded. "They torture a desperate man until he says what they want to hear. This entire performance was orchestrated to eliminate opposition to their control over our resources."

No one was listening to him.

"You betrayed us," an elder shouted. "You took Eastern silver to murder our own people. You spoke of independence while selling us out to foreign masters."

Other voices joined the condemnation.

"Where did your wealth come from?" "How long have you worked for our enemies?" "What other lies have you told us?"

The tide had turned completely. Even Beruwald's most dedicated supporters sat in stunned silence, not wanting to be caught up in the fervor coming at him.

Beruwald's composure finally cracked. Lucilla saw the moment when the conviction left his eyes, when he realized words would no longer serve his purposes.

His look shifted to something like that of a wild animal, trapped and alone.

Reaching for his belt, a knife appeared in his hand as he lunged across the intervening space toward Lucilla. The crowd scattered backward, benches overturning in the sudden chaos as Beruwald closed the distance with surprising speed.

He covered half the space before Llassar intercepted him, his sword sweeping in a horizontal arc that caught Beruwald across the chest. The nobleman's momentum carried him forward another step before he collapsed, blood spreading across the timber floor.

The assembly hall went wild. Women screamed, men shouted, bodies pressed toward the exits in panic, while others surged forward to see what had happened. Einar and the Britannian guards formed a protective circle around Lucilla while looking to Beruwald's supporters for additional threats.

There were none.

The dramatic assassination attempt had ended the Eastern-backed opposition more effectively than any amount of evidence or argument.

Several elders stared at the blood staining their sacred assembly space, their faces set in shock. Violence within these walls violated ancient customs, even when justified by circumstances.

"Order," Ragnvald commanded. "We will have order in this place. By his own hand, Beruwald is condemned. He conspired with our enemies to murder Scandi elders. This assembly is over."

And just like that, it was done. It would take some time to get everyone on board, but if anything, this would cement Scandi loyalty and more active cooperation with the Western Alliance.

By hiring Beruwald, the Easterners proved they had interest in this place, and if they won, Scandi would not be saved.

She had just started to move toward some of the more neutral elders, to begin putting words in their ears, when a young man in a Britannian naval uniform pushed through the crowd.

"Messages from Carthage, Your Majesty."

Chapter 19

Malta

"What a mess," Valdar said to himself as he looked out over the harbor, watching work crews scurry along the sides of his mauled vessels.

The damage was extensive. Half his fleet, or at least half the fleet he had left, bore visible wounds from their repeated engagements with the Eastern squadrons that seemed to continually flow into the Middle Sea. Three ships were nearly complete write-offs and would need months before they could return to service. The Gwalch lay careened on the beach, her hull split open like a gutted fish where the hasty repairs failed just as they got to the port.

"Signal the captains," Valdar told an ensign standing nearby. "I want Brigid, Fabius, Dag, and Hákon in my cabin within the hour."

The young ensign saluted and ran to the signalman. Valdar didn't watch him go. He remained at the rail, studying each vessel in turn. The Fortuna had taken the worst of it during their running battle near Crete, her mainmast reduced to a splintered stump and her foremast jury-rigged with makeshift stays. Even the Europa, one of his fastest ships, showed scars from the Eastern gunnery in her patched canvas and scarred bulwarks.

He'd hoped his speed and maneuverability would be enough to counter the enemy's growing numbers.

He'd been wrong.

The mathematics was simple and brutal. Each engagement cost them ships they could not afford to lose, while the Easterners seemed to view their vessels as expendable resources. Watchers on the Greek coast reported new warships emerging from the Black Sea almost daily.

Valdar slapped the rail once and headed toward his cabin.

The space felt cramped with charts covering every available surface, each marked with positions of enemy squadrons and patrol routes. Reports from merchant captains and fishing vessels created a picture of Eastern naval movements that grew more concerning each day.

Captain Brigid arrived first. He liked her. The Fortuna's master had served under Valdar for three years, earning her position through competence rather than connections. And her crew respected her.

"How long before she's seaworthy again?" Valdar asked as Brigid settled into a chair across from him at his desk.

"Three weeks if we can get proper timber for the mainmast. Six, if we have to make do with local materials. The rigging's completely shot, and we need new stays throughout. My carpenter says the hull damage is manageable, but we're taking on water faster than we should."

Fabius entered next, followed closely by Dag and Hákon. The four captains represented the most experienced commanders he had with him at the moment, with his fleets so spread out to now cover the African coast, the Middle Sea, combat operations in Egypt and Greece, and new operations in the Sea of Serpents.

Too many responsibilities without enough men and material to meet them.

"Gentlemen, lady," Valdar began once they had arranged themselves around his chart table. "Let's assess where we stand."

Fabius spoke first, his patrician accent marking him as one of the few Roman-born officers in the fleet. "Things are looking bad, admiral. We need extensive work below the waterline. We've plugged the worst holes, but she won't take another pounding like the last one."

Dag nodded grimly. "The same for us. I lost a third of my crew in that last action. I've got men working double watches just to sail her properly. The mizzen's cracked at the root, and we're short on everything from canvas to cordage."

229

"And you, what are your complaints?" Valdar asked, looking to Hákon.

"We're in better shape, but we've used most of our spare shot, and the port battery's down two guns. One burst when an Eastern shell hit the carriage, another's cracked at the muzzle."

Valdar nodded, looking at his people. These were solid officers who had faced storms, pirates, and enemy fleets without flinching. Now he saw something he rarely encountered in their expressions.

Doubt.

"It's not just the ships, though," Dag added. "We've lost nearly a third of our effective fighting strength between the vessels under repair and crew casualties. The men are asking questions about how long we can keep this up."

"The men aren't the only ones asking," Brigid added. "Every engagement costs us more than we can afford, while the Easterners keep sending fresh squadrons south. They're launching new ships faster than we can sink them."

Valdar had expected this conversation, though he had hoped to delay it until reinforcements arrived from Devnum. It had been clear to him for more than a week that the current strategy was unsustainable, but he'd hoped to forestall discussing it a little longer.

"Reinforcements are coming. Devnum's sending eight ships south and enough men to re-crew our ships, although I'm expecting it will be at least two weeks until they arrive."

"Eight ships won't change the fundamental problem," Hákon countered. "We're fighting a defensive campaign against an enemy who can replace their losses faster than we can inflict them. Eventually, they'll mass enough strength to break through whatever line we establish."

"Which is why I say we try and force the Hellespont again," Fabius said. "If we could force our way into the Black Sea and strike at their shipyards directly, it will take them time to replace them. This isn't like a coastline where they can make for ports a week's sail away. We control those waters, and we'll stop them cold."

"Exactly what I was thinking. We've forced worse passages before. Gather everything we have, including the incoming reinforcements, and make a concentrated push through the straits. Just sail through until we make it," Hákon added.

"Absolutely not," Valdar replied without hesitation. "That is suicide."

Brigid raised an eyebrow. "Sure, there will be losses, but …"

"We would lose half the fleet, and that is the best-case scenario. Sure, if they were still firing solid shot, we'd have a chance, back when a wooden ship could absorb dozens of hits and remain fighting. Crews could plug holes, jury-rig damage, and continue the mission. But that's not what we're facing anymore. Two days ago, the Morfudd took one hit in her side and split damn near in two, sinking straight to the bottom. One shot. A hundred men dead in an instant."

"That's the risk of naval combat," Hákon countered. "It's always been dangerous."

"Not like this," Valdar said firmly. "A single explosive shell detonating inside a wooden hull doesn't just damage the ship, it destroys it. The blast tears through compartments, starts fires that can't be controlled, and kills or maims half the crew instantly. Think of all of the fleets, the much larger fleets, we have devastated since we switched to the fused shells. They learned the lesson and have been much cagier in their engagements until this newer punch. We should be just as cagey. Besides, they have put in forts like the ones we've started using on either side of the passage. When we faced forts like that in Egypt, it wiped out even armored riverboats. The only reason those fights were possible was because we had land-based legions to take the forts. We won't have that here."

"So we accept that the Black Sea is closed to us?" Dag asked.

"For now, yes. Even if some ships made it through, they'd be trapped without support or resupply. The moment we committed to that passage, the Easterners would close it behind us."

"Which leaves us maintaining a blockade we can't sustain against an enemy that grows stronger each month," Fabius said.

He didn't blame him. These were aggressive commanders accustomed to taking the fight to the enemy. Defensive operations went against their nature, especially when those operations appeared doomed to failure over time.

"We don't have to wait forever. We just need to wait till the balance changes."

"And what will do that?" Brigid asked.

"The Victorious launches within a few weeks, maybe a month. All-steel construction, rotating turrets. She'll be able to do what our wooden ships cannot."

"One ship," Fabius said skeptically. "Against how many?"

"One ship that can absorb punishment that would sink a dozen of our current vessels," Valdar replied. "The rotating turrets mean her guns can track targets regardless of her heading. We've seen the success our ironclad riverboats have had, and this ship is steel from the keel up."

Hákon frowned. "You're putting a lot of faith in untested technology."

"The alternative is sending our fleet piecemeal into battles we cannot win." Valdar met each captain's eyes in turn. "I won't throw away ships and lives on desperate gestures."

"So what's the plan?" Brigid asked. "How do we hold out for what will probably be two months for the shakedown cruise before she arrives?"

"We establish a layered defense south of the straits. Our fastest ships patrol as scouts, providing early warning of Eastern movements. The main battle line to form a concentrated front when they come through. The coastal watchers have reported they are coming through in small groups, probably as the ships are finished. We've managed to send most of the ships they already pushed through either to the bottom or back into the Black Sea, probably headed to those same shipyards for repair, so if we bottle them up, it will stop the majority of the raids against our shipping."

"That's great," Hákon said. "Right until they realize that's what we're doing and amass enough ships to push through the small number of ships we can muster."

"True, but we don't have to hold them forever, and it will limit the problems we do have to deal with until the Victorious gets here. Hopefully, before the Easterners realize what we're doing and have the time it takes to amass a full fleet on their side of the straits."

"And if it's not here by then?" Hákon asked.

"Then we do our best to make them pay dearly," he said finally.

The captains absorbed this in silence. Everyone knew he was essentially saying they would all mostly die if that happened, but also that it was really their only choice. They needed to keep their supply lines flowing and limit the possibility of a naval landing to make an end run around their lines.

So they would just have to hold.

Northern Coast of Germania

Lucilla stepped from the narrow gangplank onto the weathered wooden dock. She didn't normally come this far east on the coast, but time was of the essence, and even with trains, it would have taken Medb time to get to Gaul or one of the major ports closer to Scandi.

The former queen turned spymaster had been very close to the front lines, in the outskirts of Sarmatia, when Lucilla's missive had found her, and this was the closest port she could get to in any reasonable amount of time.

It was a small port. Few merchants bothered with such an isolated anchorage, which at least meant there was limited pomp upon her arrival. She had not signaled ahead that she was coming, meaning there were mostly fishing trawlers and a few of the civilian-built schooners loading and unloading when she and her guard disembarked from the caravel that dwarfed the other ships.

Her ship, and her guards, did draw a fair number of eyes, giving Lucilla a moment of pause. Cynwrig and her other guards were good men, but there were not that many of them. She had left Llassar back in Scandia to finish up the dealings there so that she could deal with the new crisis brewing in Carthage.

Thankfully, Medb had given the meeting more thought, and two squads of legionaries, pulled from who knows where, were following in her wake as she made her way toward the small group.

"Thank you for coming so quickly. I hope the journey wasn't too arduous," Lucilla said, stopping in front of the fiery-haired woman.

"It was fine. Your message sounded urgent, although it was a little light on details," Medb said.

"Because I do not have a lot of details myself. I received notice, while I was in Scandi, from the commander you, or I suppose Cormac, left in charge of the city, that the situation there has deteriorated beyond his ability to handle it." Lucilla gestured toward the small building housing the harbormaster's office. "But I think we should take this conversation somewhere more private. After what happened in Scandia, I am hesitant to discuss anything important where ears can hear us."

The harbormaster's office proved cramped but adequate for their purposes, once they chased the harried man out of his own dwelling, giving them a place to talk with limited overhearing ears.

Charts of local waters covering one wall while ledgers dumped haphazardly across a wooden table spoke to the man's already frazzled state.

"So what, exactly, did the message say?" Medb asked once the door closed behind them.

Lucilla pulled out the dispatches that had prompted this meeting. "There has been an escalation in the number of resistance, or at least resistance-adjacent, actions in the city of late. Weapons caches discovered, although nothing as serious as the types of weapons you found before, propaganda leaflets distributed simultaneously across multiple districts, organized work stoppages, and questionable gatherings."

"That is roughly what was happening before. What makes this more serious?"

"I believe it's the volume and that it's spread into other districts. The commander says there is no sign of outside influence this time, but the increase in activity is coming with more unrest."

"Is he sure there is no outside activity? They were good at hiding that before."

"Yes. Ships are being inspected at a higher rate, and the quality of everything from the weapons to the flyers is low and seemingly homegrown. The increase started shortly after Cormac's departure with the bulk of the forces around the city, so the commander thinks it is opportunistic. Whoever is leading the unrest in the city is taking advantage of the sudden departure of most of our forces along with the senior leadership. My sense is, if you or Cormac were there, it could be managed and fixed, but the commander on the scene is in over his head. Which is why that city is my next destination."

The spymaster looked up from the reports, surprise evident in her green eyes. "You plan to go to Carthage yourself?"

"Yes. We need to send a clear message to any would-be rebels that this kind of thing will not be tolerated and we are willing to bring the full might of the Empire against them, which is why I intend to oversee a complete restructuring of the local administration, ensure loyal personnel are in place, and enough resources are allocated to fixing the problem once and for all."

"I'm happy to hear you say that, and I think some of those things will definitely help, but I can't leave, at least not now."

"Why?"

"I've finally got a network set up inside the Easterners' lines and have started getting the information we need to better fight them, after you not so subtly pointed out that lack a year ago. And it's been a success. We even managed to take out one of their supply depots full of the new gas shells that, according to our man, has delayed operations for almost a month, saving who knows how many lives. But, everything is still in a precarious condition. Leaving now will throw all that away and I don't know if I'll get another opportunity like this again."

Lucilla frowned. Medb was, of course, right. They'd been trying to get a source inside the Easterners' army for two years now, even longer if she included those five years since the Easterners first appeared. But she also needed her in Carthage.

"I know you keep things close to your chest, but even you have developed some capable subordinates. I know Claudius has been

235

with you here in Germania for a while. Hand over the operations to him. Unless you're saying he's not capable of the work."

"Of course he's capable. I wouldn't have asked for his transfer to work under me if I didn't believe in him, but I have assigned him to a mission that will keep him gone for a month, maybe several years."

"What mission?"

"I tasked him to lead an expedition to the far side of the world to set up a base to support the rebels inside the Eastern homeland, along with an Easterner who has agreed to get us in contact with the resistance already in place there."

Lucilla stared at her spymaster, processing this unexpected information. Ky had told her that Medb had been looking for locations for a base, but she didn't know one had been selected, let alone that the planning had progressed to this level.

"Already? I didn't know we'd already sent ships to the east."

"We haven't yet. Claudius is in Devnum now putting together a fleet and trying to pull together the resources to make this work. I'm hoping his mission will launch within the next several weeks. I'm not sure he has time to make it there before winter sets in, but my understanding from the Consul is that, at least for a lot of this trip, winter is not so bad in that part of the world and we are at the tail end of some kind of extreme rainy season that, had we gone earlier we would have had to deal with. We have a window for this mission, and this is it."

"I see."

"In fact, since you're here, we could actually use your imperial muscle. The last message he sent me was that there is a heavy call for ships and sailors to deal with that breakout in the Black Sea. While that is critical, I know the Consul's metal monstrosity will be launching soon and is tasked with defending the Middle Sea. A small fleet of wooden ships wouldn't make that much of a difference there, one way or another."

"How could you know about … never mind. I think Admiral Valdar would say that the difference would be the men killed by fighting against an enemy while under strength."

"Of course he would. He's a military man and only focused on the thing right in front of him, and yes, diverting supplies from him now will cost lives, but how many more lives will it cost if this war continues? How long and how far will we have to fight to push all the way to the heart of the enemy on foot? Based on how the Consul tells it, it's a long way. If we could end the war from the inside, in a year, maybe two, wouldn't that be worth the price the admiral has to pay now?"

"It could also amount to nothing. This is a risky play and could fail in a hundred different ways."

"To rule is to accept risk," Medb pointed out. "And I think you're just playing, what does the Consul call it, devil's advocate? You've never been overly risk-averse, and you know as well as I do that this play is worth it."

Lucilla sighed, "It is. I agreed with Ky when he mentioned it, and I agree now. I'm just not sure we will still appreciate the cost if Admiral Valdar falls and the Easterners break into the Middle Sea. So far, he's managed to hunt down and pick off most of the ships they've sent against our shipping, but he's taken a heavy pounding for that. The rail lines are good, but they are nothing compared to the volume of goods we can transport by ship."

"And yet?"

"On my way to Carthage, I will send a message to Devnum ordering them to get the tribune whatever he needs for his mission, and then I will proceed to Carthage, leaving you here to deal with your own project."

"I'm not sure going there on your own is a good idea. It is risky."

"Weren't you just lecturing me on risk versus reward?"

"Yes, but ..."

"But nothing," Lucilla interrupted her. "You said yourself I have never been risk-averse, so let me prove that to you once again. I am going to Carthage and I will see the problems there put to rest once and for all."

"Then for all our sakes, I hope you're successful," Medb said.

"For all our sakes, I hope we both are."

Chapter 21

Factorium

Sorantius stood before a row of large, interconnected glass vessels, his senior technicians assembled in a semicircle behind him, all looking at the massive apparatus that dominated the center of the facility. Standing nearly twenty meters tall with its network of pipes and collection points arrayed around it, it looked more like some sort of industrial creature than a piece of machinery. The lead operator waited beside his station, slate board ready with the day's recordings.

"Temperature readings," Sorantius said, extending his hand for the slate.

The operator handed over the board, pointing to the mercury thermometer readings marked at regular intervals. After the accident almost eight years ago, Sorantius had always been careful about the work they did, but he was taking even fewer chances here.

The Consul's repeated warnings ensured that.

Looking at the markings, he noted the gradual progression from the base heating chamber up through the various collection levels and was happy to see the numbers aligned with the Consul's instructions. One hundred and ten degrees at the base, dropping systematically to thirty-eight degrees at the highest collection point.

"Consistent throughout the run?"

"Yes, sir. No fluctuations."

Sorantius gave the man a nod, one of his highest forms of praise, before moving to the collection tanks. Stopping and picking up some of the measuring tools set out for him, he drew a sample of the naphtha feedstock from the primary tank, holding the glass vial up to examine its clarity. The liquid moved with the proper viscosity, crystal clear without any trace of contamination or unwanted compounds. He'd, of course, checked it before, when the substance was separated from the black sludge they'd been delivered, but now that it was in use, he double-checked. Again, he nodded before returning the sample to its container.

The small steam pump that moved the naphtha between stations released a rhythmic hiss as pressure built and flowed through the system. Sorantius crouched beside the mechanism, running his hands along the cylinder housing and checking the connection points.

"When did you last inspect the seals?"

"Three days ago, Sir."

"Check them again before the next run. It is feeling a little rough. Remember, this isn't like some of the other machines. Some of these chemicals are a little rough on the rubber used to keep them sealed."

Sorantius followed the transfer pipe from the collection tanks toward the next processing station, examining each bolted flange and valve connection for signs of weeping or pressure loss. He was still concerned about the seals. It was the weakest point on nearly every piece of equipment in any of his factories. And the easiest to see slack develop with use.

Satisfied with what he was seeing, he said, "Show me the priming sequence."

The operator moved to the steam pump controls, working the levers and valves with practiced motions. Steam pressure built in the cylinder chamber, then transferred through the distribution manifold to create the suction that would draw feedstock through the system.

From there, he went to the steam cracker. A hulking furnace assembly dominating the floor space with riveted iron plates and refractory brick construction. Sorantius circled the unit, checking the exterior for signs of thermal stress or structural fatigue. The internal temperatures reached levels that could weaken even the heaviest construction if not properly monitored.

Even to look into the setup after the temperatures had been allowed to cool, required extra steps, as any ports or other openings could be dangerous.

"Unbolt the inspection hatch."

A technician selected the appropriate wrench from his tool kit and began loosening the heavy iron cover that provided access to the internal chambers. The bolts required significant force to break free, having been torqued tight to maintain the pressure seals during operation. When the hatch swung open, Sorantius peered into the internal space, examining the firebrick lining for damage or excessive wear.

Carbon fouling coated the interior surfaces, a normal result of the cracking process but one that required regular attention. They had only run a few sample runs through it, so it wasn't bad, but they would have to stay on top of its performance to keep it from degrading.

"Make sure it's scraped every few days to remove the carbon buildup. Do not skimp on this," Sorantius said.

The technicians nodded. He trusted them to do their jobs, but he'd make sure his foreman double-checked in a week to ensure they were being conscientious.

He moved to the control panel where brass-rimmed pressure gauges displayed the current system status. Each gauge received a sharp tap on its glass face to ensure the needle moved freely and registered accurately.

Sorantius made another notation, then proceeded to the quenching system's water tower. The gravity-fed lines that supplied cooling water to the cracker, helping to prevent catastrophic overheating. He tested the large manual release valve, only slightly so as not to flood the system, but just enough to make sure it was working well. In the case of an emergency, this would be how they rapidly cooled the system. It would cause damage when the cracker was at full temp, but that was better than letting an out-of-control reaction burn down the whole factory.

From there, he checked the solvent extraction station that further increased the purity of the final product, which seemed to be the focus of everything he did. The final purification area was where they would isolate the toluene, since it boiled at a different point than the other chemicals mixed in with it.

As with the other stations, everything looked good, which shouldn't be a surprise since the entire factory had yet to blow up, but it was still a concern. It's why he did these inspection runs before any of the lines went into full production.

A technician drew a sample of the finished product into a small vial, which Sorantius held up to examine against the light filtering through the factory windows. The liquid displayed the water-like clarity that indicated successful removal of all colored impurities and unwanted compounds.

He uncorked the vial and tested it with a glass hydrometer, one of the many tools the Consul had them design and build for checking the array of interesting chemicals needed for nearly every level of the Britannian war machine.

It slipped into the sample with barely a ripple, settling to its equilibrium position based on the liquid's specific gravity. Again, it looked as it should.

Sorantius surveyed the entire facility one final time. The weeks of development, and months prior to that of training staff and technicians on similar procedures making all kinds of chemicals, had paid off and they managed to get through this stage without a hiccup.

"Everything looks good," Sorantius said, giving the vial back to the technician.

Then he looked over at a different set of technicians setting up yet another line that would take this product and turn it into its final form.

Or at least its final form for now.

"Let's get production ramped up so we have enough on hand for that team to begin producing," Sorantius said, before consulting his notes one last time to refresh his memory on what the Consul had called that substance, "TNT."

Devnum

Claudius pushed through the door of the port master's office, finding the seven captains already assembled around the large wooden table that dominated the cramped space. The building wasn't really made for meetings like this, but the alternative was to use one of the even more cramped cabins on one of their ships.

Claudius was already looking at a long stretch on the rolling vessels, so the longer he could stay on dry land, the better.

"Captains," he said as he took his seat with them.

The men returned his greeting with varying degrees of formality. He didn't know any of them well, having met some of them as long as a week and a half ago and others only yesterday. But he'd dealt with enough of their type to know how unique each man was.

They were unlike military men on the land, who tended to be very hierarchical; ship captains were used to being the very top of the pyramid, which allowed them to develop idiosyncrasies into their personalities.

Claudius unrolled the leather portfolio he carried and spread Ky's detailed charts over the table surface. The drawings showed coastlines and island chains that stretched far beyond any territory familiar to Britannian navigators. In a display of yet another remarkable skill, the Consul's drawings were not only incredibly intricate, but also had precise markings for distances, prevailing winds, and seasonal weather patterns that Claudius had no doubt were perfectly accurate.

"I'm happy to say the delays that have kept us in port are finally resolved," Claudius announced. "Thanks to some assistance from the Empress in clearing up the dispute about where your ships would be best used. Which means it's now time to plan our route and load up the supplies I've managed to horde for us"

"I'm not sure we can plan a route like this,' Captain Attanito said. "These waters are completely unknown to us, Tribune, far beyond where any vessel in our navy, or any of the merchants I have ever met, have traveled."

"Which is why we have these charts. I am sure it will be difficult and I have no doubt things will change along our journey as we see these places for ourselves, but I think we all know how good the Consul's information is, and I was given to understand that it would be enough information for you to at least come up with an initial plan."

The men didn't seem happy with that decision, but they also knew he wasn't wrong. The charts they had were better than their ancestors would have had charting new paths, and they knew how to read the wind and the sea.

Besides, they had a better chance of doing it right than he ever would.

"Our first objective will be to rebuild Port Amicitiae. We were unprepared to defend it three years ago, but with the new canons and fortifications, we can properly do so. We will not stay and see it done. Once we drop off the men and ships that will handle that rebuild, we will continue on and leave them to the task. Ultimately, it will be the main supply point for our eastern base.

"That is very far away for it to be any kind of supply point," Gratius said.

"It is, but it is also as close as we are going to be able to set up a port that can work in the open as a supply point. Eventually, we will probably be able to set up closer ports but the hope is that this gambit is successful enough that this war will be over before that is needed. With the new ports our captains in the African fleet are building, including the new one they have started just off the tip of Africa, we should have enough support that the rebuilt port will not be as vulnerable as it was two years ago."

"Are you leaving us much in the way of legionaries to help with the rebuilding?" Gratius asked.

"No. I know that leaves a lot on you and your sailors, but you should be able to borrow some men from the African fleet's building projects. One way or another, I need you to get it done. Once we get to our final destination, at least two of the caravels and all of the supply ships continuing with us will unload and return to you right away to load up with new supplies for a second mission. The base in the east will not just need supplies for itself. The whole point of this expedition is to set up a supply point for the rebels we have learned of in the Easterners' homeland. Rebels we hope can help take the Eastern government down from the inside."

"Do we have any idea of what presence the Easterners have in these waters? We know they are sending ships to and around Africa from their homeland, which leads me to believe they must have ships in these waters."

"Which is why it is important to avoid the mainland. As far as we can tell, their navigational aids are still limited, greatly prohibiting them from open water travel away from the coast. Still, I will admit our intelligence is limited."

"What about these proposed landing sites for this base?" Otarus asked. "We have encountered natives every time we've stopped at a new uncharted location. Do we have any information on the locations where we are planning to land?"

"Again, not really. As you said, we can assume some form of native population exists. We've been told the Easterners have not expanded out to these areas with any kind of permanent presence. But we don't know how much contact the natives may have had with the Easterners or what kinds of loyalties they might have. We think it will be like what we found along the African coast, small fishing and farming villages with minimal technology."

"Is any of this information coming from anyone local, or is this just the Consul's admittedly limited information?"

"We do have someone from that part of the world, but he is our contact with the rebels on the mainland and that is where he obtained the majority of his information. He is from an inland village and lacks maritime experience of any kind. His value is the entry it gives us with the rebels, so do not expect him to be a font of knowledge much beyond what he has already told us."

"So we're sailing blind into unknown waters based on theoretical charts, hoping to establish a secret base while avoiding enemy fleets and unknown natives," Fuscus summarized.

"That about sums it up," Claudius replied sardonically. "But consider the potential rewards. If we can establish reliable contact with the resistance networks operating within the Eastern homeland, we could take down the enemy from the inside and end this war years sooner than it would be possible if we relied only on direct conflict with them. Besides, every war is a risk. I think your real complaint is that so much of this is unknown."

Fuscus gave a half nod in agreement.

"We won't be completely alone. Aside from a complement of legionaries, our first stop will be Vikhavn, where Ekoko has agreed that some of his Mpongo people will accompany us, since this fort will have to be somewhat self-sustaining and the Consul's notes indicate the climate here should be something like what we have encountered in Africa."

The captains digested this news, clearly not happy about what they'd been asked to do, but also at least understanding the need for it. All they were being asked to do was risk their very lives on it.

"I know you are all being asked a lot," Claudius said. "But if we are successful, we could advance the winning of the war by years. This mission is worth the risk, and I trust each of you to do your best to make sure it is successful. Understood?"

The seven captains looked at each other before nodding one by one.

"Good. I want to leave by the end of the week. So let's get to it."

Chapter 22

Carthage

The last time Lucilla had been here had been at the end of the last war. Since then, she had let first Ky and then the Senate's picked administrator run the city while she worked to build the Western Alliance into what it was now, as well as help those new allies rebuild from the war. The city was much as she remembered from then, which was a worrying sign.

Smoke rose in columns from multiple places and even from the bay, she could see the rubble of buildings.

Things here were worse than she'd been told.

As if to confirm that, before her ship could align for its final approach to the main docks, a warship anchored in the deeper water of the outer bay signaled from its mast with a series of colored flags. She was not versed in the signal system Ky had introduced, but it wasn't hard to figure out that it was urgent by the way the appearance of the signal sent men scrambling on the ship, pulling the sails up until their ship slowed to a halt in the middle of the bay, instead of continuing on to the docks.

"Captain?" she questioned.

The transport ship's master glanced from the colored squares to her and said, "The Vindex is ordering us to heave to and wait for instructions."

"Orders?"

"Perhaps 'warns' is a better way to say it. We are told not to approach the docks."

She didn't ask for clarification. She knew enough about the signal flags to know there was only a limited amount of information they could pass. Besides, she would have the information in a moment, based on seeing a cutter being lowered down the Vindex's side and rowing toward them.

"Signal back that I am aboard and will transfer," she said, although it was almost certain that the captain of the warship already knew that.

"Aye, Empress," the transport's master said, and shouted orders.

The cutter slewed alongside in a spray of salt and two sailors caught the rail.

A young lieutenant in grey vaulted up, breathing fast, and saluted. "Empress. Captain Varro asks you to come aboard at once."

"Then at once," she said.

The cutter ride took less than ten minutes, but out on the water, close to the city, she could hear sporadic rifle fire. Not in concentrated volleys, however. It was more scattered shots, a pop-pop sound that broke the sound of the sea.

Things were definitely bad.

Captain Varro met her at the rail, a stocky man with graying hair and the weathered face of a man who'd spent his life on the sea.

"Empress," he said as she climbed aboard the ship. "I apologize for stopping you short of the docks, but the city is no longer safe.

"What has happened, Captain?" she asked.

"Perhaps we should discuss this in my cabin."

She looked around at all the men staring in their direction, and nodded, following him across the deck as he waved his people back to their jobs.

Once in his cabin, the man seemed to, not relax, but sag a bit from exhaustion, gesturing to a seat near a small table, and taking the spot across from her.

"What has happened here, Captain?" she asked.

"Tragedy. The rebel activity that started building after Prince Cormac left exploded in the last week and finally came to a head three days ago. We lost control of the main thoroughfare to the governmental palace yesterday afternoon. Worse, the best the praetorians assigned to the palace were able to do was pull back into the complex, which means the governor, his administrative staff, and their entire praetorian detail are cut off and surrounded."

"How did it collapse so quickly? The reports I received spoke of unrest but nothing like this."

"It wasn't a single event, more like a dam breaking in a dozen places at once. The local garrison has been stretched thin ever since Prince Cormac's legion left for Egypt. We have tried to support them as best we can, but I have limited men on board, and short of shelling the city itself, all I can do is put enough firepower down to support the men holding the immediate area around the docks."

"I understand, but you said things exploded recently. What precipitated that?"

"To counter the growing unrest, the governor re-imposed martial law. Curfews, public punishments, it was very heavy-handed, much more so than what had been in place under the prince's tenure, or so I'm given to understand. It had the opposite effect, instead of quelling the unrest, it pushed it out into the open. The only reason the entire city didn't fall is because the rebels themselves are in turmoil, and seem to have divided into three distinct factions, all hostile to us, and two of them hostile to each other."

"Really? This happened after the violence broke out?"

"It's hard to say. We became aware of it shortly before, and it was discussed in the last face-to-face conversation I had with the governor, but it became clear once the unrest became violent, as they began fighting each other as well as our men."

"I see. Do we know anything about them?"

"A little. The first group, which we're calling the Moderates, is led by a wealthy merchant named Adherbal. I actually met him once. He petitioned for more rights in shipping and trade and controlled several of the warehouses close to the docks. I'm not sure he and the people supporting him were part of the unrest prior to martial law. I know his were among many of the businesses that struggled after the orders were given. His men are mostly dockworkers and laborers. People who'd been keeping their heads down and were trying to earn a living before everything fell apart.

They're armed, and they know their district, but they aren't fanatics."

"Have we spoken to him?" Lucilla asked.

"Only enough to get a list of demands. They're asking for expanded autonomy for the city, a rollback of the military presence, an end to the martial laws, and some kind of local control over the city government itself, although they have made it clear they aren't demanding a complete break from the Empire. I think they know they have too much to gain from that. They've fortified the commercial district and have mostly stayed out of the larger street battles. Of the three, they represent the most reasonable position, but they still hold Imperial territory and show no sign of giving it up."

"I see."

"That is as close to good news as I can give you because the other two groups are much worse. The second faction has rallied itself behind a man claiming to be the illegitimate son of the former Emperor Imilcar. Calls himself Gerisbal Banaleth Azor."

"I was under the impression that Imilcar had no children. And why wait so long to come forward?"

"I'm not sure anyone other than his own men believes him. As best as the praetorians could figure out, he was some kind of functionary in the old court, which is perhaps why he seems to know so much about the former emperor. The problem is, he is also apparently very charismatic. From what I've heard, he's been giving speeches of restoring the glory of Carthage and driving us back into the sea. And it has appealed to a subset of the rebels that already existed. They have, however, come into conflict with the other part of the rebels who I guess we're calling the Hardliners. They denounce the supposed heir as a fraud, a charlatan using a dead emperor's name for his own gain, but their demands are essentially the same. Complete independence, no negotiations. They're led by a man named Mago, who, from what we've been able to find out, now that they're operating in the open, was a former officer in the Carthaginian army who either escaped or skipped the final battle for the city. Whichever it was, he is apparently ruthless. They are by far the most violent of the three groups and they are actively fighting both us and the men under

Gerisbal, who we've been calling the Restorationists. That internal conflict is the only thing that has prevented either of them from fully consolidating their power and overwhelming our positions, honestly."

"What exactly are our positions?"

"The praetorians who were stationed near us managed to fall back here and we were able to secure the immediate area around the docks. We've managed to create a small, defensible perimeter. We are keeping them supplied and can offer support from our guns, but we don't have enough men to break through to the governmental palace, which is the other place we hold. That has a larger contingent, nearly two hundred praetorians, but they have a lot of injured and based on the supplies I know they were sent, they are low on everything. They lost the warehouses, most of their extra gunpowder, and even some of the new rifles were stored in to the Hardliners in the first push, which made things worse."

"They have the new repeating rifles?"

"Yes. A fair number, which is why we haven't had any luck breaking through. Eventually, they will run out of ammunition, but it was a pretty significant depot that they took. It's allowed them to hold the quarter around the government palace and push the Restorationists back quite a bit. They definitely have the strongest hand of the three."

Lucilla absorbed the information. To say it was grim was an understatement. If they could get their people out of the center of the city, that would be her first choice, just pull back to here and then retake the city block by block.

Of course, that might not even be an option. With their forces falling back across nearly all fronts of the war and the casualty numbers going up faster than they could recruit more men, thanks to the poison gas, there weren't any forces for her to use to retake the city.

The only good thing was that they were distracted by killing each other, buying her some time to figure out how she could retake the city with the meager forces she had at her disposal.

"Do we have any communication line open to any of the three factions?"

"Partially. Mago and the claimant won't even accept a parley and they'd rather shoot any of our messengers than talk, but Adherbal and the Moderates have indicated they'd be willing to negotiate their way out of this."

"Well then," Lucilla said. "We'll start there."

Factorium

Hortensius stood beside the sealed testing chamber, its thick wooden planks reinforced with iron bands to contain whatever might happen inside. The structure dominated the eastern corner of the Factorium grounds, built specifically for this purpose over the past three days. His lead technician, Marcus, adjusted valves on the smoke generation apparatus while a weathered centurion from the Germania front watched with barely concealed impatience.

"I just need your man to put this on and stand inside this room for several minutes," Hortensius said. "If everything goes well, then this will save a lot of men at the front."

"And if not, is this going to kill my man?" the centurion asked. "We've seen the men who didn't die from the gas. It's not pretty."

Both he and the legionary with him had come from the front a month ago, both with serious injuries. The centurion was missing his foot, blown off by a shell, or so Hortensius had heard. The legionary was missing an ear, and his left eye was in bad shape.

The fact that both men still wanted to do their duty to the Empire, to serve it, in spite of their injuries said something about them.

"Of course, of course. We wouldn't use the Easterners' gas for this kind of test; the risk is much too great. We'll use sulfur smoke mixed with damp straw. It will create a thick, choking cloud that will not harm him, but he will be able to tell if any leaks through the mask's seals or isn't properly filtered out."

"If you say so," the centurion said, still clearly uncertain but nodding at his man, as if giving permission.

Hortensius lifted the prototype respirator from the workbench. The device looked crude but functional, leather and canvas formed the facepiece, with double-paned glass discs set where the eyes would be. A metal canister about the size of a man's fist hung below where the mouth would sit.

The glass eye pieces were the part that worried Hortensius the most. The Consul's original design called for a single pane, but the more Hortensius looked at the seals around it, the more he was concerned they wouldn't hold out the gas. Also, the glass was thick, but still could shatter, and a second pane would give the soldier a chance if the outer one cracked or broke.

It was well-made glass, thanks to the advances they'd made in glassblowing, but the two panes together would make it hard to see. Not impossible, but everything would be a little blurry.

Still, that was far superior to dying, choking on your own fluids.

He turned the mask over, showing the centurion the intake valve. "Air enters here, passes through layers of activated charcoal mixed with chemical neutralizing agents, which should clean it of any kind of harmful substance, from thick smoke to poison, before it reaches the wearer."

Both men looked at him a little perplexed that he was explaining the workings of the device, but he'd felt that if they were concerned about it harming the younger man, that knowing how it worked might settle those nerves.

He was, apparently, wrong.

"But will it work?" the centurion asked.

"The Consul's designs have never failed us before. I will admit we've never had to do something this hasty before, and the notes were less thorough than they have been on other projects, but I suspect that is also because of the need to do this quickly. Still, from my understanding, yes. The design is sound and has worked on a smaller scale, non-human tests we have conducted."

Again, the centurion gave the younger man a nod.

"We will just fit you with it," Hortensius said to the younger man. "You only have to breathe normally. We will light the fire that will release the smoke and then leave you here in this room, sealing you in so the smoke builds up. My understanding is that this will make it slightly harder for you to breathe than it would be if you were breathing normally, so that is expected. However, the moment you feel any discomfort beyond simple breathing restriction, signal through the viewing port. We'll have you out immediately."

The man nodded. Hortensius and his technician settled the mask over the soldier's face. The leather had been softened with oil to create a better seal against the skin, but it still had to be strapped down tight and each connection point checked individually. He was still working on notes of how soldiers might do this quickly in the field and had sent several questions back to the Consul looking for some clarification on the mask's design, but the design was far enough along to test before those answers came back.

"Can you breathe?" Hortensius asked once the mask was fully secured.

The soldier's response came muffled but clear enough. "Yes. Feels strange. Like breathing through cloth."

"That's expected. Try turning your head. Any gaps?"

The legionary moved his head from side to side, then up and down. He gave a thumbs-up.

Hortensius patted him on the shoulder and then directed the other men to leave. The technician stopped by the small pot on one side of the room and lit it before hurrying out after them, sealing the door behind him. There was a thick pane of glass that allowed them to look in through the door at the man inside.

The chamber had been designed hastily, but they had tested it once to ensure the room was completely sealed when the smoke started filling it.

Hortensius waved to get the man's attention, who raised his thumb again, indicating he was alright.

The smoke from the mixture of sulfur and burning straw had already begun to fill the room, creating a yellowish black vapor that began to obscure everything inside. They could still see the man, standing there in the middle of the room, but he was more of a vague shape than a full person.

For thirty seconds, everything proceeded as expected. The legionary remained still, arms at his sides, breathing steadily through the mask.

Then his entire body jerked, and he dropped to his knees. Through the smoke, they could see him pulling at the mask, trying to tear it free.

"Something's wrong," the centurion said.

"Get him out!" Hortensius shouted.

Hortensius and the technician heaved the heavy beam helping keep the door well sealed and yanked it open. Smoke flowed over them in a choking wave as they plunged inside, grabbed the soldier under his arms, and dragged him into the open air.

The moment they cleared the doorway, the legionary succeeded in ripping the mask away. He hurled it aside and collapsed onto his hands and knees, gasping. His face had turned an alarming shade of red.

"Water," he croaked.

A medicus, who'd been standing by, rushed forward with a canteen. The soldier drank greedily, water running down his chin.

"Felt like breathing fire," he managed between gulps. "Scorching hot."

Hortensius looked at him and then reached carefully for the discarded respirator. Even several hand spans away he could feel heat radiating from the metal canister. Reaching into his belt, he pulled on a thick leather glove before picking it up.

Even through the leather, he could feel the intense heat.

It took a moment for him to realize what had happened, why the metal casing would be hot at all. He knew from the early experiments that he and Sorantius had conducted the first few days after they received the Consul's instructions that the chemical reaction that eliminated the impurities in the air could cause the chemicals to release heat.

He'd assumed it was part of the process, but something must be wrong. Perhaps they used the wrong chemicals in the reaction.

The centurion's face had gone dark with anger. "You nearly cooked that boy's lungs."

"The filter worked perfectly. Look, he wasn't coughing. The smoke never reached his lungs. But the air passing through the canister was hot; this didn't happen in our initial testing. I am so sorry."

"You're sorry? You just tortured one of my men with your untested device."

"I apologize. To both of you." Hortensius looked at the recovering soldier, who was now sitting upright, breathing more normally. "The failure is mine. We will get this fixed."

The soldier waved a hand weakly. "I'm alright, sir. Just maybe ... find someone else to test it next time."

"We will, but the next time will go much better. We won't make the same mistake twice."

"I certainly hope not," the centurion helped the young legionary to his feet. "Come on, boy. Let's get you checked properly by the medicus."

As they walked away, Hortensius turned back to the apparatus. He would have to take it apart again and work on what caused it to heat like that after he sent word of the test and its results to the Consul.

Maybe it had something to do with the smoke he used, the sulfur, and the chemicals in the case itself. They had learned, both from the Consul's warnings and from their own tests, that some chemicals, when combined, could generate heat, or even toxins, as the Easterners had exploited for their weapons.

He would have to figure out what combination created the heat and find a way to neutralize it.

Chapter 23

Testing Range, Outside Factorium

The artillery range stretched across three kilometers of cleared land, on the other side of the river from the main complexes of Factorium, for safety. The brown earth was scarred from months of testing, divots and craters dug out of it by bullets, shells, and raw explosives, each delivering information for the designers to build from.

Hortensius stood beside two howitzers waiting as the carriage carrying the chieftain pulled across the bridge, stopping next to the test and viewing platform.

The Caledonian was a few more minutes behind schedule than the Empress would have been and with several more aides and hangers-on than she traveled with. Not that he had complaints with the job the man had been doing. He'd only ever had good experiences with the chieftain since his elevation in status with the formation of the Empire, but the man had taken to his new administrative duties with unexpected diligence following the Empress's departure.

"You have something to show me?" Talogren said in his very direct way as he exited the carriage and made his way to the viewing platform.

"I most certainly do. Have a look at this," Hortensius said, taking the man by his elbow and showing him two shells sitting on top of nearby crates. "On the left is the standard black powder shell we have been producing for the last two years. On the right is a new shell filled with a compound the Consul calls trinitro-toluene and that we call TNT."

"They look identical."

"Only on the outside. The outer shell of the one with the TNT is thinner, giving us room for more explosive, which would be notable in and of itself if it wasn't for the other differences."

"What differences?"

"For one, the explosion is significantly more powerful. One for one, the TNT expels three to four times the force when set off as the black powder, and that doesn't take into account that we are using more of it. For another, black powder burns rapidly in a process called deflagration, that releases a great deal of gas and energy. The pressure shatters the casing and propels the fragments outward, along with the burning gases. The TNT, on the other hand, detonates. Instead of fire burning from grain to grain, a chemical reaction travels through it faster than that of sound, before the compound releases a powerful, explosive force outward from it. This isn't compressed gas, but a shockwave of force that radiates from the point of detonation, traveling so fast that the shockwave will hit you before you hear the sound of the explosion. The shrapnel is deadly, but the shockwave has such power that it can pulverize a man, rip limbs asunder, and liquefy organs. And then there is the shrapnel. That shockwave also rips the metal shell into many more pieces, smaller and traveling at a much higher velocity. The danger zone for infantry is significantly larger and the fragments much more lethal."

"The good thing is that it's also much more stable and safer to handle. It is much less likely to go off at the slightest disturbance, which means less of a chance of rounds going off in the tube, less likely for a dropped round to explode, killing the handlers, and a near miss on a caisson won't set off the whole lot, though a direct hit will still be catastrophic, maybe more so."

"Ohh."

"On top of that, we've also developed a new propellant charge with the smokeless powder the Consul had us develop. It produces a much higher pressure than the black powder charges, which means the cannons can fire much farther. We couldn't use these more powerful charges with the old black powder shells. The initial shock from the increased kick was enough to risk setting off the black powder in the old shells prematurely. With the stable TNT that is no longer a concern. We can fire farther, with greater accuracy, and deliver a vastly more destructive payload when it arrives at the target."

"Well, I believe all this talk deserves a demonstration," Talogren said. "Or was this something that could be put in a telegram."

"No sir, we did prepare a demonstration for you," he said, holding out his hand and directing the chieftain to the viewing platform before turning to a soldier nearby. "Lieutenant, you may proceed. Target Alpha. Standard black powder shells. Fire for effect."

The lieutenant saluted and trotted back to the gun line, giving out orders to two teams. One man sponged the barrel, another inserted the shell, seating it firmly. A third rammed home the cloth-wrapped propellant charge. The gun captain adjusted the elevation with a hand crank, checked his sights, then stepped back, lanyard in hand.

"Battery, fire!" the lieutenant yelled.

The two cannons discharged in a rolling thunder that shook the ground. A dense cloud of grey-black smoke billowed from the muzzles, obscuring the gun line for a moment before the wind began to shred it. Hortensius watched the shells arc through the sky, small dark specks against the grey clouds.

They landed in a tight grouping around the first structure set up downrange. Both impacts were direct hits. The explosions were loud, concussive booms followed by the crackle of splintering wood. Large sections of the target's frame were blown inward, and the roof sagged where one shell had torn through it. Smoke and dust rose from the wreckage. The structure was heavily damaged, ruined, but it was still recognizably a structure.

"Excellent," Talogren said.

"You haven't seen anything yet," Hortensius said. "Lieutenant, reload with the new ordnance. Target Bravo."

Again, the gun crews went to work. This time, the propellant charges were slimmer, more compact, although the shells were visually identical.

The lieutenant waited for the all-clear from each gun captain before yelling, "Battery, fire!"

The report was entirely different. It was not a rolling boom but a single, violent crack, sharp and loud. There was almost no smoke, just a brief flicker of orange at the cannon muzzles and two thin wisps that dissipated almost instantly. Hortensius could track the shells in flight for their entire journey.

The shells struck the second structure dead center.

There was a flash of light followed by a thump against his chest, a solid, physical blow, a moment before the sound arrived, a loud, physical boom that shook the ground and the people.

The target structure did not break apart. It ceased to exist. One moment, it was there, a solid frame of timber and planking. The next, it was a rapidly expanding cloud of dust and splinters thrown high into the sky. The shockwave rolled across the field, flattening the tall grass in a visible wave. Even from hundreds of meters away, Hortensius felt the air compress around him, a pressure against his skin.

Silence descended on the field, broken only by the faint patter of falling debris. Where the second structure had stood, there was now only a deep crater. Not a single piece of timber larger than a man's hand remained.

Talogren stood motionless for a long moment, his expression unreadable as he stared at the utter devastation. The difference was not one of degree. It was absolute.

Finally, he turned to Hortensius, his voice low. "When can this go into production?"

"It already is," Hortensius replied, unable to keep the pride from his voice. "We began full-scale manufacturing of both the shells and the new propellant charges a week ago, as soon as Sorantius finalized the chemical processes. We are already producing enough to fill the magazines and at least one supply tiller for the *Victorious* before she finishes her sea trials."

"Good. As I understood from Lucan's report, the ship was made to fire these new shells and charges."

"Yes, it was," Hortensius confirmed. "We could fire the old ones, but we ideally need the new charges to push the shells out of the longer tubes, which were made to internally recoil so they could be fired again quickly. For the rest of the army, though, we will need to begin changing out the artillery tubes we have. The guns we use now were not meant to deal with the pressure generated by the new charges, and we will start having guns fail. The Consul has already sent plans for a new type of cannon, one with the shells loaded from an opening in the rear ... a 'breech', he calls it. Beyond being able to handle the new shells, it will increase the rate of fire dramatically."

"Until then?"

"Until then, we are manufacturing some special shells for the existing guns. They are packed with additional shrapnel and smaller TNT charges. They won't have the same range as they would with the new propellant, but they will still be far more effective against infantry than the old black powder rounds."

Talogren nodded, his gaze returning to the smoking crater downrange. "Good. Do what you have to do, but get this deployed as fast as possible. What about the other thing you've been working on? The masks, to protect against the Easterners' gas."

"Soon," he said, almost apologetically. "We had an issue with the chemical neutralizers in the filter canisters and are re-manufacturing the filter media with a new composition. It's taking time. Perhaps in the next week, we will be ready for another test."

"Hurry," Talogren said, his voice flat and hard. "The boys can't wait long for it."

"I know. We are on it."

Carthage

It was not hard to tell what this warehouse was normally used for, not with the smells of salt, dried fish, and cedarwood crates. It had sat empty long enough that most of the actual product had been removed, either by owners hustling it out while they still could or looters, although both would have been high risk.

It sat two blocks in from the docks, just outside of the small perimeter the praetorians and marines off the ships had managed to hold while the city fell apart. It was technically considered a no-man's land, with a block separating it from the territory currently claimed by the 'Moderates.'

The centurion commanding these praetorians, the warship captains, and her own guards had all argued against her being here, but she wasn't particularly worried.

True, there was a danger of one of the rebels deciding now would be the time to take their shot and get rid of the head of their enemy, but she didn't think that likely. For one, this group was, if their demands were to be believed, not asking for autonomy from Britannia. And two, they were mostly armed with muskets, not even the now-outdated rifles. Those weapons had a fairly short range, an accuracy that left much to be desired, and a very low rate of fire compared to the repeating rifles the dozen men she brought with her carried.

And of course, there was the fact that anything short of an instantly mortal blow would be unlikely to do her in before the small machines that Ky had filled her with could repair the damage.

She'd survived an assassin's blade, and that had been well-positioned and targeted.

In any event, she wasn't taking too many chances.

The man she was there to meet, the merchant turned rebel named Adherbal, was already there, waiting for her near a broad table. He was a heavy-set man who'd let himself go recently, or so it seemed. His fine tunic spoke of wealth but his hands and physique said that wealth was something more recent; he had known hard labor in his life.

Behind him stood a handful of men. She'd had her people check out the building as much as possible without being too obvious about it, and it seemed pretty clear this was all he had brought with him. Based on the intelligence they had gathered, this group was spread thin, as most of the people who supported this faction were not zealots and few wanted to actually put their lives on the line, making them much shorter on manpower than the other two factions.

Adherbal inclined his head as she approached. "Empress. Thank you for agreeing to meet on our ground."

"It is your city as much as mine, Adherbal," Lucilla said as she stopped in front of the table, her guards forming a loose semicircle behind her. "I hope we can find a way to restore its peace."

"That is my hope as well," he said. He gestured to her guards. "But it is difficult to speak of peace when surrounded by so many soldiers. It puts men on edge."

"My guards are here for my protection. Nothing more. I gave you my word you would have safe conduct to and from this meeting and I intend to keep it. The question is whether you will give me something in return, a reason to believe this unrest can end before more people are hurt."

"The people of Carthage have grievances, Empress. Serious ones. They feel their role in this Empire is one of subjugation, not partnership."

"I can understand that, to some degree, although you must also understand that we came to this city in order to defend our own homes. We have been here for seven years while the former rulers of this place had their boot on the neck of the known world for generations. You have to allow that it will take time for the people at the heart of that former empire to show enough faith that they do not want to return things to how they had been.

"We lived under the same oppression and just want to be allowed some say in our lives."

"What kind of say?"

"For starters, we'd like the money from taxes here to stay here. We'd like all the taxation and duties collected at the port to be administered by a Carthaginian council, with funds used for the betterment of this city and its people, not to fund a war in another part of the world. Additionally, we don't want to see Britannian soldiers marching through our streets, accosting its citizens and telling us who is allowed to go where. We are not so naive that some kind of guard force isn't needed, to keep criminal acts under control, but they should be housed outside of the city walls and their patrols and tasks should be controlled by a Carthaginian council. And lastly, we understand that as part of a wider Britannia there will have to be some kind of administration, like a governor-ship or praetorship or whatever you call it, but we would like a say in who is appointed, and the right to remove them and request a new one if we feel that person is working against the best interests of our people."

"Those are very big requests. Put together, you are asking me to give Carthage the means to arm itself, fund itself, and staff itself with men of its own choosing, with no oversight from the Empire it is supposedly a part of. You don't ask for partnership. You ask for the keys to the city and the gold in its treasury."

"We only ask for self-determination and the respect due to all people."

"What you are asking for is to be allowed the tools of secession and the ability for the Carthage of old to rise again and try to reconquer the world. Millions lost their lives to that empire and I cannot allow that to happen again. No sane ruler would."

"Then I have nothing to offer you and I fear I will have nothing to offer my own people, Empress. You must understand my po-sition. The Moderates, my faction ... we are losing ground every day. Gerisbal speaks of restoring the throne of Imilcar. Mago preaches a war of total independence. They tell their people that negotiation is weakness and that the only thing you understand is force. Every day, more of my own supporters listen to them. They see your legions bottled up on the docks and your governor trapped in his palace. They start to believe the Hardliners are right. If I return to them with empty hands, they will abandon me. They will go to Mago. The fighting you see now will become a war."

"And what do you think the result of that war will be? You need to understand the situation, Adherbal. The real situation, not the one Mago sells to angry young men in the alleys. Britannia will not, *cannot*, allow a rebirth of the Carthaginian danger. We fought one war to end that threat forever. We will not stand by and watch it rise again, not in our own territory." She took a step forward, to the edge of the table between them. "I am not unreasonable and I am not here to offer you continued subjugation. What I want is to help you find a real place in the Empire, not as vassals, but as participants with a voice in your own governance and representation in the Senate. But I cannot do that in a way that weakens the whole of the Empire. That is the road to ruin, for all of us."

"I want that partnership. I truly do. But we are told to wait. To give it time. My people demand proof."

"I can increase the authority of the local council and I can designate a portion of port revenue to be managed locally for civic projects. I can even ensure the next governor is a man of Carthaginian birth, acceptable to you, although one who we know will be loyal to the Empire. I would say that is significant proof of my goodwill, and I urge you to take the gift you are being offered, Adherbal. I am trying to find a way that does not involve bringing the hammer down on Carthage."

"My people will say it is not enough," he said, shaking his head.

"Then you must be a leader and convince them. Do not think for a moment that because our main armies are occupied in the east that this Empire is weak. Do not mistake our desire for a peaceful solution for an inability to impose a violent one. This unrest has been problematic so far, but is not yet critical. If it becomes a genuine threat, if it forces me to divert ships and legions from the war front, do you think I will be in a generous mood when they arrive?"

"Force is not the answer, Empress."

"That is true only until there are no possible other answers. If this rebellion continues, if it grows, then the calculation changes. It will tie my hands and force me to shift the necessary resources here to excise the threat completely and permanently, which would be terrible for your people. And it will be your doing, because you refused to accept a reasonable peace when it was offered."

She paused a moment, holding his eye contact, making sure he understood how serious she was.

"Make your decision, Adherbal. You can gain real power for yourself and your people. You can secure a better future for Carthage within the Empire. Or you can throw it all away in search of a perfect solution that does not exist for anyone and, in doing so, put your people in more danger than they have faced since the last war. The choice is yours."

With a final, level look, Lucilla turned and walked out of the warehouse, her guards falling in behind her. She had said her piece and could now only hope he came to the sane conclusion.

And that he would do it quickly.

Chapter 24

East Indies

Claudius wiped his brow for the hundredth time.

The heat was a physical weight. He felt it pressing down on him, a damp, suffocating blanket that clung to his tunic and slicked his skin with a perpetual film of sweat. It was strange, the heat. Back home, the first snows of the year should have fallen, and yet here it was as if the rules of nature and time no longer existed.

For weeks, they had sailed east across an endless blue expanse, the sun a relentless hammer in a cloudless sky. Captain Crispinus might not have been worried, trusting the Consul's navigational tools, but Claudius had wondered if they would ever see land again.

Thankfully, yesterday they'd seen a gull, which apparently was a sign of land. The captain had been right.

"Mountains," the captain said, staring through the seeing glass. "Probably an island by the look of these waters."

Claudius had noticed the color of the water changing from a dark near black, lightening to a murky turquoise. The other thing he noticed was that the captain didn't sound pleased that they'd finally found land again after traveling for so long.

Or at least not as pleased as he would have thought the man would be.

"What?" Claudius asked.

"Can you smell it? The pressure just fell out from under us. The sky is turning. A storm is coming."

They had been sailing toward some dark clouds for a while, but it was hard to tell how far away they were, and they seemed to be moving away from them. The sky had taken on a greenish-yellow tint shortly before they'd seen the shape on the horizon the captain had confirmed to be mountains.

"According to the Consul's map, assuming we are where you say we are, there should be a deep cove about three kilometers ahead, on the north side of that large island. If a storm is coming, we should be able to make it there."

"We won't make it," the captain said. "All hands! Secure for heavy weather! Take those sails in, now!"

The lethargy the crew had been under for most of the long trip across open ocean shifted almost instantly to immediate, frantic action. Sailors scrambled up the rigging while others began lashing down everything movable on the deck.

As if it were waiting for the captain's words, the wind shifted without warning. One moment it blew steadily from the west, the next it came from the north with enough force to heel the *Nauta* over. A sailor working on the main topsail lost his grip and would have fallen if not for the safety line around his waist.

"Faster!" Crispinus roared. "Get those sails in!"

The sea changed color too, going from green to gray in minutes. Waves that had been a few hands high suddenly doubled, then tripled in size. The *Nauta* began to pitch violently, her bow diving into troughs before climbing the next wave.

Signal flags went up on the other ships. Claudius could make out the *Vires* and *Asturia* nearby, both frantically working to prepare for the storm. Further away, barely visible through the increasing spray, the *Doirinn* and *Ulderica* struggled to keep formation.

The rain started as scattered drops, then became a wall of water. Visibility dropped to fifty meters, then twenty, then less. The deck became treacherous, water sluicing across the planks with each roll of the ship.

Claudius grabbed a rope as the ship rolled hard to port. One of his legionaries slid across the deck until he fetched up against the rail. Blood ran from a gash on his forehead where he'd struck something.

"Get below if you're injured," Claudius ordered.

"I can still work, Tribune."

"Then tie yourself to something solid and help with those water barrels."

The wind increased again, going from a howl to something beyond sound, a physical force that threatened to tear the men from the deck. The *Nauta* climbed a wave that seemed to go on forever, her bow pointing at the dark sky. At the crest, Claudius caught a glimpse of the other ships through the rain.

The schooner *Ulderica* was being driven sideways, her smaller size making her vulnerable to the wind. The *Doirinn* disappeared completely behind a wall of water. As Claudius watched, the *Ulderica* vanished into the storm, swallowed by rain and waves.

"She's gone!" one of the sailors shouted.

"Focus on our ship!" Crispinus replied. "Helmsman, keep her nose into the waves or we'll broach!"

The helmsman and two other sailors fought the wheel, muscles straining against the forces trying to turn the ship broadside to the waves. If that happened, if they broached, the next wave would roll them over.

A wave larger than anything Claudius had imagined possible rose before them. The *Nauta* began to climb, her bow going up and up until it seemed they would flip over backward. Men clung to whatever they could find, feet sliding on the wet deck.

The wave broke over the bow.

Tons of water crashed down on the foredeck. The sound was tremendous, drowning out even the wind. Claudius saw men disappear under the green water, their safety lines the only thing keeping them from being swept overboard. Crates that had been double-lashed tore free and went over the side.

The foremast made a sound like a tree breaking in a forest.

"Watch out!" someone screamed.

The thick wood had cracked halfway up its length. It hung at an angle, held up only by the rigging on one side. With each roll of the ship, it swayed dangerously.

"Cut it loose before it comes through the deck!" Crispinus ordered. "Bosun, get men up there with axes!"

"In this?" Claudius asked.

"Now, or we all die!"

Three sailors grabbed axes and began climbing the rigging. The ship's motion threw them about, slamming them into the mast and lines. One man made it to the damaged section and began chopping at the supporting lines while clinging to the mast with his legs.

"Get guide ropes on it!" Crispinus shouted. "When it goes, we need to control where!"

Claudius organized his men to handle the ropes. They fought to get lines around the broken section while waves continued to pound the ship. The *Nauta* took on a list as water poured through the damaged bow area.

"Claudius, send your men down to help man the pumps!"

Claudius yelled and directed his men who'd been on deck helping get things stowed to go below. Half of Claudius's legionaries went below to work the manual pumps. The others continued helping topside, bailing water with buckets, securing loose debris, anything to keep the ship afloat.

The sailor with the axe finally cut through the last supporting line. The broken section of mast swayed, held now only by the guide ropes Claudius's men controlled.

"Let it go to starboard!" Crispinus commanded. "Easy! Control it!"

The men paid out rope gradually, fighting to keep the massive piece of timber from swinging wildly. It scraped along the deck, gouging deep furrows in the wood, before finally sliding over the side with a splash lost in the chaos of the storm.

The storm raged for six more hours. The captain worked hard to keep them moving away from the islands they had seen in the distance, instead of going for the protected cove, deciding it was too dangerous to get close to land with waves like this.

The sea continued to batter the *Nauta*, though none were as large as the monster that had damaged the foremast. The men worked the pumps continuously, barely keeping ahead of the water coming in through various breaches in the hull, working in shifts, exhausted legionaries replacing exhausted sailors in an endless cycle.

Finally, gradually, the wind began to decrease. The waves, while still dangerous, lost some of their towering height. The rain eased from a battering torrent to merely heavy.

"I think we're through the worst of it," Crispinus said.

Claudius surveyed the damage. The deck was a disaster of tangled rigging, broken wood, and debris. The missing foremast left the ship looking unbalanced, wrong. Water still sloshed in the hold despite the pumps working continuously.

"Can you see the others?" he asked.

Crispinus raised a brass telescope. "The *Vires* is off our port quarter. She's lost her mainmast from the look of it. The *Asturia* is ... there, to starboard. Down by the bow but still floating. I see, five ... no six of the supply ships. They look to have all made it through."

"The *Ulderica*?"

"No sign of her. Or the *Doirinn*."

Claudius nodded grimly. It didn't mean they were sunk, of course. The storm had gone on for hours. They could easily have been blown off course. The captains knew where they were headed, so it was possible that if they had been blown off course, they would be able to catch up.

Although it was also very possible they would never see those ships again.

Signal flags went up as the three surviving ships communicated their damage. The reports were uniformly troubling.

"How bad is it?" Claudius asked.

"Very. We've lost the foremast completely," Crispinus began. "Three sails are shredded beyond repair. We're taking on water faster than we should; probably sprung planks below the waterline. The pumps are keeping up, but only just."

"Can we make repairs?"

"Some. We can patch the worst of the hull damage if we can find a calm bay. Jury-rig masts to replace some of what we've lost. But Tribune, we're not going to be fighting any naval battles. We can barely sail, let alone maneuver in combat."

"What about the others?"

"Forannan signals that the *Vires* is in worse shape than us. Lost the mainmast entirely, and he's got flooding in two compartments.

270

Fuscus on the *Asturia* reports structural damage to his bow from that big wave. He's holding together, but one more storm like that ..." Crispinus shrugged.

"Your recommendation?"

"We turn back. Now. Make for Port Amicitiae, get proper repairs. We've two ships completely unaccounted for and the three ships we have left aren't fit for anything but limping home. Continuing east into unknown waters with hostile forces, I don't recommend it."

Claudius looked at the battered remnants of his fleet. The captain made sense. Every logical argument said to turn back.

And yet.

"No," he said finally.

"Tribune ..."

"I understand your point, Captain, but we continue on our original course. If we turn back now, it'll be a year before another expedition can be mounted, maybe longer, and one of the goals of this whole thing is to end the war sooner ... not later."

"We'll be no good to the Empire if we sink."

"Then we won't sink." Claudius pointed to a dark land mass on the horizon. "The cove is still ahead of us, yes? We can cut timber and use what we find there to repair the ships as best we can."

"And then?"

"Then we complete the mission."

Crispinus stood rigid for a long moment, clearly fighting between his duty as a sailor and following orders.

Finally, he nodded and said, "Of course."

He turned and began issuing orders. The helmsman adjusted their heading, pointing the battered *Nauta* toward the island as signal flags went up, directing the other two to follow.

Claudius remained at the rail, studying the jungle-covered island ahead. The missing two ships were a problem. Not insurmountable, but it would make their job here harder.

But what other choice did they have?

Carthage

Praetorian Commander Pinarius finished his mental calculation. "Cut everyone down to quarter rations. That might buy us another week. The children get half-ration shares."

He wished he didn't have civilians here, but when the quarter fell to the rebels and they'd pulled back to the palace, the Hardliners had started executing 'collaborators.'

He couldn't throw the administrative staff that had been in the building to their deaths, or deny the families that had been able to make it here from gaining protection.

Which left him too many mouths to feed and not enough supplies to do it with.

"The men won't fight well on empty stomachs."

"They will fight worse with no stomachs at all," Pinarius said. "We need time. We still have ships in the harbor. We just need to wait for them to relieve us."

A young legionary, his face smudged with dirt, appeared at the larder's arched entrance, his chest heaving from a hard run. "Commander. Sentries report movement on the south lane."

"Understood," he said, giving one last look at the quartermaster. "Get it taken care of."

With that, Pinarius left him to it.

The government complex had never been a fort. It had been designed to show the wealth and opulence of the Carthaginian emperors and was a sprawl of marble courts and offices layered with ornamental ponds and a colonnade that had impressed petitioners for a century.

When the quarter began to burn, the Praetorians had pulled back through those lanes inside the complex and made the place into a barricaded warren using pieces of furniture, carts and

272

everything in between to create firing alleys and walls to stop the enemy from just running right in.

He crossed to the central tower on top of the forum, taking the spiral steps two at a time until he reached the platform where his lookout maintained his post. From here, he could see the harbor out in the distance, Britannian ships riding at anchor.

The ships might as well have been in Devnum for all the good they did him.

"Report," Pinarius said.

The sentry pointed southeast toward the commercial quarter, where a wider street led to the palace's outer wall. "Movement all night, Commander. They've been dragging something heavy through the streets. They've been gathering since midnight."

A team of oxen emerged from behind a row of shops, straining against their harnesses as they pulled a wheeled platform. Even in the dim light, Pinarius recognized the distinctive barrel shape mounted on the carriage.

"So they did get the cannon when Cossus's men retreated."

"They won't have much ammunition for it," the sentry said. "He only had a handful of gunpowder charges, and if they try to use loose powder to make their own, they're going to get the ratios wrong and crack the tubes."

Pinarius nodded, not that it offered much comfort. The makeshift walls they had built could withstand musket balls, but they weren't made to withstand artillery. Even a few cannonballs could breach their defenses.

They were just straight tubes, thankfully. Cormac had taken all of the actual artillery with him when he'd left the city. While he watched, teams of rebels worked to position the cannon, while others hauled wooden barriers into place around it.

"How many are coming?" Pinarius asked.

"Based on the movement I've seen, I'd say three hundred. Maybe four."

A second artillery piece appeared as the eastern horizon began to lighten. Another howitzer, dragged into position fifty meters from the first. The rebels had found both guns that had been lost in the western quarter's collapse.

The men manning the guns finished their preparations as dawn approached and loaded the first shell. It wasn't pretty. These weren't trained artillerymen, but they didn't need to be experts to pound the palace at close range.

"Signal the guard posts," he ordered. "All men to defensive positions. Send runners to the barricades and tell the squad leaders to distribute ammunition. Try to get every man sixty rounds, or as close to that as they can before the stores run out."

The sentry dispatched a legionary with the orders while Pinarius studied the rebel positions. They'd chosen their spots well, placing the cannons where they could target the main avenue and the adjacent courtyards. The outer defensive positions would crumble under concentrated fire.

Throughout the complex, praetorians took positions behind the improvised barricades they'd constructed over the past week. They were as ready as they'd ever be when the first shell screamed overhead.

Pinarius threw himself flat as the projectile struck the complex's eastern colonnade. Marble columns shattered under the impact, cascading debris flew across the courtyard while dust and smoke billowed from the destruction. The explosion left his ears ringing, but through the noise, he heard shouts from the defenders manning the outer barricades.

"Return fire!" he yelled.

The complex's two remaining cannons replied from positions near the central buildings. As with the ones the rebels had, they were old pieces firing solid shot and not the new guns firing the fused shells.

He'd give his left arm for one of those.

Their barrels spit flame and smoke toward the rebel positions. One shot fell short, gouging a crater in the avenue's paving stones. The other struck a building corner, showering the first cannon crew with debris but leaving the gun intact.

The second rebel cannon fired thirty seconds later.

This time, they'd found the range. The projectile slammed into the ornamental fountain at the complex's main entrance, sending water and marble fragments in all directions. The decorative structure collapsed completely, its rubble blocking part of the avenue while creating new cover for advancing infantry.

He scrambled to his feet and grabbed the sentry by the shoulder. "Get down to the outer courtyards. Check our firing positions and make sure the men understand their withdrawal routes. Once they start their assault, we'll have to fall back through the defensive lanes."

The soldier nodded and disappeared down the stairs while Pinarius remained on the platform. From here, he could direct the defense and coordinate with his scattered units positioned throughout the complex's maze of buildings and courtyards.

The third shell struck, hitting the marble portico that covered the main avenue's entrance to the government buildings. Ancient columns cracked and toppled, their capitals crashing into the courtyard with thunderous impacts that shook the ground beneath his feet.

In the courtyards below, praetorians emerged from covered positions and took their places behind the improvised barricades. Most carried the new lever-action rifles, their bronze mechanisms designed for rapid, sustained fire. The defensive positions had been arranged to create interlocking fields of fire throughout the complex's open spaces.

The fourth cannon shot accomplished what the previous three had started. The impact brought down the remaining section of the entrance portico, completely blocking the main avenue with fallen marble and creating a rubble barrier that infantry would have to climb over to advance.

Pinarius allowed himself a small smile. If they wanted to help him create more barricades, they were welcome to it.

The prelude done, the attack came.

Unfortunately, the rebels had planned for the damage done by their pilfered cannons. Instead of charging straight down the blocked avenue, they spread out through the side passages and smaller courtyards, approaching the defensive positions from multiple directions simultaneously.

Mago's Hardliners poured into the complex like floodwater through broken channels. Some clambered over the rubble barrier in the main avenue while others filtered through the narrow passages between buildings. Their black banners streamed behind them as they rushed toward the first line of barricades.

The distinctive sharp cracks of lever-action rifles erupted from defensive positions throughout the outer courtyards. Bullets tore into the advancing rebels, dropping men among the ornamental gardens and marble walkways. Bodies fell beside decorative pools while the surviving attackers used whatever cover they could find.

The rebels had courage and numbers, but the praetorians held superior positions with better weapons. Concentrated rifle fire from behind solid barricades cut down the first assault waves before they could reach the defensive line.

It wouldn't stop them forever.

The complex was too large to defend completely. Hardliners found gaps between the barricaded positions, slipping through unguarded passages and emerging behind some of the outer defensive posts. Hand-to-hand fighting erupted in the eastern courtyard as rebels overran an isolated position.

The cannons had fallen silent after their initial bombardment, their limited ammunition reserves forcing the attackers to conserve shells or maybe a reticence to hit their own men. Not that it mattered. The enemy still had hundreds of fighters who pressed forward despite heavy casualties.

Pinarius descended from the tower and made his way through the maze of defensive positions toward the sound of the heaviest fighting. The eastern courtyard had become a killing ground where praetorians fired from behind overturned marble benches and windows of the adjacent buildings while rebels advanced through the formal gardens.

"How are we on ammunition?" he asked the centurion commanding the position.

"Down to about thirty rounds per man," came the reply.

The officer squeezed his trigger and a rebel attempting to cross between two ornamental trees fell backward into a flower bed.

The second wave had spread out across multiple courtyards, taking shelter behind decorative walls and garden features while working their way toward the defended positions. Some carried muskets and fired at the praetorians whenever they exposed themselves to shoot.

His men were going to run out of ammunition before they ran out of targets.

"Signal the withdrawal," Pinarius ordered. "Pull back to the second line. Use the prepared routes through the central building."

The order passed from position to position while the battle continued. Praetorians began their fighting retreat through the complex's interior passages, moving from the outer courtyards toward the central administrative areas where additional barricades had been prepared.

The withdrawal became a running battle through marble corridors and office chambers. Rebels pursued aggressively, maybe feeling victory was close with the defenders giving up ground.

Not that it all went smoothly. Some Hardliners found alternate routes through the building complex, forcing firefights in unexpected locations.

It was unavoidable. He just didn't have enough men to guard every possible entrance.

Pinarius found himself directing traffic at an intersection where three withdrawal routes converged. Wounded praetorians limped past while their comrades provided covering fire down the corridors they'd just abandoned. The sound of breaking furniture and shattering marble sounded through the buildings as rebels smashed their way through abandoned barricades.

A group of Hardliners appeared at the far end of the main corridor. Pinarius threw himself behind a marble pillar as musket-fired bullets chipped stone fragments from its surface. He returned fire, forcing the attackers to seek cover among the office doorways.

"This position's compromised," he shouted to the retreating praetorians. "Move to the central building."

The second defensive line held for perhaps an hour before pressure from multiple directions forced another withdrawal. Someone in the rebel forces must have spent time in the complex, maybe during the tenure of the previous owners.

Not all of the men from the old regime were with the pretender's people, after all.

Either way, they knew the complex's layout and were using that knowledge to their advantage, hitting several positions simultaneously to prevent mutual support during the withdrawal.

By midmorning, the defenders had been pushed back to the central administrative building and its immediate courtyards. He'd lost two-thirds of the complex in one attack.

The rebels brought up their artillery for the final phase of the assault. Both cannons were positioned in courtyards with clear fields of fire toward the administrative building's main entrances. The crews couldn't have much powder or ball left, but they clearly still planned to make the stolen weapons count.

"Get everyone inside," Pinarius ordered. "Barricade the main entrances and prepare firing positions at the windows. We'll make our stand here."

The first cannon shot struck the building's eastern wing, bringing down part of the outer wall and filling several offices with debris. The marble facings that had once displayed Carthaginian wealth shook under the impact.

Civilians screamed in the interior chambers while praetorians helped dig out anyone trapped by falling masonry. The complex's staff, their families, and various petitioners who had been caught in the building when the rebellion began huddled in the central rooms while the battle raged around them.

There was nowhere else to fall back to now.

A second shell followed three minutes later. The impact punched through a large window and exploded inside what had been the treasury office, killing two defenders and wounding several others. The blast brought down a section of ceiling, making part of the first floor too dangerous to occupy.

"We can't take much more of this," a centurion said, blood trickling from a cut on his forehead where flying stone had grazed him. "The whole building's shaking apart."

As if to prove his point, another shell struck near the main entrance, collapsing the ornate doorframe and part of the adjoining wall.

Pinarius surveyed their shrinking defensive perimeter. They'd been pushed back from the outer rooms to the central offices, and even those wouldn't be defendable if the artillery continued. Perhaps fifty effective fighters remained, plus the wounded who could still hold weapons, and civilians.

The rebels must have realized their ammunition situation was critical. Instead of wasting their final shells on individual rooms, they positioned both cannons for a strike against the building's main support structure.

"Get everyone to the administrative building," Pinarius ordered. "Move the wounded and the civilians to the basement but hold the stairs. We'll make our final stand there."

The administrative building sat in the center of the palace complex. A small building that mostly held the central tower and stairwells leading down to a basement and up to the tower, along with maybe half a dozen offices. It was more a central node than a building in its own right.

It meant he'd be completely locked in, with minimal supplies in the basement and no way to get out, as the only entrances into the administrative wing were through the parts of the complex the rebels now held.

Unless his people wanted to start jumping out of windows into courtyards that the rebels also held.

The evacuation proceeded while rebel musket fire kept the defenders pinned at their window positions. Women carried children down narrow service stairs while praetorians provided covering fire from the upper floors. Several men were hit during the movement, but all the civilians reached the relative safety of the basement chambers.

Both cannons fired shells that struck within seconds of each other, targeting the building's central supports. The entire structure shuddered as load-bearing pillars cracked and shifted, but held.

Mostly.

The building's partial collapse sealed several entrances while leaving others partially blocked. Rebels would need time to clear passages or find alternate routes inside, but they controlled the entire government complex except for the damaged administrative center.

Pinarius climbed back through the wreckage until he reached what remained of the signal tower. The tower still rose above the surrounding debris, and it still had the flagpole in place, stretching even higher than the rest of the buildings. He pulled out several flags, hoping the ships in the harbor were still watching as he started sending them up in order.

The run of flags spelled out a message.

"PALACE FALLING, COMPLEX LOST, CAN HOLD WEEK MAXIMUM, REQUIRE IMMEDIATE RELIEF."

Once that was done, he put up one last flag, leaving it in place instead of pulling it back down.

It only read, DANGER.

He just hoped those people in the ships could figure something out, or this place would end up being his tomb.

Chapter 25

Hellespont, Middle Sea

"Message from the *Ghaoth Álainn*, Admiral," Valdar's first mate said.

Valdar looked up to the signal mast and then out to the distance where the smaller schooner was cutting through the waves toward them.

"They report fifteen Eastern warships clearing the narrows in line of battle. He believes it isn't a feint this time, they've decided to finally make the breakthrough."

Valerius was a good man. If he said they were finally making their play, then they probably were.

"It was bound to happen sooner or later," Valdar said. "Signal the fleet to form line of battle. Include the number estimates and make it clear we're about to be outnumbered and in serious action."

Outnumbered was an understatement. After a series of probing actions over the last month, his fleet had been whittled down. Even with reinforcements from the African fleet, he had fewer ships now than when he'd set out from Malta a month ago to block the path from the Black Sea.

He'd hoped new ships coming out of the drydocks would have increased his numbers, but a terse message from the Empress apologized that the ships had been reassigned to a higher priority and he would have to make do with what he had.

He wasn't sure what higher priority there could be than keeping the enemy out of their shipping lanes, but it wasn't his place to question royal authority. Just to carry out his orders.

Although it looked like it might be the end of him and his men. In the days of solid shot, clever tactics let him take out enemy ships, but explosive shells meant death for a wooden ship.

If he was lucky, he'd take out most of the enemy before the last of his ships were sent to the bottom.

But it was his duty, and he'd do it.

By the time his ships were in line, the Eastern fleet was already visible as dark shapes against the grey waters, their square-rigged sails bellied with the morning wind. They sailed in loose formation. It was sloppy, but with their numbers, they could be.

Valdar collapsed his spyglass. "Signal the line to close up. We'll give them a proper broadside before they scatter us."

He was proud of his captains, who formed up the battle line well, holding good position thanks to the constant drilling they did. Each caravel settled into position exactly two ship-lengths behind the vessel ahead, their gun ports open and cannons run out. The *Bellona* led the line, followed by the *Aquila, Aeolus, Europa, Hasta, Spes, Dumnos*, with the *Praetor* bringing up the rear.

The range closed steadily. Three thousand meters. Two thousand five hundred. The Eastern formation began to tighten as their commanders seemed to realize his ships were going to stand and fight, rather than scatter and flee.

"Gun crews to stations," Valdar called.

The men had almost certainly been by their guns ever since they began to sail into formation, but he was a believer that there was a comfort in tradition and protocol.

Two thousand meters. The Eastern fleet stretched across a front nearly twice as wide as his own line. Their lead ships would be able to concentrate fire on his van while their trailing vessels swept around his flanks.

At eighteen hundred meters, flashes erupted along the Eastern line as it began to turn slightly, allowing broadsides of the front ships to come to bear. Cannon smoke billowed across the water, followed seconds later by the rolling thunder of their broadsides. Waterspouts erupted around his ship as the initial salvos fell short, though several shells burst close enough to shower the *Bellona's* deck with spray.

"Steady as she goes," Valdar told his helmsman. "Wait for the command."

Another Eastern broadside crashed out. This time, the range was better. A shell burst against the *Aquila's* bow, sending splinters flying across her forecastle. Another exploded just off the *Europa's* starboard quarter, close enough to tear holes in her sail.

Fifteen hundred meters. The Eastern ships were close enough now that Valdar could make out individual figures on their quarterdecks.

"Signal the fleet," Valdar commanded. "Engage the enemy."

The signal flags whipped up to the masthead. Along the Britannian line, gun captains raised their slow matches.

"Fire!"

Eight broadsides erupted nearly simultaneously, starting with the *Bellona* and rattling out from there. The *Bellona* shuddered as her fourteen guns discharged in sequence, the explosive shells arcing across the diminishing gap between the fleets. Valdar watched through the smoke as his shots found their targets.

Not all of them, of course, but enough.

The lead Eastern ship staggered as two shells burst against her hull near the waterline. Another enemy vessel's mainmast toppled as a shell exploded among her rigging.

The Easterners replied immediately. Their superior numbers allowed them to pour a devastating volume of fire into the Britannian line. The *Bellona* rocked as shells burst around her, one explosion close enough to the starboard rail that Valdar felt the heat wash across his face.

"Reload and fire as you bear," he shouted to his gun captains.

The battle settled into a thunderous exchange of broadsides. Smoke from hundreds of cannon obscured the water between the fleets, turning the morning into artificial twilight. Through the haze, Valdar caught glimpses of damaged rigging and splintered hulls on both sides.

The *Aquila* had taken position at the head of the Eastern line where she could support the flagship. Now three enemy vessels converged their fire on her, recognizing the threat posed by Captain Einar's accurate gunnery. Shell after shell crashed into the *Aquila*'s hull, each explosion sending up gouts of smoke and debris.

"She's taking too much punishment," Valdar muttered, watching through his glass as another salvo struck home.

A massive detonation erupted amidships on the *Aquila*. When the smoke cleared, Valdar could see water already pouring through a gaping hole in her starboard side. The ship listed heavily to starboard as her crew fought desperately to plug the breach.

"Signal to *Aquila*," Valdar ordered. "Can they maintain station?"

Before the signal could be sent, another concentrated salvo struck the damaged ship. The explosive shells opened her hull like a flower, and thousands of tons of seawater rushed into her lower decks. The *Aquila* rolled onto her side with terrible slowness. Men leaped from her deck as she capsized completely, her masts disappearing beneath the churning surface. In less than three minutes, she was gone.

"Close the gap," Valdar commanded his flag captain. The *Bellona* and *Aeolus* moved to fill the hole left by the *Aquila*'s destruction, but the Eastern fleet had already recognized the opportunity.

Two enemy ships pressed forward against the weakened Britannian left flank. Their concentrated fire fell upon the *Aeolus*, Captain Fabius's vessel, struggling to maintain position as shells burst around her.

The mainmast of the *Aeolus* cracked, the entire spar toppled forward, dragging a tangle of rigging and canvas across her gun deck. Fires started immediately as burning wadding from the enemy shells ignited the fallen sailcloth.

Through the smoke, Valdar saw Fabius on his quarterdeck, sword raised as he directed his crew's firefighting efforts. The *Aeolus* continued to fire even as flames spread across her deck, her gun crews working their cannons despite the chaos around them.

But the Eastern advantage in numbers was beginning to tell. Their ships could concentrate overwhelming firepower on individual Britannian vessels while his own line was forced to spread their fire across too many targets.

The *Europa* suffered the next major damage. A shell burst directly against her stern, destroying her rudder and tiller mechanism. The ship began to drift sideways between the two fleets, unable to maintain her position in the line.

"She's out of control," the *Bellona's* sailing master called.

Captain Hakon and his crew fought desperately to rig an emergency steering system, but more shells found the helpless vessel. Fires erupted below her quarterdeck, sending dense smoke streaming from her companionways. The *Europa* drifted directly into the field of fire between the two fleets, taking hits from both sides as she wallowed helplessly.

Not that all of the damage was limited to his own ships.

An Eastern ship took a direct hit from one of Valdar's broadsides and began settling at the stern, her crew abandoning ship as water flooded her magazines. Another took three shells on its deck, toppling its masts and killing most of its sailors in one go, but it was small consolation. The Britannian line was disintegrating under the weight of superior numbers.

The *Bellona* herself had taken multiple hits. Her starboard bulwark was shattered for twenty feet where another blast had swept away two gun crews. Blood slicked the deck planking around the dismounted cannons.

"Signal the fleet," Valdar decided. "Close with the enemy. Take them to grips."

If his ships were going to die, they would die fighting at close range where their fellows would hesitate to fire lest they hit their friends and cannon fire itself would be as dangerous for the firing ship as the target. The signal flags went up, and his surviving captains acknowledged immediately.

The *Praetor* was the first to respond. Captain Livia brought her ship around in a tight turn that put her directly alongside an Eastern vessel. At a range of less than fifty meters, she fired her full broadside into her opponent's gun deck.

The Eastern ship's side exploded inward. Her cannons were dismounted, and her crew devastated by the point-blank fire. Flames immediately spread through her shattered interior as the *Praetor* sailed past, already reloading for another target.

But even this aggressive tactic couldn't overcome the numerical disparity. Two Eastern ships broke free from the main battle and made directly for the *Bellona*, recognizing that destroying the flagship would collapse Britannian resistance entirely.

Shell after shell crashed into the *Bellona's* hull. Her mizzen mast went over the side, taking her sailors with it. An explosion on her gun deck wiped out an entire cannon crew and started a fire near the magazine that had her crew frantically forming bucket chains.

Valdar found himself gripping the quarterdeck rail as his flagship absorbed punishment. The battle was clearly lost. The *Aeolus* had struck her colors, her hull too damaged to continue fighting. The *Europa* was sinking by the bow, her crew abandoning ship. Only five Britannian vessels remained even partially effective against at least ten Eastern ships that were already beginning to push past his shattered formation.

The only solace he had was that he wouldn't be around to see the disaster that would result from his failure.

"Admiral," called his flag captain. "Two enemy vessels are closing to finish us."

Valdar could see them through the smoke, fresh Eastern ships with undamaged hulls converging on his crippled flagship. In minutes, the *Bellona* would follow the *Aquila* to the bottom.

Not that he was giving up. He was ready to fight to the end.

"All guns," Valdar commanded. "Fire as you bear."

The surviving cannons of his flagship discharged one final broadside. Several shots struck home, but it was futile. The Eastern ships continued their approach, their gun crews preparing for the killing salvo.

Then the world exploded!

A series of detonations erupted through the Eastern vanguard, each far more violent than any explosive shell Valdar had ever witnessed. The blasts were so powerful they seemed to tear holes in the air itself. One Eastern caravel seemed to break in half in a ball of fire and debris. Another had her entire starboard side ripped away, her hull opening like a gutted fish.

Valdar stared in shock at the destruction. The explosive shells were deadly, but his ships weren't doing this kind of damage. No cannon he'd ever seen had. Through the smoke and confusion, he searched for the source of this impossible bombardment.

Even following the trajectory back, it took a minute for him to find the ship, mostly because it was much, much further back than any of his ships would have been able to fire from, let alone fire with any kind of accuracy.

The vessel that emerged from the haze bore no resemblance to any warship he had ever seen. Long and sleek, she rode low in the water with a profile that made every surrounding caravel look clumsy and slow. No masts rose from her deck, instead, a pair of funnels poured dark smoke into the morning air as she moved with impossible speed through the battle, more like one of the river boats than a sailing ship.

"By the gods ..." breathed the sailing master.

Before anyone could answer, the strange vessel fired again. Valdar saw her guns, not pointing out of ports in the side but from a large turtle-like thing sitting on the bow with long tubes sticking out that turned slightly as it hunted for a new target. The cannon didn't roll back when it fired. The tubes kind of compressed for a moment before the entire thing was washed out in a bright light. The sound of their discharge was unlike anything he'd heard before, a deeper, more violent roar that seemed to shake the water itself.

One of the two shells struck their target with horrific effect. The Eastern ship erupted in flames as the entire bow was ripped apart in a tremendous explosion. And then, in less than a minute, it fired again. Another vessel staggered, struck by a single shell, broke completely in half, her bow and stern sections rising at impossible angles before sliding beneath the surface.

"The *Victorious*," Valdar said. "The new warship we were promised."

He'd been expecting the thing for a month. It had been described as a new all-steel warship, but he'd expected something squat and fat, like a larger version of the riverboats.

He'd never expected something like this.

It was a predator, hunting through the enemy fleet, taking down ships one after another, moving faster than any of the other ships around it, friend or foe, completely ignoring wind and tide.

The Eastern formation, moments before on the verge of total victory, dissolved into chaos and panic. Their commanders, faced with a threat they could not comprehend, lost all coordination. Some ships turned to engage the newcomer while others maintained their attacks on the surviving Britannian vessels, creating confusion that the steel warship exploited ruthlessly.

Now mixed in the enemy formation, the rear turret was able to get into the action, allowing it an almost constant barrage of fire. Each shell that struck an enemy vessel produced catastrophic damage.

Several Eastern captains, showing admirable courage if poor judgment, attempted to engage the *Victorious* directly. Their broadsides erupted against her gray hull in bright flashes of fire and smoke. Valdar expected to see damage, some sign that conventional weapons could still affect this revolutionary warship.

The shells exploded against the side of the ship and … apparently had no impact on the vessel at all. What would have shattered wooden hulls and killed dozens of men just left dents in the steel plating. The *Victorious* continued her path of destruction without pause, her turrets rotating to engage new targets while her hull shrugged off hits.

The slaughter was complete. Eastern ships died one after another, their crews helpless against weapons they could neither match nor survive. The few vessels that attempted to flee found the steel warship firing after them, its new cannon apparently not just more powerful, but with a longer range and better accuracy.

Within twenty minutes of her arrival, the *Victorious* had reduced the Eastern fleet to scattered wreckage. A handful of survivors turned and ran for the safety of the Black Sea, their breakout attempt utterly crushed. The steel warship pursued them briefly, her guns claiming one final victim before she turned back toward the battle zone.

"Lower boats for search and rescue. Survivors take priority," Valdar said, his senses coming back to him.

The *Europa* was settling rapidly by the bow, her crew already in the water. The *Aeolus* might be saved if they could get pumps aboard quickly enough. Throughout the battle zone, men clung to debris and called for help.

His fleet had been destroyed, but he wasn't even sure that mattered.

They'd just changed naval combat. Permanently.

East Indies

"Keep those supports steady," Claudius called to the work crew bracing the ship's starboard side.

The vessel listed badly where storm damage had torn through her planking. Two carpenters worked with adzes, shaping a replacement beam from the jungle wood while others heated tar in iron pots over driftwood fires.

Fourteen men were working on the *Nauta* alone, with similar crews spread across the other damaged vessels. They'd been at it for more than a week, trying to get his ships back in shape to sail after the storm.

They almost hadn't made it to the protected cove at all. The ships had been so badly damaged. The fact that he'd only lost two was honestly a miracle.

Crispinus emerged from beneath the *Nauta's* hull, wood shavings clinging to his tunic. "Six more planks on the port side and she'll be seaworthy, I think."

"How long?"

"Two days if the wood holds. These jungle trees aren't oak. The grain's different, softer in places, and it's got to be treated and dried."

Claudius nodded. It wasn't like he had much of a choice. The ships would take as long as they would take to repair. He had no doubt the captains were working as hard as they could to get the small fleet seaworthy.

He turned his attention to a group of legionaries sawing through a massive trunk with a two-man saw. Thankfully, the carpenter, Asturia, had been with Valdar in Africa and had a wider understanding of timber from outside of the continent.

Further down the beach, smoke rose from the tar fires where crews worked on other vessels. The *Vires* sat higher in the water after they'd pumped out most of the seawater from her holds. Her crew had lashed together a crude mast from three smaller trees, not pretty but functional enough to carry canvas.

"Tribune." One of the Mpongo scouts jogged toward him from the jungle edge.

He'd sent their tribal allies to scout the jungle around them, just in case there were natives that might cause them issues.

"Problems?"

"Ships. Two of them, from that way," he said, pointing to the southern edge of the cove entrance. "They look to be coming straight here."

Claudius grabbed his spyglass from where it hung on a salvaged piece of rigging.

"Eastern vessels?" he asked, hoping the scout knew the difference.

"No, like yours."

Could it be? Without waiting for more answers, Claudius jogged around the edge of the cove, followed by the tribesman, and climbed the rocky outcrop that formed the cove's southern boundary. Once at the top, he extended the spyglass and swept it across the horizon.

There. Two sets of sails, both showing damage but unmistakably not the square, ribbed sails the Easterners used. Claudius searched the sea around them, but it looked clear. They were not followed.

Hopefully.

The *Ulderica* limped badly, her mainsail gone entirely. In its place, they'd rigged what looked like spare canvas from belowdecks, barely enough to catch wind. The *Doirinn* followed close behind, riding lower in the water than she should.

"They're taking on water," he said to no one in particular.

The *Ulderica* entered the cove first, her reduced sail making navigation easier in the confined space. Otarus brought her straight toward the beach, not bothering with an anchor. The ship's keel scraped sand fifty meters from shore, grinding to a halt in the shallows.

Claudius hurried back around the cove to the beach where they'd landed. Otarus was coming over the side when he got to them, not waiting for a ladder, wading through waist-deep water.

"Thought we'd lost you," Claudius said, as the man made it to dry land.

Otarus wrung water from his tunic. "Thought the same about you. That storm was like nothing I've ever seen. Waves tall as buildings, wind that could tear the clothes off your back."

"I know. We barely made it ourselves. Lost a lot of men and took almost as much damage as you."

Behind him, the *Doirinn* approached the beach. Captain Brocan brought her in more carefully, but Claudius could see the strain in how the ship moved. She sat too low, sluggish in her responses.

"What happened to your mainsail?"

"Torn away completely. We tried to reef it when the wind picked up, but it went all at once. Lost two men who were trying to secure the lines."

Brocan waded ashore, his round face haggard. A fresh scar ran along his left cheek, still pink and healing.

"How is she?" Claudius asked.

"She's taking water badly. We've been bailing constantly for eight days and there's a crack along the starboard side you could put your fist through."

"Show me," Claudius said, waving over his carpenter.

They walked first to the *Ulderica*. Up close, the battering she'd taken was even more apparent. Gouges ran along her hull where debris had struck during the storm. The rudder assembly hung at an odd angle, held by a single pin that had somehow survived.

"We lost steering on day four," Otarus explained. "Been using sweeps and what little sail we could rig to maintain direction. Takes six men working constantly just to keep her on course."

Claudius ran his hand along a section of damaged planking. The wood felt soft, waterlogged. "You're lucky she held together."

"Lucky. Yes." Otarus's tone suggested he didn't feel particularly fortunate.

The *Doirinn* was even worse. The crack Brocan had mentioned ran for seven meters along the starboard side, starting above the waterline but descending below it amidships. Seawater seeped through despite the canvas and tar they'd packed into the gap.

"Started small," Brocan said. "Just a split in the wood when we hit that first big wave. But it kept working itself wider. We've stuffed everything we could find into it. Spare clothes, sailcloth, even pages from the navigation logs."

"Your cargo?"

"Most of it's gone. The waves breached our forward hold on the first night. Washed out near everything. Food, water barrels, medical supplies. We saved the weapons and powder, kept those in the aft hold, but ..." He spread his hands helplessly.

Otarus confirmed similar losses. "We managed to keep more of our water, but the food's mostly gone. Been living on half rations for several days."

"Crispinus," he called to the captain. "Get these men food and fresh water, whatever we can spare."

"That won't be much," Crispinus warned quietly.

"I know, but they need something, and they need it now."

Claudius considered their situation. He still had all of his ships, although all were damaged to varying degrees. Between what these ships lost and the losses from flooded holds and goods swept over, he was down maybe fifteen percent of his supplies. That was bad, of course, but not critical.

They could still do this.

"We'll get your ships repaired," he said, "and hopefully be on our way in a week, maybe two."

"With what?" Brocan gestured at the jungle. "These trees? They're not made for shipbuilding."

"They'll have to do."

Forannan approached from where he'd been supervising repairs on the *Vires*. The stocky captain had lost weight during their voyage, his belt pulled tight to keep his trousers in place. "Good to see you both alive," he said to Otarus and Brocan. "We'd given up hope."

"As we had for you," Otarus replied. "That storm scattered us across half the ocean."

A group of Mpongo warriors emerged from the jungle, carrying the carcass of a wild boar between them. Others followed with gathered fruits and what appeared to be edible roots. That solved some of the supply issues. The lost food could be replaced by hunting and fishing here. Since they needed at least a week to repair the boats, it wouldn't be that hard to build a temporary smokehouse and dry some of the meat for the voyage.

He'd have to talk to some of the tribesmen, but they might even be able to find fruit or the like, which the Consul had stressed years ago as being critical on long sea voyages.

"There's another issue," Otarus said quietly. "Some of my men are talking about turning back. They say these are all bad omens and signs we shouldn't be out here any longer."

"Mine, too," Brocan admitted. "Hard to blame them after what we've been through."

Claudius had expected this. Sailors were superstitious by nature, and this expedition had already faced more hardships than most. "Gather all the crews. I need to address them."

The crews formed a rough semicircle on the beach, perhaps five hundred men in total between sailors, legionaries, and tribesmen. Many bore injuries from the storm or the repair work.

"I know what some of you are thinking," Claudius began. "It looked as if we'd lost ships, supplies, and good men, and while our lost ships have returned to us, the rest is true. I know for many of you, the smart move would be to turn back, return to Devnum, and report that the mission was impossible, but consider this: We've sailed further than any Britannian vessel in history. We've survived a storm that should have killed us all, and we're still here, still capable of continuing."

"Capable of dying is more like it," someone called out.

"You're right. We might die. But every soldier and sailor who serves the Empire accepts that risk. The question is whether we die trying to accomplish something important, or whether we turn back and let fear make that decision for us. The war against the Easterners has dragged on for two years, and it could drag on for many more. We know the Easterners' homeland is out here, months of marching for our furthest forces in Sardinia to get there, and that would only be if there was no one to oppose them. With the Easterners fighting us every step of the way, it could take a decade to reach their home and finally end them as a threat.

The Consul believes this mission we have been sent on will allow us to take the fight to them right away, much sooner than if we have to fight our way here. For each man we lose on this trip, how many thousands do we save back home? We've come too far to quit now. Yes, the repairs will be difficult. Yes, we've lost supplies. But we're not defeated. We have skilled craftsmen among us, we have the Mpongo warriors to help us hunt and forage, and we have the knowledge that what we're doing matters."

He paused, meeting as many eyes as he could. "I won't force anyone to continue. When we leave this cove, any man who wants to remain behind can do so. We'll leave what supplies we can spare, and you can wait for the next supply convoy to pass through. But I believe most of you are made of stronger stuff than that."

No one made to counter him. He didn't think they would. As offers go, it wasn't a fair one, being marooned here on an island that may well never see one of their convoys and could as easily mean their deaths as continuing with the fleet. Even the most superstitious among them would take staying with their comrades over being left behind.

But it did distract them, for now. They needed to be focused on their jobs, on repairing their ships, and he wasn't about to give up this mission now.

Not when they'd come so far.

Chapter 26

Carthage

The warehouse was the same one where they met the first time, still with the same stink of old fish and sea. It seemed unlikely it was being used during all this turmoil, and a part of Lucilla's brain wondered if that was a smell that went away.

The rest of her, however, was focused on the man standing in the center of the building, a loose rabble of men spread out behind him.

Lucilla entered with only two praetorians this time, which caused some consternation among her guards. She wanted to send a message of confidence, and she didn't have time to do this carefully anymore. Still, there was a whole contingent waiting outside of the warehouse, ready to storm it, should things go badly.

"Thank you for coming," she said when she reached Adherbal. "I have given your offer some thought and, while I cannot agree to the terms as you gave them, I am willing to recognize that Carthage requires special consideration given its history and current circumstances."

"What does special consideration mean?" he asked.

"That you are right, Carthage needs to be headed by one of its own. Someone who knows the city's troubles and needs and can best keep it from devolving into this kind of chaos. Which is why I am prepared to offer you the governorship of Carthage."

"What?" he said, completely surprised. "Me?"

"Yes. You. I know you are no politician, but the last thing this city needs is someone who wants to control the city for their own power. You have put your neck out for your people, and that speaks to your character. To be clear, the city will still be under Britannian rule, and you will be, in effect, a Britannian civil servant, but you'll serve as governor with full authority over internal civil administration. Tax collection, civic projects, trade regulations within the city proper. These will be yours to manage, although there will be requirements handed down to you from the Senate and myself that you will be responsible for carrying out if you are to remain in that position. In addition, the port remains under direct Imperial control, as does the military garrison. I know that takes away some of your autonomy, but it is our security guarantee that the city will not fall to fracture again."

"So I would be a Britannian puppet."

"No, you would be its governor with the same responsibilities and authorities as any provincial governor in the Empire. You'll report to me and the Senate, yes, and you'll be expected to meet Imperial standards for governance, but within those parameters, Carthage's internal affairs would be yours to direct."

"And what of representation? My people want their voices heard in decisions that affect them."

"Every major administrative position in your administration, aside from military, will be available to Carthaginian representation. You are free to form a council of citizens to help guide your decisions if you like, although that council cannot overrule the requirements handed down to you from the Empire. But your people will have the opportunity to shape policy as you see fit, under those restrictions."

Adherbal walked to one of the warehouse's broken windows, looking out toward the smoke rising from various districts. "These terms, even if I could accept them, might not be accepted by my supporters. Many of them have suffered under the hands of your rule, and they want the occupiers gone, not legitimized under a puppet government."

"I understand that, but this is the best offer you are going to get. Let me clarify the situation for you. The assault on the palace recently nearly succeeded. Your faction wasn't part of it, but both of the other factions were, which is why they were able to almost take it."

"Impossible. They hate each other more than they hate you."

"It seems they have put those differences aside for the time being, because what I am saying is true."

Adherbal turned back to face her, a new concern on his face. Lucilla, however, wasn't done laying out the facts.

"If those two factions have found common cause, even temporarily, they have the combined strength to take the palace. It will fall soon, and I will not abandon my people. What's more, I want you to consider what happens after the palace falls. Do you imagine Gerisbal and Mago will share power? The moment they have finished off one enemy in the city, they'll turn on their next one. You. The city will burn while they fight for supremacy."

"They might ..."

"Don't be naive. You're already branded as collaborators by both sides. They will not tolerate a third power base in the city, especially one that tried to negotiate with the Empire. It is true that as soon as they have the city, they will fall into fighting each other again, but what does this do for your people? Both those civilians hiding now and the ones following you?"

"You're trying to frighten me into acceptance."

"I'm explaining reality. You have perhaps one day, two at most, before this situation resolves itself. When it does, you have three possible outcomes. First, you accept my offer, help me retake the palace, and govern Carthage as part of the Empire with significant autonomy."

"Second?"

"Second, you reject my offer and try to maintain neutrality while the extremists tear the city apart. When one of them wins, they'll eliminate your faction as a threat. Your supporters will die, and Carthage will fall under the rule of fanatics. However, I will not allow this option to happen."

"So what will you do?"

Lucilla walked closer to him, close enough that her guards tensed. "I will not allow the palace to fall. If it looks like it might, I have warships in the harbor with enough shells to level half the city. I'll create a wall of fire around that palace to protect them that nothing living can cross, regardless of the collateral damage that will cause. Then I'll recall legions from Egypt to retake the city and clean out all rebels."

"You would slaughter thousands of innocents."

"Probably, which is why I haven't done that yet, but I will not allow my people to be butchered, and I will not allow extremists to control this city. If the palace starts to fall, I'll have no choice but to begin full military suppression."

"You're asking me to betray my own people."

"I'm asking you to save them. Work with me now, and Carthage remains largely intact with meaningful self-governance. Force my hand, and I'll have no option but wholesale reconquest."

"Even if I agreed, I don't have the military strength to break the siege."

"But you can open a corridor. Your people control the merchant district between the docks and the palace. Create a path for my troops to reach the palace, and we'll do the rest and rejoin with our men here in the city. Work as an auxiliary with my people. Help us root out who is a citizen and who is a rebel. Once we break the siege and secure the palace, we'll have the combined strength to restore order throughout the city."

"I need to consult with ..."

"No," Lucilla said, cutting him off short. "The time for talk has passed. If you leave this warehouse without an agreement, I'll assume you've chosen to stand aside, and I'll act accordingly."

"You're not giving me any real choice."

Adherbal stood in silence for a long moment. Outside, the distant sound of small arms fire could be heard. Someone was testing their positions, or perhaps beginning another assault.

"If I agree," he said slowly, "I need guarantees."

"You have my word as Empress."

"And my people who participated in the initial uprising?"

"Amnesty for anyone who didn't directly kill Imperial soldiers or citizens. Those who did will face trial, but under Carthaginian judges with Imperial oversight. Decide, Adherbal. Now."

Adherbal closed his eyes, his lips moving in what might have been a prayer or a curse.

"I accept your terms."

"Good. Then we need to get in place to relieve my people."

Central Macedonia

Ky stood outside the command tent, winter mud clinging to his boots as he reviewed the tactical situation with his senior officers. The defensive line stretched across the Macedonian highlands, but each day brought fresh reports of Eastern forces massing beyond their forward positions.

"We just can't stop them. We're making them pay for each step, shelling as they move up, but they're willing to take that pounding to keep pushing us. And even then, sometimes they get a march on us, or our people are slow, and we lose more men to the gas. We lost an entire battery yesterday, and they took the guns after our men fled."

Ky nodded, his dark eyes fixed on the distant ridgelines where enemy scouts had been reported. The situation had deteriorated rapidly since the first gas attacks, and none of the stopgap measures were working. They were now all the way back to the Macedonian highlands. Another two months of this, even at the slow pace they were keeping, and they would be back at the trenches they'd pushed out of at the end of the summer.

Worse, winter had set in, and the enemy had not decreased their pace of operations. And with them having the gas, he couldn't just sit behind fortifications and let the enemy freeze.

So he was losing men to accidents and frostbite as well.

If not for the good news of the Victorious's success near the Dardanelles, things would be reaching an overwhelming point.

"If we lose Thessalonica, we also lose our only viable port short of Athens. We will have to bring everything up by pack mule, at least until we have time to blast enough grading to put down tracks. It will make the supply situation worse," one of the commanders said.

Ky had already considered this. Losing Macedonia would surrender the entire northern approach to Greece, forcing the Western Alliance back into a purely defensive posture. The forces in Sardinia were already back over the Vistula, and only the riverboats had contained a further breakthrough, since they had found a way to mostly seal those off and could quickly sail away from shelling.

"How long can we hold current positions?"

"Two weeks, maybe three if the weather slows their advance as much as it is slowing our retreat," Modius answered. "But they're bringing up more gas batteries."

Before Ky could answer, the conversation was interrupted by the sound of approaching hoofbeats. A dispatch rider appeared through the morning mist.

"Sir, a package from the rail depot at Pella. They said it was urgent," the rider said.

Ky accepted the package and sealed dispatch, and broke it open, scanning the contents quickly.

"This might be the answer we needed," he said, unwrapping the package, revealing a strange contraption.

The device consisted of a black leather mask that would cover the entire face, with two round glass eyepieces and a cylindrical filter canister attached below the mouth area. Leather straps would secure it around the head, and a flexible tube connected the filter to the mask interior.

"What in the gods is that?"

"This, my friends, is a gas mask, courtesy of our friends in Factorium. It filters out toxins in the air, allowing the wearer to breathe normally."

"Does it work?" one of the officers asked skeptically.

"Sophus?" he subvocalized.

The AI's response was instantaneous: *"Filter composition is a layered matrix of activated carbon and a granular sodium bicarbonate compound. It is optimized to neutralize chlorine and phosgene agents through chemical absorption and reaction, although it will perform well against other agents as well. The perforated canister casing allows it to dissipate the heat generated by the exothermic reaction within the filter. Airflow dynamics suggest it will remain below the threshold for user discomfort, although that can vary from user to user, so some may find it intolerable still. The leather construction does leave something to be desired over a rubberized one, but the double layering should be sufficient, and the rubber seals should be enough to keep it from leaking toxins into the mask. It should be enough to stop the majority of chemical agents, although there is an expected number of failures, both technical and from incorrect use by soldiers. Overall, it should allow for a possible eighty to ninety percent reduction in chemical-related exposure. It will work."*

Ky turned the mask over in his hands, then looked at Modius, whose own hard eyes were fixed on the device.

"Yes. It won't be perfect, and the men have to use it correctly for it to work, but it will protect most of them," Ky said.

"That glass seems rather thick," Modius pointed out.

"It is, and I know what you're thinking, and you're right. It will make shooting accuracy for soldiers wearing it much lower. Even the best glass we can make has some distortion, and fogging is going to be an issue as men breathe, but there is little choice in that. We already saw that even with the soaked cloth, the eyes are one of the vulnerable points."

"True," Modius said, although he looked at the mask skeptically.

"Sir," the messenger said. "There was another manifest they wanted me to bring."

Ky took it and unfolded the paper.

"When it rains, it pours," he said. "It seems Hortensius and the rest have been hard at work trying to give us the edge again. In addition to the masks, they finished the work on the new explosive in time for the *Victorious* to use it to good effect. If you haven't already, you should all look at Admiral Valdar's report on that."

"I saw it, and honestly, I wasn't sure if I should believe it," Modius said. "The level of damage it inflicted seemed improbable."

"It's not. This new compound is several times more effective than our current powder. Unfortunately, we can't use it in our cannons directly right now, as the charge would split the tubes in two, but they did see fit to start producing some shells with a mixture of some of this new compound and black powder, giving some added punch to our artillery."

"How many shells? Enough to make a difference?" one of the officers asked.

"Right now, only a few hundred, but I believe this is only the first shipment. Considering they sent five thousand of these masks to us, and another five thousand to Bomilcar's people in Sardinia, it's clear that was their priority."

"Probably for the best," Modius said.

Ky folded the manifest and handed it to one of his aides.

"Get all of this up to the front as soon as possible. Bring the masks to the quartermasters. I want them distributed immediately, priority to the cohorts holding the forward lines. I want every legionary on the line to have one by nightfall tomorrow until we run out, and then I want a man stationed by the train depot day and night to bring up more as soon as the next load comes in. Assign someone in each unit to read the instructions that were sent with it, learn how to use it, put their face over smoke if they have to, but they need to know what they're doing, and then train their men on how to wear them. This takes priority."

He turned to another aide.

"Send a directive to the artillery commanders. Have them send back their wagons for the next reload. Bring up the new shells, but hold off on using them. When we make our push, I want each battery to have as many as possible, and I want to open with them. It's time for a little shock and awe of our own."

Chapter 27

East Indies

"Here they come," the first mate said, staring off the starboard railing.

They had finally finished the repairs, but had only been out of the cove for two hours before the first of these small boats started harassing them. Normally, he would put on full sail and try to outsail them, but even repaired, his ships were not in the best shape, and his ships in better shape had to slow to keep the fleet together.

The small boats were making a play for his supply ships, and it was all his warships could do to interpose against them. Unfortunately, they were too small and coming in much too close to get cannon on them.

"Repel boarders," Claudius said.

Luckily, the legionaries were armed with repeating rifles, letting them put pressure on the boats harrying them. Equally as helpful, the pirates, and that was what these must be, were not similarly armed. They carried bows, spears, and swords that looked like cleavers.

They made up for that lack with numbers. There were fifty, maybe sixty of the small craft, splitting to either side of his 'fleet' to rake and probe.

"I've seen this before," Crispinus said. "This was what it was like in the Sea of Serpents before our navy began to patrol so heavily. They would come out of their coves and hiding spots like flies and swarm you, grappling and boarding the ships."

The first skiffs came within two hundred meters, the archers in their bows leaning to draw. The Easterners really must not have a presence out here if these people had yet to learn to be wary of using bows against firearms.

Of course, it was easier to shoot at a warship than a small canoe. He waited as he let the archers loose their arrows; he wanted them to get closer. A scatter of arrows pattered along the forward rail and rattled off the iron strakes around the mid-deck gun. A sailor made a rude gesture and grinned.

"Now," Claudius said as the small ships got closer.

Shots cracked along the starboard rail of the *Nauta*. Not a volley like muskets, but a scattering and continuous crack-clack-crack-clack of firing and working levers. The closest skiff's bowman toppled backward, legs kicking, and the two men behind him tried to swing the boat alongside anyway, only to be peppered with bullets themselves.

In moments, the closest of the skiffs began to drift off, no one alive aboard it to steer any longer.

More boats came at them, trying to push through the fire to the prizes beyond.

Shots began to crack out of the *Vires* ahead and the *Doirinn* behind as the legionaries on each began to take shots, aiming as best they could at the bobbing targets.

More skiffs floated off as bodies slipped beneath the waves. There were, however, too many of them. Near the port beam, a bundled grapnel sailed toward the railing.

Claudius leaned over the rail, raising his own rifle, and fired. The grapnel-man's shoulder turned into a wet, dark patch, and the iron tumbled backward with a hollow clank.

"Spare your cartridges," Claudius said three minutes later when the first rush slowed and the pirates began to give them more space. "Shoot when you can see faces."

He watched men drop into the bottom of their boats and pull back. A captain on a high-sterned dhow stood out in his white robe with a red sash, gesturing, angry arms cutting through the air. His boat blew the brass-throated horn, and the skiffs formed in a loose chevron that would draft behind them.

"They'll try the wake," Crispinus said. "Coming up our stern."

Unfortunately for them, they had also pulled back far enough to put them in range of his cannons.

The stern gun fired, and the foe got another lesson. Case and shell chewed water, jounced skiffs, tore oars from hands, drew blood and scattered fragments as men screamed.

They were, however, a distraction, one Claudius almost fell for.

"Boat starboard low!" a lookout called.

Claudius turned and saw one skiff hugging the shadow of *Nauta's* own hull, so close the men at oars could almost reach out and touch tar and iron. They'd pulled their focus and used the distraction to get in under the angle for rifle fire.

"Hooks," Claudius said.

Two marines reached down and dipped their own grapnels. There was a clank and a grunt and then a flurry of curses as the hooks bit and men on the skiff yanked back harder. Then another thump, more a wet slap really, and a pirate sprang up with a short, barbed spear, driving it into the wrist of a marine, and the hook went slack.

"Back!" Claudius said.

The first of the pirates had already leaped onto the deck, bare feet finding purchase on wood made gritty for this very moment. The man carried a curved blade with a notch close to the hilt; his eyes were wild and his mouth wide in a yell that failed to be a word. He had a scrap of blue cloth tied around his forehead and a scar that dragged his left earlobe down.

Claudius spared him one look before firing his rifle, sending the man falling backward over the railing. Another came up, and another, and learned just how difficult it was for men with swords to fight men with rifles.

What had the Consul said one time? Don't bring a knife to a gunfight.

It went like that for a stretch. They tried along both beams and over the stern at once. *Nauta's* deck ran with spilled water and blood, and the sand turned muddy underfoot. Not that all the blood was the pirates'. They had managed to score a lucky hit here and there.

A sailor dragged a wounded man by the back of his coat toward the midships hatch while another sailor hammered a knife into a grapnel rope, severing it with three blows. A bugle down the line sounded two short notes; *Vires* had copycats on her own rails.

Then the pressure eased. The pirates had their own tally, and however cheap human life was to them, there were limits to how many they could spend on a single prize.

Claudius let his men breathe. He took a wineskin from a messenger and spit into the scuppers. "Get the medicos up here."

He looked along-column again, making his own quick count. He knew the pirates were still out there, probably following along their progress, waiting to strike again.

This would be much harder in the dark, and would cost many more men if they decided to wait until then to attempt it again. A warship stood out well against the moon, but those small skiffs practically disappeared against the waves below them.

He called his officers aboard while it was quiet. It wasn't difficult, as slow as the fleet was moving.

"We can't keep doing this," Crispinus said. "They're going to try to make another play for us."

"My thought exactly," Claudius said. "We keep moving, sail through the night. It's harder to chase a moving target."

"We don't know these waters well enough," Forannan said. "We'd pile up on a sandbar or catch a reef in the dark. And if the tide turns, we'll drag keels and they'll swarm."

"I was worried about that. Then we try another tack. We don't have time to keep fighting them all the way to our destination, and we can't afford to take more losses or lose any of our supplies. When they retreated, they pulled back to those islands, so they must be camping somewhere in this area, yes? Probably on that land, there, since they came out ahead of us and then retreated behind us. Jian, how many languages do they speak along here?"

"I have no idea," Fa Jian said. "I know several, although this area does see trading, and if they're pirates, the only reasonable ships for them to steal from like this would be my people's. It stands to reason they speak my language."

"Probably. Then what we need to do is convince them this isn't worth it. That there are better ways to earn money."

"How exactly do we do that?"

"We get close to shore and huddle up while sending our Mpongo friends and some of the legionaries to find these pirates and pay them a visit."

"They'll scatter once we attack in force."

"I'm not planning an attack. I want a smash and grab. Did you all see that man giving orders, the one in the fancy garb?"

The captains all nodded in the affirmative.

"We need to take him and convince him that he is tempting a worse fate if they continue their harassment. They need to believe that we are an Easterner convoy and they are going to draw the might of that empire down on them. Hopefully, they are smart enough to fear that and decide this isn't worth the effort."

"How in the world do you plan on doing that?" Captain Attantio asked.

"Using him," he said, pointing at Fa. "We dress him up nice, make him look official, and he can explain it to them."

"No," Fa said.

"Yes. It's our best chance. Unless you want to give up and turn back."

Fa glared at him but nodded.

"Good," Claudius said.

Harder than fighting off the pirates was sitting on his ship while a centurion took fifty legionaries and thirty of the Mpongo tribesmen and disappeared in their small launches toward the island in question.

Claudius was pretty sure he was right, but they would know soon enough. He'd kept half his legionaries on the ships, in case another attack came, but he was mostly relying on the Mpongo, who knew how to track in these conditions better than any of his people.

An hour passed, and then two, without the hint of any kind of sound.

And then in the distance he heard the crack of a rifle. And then another, coming toward him. The sun had fallen, and it was hard to see exactly what was happening on the beach as his men made it back to their longboats, with the exception of the occasional tongue of fire that would leap out from one of their guns.

They were moving fast, however; the flashes of fire retreated to the beach and then onto the waves as they boarded their boats and made their way back to the ships.

He just hoped they would make it back without being followed too quickly. He wanted some time to talk to this man before the pirates tried to take him back.

As his force boarded the ship, he saw that one of the Mpongo and two of his legionaries were clutching wounds, but they all looked to have returned from the raid.

In between two of his men, they carried the man in colorful clothing with a gold ring in one ear. He had his head wrapped in a cloth stained red but looked conscious enough to parley.

"Bring him to my cabin," Claudius ordered. "And fetch Fa Jian."

The pirate leader said nothing as they hauled him below decks, though his head turned constantly, taking in the ship's armaments and crew. Claudius had chosen his best-equipped legionaries for deck duty during this encounter, men whose gear and bearing would suggest wealth and organization.

In his cabin, Claudius had already prepared the stage. Official-looking documents written in Chinese characters sat open on the table, the ink thankfully dry by the time his men returned to the ship.

When Fa Jian entered, Claudius was pleased to see that the man had already begun his transformation. Gone was the simple prisoner's tunic, replaced by the nicest clothes he could put together, thankful for once that Captain Attanito's preference for flamboyant dress had finally come into use. It wasn't exactly what they'd be wearing to court in the East, he had to assume, but it looked impressive, nonetheless.

As more of an exercise to pass the time than anything else, Claudius had been learning the Easterners' tongue, thinking it might come in handy to be able to understand some of what the people they would come into contact with said.

That intent suddenly became useful.

"We have found the man responsible and brought him to you, Inspector General Li." Claudius said in Jian's language, the words still awkward in his mouth.

308

The pirate leader's eyes widened at the exchange, which thankfully meant their guess was correct, and he did speak Jian's language.

"Good. I am tired of this foolishness. What is your name?"

They had brought the pirate in and seated him on a wooden stool while Fa Jian took his chair behind the table, and Claudius stood at his right shoulder.

"I am Captain Rajan. You have no right to hold me; these are my waters."

"Your waters? The empire is the master of all it sees, the ruler of every place the sun touches. And you have made a grave error attacking vessels under Imperial protection."

Captain Rajan interrupted with rapid speech, his voice rising in what sounded like protest or explanation.

"We mean no offense. These look nothing like the empire's ships. Had we known, we would never have dared challenge them. Please, I beg your forgiveness."

Claudius highly doubted they thought anything of the sort. If he had to guess, they had attacked Easterner ships before and gotten away with it. They just hadn't expected these to be so difficult.

"Your ignorance does not excuse your actions. I have already sent my fastest ship ahead to request a larger force to come and teach you some manners."

"Please, that isn't necessary."

"Of course it is," Fa said. "How else can we assure you will not attack more of our ships in these waters? These vessels may seem unusual, but only because they were built by our new allies to the West. That doesn't make them any less ours."

"We can see that now and will be more careful not to interfere with your ships in the future."

Fa stared at him for a long moment, considering.

"I doubt a thief like yourself has an ounce of honesty in him. I do, however, believe you have some measure of prudence when it comes to your own self-interest. The empire is engaged in important business that would generally supersede dealing with the likes of you. So I will give you this one chance. I will put you ashore and you can tell your men to never again touch a ship belonging to the empire, and you can go on raiding the other tribes and pirates in the area. Or I can kill you now and bring in enough men to wipe your entire band from the face of the planet. Which will it be?"

"Yes, of course. Thank you, my lord. I am your humble servant."

"Take him away," Fa said, waving.

The legionaries had been instructed what to do and picked up the man by his arms, lifting him off the ground and dragging him out of the cabin as he continued to offer his profuse thanks.

"I can't believe that worked," Fa said.

"There's something to be said for the power of fear. They may still try for our boats in the future, so we will have to make sure all supply ships coming this way are alerted, but I think we can count on these pirates being somewhat cautious for the time being."

"And if they realize we aren't from the empire and try and sell that information?"

"Then we will deal with that when we have to. I don't see that we have any choice."

Fa made a face like he was unsure this was a wise idea, but Claudius stood by his statement. They didn't have the time or the wherewithal to deal with these people the whole way to their new home.

Still, he couldn't help but feel a little of the same dread.

Carthage

The first Britannian marines hit the docks running. Within minutes, one hundred soldiers had formed up into columns. From the harbor's northern edge, another wave of troops disembarked from transport vessels that had been waiting offshore for the signal.

Lucilla checked her rifle's action one more time. Ky had shown her how to use it the last time they were together, and she'd browbeat Cynwrig into giving her a few more lessons when they'd been in Scandia. It seemed like they might have to defend themselves.

Still, while she'd fought with arcuballistæ and swords, that had been years ago. She hadn't been in a fight personally in more than seven years, and never with a weapon like this.

Cynwrig was clearly thinking the same thing.

"This is foolish. There's absolutely no reason for you to go in with the praetorians. They know what they're doing, and losing you will be a much bigger win than anything these rebels could do in the city itself. You're not a soldier. We need you to do the politics and leave the fighting to the rest of us."

"I'm not here out of military necessity. I'm here because of the politics. The Moderates need to see Imperial authority fighting alongside them, not hiding behind them, to show we are willing to put everything on the line."

"Cynwrig is correct, Lucilla. The probability of injury increases exponentially with proximity to combat zones. You should stay aboard the ship."

She ignored both the protest of the man next to her and the protest in her ear, walking over to Adherbal, who stood nearby with several of his people, sweat beading on his forehead despite the cold winter morning air. The merchant leader held a curved blade that looked more ornamental than practical.

"Your people are moving into position?"

Adherbal nodded, though his grip on the sword suggested nervousness. "Yes. I have them advancing from the merchant quarter and the old temple."

"Don't have them just charge up the streets. We know they have cannon, but we don't know how many shells. They can wipe out a lot of you if you're caught in the open."

"I know. My people know to avoid the main boulevards where the Hardliners have positioned their cannon."

"Good." Lucilla raised her voice to address the assembled praetorians. "Form up! Our people are in a bad situation, and we need to relieve them. We move for the government complex immediately!"

The column of one hundred praetorians began marching through the streets closest to the docks already secured by Adherbal's moderate faction fighters. Local militia in mismatched armor and civilian clothes held intersections, waving the Imperial forces through. From several blocks away, the boom of cannon fire and the cracks of rifles and muskets could be heard.

They'd covered half the distance when the first shots rang out in their direction from a side street. A praetorian dropped, blood spreading across his uniform. The men scattered, finding cover as return fire erupted from their new positions.

They'd moved out of the area controlled by the Moderates and into enemy territory. The ambushers, Hardliner rebels with older muskets, managed only one more ragged volley before Britannian firepower drove them back. Each praetorian could fire seven rounds without reloading, and the rebels with their single-shot muskets and rifles couldn't match that volume of fire.

"Keep moving!" Lucilla shouted, stepping over a fallen rebel whose chest had been torn open by multiple rounds.

A three-story building ahead suddenly erupted with activity. Rebels appeared at every window, pouring water from buckets and clay pots onto the street below. More rebels emerged on the roof, hurling roof tiles down at the disorganized soldiers.

"Back! Get back!" one of the praetorian commanders yelled.

A praetorian took a shot in the leg and went down hard, his rifle skittering away. A tile struck another soldier's shoulder, spinning him around. The rebels had turned the street into a trap with crossfire well directed from elevated positions. From the windows, in addition to bullets, arcuballista bolts and arrows began flying.

They were throwing everything they had at them.

Several praetorians ran into the building, but the rebels had blocked off the stairs and lower floors. It was going to take time to fight up from the bottom.

Time they didn't have.

Lucilla grabbed a soldier carrying a rope. "The balcony across the street – can you make that throw?"

The man studied the distance and nodded, then tied a grappling hook to the rope's end. His first throw fell short, the hook clanging off the building's wall. The second caught the balcony's iron railing. Three praetorians hauled themselves up while their comrades provided covering fire, forcing the rebels back from the windows.

Once on the balcony, the soldiers kicked in the door and cleared the building room by room. The rebels on the roof, realizing their trap had failed, retreated across the roofs of adjoining buildings, jumping from roof to roof.

A Moderate militiaman came sprinting toward them from ahead, nearly getting shot by nervous praetorians before Adherbal recognized him. The man gasped out his report in rapid Carthaginian.

Adherbal translated quickly. "The Hardliners have barricaded the streets around the market with overturned carts. They've got at least forty men behind them."

Lucilla turned to the praetorian centurion beside her. "Take a squad around and come in the other side of the market. Wait for our fire, then hit their flank."

The officer nodded and peeled off with a dozen men, disappearing down a side alley. Lucilla led the main force forward until the barricade came into view, a jumbled mass of merchant carts, furniture, and broken masonry blocking the entire street. Rebel muskets, rifles, and a few stolen arcuballista protruded from gaps in the obstacle.

But the rebels had prepared more than just a simple barricade. They'd strung ropes between buildings at neck height, nearly invisible in the shadows. The first praetorian to advance hit the rope at full speed, flipping backward. He wasn't moving fast enough to get seriously injured, luckily, but the ropes would slow them down. Others saw the trap just in time, ducking under or cutting through the ropes with bayonets.

"Spread out! Use the doorways!" Cynwrig yelled.

The praetorians scattered just as the rebels fired their first volley. Lead balls smashed into stone walls and whistled around them. The rebels immediately began the laborious process of reloading, pouring powder, ramming wadding and ball, priming the pan.

From a side alley, a rebel pushed a cart loaded with burning straw into the street. The improvised firewagon rolled toward the Britannian position, smoke billowing from its cargo. As a danger, it was only moderately a problem, but the volume of smoke it put out made it hard to see who was shooting at them, and the enemy had cover while her people didn't.

A praetorian sergeant sprinted forward, rifle slung over his shoulder, and grabbed the cart's handles. Muscles straining, he redirected it into a wall where it crashed and spilled its burning contents harmlessly into an empty doorway, starting a fire in the building.

The fire would spread and cause serious damage in this section of the city, but for now, she couldn't worry about that.

They kept the pressure on, not giving the barricaded defenders time to reload. Britannian rifles cracked, each soldier putting multiple rounds downrange. Wood splintered, stones sparked, and rebels fell. The rebels managed to send a few shots and bolts downrange, but the difference in volume was striking.

Then the flanking century struck. They came from the perpendicular street, catching the rebels completely exposed. The crossfire was devastating. Men armed with muskets tried to return fire but were cut down. Some drew swords and tried to charge, but the praetorians simply stepped back and shot them down at twenty paces.

A rebel officer, recognizing the hopelessness, stood up waving a white cloth tied to his sword. "Quarter! We ask for quarter!"

"Weapons down! All weapons on the ground!" a praetorian commanded.

Twenty-three rebels emerged from behind the barricade, hands raised. The rest lay dead or dying in the street. Adherbal's militiamen moved in to secure the prisoners while praetorians kicked apart sections of the barricade to clear the path.

They pressed deeper into contested territory, past the market square where overturned stalls created a maze of obstacles. Rebels had positioned themselves in the stores and buildings beyond, using the doorways and windows as cover. A praetorian stepped around a corner and found himself facing a rebel with a loaded crossbow at point-blank range. Before the rebel could fire, the soldier grabbed hold of the weapon, forcing it upward. The bolt shot harmlessly into the air as the two men wrestled for control.

The praetorian won by abandoning the struggle entirely, letting go of the crossbow to draw his bayonet. He pushed the blade in under the rebel's ribs, dropping him instantly. But more rebels were emerging from hiding spots. They'd prepared another ambush.

"Don't get separated! Squad formations, clear by sections!" Lucilla ordered.

The praetorians formed tight groups of ten, sweeping through the streets. When rebels popped up to fire, they met concentrated return fire from entire squads. The rebels' coordination broke down under the pressure. The ambush turned into a series of isolated skirmishes that the better-armed Britannians won decisively.

At one intersection, Moderate faction fighters had pinned down a squad of Restorationist troops behind an overturned wagon. The rebels wore blue sashes, the color of the supposed Carthaginian heir, which was helpful in knowing who was friend and who was foe. They were trying to load their muskets while the Moderate militiamen kept them pinned down with sporadic fire from their own collection of now antiquated firearms.

The wagon suddenly lurched forward. The rebels were using it as mobile cover, pushing it toward the Moderate position while crouched behind its bulk. The Moderates' musket balls thudded harmlessly into thick wood. When the praetorians arrived, they didn't target the wagon. Instead, they shot at the ground beneath it, their rounds ricocheting and sending up shards of stone striking the rebels' feet and ankles. Screaming men fell, the wagon rolling over two of them before coming to rest.

They started to make progress again. Slowly, but pushing the rebels back.

Cannon fire suddenly erupted from ahead. An explosion shook the ground as a shell detonated against a building twenty meters from Lucilla's position, blowing out windows and showering the street with fragments of stone and mortar. Through the smoke and dust, she could see the rebels, a hastily constructed barricade defending the single cannon.

The rebel gun crew was already loading a second shot, one man holding a canvas bag of powder while another prepared to ram it home. Behind them, Lucilla could see only a small stack of shells remaining, perhaps four or five.

The rebels had learned from earlier fights. They'd positioned sharpshooters with rifles on nearby roofs to protect the gun. Every time a praetorian showed himself to aim, fire would force him back into cover.

"Suppressing fire on those rooftops," she ordered.

Half the praetorians engaged the riflemen while others targeted the gun crews. The rebels managed to fire their gun again, the shell arcing over the Britannian position to explode in the street behind them.

It was lucky these were amateurs who hadn't spent time training with these weapons. Her own artillerymen would have made this standoff much more dangerous. As it was, shrapnel rattled off walls and roof tiles, wounding three soldiers who'd thought themselves safely out of the line of fire.

A praetorian squad worked its way through a bakery, climbing an internal stairway to reach the upper floors. They kicked open shutters and fired down at the gun position from an unexpected angle. The rebel gunners, focused on threats from street level, didn't see the danger until it was too late.

Meanwhile, two more squads had found a narrow alley that led behind the rebel position. They emerged to find rebels frantically trying to turn the cannon to face the new threat. The gun was heavy, requiring two men to rotate it on its carriage. They'd managed only a quarter turn before rifle fire cut them down.

With most of the gunners dead, the surviving rebels had only swords and knives left and opted to run for it.

"Secure that gun and any remaining shells," Lucilla ordered. "We might need them ourselves."

They joined with the men of Pinarius's breakthrough attempt two streets from the palace. The garrison commander led his forty praetorians in a sortie from the administrative building as soon as his relief force came into view. They'd used a wagon as a battering ram, six men pushing it at a run to smash through a rebel barricade. The impact scattered defenders and opened a gap for the garrison troops to pour through.

The rebels, armed mostly with melee weapons, had tried to counter. They'd overturned market stalls and doors torn from buildings to create obstacles that would force the praetorians to slow down, hoping to engage in close combat where swords might have a chance. But Pinarius's men simply shot through the flimsy barriers, their rounds punching through the wood and striking the rebels crouched behind them.

A group of rebels had climbed onto a building's awning, planning to drop onto the praetorians as they passed below. But the cloth and wood structure couldn't support their weight. It collapsed, sending the rebels tumbling into the street where they lay stunned and were easy targets.

The Hardliners made their last major stand at the old Carthaginian War Ministry, a squat stone building they had overrun in their last push before they took the palace. They'd barricaded every entrance and created a killing field in front.

Through the windows, Lucilla could see rebels pouring oil onto the building's wooden floors, preparing to burn the structure with themselves inside. Foolish, probably hoping to make themselves martyrs.

But they'd made an error; the oil was spreading toward the windows, seeping through gaps in the ancient stonework, which gave her an idea.

"Your men with bows. Have them put fire arrows into those windows," she told a Moderate militia captain.

The militiaman looked confused. "But they want to burn it …"

"Not yet, they don't. Trust me."

Flaming arrows arced through windows, igniting the oil prematurely. They hadn't soaked everything, and most of the building was stone. It wasn't going to burn around them, and there wasn't enough oil poured yet to gut the structure.

The rebels inside suddenly found themselves dealing with fires they hadn't planned to start yet. Smoke began pouring from the building.

In the confusion, praetorians rushed forward. Some rebels tried to hold the doorways but they were firing blind through smoke, their plan now an obstacle. Others abandoned their posts to fight the fires, fearing the building would collapse before they could achieve their martyrdom.

The assailants went in through every entrance simultaneously. The smoke that hindered the rebels also concealed the praetorians' approach until they were at point-blank range. Rebels with swords found themselves facing rifles in narrow doorways where they couldn't dodge or advance.

Mago, the Hardliner military leader, stood in the main hall with a torch, trying to reach the oil barrels that hadn't yet caught fire. Five praetorians fired at once. He fell three meters from his goal, the torch rolling harmlessly away across the stone floors.

Word came in from other sections of the city. Her praetorians and the Moderates had cleared most of the city.

The battle for Carthage was effectively over. Now the real work would begin.

Chapter 28

Callipolis, Sardinia

The predawn darkness was lit up as cannons along the Britannian line fired, then orange light spat from the wall towers in answer. They had sixty pieces firing in a staggered roll, all of the batteries laid for one target along the western curtain of Callipolis, the largest Greek city on this side of the Hellespont. He'd picked the old brickwork there, the weak seam between two rebuilt sections, a cheap repair made after an earthquake sometime in the last few years. Ancient stone and fired clay might have stood up for a time against solid shot or even black powder rounds, but they were no match for TNT.

"Keep it on that seam," Ky said.

The chronometer counted down in the corner of his vision, along with projections for wind from the harbor, which drifted in from the coast moving north through the city.

That would help dissipate the gas when they deployed it, to a degree.

Modius stood at his shoulder. "They're ready."

"Good. Make sure they have their masks on tight. They should start their gas bombardment soon. The masks won't save all of them, but it will be enough."

As if on cue, the first Eastern gas barrage came like a curtain dropping. The shells fell along his line releasing a green-yellow cloud that flowed down into the broken ground between the farms and the outer ditch.

Men on the forward slope held their ground, thick glass plates fogging along the edges, rubberized cloth straps snugged behind heads. As predicted, here and there, a man went down from a mask not cinched tight enough or a small, fatal gap.

319

But most held, guns in hand, ignoring the smoke that rolled over them.

The gas moved like a tide in the draws and low places. Some of it went stagnant and pooled; more slid toward their trenches, spilled over and then started to dissipate as the breeze from the south pushed it away.

His guns fired on, the shells blasting the fired brick to shards, a hole opening here and there as the wall began to break from the pounding.

"We go in on the collapse," Ky said.

"They'll still be up on either side," Modius said. "Shooting down on us."

"I know. Keep up the fire."

The seam gaped, edges sagging as more holes appeared in the wall and the layered masonry started to become unstable, brick dust pouring down and accumulating into a slope over the ditch. They kept punching until the edge on the right fell and the left hung by a thread of mortar. Another hit took that out and the whole face came down. A roar, a slide of rock, crushed clay and timber beams, a cloud of dust that changed the dark to a grit storm in the lantern glow from the wall.

"Go," Modius said.

At the sound of the trumpet, the first cohorts rose from their positions and ran.

The first teams went out steadily, without the normal cheer. Not with the masks. They took the breach like a file through a knot, narrow, careful, and then widening as the first men scrambled up and over. The engineers with the big hooks and short shovels dragged timbers and cut away crushed clay and debris, making it easier for the men behind them to get through. Then the gunfire started. The enemy wasn't on them directly, having to stay back for their own safety, away from the gas, but they were on the walls on either side, high above the gas, they had flanking towers, and they had men in the city itself.

The gunfire had its effect as his men began to bunch, trying to take cover from the shots.

Which was exactly what they weren't supposed to do.

"Suppress flanking towers," he said.

Moments later, shells began to smash against the towers and walls.

Ky waited, hoping his men's training and confidence would carry them through as the gunfire slackened. When it was clear they would not carry on momentum alone, he began to move, running down the slope and pushing through the men in the rear lines.

Men made space for him without looking around. They knew him and knew he was here to save them. Unlike his men, he wore no mask. The clouds of sick-colored wisps moved around him, around his head, and he ignored them. He had nothing to fear from the gas. His nanites would filter out the toxins.

Men bunched at the foot of the breach where the rubble shifted under their feet. The ditch still had water in the bottom; two fell in the muck and went under, then hands pulled them up and shoved them forward again.

Shrapnel hissed and chipped the stones. Men vanished into the dust boils and came out crawling, then up again. A few lay down and didn't rise. The first volley from the parapet above chewed the top of the rubble. A centurion with the 18th got a hole drilled through the glass plate of his mask and dropped like a cut rope. The man behind him stepped into his place and fired up at the shooter.

"Forward. Staying put is death. Move," he shouted, pushing men through the breach.

The men found their courage, hearing his voice.

They made the lip and tumbled over, then fanned across what had been a walkway. The city inside was a tight grid of narrow streets, tiled roofs, and courtyards sunk behind the walls. This had been Greek first, then Punic, then a Greek/Roman fusion, history layered in stone and plaster. Now the houses created bastions, chokepoints, and murder lanes.

Ky's first squad cleared the stair tower. A man yanked the safety strip on a one-finned grenade and underhanded it through the door, then flattened himself against the wall. The percussion came quick and hard, and three Eastern rifles clattered down the stairs with chunks of bone and wood. The second grenade was thrown at the next landing. The squad went in, stepping over bodies, getting off shots into bodies that twitched.

Ky pointed down the slope to the street that ran like a dry stream under the wall and then bent toward the center. "Take the line to the central temple. Send men up left and right, clear the wall for the units coming behind us. You lot, follow me."

He started down the street with a dozen men around him, in the ad hoc wedge that always formed when he moved forward, with him at the fore. The rifle was an extension of him, firing as fast as the rifle could cycle, Eastern soldiers fell everywhere they showed themselves.

The air here was clearer of shell dust. The wind pushed the smoke toward the northern end of the city. That spared the vanguard, mostly, but the rear ranks got the choke of pulverized brick and poison gas.

The right-hand alley had a barricade of barrow carts and a wood door ripped off its hinges. An Eastern unit had turned a wine shop into a redoubt. They fired through the shutters at waist height. A boy fell with a sound like something breaking and kept trying to get up. The man at Ky's elbow, a veteran who wore no badge beyond scars, put three rounds through the shutter and made a hole, then another. Ky put one through the hole, and a man inside screamed.

"Grenade," someone said.

"Not in wood," Ky said. "We don't want to set half the street on fire with our own men coming up behind us."

He moved up to the doorframe and snapped one shot into the hinge-side gap as the Eastern soldier inside leveled his weapon. The shot inside went wild. The veteran followed with a thrust under the enemy's arm and a snap-wrist twist that tore the rifle free. Another man vaulted through the window and landed hard, bayonet first. The interior of the wine shop went to silence fast. Ky stepped in, kicked a still-moving hand and checked the corners. He stepped back out before the men could speak.

"Keep moving," he said. "Don't clear deep. Take the frontage and the next corner and leave the rest to the men behind us to clean up."

322

Ahead of them, Eastern artillery crews were hauling a field gun into position at the intersection, the straight tube swinging toward the Britannian advance.

Ky's rifle came up lightning fast, cracking off a shot in the blink of an eye. The crew chief fell backward off the limber. Before anyone could react, two more shots dropped the loaders. The remaining crew scattered, abandoning the gun halfway into the intersection.

"Forward!" Ky shouted, leading his men in a rush across the open ground.

They vaulted the abandoned gun carriage and spread out under cover as Eastern rifles opened up from windows above. Bullets sparked off cobblestones, sending chips of stone whining through the air.

The first organized resistance came at a marketplace two blocks further in. Eastern troops had overturned market stalls to create a maze of barriers, forcing the Britannians to advance through narrow channels between wooden frames and scattered produce. As Ky's lead squad pushed through, Eastern soldiers rose from behind the barriers on three sides.

They were still making a good push, right up until a group of Easterners appeared out of a side alley, in their midst before anyone could turn a barrel toward them. The ambush turned into a melee. Britannians used their weapons as clubs when they couldn't get enough distance to get a shot off, but the Eastern troops kept coming, using bayonets when their single-shot rifles emptied. A young Britannian soldier went down with a blade through his chest, screaming as an Eastern soldier tried to wrench it free. The Britannian next to him put his rifle barrel against the attacker's temple and fired.

Ky circled back, leaping two stalls in a single bound, landing with his foot on the chest of one of the attackers, collapsing his chest, and then shooting two more while still standing on the body. Ky fired over and over, running through most of his ammunition as fast as the lever could fire and the tube could take new rounds. An Eastern officer tried to rally his men from atop an overturned wagon. Ky's shot took him in the chest mid-shout, sending him tumbling backward into his own troops.

"Grenades!" someone yelled. Three Eastern soldiers were pulling pins on their own finned explosives, copied from the Britannian design. Britannian soldiers dove behind whatever cover they could find as the grenades sailed through the air. The explosions shattered market stalls and sent wooden splinters flying like arrows.

They fought through the marketplace stall by stall, barrel by barrel. An Eastern squad had fortified a shop, firing through the windows while others threw clay pots filled with lamp oil that shattered and spread fire across the cobblestones. Britannian soldiers had to dodge between the spreading pools of flame while continuing to advance.

Ky stopped next to a few of his fallen men, pulling ammo out of pockets and wrapping bandoliers over his shoulder. He needed the rounds if he was going to keep his men from bogging down, which was the entire goal of the Eastern defenders.

Now that their troops were mixed together, the Easterners had stopped firing their gas shells, afraid of hitting their own people, and the more he kept the pressure on, the longer they'd go without more of the gas being fired.

Even better would be to overrun the gun emplacements entirely.

First, he needed to break the enemy.

The approach ahead was blocked. Eastern forces had pulled three guns into battery formation, covering the entire avenue. The position was too strong for a frontal assault, and he didn't feel like having to rebuild parts of himself after taking a shell.

"Through here," Ky ordered, pointing to a narrow alley between two stone buildings. "We'll circle behind."

The enemy had been waiting for that. The alley was a clever trap. Eastern soldiers on the rooftops fired rifles and dropped stones and tiles onto the Britannians below. His men raised their rifles to fire back, but the angle was bad and the defenders had solid cover. A tile caught a soldier across the forehead, dropping him. Another man's rifle was knocked from his hands by a falling brick.

"Back!" Ky ordered, but Eastern troops had moved to block their retreat, setting up a firing line at the alley mouth. They were boxed in, taking fire from above and behind.

Ky grabbed a grenade from a soldier's belt, pulled the pin, and held it for two seconds before hurling it onto the roof, much farther than any of his men would have been able to throw it. The explosion sent bodies and debris raining down.

"Now! Through them!"

The charge out of the alley was brutal. Men ran straight into Eastern bayonets, using rifle butts as clubs when there wasn't room to shoot. A Britannian corporal took a bayonet through the thigh but kept fighting, smashing his rifle stock into his attacker's jaw.

They'd just cleared the alley when an Eastern platoon burst from a side street, catching them in the open. Thirty Eastern soldiers with bayonets fixed, charging at a dead run.

Ky moved faster than seemed possible, his rifle dropping as he drew his sidearm and combat knife in one fluid motion. The first Eastern soldier to reach him tried to thrust with his bayonet. Ky sidestepped, grabbed the rifle barrel with his left hand, and yanked. The soldier flew forward off balance straight into Ky's fist, which snapped his head back so hard it broke his neck.

He dropped ten more in seconds, tearing through them before the remaining Easterners broke. They'd seen twenty of their comrades ripped apart in less than thirty seconds by one man who moved like nothing human. They ran, and Ky let them go, already turning back to his own forces.

They still had a goal.

"The battery," he said simply, as if he hadn't just torn through an entire platoon. "We take it now."

They circled behind the three-gun battery which was firing down the avenue at his people, holding down the rest of the line.

"Grenade the powder!" Ky shouted, pointing at a cart loaded with bagged powder charges and shells.

A soldier pulled a pin and lobbed the finned explosive toward the ammunition limber. The explosion lifted the nearest gun off its carriage, flipping it backward. The blast wave knocked men flat for thirty meters in every direction, windows shattering in an expanding ring of destruction.

With the battery destroyed, Britannian forces pushed deeper into the city.

A courtyard that should have been a simple crossing became a deathtrap. Eastern troops held every window of the surrounding three-story buildings, creating interlocking fields of fire. The first Britannian squad to enter was cut down before they made it ten meters.

"Smoke!" Ky ordered.

Soldiers threw grenades filled with a chemical mixture instead of black powder. A moment later, the courtyard filled with gray clouds. Under cover, men sprinted across in small groups while others hammered the windows with suppressing fire.

Building by building, room by room, they cleared a path toward the temple.

The bathhouse proved the worst. Eastern forces had turned it into a fortress, with metal plates covering windows and water-filled trenches dug in the main chamber that forced attackers into predictable paths. The first assault failed completely; men driven back by concentrated fire from protected positions.

"We go over," Ky decided.

The assault team crashed through an adjacent pottery workshop. Eastern soldiers waited behind overturned kilns, and the firefight in the confined space shattered hundreds of clay pots, filling the air with ceramic dust. They fought up the stairs and across the roof, dropping grenades through the bathhouse skylights. The explosions finally silenced the strong point.

The temple square was the final position. Eastern forces had prepared it, as soon as it was clear the Britannian line was pushing toward it, with artillery at four corners, rifle pits between, every approach a killing field. As his forces converged from multiple streets, they met devastating volleys.

The assault stalled. Men hugged walls as Eastern artillery fired canister shot, turning streets into corridors of death. Bodies piled at the mouth of each approach where soldiers had tried to rush across.

His men wanted to storm it, to charge in and overrun it now that they had a numerical advantage. Most of the enemy had fled the city, and whole sections had surrendered as his men swept through the city, surrounding the temple.

Ky sent a messenger back to outside the walls and waited while men peppered the building with small arms fire, mostly to keep the enemy occupied.

"Incoming," one of his men yelled as everyone took cover.

Ky didn't. He'd been waiting for this. Beyond introducing new types of cannons and shells, one of the bigger additions was the calculations to make much more precise shots. Not so much to hit a group of attackers within meters of them, but rather to hit a building surrounded but with an open square around it, giving his men almost sixty or so meters away from the building on all sides.

His men could maintain the distance that isolated them from the target, and the new shells had a punch that the old ones never did. Not all of the blasts hit the building directly, but the ones that did connect caused massive damage. By the fourth hit, the domed ceiling collapsed. By the tenth, almost none of the building was standing, flattened by high explosives and turned into a pile of rubble.

The shells stopped, and Ky sent his men in. To everyone's surprise, there were still a few enemy soldiers alive, in sections that managed to have enough structure left to protect them from the collapse.

They were in shock and easily subdued.

As dusk settled over the city, Ky stood in the temple square amid the devastation. The city had taken pretty extreme damage, and bodies covered every street where the fighting had raged, but the battle had proved that the masks worked.

They had neutralized the enemy's new weapon and would be able to go on the offensive again.

Chapter 29

Port Versteck

The lead ship rounded the headland and Claudius saw exactly what Ky's charts had promised. The bay opened before them, almost completely enclosed by vertical cliffs that rose two hundred meters from the water, their faces covered in dense jungle vegetation that spilled down in green cascades wherever the rock allowed purchase. The entrance itself was no more than three hundred meters wide at its broadest point, narrowing to half that where the current ran the strongest.

"Bring us through steady," Claudius called to Captain Crispinus.

The *Nauta* led the way, her patched hull and jury-rigged foremast testament to everything they'd weathered. Behind her came the rest of his battered fleet, each ship bearing scars from their passage across half the world's oceans and the fight with the pirates.

Inside the bay, the water lay still and dark, protected from ocean swells by the encircling cliffs. Claudius studied the shoreline through his field glass, noting several beaches suitable for landing where streams cut through the jungle to reach the sea. The largest of these lay on the eastern shore, a crescent of sand perhaps four hundred meters long, backed by relatively level ground before the jungle proper began.

"That's our landing site," he told Crispinus, pointing to the beach. "Signal the others. We'll anchor the fleet and use the boats to ferry everything ashore."

The work began immediately. Sailors loaded into longboats with their equipment while legionaries and their Mpongo allies put ashore to start setting up some security and begin exploring inland.

Claudius waded ashore from the third boat. It was a good location, but it was going to take some work to cut any kind of livable area out of it.

He set the men to work as soon as they were ashore, cutting areas clean and putting aside the wood for later use. The men had been crammed on these ships for a month and a half, and they couldn't stay living like that much longer. He needed to get some temporary shelters set up while they built out the port properly.

Thankfully, many of these men had taken part in building some of the ports along the coast of Africa, and by now they knew the routine well.

Once they had livable conditions, the next priority would be the fort. They couldn't have it at the mouth of the harbor, which was the smartest place tactically for it, since that would be too much of a giveaway for any Eastern ships that might sail into this area, but he wanted one inside to offer both protection if someone did sail into the harbor and as a point for the people here to fall back to if things went badly.

It was hard work, especially in the heat and damp. The forest here was like nothing he'd experienced in Britannia, Carthage, or Germania.

Progress was made, however.

By late afternoon, the basic camp had taken shape. Canvas shelters arranged in neat rows, cooking fires established in cleared areas, and the beginnings of a few more permanent wooden buildings.

Claudius found Fa Jian standing at the edge of the cleared area, staring at the water and out the portage to the sea beyond.

"We're still a good way from your homeland. A lot of water between us and it," Claudius said, joining him.

"I know. Still, this is closer than I have been to my home in over three years." Fa Jian's Latin had improved considerably during their voyage, though his accent remained strong. "You know this will not be easy. Most of the people in my homeland, even those in the Han resistance, have never dealt with foreigners before. They will be distrustful of your help."

"You're going to have to convince them. This is their only chance to free themselves from their emperor. If they were able to do it on their own, I'm sure they would have by now."

"That is true. How long will it take to get enough built so that you are able to take me to the mainland?"

"Several weeks at the least. We need to send one of the schooners out scouting, so we know where we're headed and what the opposition looks like. And we need to get things built out here, especially the docks, so we can repair the ships enough to send the supply ships and two of the caravels back to let them know we made it and to get the next round of supplies."

"Then I guess this is where the real work begins," Jian said.

Carthage

The governmental palace of Carthage bore the scars of recent battle, though the worst of the debris had been cleared away. Marble columns showed chips from stray bullets, and several walls displayed fresh patches where cannon fire had torn through the ancient stonework. Yet, the great reception hall retained its grandeur, its vaulted ceiling and intricate mosaics speaking to the power that had once ruled much of the known world.

Lucilla stood at the head of the hall, wearing the deep purple robes of Imperial authority. Behind her, the banners of Britannia hung alongside those of Carthage, not replacing them, but sharing space in careful equilibrium.

The assembled crowd filled the hall completely. Carthaginian merchants and nobles occupied the front rows, looking weary and tired, but also, maybe a bit hopeful. Behind them stood the administrators and clerks who would be running the city from here on, made up of both Britannians and Carthaginians. At the sides of the hall, Praetorian guards maintained a watch, their presence a reminder that peace had been won through strength.

The doors opened, and all eyes turned as Adherbal entered and approached the dais. He had exchanged his merchant's clothes for formal Carthaginian robes of office, the purple trim marking his new status.

"Citizens of Carthage," Lucilla began. "We gather today to mark a new day in this city's history, and an end to the troubles that have been killing so many, for so long. At the heart of these troubles were legitimate concerns about governance and representation. The Crown has heard these concerns, and we have listened. These concerns deserve answers, not suppression. Therefore, it is my pleasure to announce the appointment of Adherbal, whom many of you joined with rather than supporting the more violent factions that fought over the city, as Governor of Carthage under Imperial authority."

The response was immediate and positive. Applause broke out among the Carthaginians, genuine in its enthusiasm. Here was one of their own, elevated to real power rather than a mere ceremonial position.

Adherbal knelt before the dais as protocol demanded.

"Do you swear to govern justly and wisely, respecting both Imperial law and local custom?" she asked.

"I do so swear, Majesty."

"Do you pledge to maintain the peace between all peoples under your administration?"

"I pledge this, Majesty."

"Then rise, Governor Adherbal, and receive the symbols of your office."

A praetorian stepped forward bearing a polished wooden case. Inside lay the governor's seal, carved from local stone but set in Imperial gold. Adherbal accepted them with steady hands, then turned to face the crowd.

"Citizens of Carthage," he said, still sounding nervous and off kilter. He was a merchant at heart, after all, and this kind of thing did not come naturally. "I accept this responsibility knowing the trust you place in me. Our city has suffered, but it endures.

Together, we will rebuild what was damaged and strengthen what remains. I tell you now, we will be working to set things right. The first priority will be repairing the damage from the recent fighting. Streets must be cleared, buildings rebuilt, markets reopened. Every citizen who wishes to contribute to this effort will find opportunity for honest work at fair wages. We do this because much of the city's tax revenue is coming back to our people. On top of this, the Empress has agreed that Carthaginian representatives will have a voice in the decisions that directly impact our community. We hope these new resources and authority will give our people a chance to be a people again. To that end, amnesty extends to all citizens who accept the new arrangement. Past allegiances matter less than future conduct. Those who work for Carthage's prosperity under Imperial law will find welcome and opportunity. However, those who choose violence or sedition will face the full consequences of their actions. We are part of the Empire and will protect those who live peacefully within its bounds, but we will not tolerate threats to that peace."

His speech finished, but as the formal proceedings concluded, Adherbal stepped to the front of the dais.

"Citizens, the path forward requires effort from all of us. The Empire offers opportunity, but we must seize it. Our city can prosper again, but only through unity and dedication to a common purpose."

The final applause was sustained and genuine.

As the crowd began to disperse, Lucilla felt a measure of satisfaction. The ceremony had accomplished its purpose. Adherbal possessed real authority to govern; the Carthaginians felt heard and respected, which meant Imperial control should be back in place.

The Hardline faction had collapsed with the death of their leader, and the false heir, who had fled the city entirely, had been grabbed up by a patrol the day after the battle.

The year was ending, and things were looking up. The Carthaginian problem, as some had called it, might finally be solved. The *Victorious* had cleared out the enemy fleet coming out of the Black Sea and would soon be going in to deal with whatever port they had built there, and Ky and Bomilcar had both resumed the offensive now that the gas masks had proved effective.

After almost one year of being on the back foot, constantly falling back and struggling, they were moving forward again.

She hoped that meant the war might soon be over, and her people could return to peace.

To Be Continued ...

About the Author

Travis writes science fiction, fantasy, and thriller novels (and the occasional coming-of-age story), with the hope of transporting and enthralling readers. Publishing novels since 2015, Travis's passion is creating worlds and characters that live and breathe, and experiencing the joy of those stories with his readers. When not writing, Travis enjoys connecting with readers and other writers, managing the popular Complete Marvel Reading Order website, where he works on his other passion for comics and graphic novels, and spending time with his family. If you have enjoyed this book, please consider taking a moment to rate or review it wherever you found your copy, as it helps new readers find my works and ensures I can continue writing book into the future.

Find out more at:
amazon.com/TravisStarnes/e/B072YBDC3S/

Or visit
https://tstarnes.com

Maps available at
https://tstarnes.com/book-series/imperium/

Signup to get free previews and notifications of upcoming books at
http://tstarnes.com/preview-notification-newsletter/

Also by

John Taylor Stories

Rebirth
False Signs
The Wrong Girl
Burying the Past
Family Ties
Election Day
Danger Close
Extraction
Designated Target
Border Crossed
Desperate Rendition
Broken Ground

Country Roads Series

Playing by Ear
Fanfare
Dissonance
Elegy
From the Top
Center Stage

Imperium Series

Volume 1
The Sword of Jupiter
The Trumpets of Mars
The Sands of Saturn
The Depths of Neptune
The Fires of Vulcan
The Triumph of Venus
Volume 2
The Wings of Mercury
The Plains of Pluto
The Clouds of Caelus

Shattered Lands Series

In the Shadow of Lions
An Ending of Oaths
The Barons' War
Heavy Lies the Crown

False Start Series

Second Down
Scramble
Loss of Down

The Veilguard Saga

Threads of Destiny
The Blackstar Legacy

Stand Alone

Going Home

www.ingramcontent.com/pod-product-compliance
Lightning Source LLC
Chambersburg PA
CBHW070626260626
47161CB00007B/2599